THE
TELEGRAPH

STENDHAL

Lucien Leuwen

BOOK TWO

THE
TELEGRAPH

TRANSLATED BY LOUISE VARÈSE

A NEW DIRECTIONS PAPERBOOK

First published as ND Paperbook 108 in 1961

Second Printing, 1962

Book design by Maurice Serle Kaplan

Manufactured in the United States of America by
Quinn & Boden Company, Inc., Rahway, N. J.

New Directions Books are published by James Laughlin at
Norfolk, Connecticut. New York Office: 333 Sixth Avenue (14)

INTRODUCTION

LUCIEN LEUWEN IN THE MAKING

IN 1833 Henri Beyle (or Stendhal, as he is better known today), then Consul at Civita-Vecchia, the little port of Rome, spent a brief leave of absence in Paris, and brought back with him the manuscript of a novel, entitled *The Lieutenant,* by his old friend Madame Jules Gauthier. He promised to read the lady's manuscript and to send her a detailed criticism. The brutally frank letter he finally wrote her must have discouraged the "adorable Jules" for there is no record of any further literary effort on her part. Stendhal's criticism is especially interesting as disclosing the principles of writing which he himself invariably followed.

"I read *The Lieutenant,* dear charming friend. You must rewrite it entirely, imagining that you are translating from the German. The language to my mind is horribly grandiloquent and stilted; I have heartlessly scribbled all over it. You mustn't be lazy; you are writing only for the sake of writing: for you it is an amusement. So then, put it in dialogue form—the entire last part of the second note-book: Versailles, Hélène, Sophie, the comedy scenes of society. All this is too heavy in narrative form. The dénouement is flat. . . . In every chapter you must take out at least fifty superlatives. Never say: 'Olivier's burning passion for Hélène.' We poor novelists must try to make people believe in a burning passion, but never mention it. It's indecent. If you say 'The passion which consumed him' you sink to the level of the novels for chambermaids printed in duodecimo by M. Pigoreau. But for chambermaids, *The Lieutenant* offers too few corpses, elopements and such normal things, which are to be found in the novels of old man Pigoreau.

LEUWEN
or
The Student Expelled from the École Polytechnique

That is the title I should adopt. . . . Write it all as though you were writing to me. . . . In describing a man, a woman, a setting, think of a real person or place."

But now, having scribbled all over the margins and between the lines of Jules' manuscript, Stendhal suddenly realized that the subject had taken possession of him, and he sat down to rewrite it himself. Quite shamelessly he confessed his theft: "Night of May 8-9, can't sleep from eleven-thirty to one-thirty. To relieve my boredom, I think of this: not *to send it* to Mme. Jules, but *to make* of it an opus. With *that lady* it would quickly become one of the reading-rooms' not-reads for chambermaids. Provided the idea lasts." (The words in italics are English in the original—only Stendhal could say why!) Paradoxically, Stendhal is as notorious for his thefts and plagiarisms as he is famous for his originality. Paul Valéry comes to his defense: "In all such criminal matters, the main thing is for the accused to show himself infinitely more entertaining than his victims." By this test, Stendhal stands acquitted.

No one knows just how much *The Green Huntsman* (for the question hardly goes beyond the first volume) owes to Mme. Gauthier's *Lieutenant,* since the manuscript (which, let me say in passing, Stendhal, more honest in deed than in intention, did return) has never been found. There does, however, exist a passage in Stendhal's *Racine and Shakespeare* to indicate that the theme of his romance is his own, conceived as far back as 1825: "Thus it is that a young man, if fate should place him in a garrison town in the society of women of a certain type, on witnessing the success of his comrades, and observing the kind of pleasures that amuse them, sincerely believes that he is incapable of love. Then, by chance, one day he meets a simple, natural, virtuous woman, worthy of being loved, and he realizes that he has a heart."

* * *

From the innumerable notes dotted through the manuscript, it is evident that Stendhal intended from the outset to use his Lieutenant not merely as the hero of a charming love story, but as the unifying element of a work of grand proportions. In his mind the novel was to be a continuation of the "chronicle of the Nineteenth Century" which he had begun in *The Red and the Black*. The overall plan, which he must have conceived soon after he started work on Jules' manuscript, never varied in its general lines, but the endless changes he suggests or interpolates without revising what went before, have occasioned many minor inconsistencies and lapses which, without a complete revision, are in most cases impossible to rectify. These do not affect the book's readability nor its importance, but constitute hurdles for the baffled translator.

Stendhal's first idea was to write a sort of triptych, three volumes with three different environments: I. An ultra-legitimist provincial town in France (he finally settled on Nancy); II. Bourgeois Paris, its society, finance and politics; III. Diplomatic circles in Rome (referred to as Omar [Roma], later called Capel or Madrid); each volume with a fresh set of characters, a fresh love intrigue, and a fresh subject for satire. After practically finishing the first two volumes, Stendhal suddenly decided that it would be a mistake to introduce a whole new set of characters at this stage. "Therefore, no more Duchesse de Saint-Mégrin, no more third volume. Reserve for another novel."

Lucien Leuwen, like Fabrice and Julien, Stendhal's other heroes, is Henri Beyle himself starting out in life with a guileless heart bursting with enthusiasm—but an idealized Beyle such as he would have liked to be. In this case Lucien is handsome and rich (which Beyle was not), enthusiastic, romantic, and republican (which Beyle was). After being expelled from the École Polytechnique for having participated in republican riots, Lucien gets a commission through the influence of his rich banker father and, happy as a child over his handsome Lancer's uniform, goes to join his regiment in the garrison town of Nancy. Here, partly through pique, accepting his father's teasing challenge, partly in order to meet the lady under whose parrot-green shutters his horse had thrown him the day he marched into the city with his regiment, he breaks into Nancy's ultra-legitimist society which looks down its nose at Louis-Philippe's *Juste-milieu* army. He falls in love with the lady of the parrot-green shutters, who turns out to be the ultras' most beautiful and wealthiest heiress, a young widow with the charming name of Bathilde de Chasteller. And although Lucien is never quite sure of it, he is passionately loved in return. The young aristocrats of Nancy become worried, and appeal to their vulgar, unscrupulous, but clever mentor, Dr. Du Poirier, to find some way of getting rid of this dangerous rival and of preventing him from carrying off their best "catch." The device hit upon by the rascally doctor, by which Lucien is made to believe that his pure, beautiful Bathilde has had an illegitimate child, is one of Stendhal's worst descents into irrealism. Without seeing his beloved, Lucien jumps on his horse and gallops back to Paris with a broken heart. So ends *The Green Huntsman,* the first volume of *Lucien Leuwen.*

With the second part, which in this edition is given one of Stendhal's many suggested titles, *The Telegraph,* the scene shifts to Paris. Stendhal has had his fun with the *Juste-milieu* officers and generals, and with the aristocrats who live in constant fear of another Reign of Terror, or, as Stendhal says, "who hate and are afraid," adding, "and therein lies their misfortune." (Stendhal would have agreed with Disraeli that "there is scarcely a less dignified entity than a patrician in a panic.") He now turns his x-ray eye on the ruling class of Paris, the rich bourgeoisie which came into power with that businessman King, Louis-Philippe. Although Stendhal's idealist young hero does not become a rogue as his father advises, he does learn (sadly philosophizing all the while) to find his way about in the venal world of high finance and high politics, which have joined forces in order to make as much money as quickly as possible.

Stendhal began writing *Lucien Leuwen* in May 1834 and continued, with only one serious interruption caused by an attack of gout, until November 1835, when he set it aside to begin his second autobiographical attempt, *La Vie de Henri Brulard.* Part of that time was spent correcting and dictating the first eighteen chapters. He took up *Lucien Leuwen* again and for the last time, on his return to Paris in September 1836, but did little more than add one unco-ordinated chapter, the one on Menuel to be found in the Appendix of *The Green Huntsman.*

* * *

Stendhal was not happy at his Consulate. He suffered from the heat in summer, the sirocco in winter, and worst of all there were no intellectual cronies, no witty women. He escaped to Rome as often as possible—much too often, officialdom reported—where he was cordially received by the French Ambassador, the Comte de Sainte-Aulaire and his attractive wife. With his customary dash, he entered into the social life of the diplomatic circle, and assuaged his esthetic cravings in the company of his friend, the Swiss painter Abraham Constantin, mentioned in *The Telegraph* as the "divine painter on porcelain." But, in spite of Roman society and Roman art, he was bored and homesick for Paris. The former "Milanese," as he had once styled himself when he was in love with Italy and everything Italian, could not wait to get back to that Paris which had caused him such "deadly disgust" in 1821. But now from Civita-Vecchia Paris appeared to him the Eden of the élite. To relieve his boredom and give vent to his endlessly swarming thoughts which, disparaging as so many of them were to the government he represented, could hardly be voiced in the diplomatic drawing rooms of Rome, he wrote continuously. But of all the works begun at Civita-Vecchia—two autobiographies (*Souvenirs d'Egotisme* and *La Vie de Henri Brulard*), three novels (the fragmentary *Une Position Sociale, Lamiel* and *Lucien Leuwen*) not one was completed. Yet, when he at last got back to Paris in 1836 on a leave of absence which lasted more than three years, he began and finished the *Chartreuse de Parme* (in only seven weeks), as well as writing and publishing *Mémoires d'un Touriste* and *Chroniques Italiennes.* A common factor to be found in all the works written at Civita-Vecchia and one which explains their unfinished state, is the merciless lampooning of Louis-Philippe and his government. It would have been impossible for Stendhal to publish any of them while, as he liked to phrase it, he was "feeding on the Budget." "I expect to be silent for eight or ten years," he wrote to his publisher soon after he became Consul, prophetically looking forward to the collapse of the July Monarchy.

Stendhal also indicates other reasons for not finishing *Lucien Leuwen:* his consular duties, with all their interruptions, not being conducive to a work of the imagination, the lack of any intellectual stimulus, and the need for documentation to be found only in Paris. "The boredom I wallow in here," he wrote, "does not stimulate me for this work. Paris has the opposite effect . . . I shall have to wait till I get back to Paris to correct it for style and pleasing form." And the notes scattered through his manuscripts bristle with such observations as: "Get the 'A' in Paris for these conversations at the time of publication." "In four years in Rome I've scarcely heard a single light, amusing conversation. What salon here could give me the 'A'?" "In Paris consult a clever woman about this dialogue —Mme. Lanekaste [Castellane]." But, as we have seen, when he finally got back to Paris, instead of finishing *Lucien Leuwen* his mind turned to fresh themes, and with youthful exuberance he plunged into his last great work, the most bewitching of his novels, *La Chartreuse de Parme,* his swan song. Curiously enough, its setting is Italy!

* * *

In *The Telegraph* it is not always easy to follow Stendhal's innumerable political and historical innuendoes. His many references to political events and scandals familiar at the time to anyone who could read a newspaper or gossip with his neighbor, are sometimes puzzling to a modern reader who, though up on the latest antics of our own representatives, may never, for example, have heard of the once well-known Deputy, Monsieur Piet. Suggested explanations of many of these references will be found at the back of the book opposite the number of the page on which they occur. But to enjoy Stendhal's quiet satire or bitter irony, it is by no means necessary to understand all these passing allusions to historical events and people. It is quite enough to keep in mind one or two salient characteristics of the period. One should not forget, for example, that the Revolution of 1830, which ousted the autocratic Bourbons, was a failure in the eyes of the republicans and the working classes. They had done the fighting, and the bourgeois politicians had divided the spoils. The people had been deceived by their idol, Lafayette (himself duped by his vanity) who had vouched for Louis-Philippe as "the best of republicans." But they soon discovered that the "King of the barricades" was extremely Bourbon in his love of power, and bourgeois in his love of money. As for Louis-Philippe, finding the throne anything but an easy chair, he was not long in forswearing his solemn vows to uphold the reform Charter of 1830, and the freedoms curtailed by Charles X. He was forced to show his true colors which were certainly not *tri-colore*. The government was afraid that if it kept all its liberal promises it would soon be out. With each new uprising, some of the precious freedoms were lopped off with the approval of the very men who, liberals under the Restoration, had in their name plotted the overthrow of the autocratic Charles. Although the government's policy was "peace at any price" (much to the disgust of the republicans who were still in heroic mood and wanted to avenge the humiliating Treaty of 1815, which penalized France for the final Napoleonic conflagration) it felt obliged to mantain an enormous standing army to cope with the country's volcanic unrest. The bitterness of the impoverished working classes was kept in ebullition both by the trade unions and by the constant prodding of the republicans through their courageous and able journalists. It was one of Lucien's repeated complaints against the government that this army was used exclusively to put down strikes and insurrections or, as he put it, "to wage cabbage wars," instead of fighting for the glory of France. But besides this regular military force and the gendarmerie (a police force controlled by the army), there were other police forces—small armies of secret agents who were employed not only to spy on the republicans but to keep the military from hobnobbing with the citizenry. The government's constant fear was that in a popular uprising the soldiers would go over to the people. In the "Kortis affair," narrated at some length, we are taken behind the scenes and shown how this system of agents provocateurs functioned. Not only did the King have his agents, but each of the important Ministries had its own secret police. As M. de Vaize says to Lucien: "We live under five police forces." The wealthy rulers of France were fully conscious of the precariousness of their tenure, which made for a reckless unscrupulousness among the happy "Haves." The order of the day was, "make hay while the sun shines." The semaphore telegraph, which had been set up in France for the exclusive use of the government, was bringing new techniques for acquiring fortunes quickly and making life pleasant and exciting for Ministers with friendly bankers, as well as for the bankers who received telegraphic tips from friendly Ministers. All this is fully described in the second part of *Lucien Leuwen,* in which the telegraph is the *deus ex machina* of this Louis-Philippe epic.

As for the political situation described in *The Telegraph,* it is based on the actual state of affairs during the first part of the July Monarchy. The King and his Ministers were constantly at odds. Louis-Philippe regarded himself as the permanent President of the Council, his Ministers merely as administrators; while the Ministers' slogan was: "The King reigns but does not rule." The endless bickerings, described by Stendhal, between the Minister of War, Soult (the only Minister Stendhal mentions by his real name) and the Minister of Foreign Affairs, as well as the ministerial crisis in which M. Leuwen père becomes involved, are political *reportage* rather than fiction. Now that the legitimists no longer counted, political power was in the hands of the two rival bourgeois parties in the Chamber: the "party of resistance" with the conservatives Casimir Périèr and Guizot at their head, and the "party of progress," led by the former liberals, Lafayette and Laffitte. But both parties agreed in being against any change in the status quo, the liberalism of the "party of progress" not going beyond a representative monarchy and the Charter of 1830.

Another feature of the time which should be borne in mind, is the very limited electoral system. Otherwise the figures cited in the provincial elections at Champagnier and at Caen will seem unbelievably small. Although the government in 1831 had passed an electoral law which considerably reduced assessments for electors, thus adding voters of a somewhat lower income bracket and giving a certain liberal aura to the measure, voting remained entirely in the hands of a comparatively small number of men whose interests corresponded to those of the ruling class. A great many legitimists sacrificed their right to vote rather than take the oath of allegiance to the "Usurper." Neither they, nor the few Deputies who raised their voices on behalf of the disenfranchised working classes, counted in the Chamber. Although 1830 had instituted a representative monarchy, and further limited the power of royalty, the government still represented a very small minority. France was governed by money. The law was as liberal a concession as the government, none too popular, dared to make. The hypocrisy so bitterly complained of by Stendhal is hardly surprising in a government which owed its power to a popular revolution, but whose chief concern was the bourgeois Bourse. It could hardly be frank about such a preference. According to Stendhal the society of his day was based on "charlatanism and endless intrigue without which talent has no chance." It was ideal, he says, "for intrigants without talent like M. de Salvandy . . . and gifted men with a talent for charlatanism like M. de Chateaubriand and Victor Hugo . . ." These are the recurring themes of his indictment of the Louis-Philippe regime. The out-and-out rogues mentioned by Lucien's father—the Talleyrands of varying stature—so far outnumbered patriotic men like the fictitious Mairobert, or the real Dupont de l'Eure, famous for his disinterestedness, that they only serve as a contrast to heighten the cynical picture Stendhal paints of his period.

*   *   *

When Stendhal went to Paris on his long leave of absence in 1836, he took with him his manuscript of *Lucien Leuwen,* intending (for had he not been waiting for just such an opportunity?) to get the "A" from those clever and sophisticated women whose society he had so longed for at Civita-Vecchia. Having abandoned the third volume, he must also have thought of revising the other two. He worked on the book for a short time after his arrival, only to set it aside for good before ever starting on the arduous task of revision. From his notes we know that he intended to bring many of his Nancy characters to Paris. Madame de Chasteller was finally to come with her friend Madame de Constantin, and the finished version was to have ended with the reconciliation and marriage of Bathilde and Lucien. For through all the variations and changes suggested in his notes, there is never a hint of any other ending. That is all we are sure of, but we cannot help speculating on just how the united lovers lived happily ever after. Did Lucien continue his diplomatic career, or did he retire with his adoring bride to the country, as he had once dreamed of doing, to become a philosopher-farmer? Did he, in his happiness, resign himself to things as they are, or did he continue to blast the mediocrity, venality and barbarity of the Louis-Philippe age? Did he continue to applaud America's "liberté, liberté cherie" while thanking his lucky stars for giving him an aristocratic wife and the tangible liberty that goes with wealth, whether of bourgeois, proletarian, or Bourbon origin?

* * *

It has often been said that Stendhal has no style, that he has a bad style, that he could not write. Once Pierre Louys became so violently incensed at Stendhal's "intolerable prose" that he flung *Le Rouge et le Noir* to the floor and stamped on it in a fury of offended purism. And because of its unfinished state, *Lucien Leuwen,* more than any other work, fairly bristles with all the faults which infuriated the precious author of *Bilitis*. In it Stendhal is careless, inaccurate, contradictory, often obscure, and his *non sequiturs* are the despair of a translator. Stendhal was by nature an improvisor. As he deplores over and over again, he had a bad memory, and he wrote rapidly, almost feverishly, as though afraid of losing his ideas before committing them safely to paper. "I put down everything, note everything, sometimes crudely—for fear of forgetting—I'll polish later." Nor did Stendhal have facility; but neither did he have its faults. He struggled with his ideas to present them honestly, stripped of cant and convention. The question of style was always secondary. "There are many haphazard sentences and I shall leave them. I want to leave the sentiment. I'll correct the expression on the proofs. . . ." But the "expression" never came easily: "I only succeed," he says, "in getting some brilliance after correcting for the fourth time when I have forgotten the substance." But what he succeeded in acquiring is something far more important— an inimitable "tone," as Valéry calls it, which makes him a much better writer than "good" writers. Literature seems to have so many examples of this paradox that one is sometimes almost tempted to say that the bad writers are the great writers. America has her Faulkner. As a matter of fact, Stendhal generally achieved the easy, conversational style which he aimed at, and which is so well suited to his unemphatic humor. His ideal was to write as one speaks, or, as Valéry adds, "almost as one speaks to oneself." He wrote what might have been called, in this age of tags and slogans, "shirt-sleeve" French. That in itself was a mark of originality in a day of extravagantly florid prose. He scorned the purely formal felicities of expression, and loathed the poetic and rhetorical style in vogue. Chateaubriand was for him a horrible example of how not to write. Refreshingly independent in his judgments, at a time when Walter Scott, the "ultra Baronet" as Stendhal calls him, was accorded a place only second to Shakespeare by his contemporaries, Stendhal, in *Souvenirs d'Egotisme,* quoting a discussion he had had with a friend, says: "I claimed that at least a third of Scott's merit was due to some secretary who jotted down exact descriptions of the natural scenery he saw. I found him (and still do) weak in the delineation of passion and the human heart." Happily, Stendhal himself spares us those long descriptions, so tedious in early Nineteenth Century literature, while he lays bare the human heart with an almost Freudian ruthlessness. He is perhaps the first novelist to draw characters so true to nature that they are a mass of contradictions (like Stendhal himself), and absurd in the way we ourselves, if the truth were known, are. That Stendhal is exasperating no one can deny. His faults are glaring and his virtues subtle. In the end you must simply take him or leave him. But if you take him it is fatal. To quote Valéry's final verdict: "We shall never have done with Stendhal. And I can't imagine higher praise."

* * *

In his preface to *The Telegraph,* Stendhal ironically protests that his characters are not intended to be likenesses of any living persons. The contrary, of course, is true. He invariably follows his own advice to his friend Jules, and picks a living model, or several, for most of his characters. He himself has mentioned many of their names in his notes, often transparently concealed by anagrammatical spelling. M. de Vaize, the Minister obliquely referred to, while probably intended also as a prototype of the animal, Minister of the Interior, was a caricature of a living Minister Stendhal had in mind. For, in one of his notes, debating whether or not it is advisable to make use of the Bassano "three day Ministry" as a model for the one M. Leuwen is preparing to form, Stendhal says: "It has only one disadvantage—that of giving a name to MM. de Vaize and Bardoux." Naturally, at the time, caricatures of the fallen Ministers would have been recognized by everyone. Why Stendhal should have been at such pains to conceal their identities, since he had no intention of publishing the book during the Louis-Philippe regime, is just one of those Stendhalian anomalies. One no sooner gets Stendhal pigeon-holed as subtle than he behaves like a child—a child playing a game which seems foolish to adults who aren't playing, but serious to the child because, to be fun, a game has to be serious. The indefatigable Henri Martineau has compiled a Stendhal Dictionary which tabulates most of Stendhal's characters with their flesh-and-blood models tracked down and described.

* * *

The first of any part of *Lucien Leuwen* to be published appeared in 1855 under the title, *Le Chasseur Vert (The Green Huntsman).* It was edited by Stendhal's cousin Romain Colomb with a few minor corrections (authorized in Stendhal's will), and printed as the first of the *Unpublished Stories* in an edition of Stendhal's works published by Michel Levy. This first *Chasseur Vert* consisted of the first eighteen chapters only, the ones corrected and dictated by Stendhal in the summer of 1835. Stendhal's next editor, Jean de Mitty, brought out what purported to be the first complete and accurate transcription of the entire manuscript, choosing for the novel, from among Stendhal's many titles, *Lucien Leuwen*. This version was reprinted in 1901 and again in 1923 with the title *Lucien Leuwen or The Magenta and the Black,* the supplementary title being another of the many Stendhal had considered for a time. This version is neither complete nor accurate as de Mitty claimed, and has called forth the indignant censure of all later Beylists, notably Henri Martineau and Henry Debraye who, with such infinite patience, have transcribed every word as well as all the notes of Stendhal's almost illegible manuscripts, now conserved in the Museum of Grenoble.

In making this first English translation I have followed, for the most part, Henri Martineau's version in the Editions du Rocher, Monte Carlo, 1945, but with frequent reference to the Champion edition of 1927 edited by Henry Debraye.

I wish once more to acknowledge my indebtedness to Robert Allerton Parker who, for *The Telegraph* as for *The Green Huntsman,* has most generously given me the benefit of his critical advice. I should also like to thank Jacques Barzun for helping me untangle some of Stendhal's historical and linguistic knots.

L. V.

THE AUTHOR TO THE READER

INDULGENT READER:

Now that we are back in Paris, I shall have to make a great effort to avoid resemblances. Not that I dislike satire—on the contrary! But in focusing the reader's attention on the grotesque figure of some actual Minister, his mind will be bankrupt in interest, and have none left for my other characters. Although most amusing, personal satire is out of place in a work of fiction. The reader becomes entirely engrossed in comparing my character with some unprepossessing or even odious original he knows so well, and will think of him as disgusting or evil according to the way my story depicts him.

When they are true to life and not exaggerated, personal characterizations are charming. But what we have witnessed in the last twenty years is calculated to cure us of this temptation.

"How futile," said Montaigne, "to slander the Inquisition!" In our day he would have said: "How impossible to add anything to the current passion for money, the fear of losing one's job, or eagerness to anticipate one's employer's slightest wish, all things which constitute the soul of those hypocritical speeches of the men who feed upon over fifty thousand francs' worth of the Budget?"

I admit that at over fifty thousand francs private life ceases to be private.

But it is no part of my plan to satirize those happy souls on the Budget! Vinegar is in itself an excellent thing, but mixed with cream it will spoil anything. Therefore, O Indulgent Reader, I have made a great effort to keep you from recogniz-

3

ing any recent Minister in the one who tried to do Lucien some very ill turns. What possible pleasure would it be for you to have me point out that a particular Minister was a thief, that he was scared to death of losing his job, that he scarcely ever indulged in one word that was not a lie? Such people are really only good for something to their heirs. And since their souls have never known a moment of spontaneity, the view of the interior of those souls would disgust you, O Indulgent Reader, and all the more were I so unfortunate as to make those suave and ignoble features masking their baseness recognizable.

It is quite enough to be forced to see such people mornings when one goes to solicit their favor.

Non ragioniam di loro, ma guarda e passa.

THE TELEGRAPH

CHAPTER ONE

I DON'T MEAN to take advantage of my title of father to interfere with you, my son. You are free."

Thus, seated in a comfortable armchair in front of a good fire, gaily spoke the great banker M. François Leuwen, already past his prime, to Lucien his son and our hero.

The room in which this interview between father and son was taking place had just been done over with the greatest possible luxury from M. Leuwen's own designs. He had hung on the walls the three or four good engravings which had appeared during the year in France and Italy, and an admirable painting of the Roman school which he had just acquired. The white marble mantelpiece on which Lucien was leaning had been carved in Tenerani's studio, and the mirror, eight feet high by six wide, hanging over it, had been cited at the Exposition of 1834 as absolutely flawless. It was a far cry from the miserable drawing rooms of Nancy where Lucien had lived through such disquieting moments. In spite of his profound suffering, the vain and Parisian side of his nature appreciated the difference. He was no longer in the country of the barbarians; he had returned to the bosom of his native land.

"The thermometer," remarked M. Leuwen, "seems to be rising too rapidly. Will you just press that button, my dear boy— ventilator number 2 . . . there . . . back of the mantelpiece. . . . That's it. As I have said, I have no intention whatever of taking advantage of my title to *curtail* your liberty. Do exactly as you please."

Leaning on the mantelpiece, Lucien wore a somber, harried, tragic air—in short, the air we should expect in an actor playing the young, love-sick hero of a tragedy. He made a painful and visible effort to alter his melancholy mien and to present an appearance of respect and that sincere filial love which, in his heart, he really felt. But the horror of his position since that last evening in Nancy had changed the well-bred expression he habitually wore in society to that of a youthful criminal appearing before his judges.

"Your mother," continued M. Leuwen, "says that you do not want to return to Nancy. Well then, by all means, don't go back to the provinces. God forbid that I should set myself up as a tyrant. Why shouldn't you commit follies, and even stupidities? There is one, however, but only one, which I should not consent to, because it entails consequences: that is marriage. You can, of course, always have recourse to *sommations respectueuses* . . . and I wouldn't quarrel with you for that. We'd argue it out together over dinner."

"But, my dear father," replied Lucien, bringing himself back from far away, "I am not thinking of marriage."

"Well, if you aren't thinking of marriage, I'll think of it for you. Consider this: I can marry you to a rich girl, and no stupider than a poor one. For it is possible that you may not be a rich man when I die. Of course, in a crazy country like this, it's quite enough to have epaulets for pride to put up with a restricted income. Clothed in a uniform, poverty is only poverty, it doesn't count, it's not a disgrace. But," continued M. Leuwen, changing his tone, "you will believe these things when you have experienced them for yourself. . . . I must seem to you an old dotard. . . . So then, brave Lieutenant, you want no more of the military state?"

"Since you are good enough to discuss things with me instead of commanding, no, I want no more of the military state. At least, not in peace time—spending all my evenings playing billiards and getting drunk in some café, and even forbidden to pick up any newspaper but the *Journal de Paris* off their dirty marble tables. Whenever three of us officers take a stroll together, one, at least, is suspected by the other two of being a spy. The Colonel, who was once a brave soldier, under the magic wand of the *Juste-milieu* is transformed into a filthy policeman."

M. Leuwen could not help smiling. Lucien understood, and quickly added:

"Oh, I wouldn't even try to deceive so discerning a person as yourself. Believe me, father, I am not so presumptuous! But, after all, I had to begin my story somewhere. Admitted: it isn't for any reasonable reason that I want to quit the army. But it's a reasonable step I want to take, nevertheless. I have learned how to handle a lance and how to command fifty men who can do likewise. I know how to get along passably with thirty-five comrades of whom five or six are police informers. So, you see, I do know my *trade*. If there should be a war—but a real war, in which the General-in-chief does not betray his army—and if I still feel as I do today, I shall ask your permission to serve in a campaign or two. The war, as I see it, could not last longer than that, provided the General-in-chief is anything like Washington. If he is nothing but a clever and brave freebooter, like Soult, I shall retire a second time."

"Ah! so that's your political stand!" rejoined his father ironically. "The devil! it's unadulterated virtue! But politics is long! What do you want for yourself personally?"

"To live in Paris or else to go on long voyages—America, China . . ."

"Considering my age, and that of your mother, let's make it Paris. If I were Merlin, and you had but to say the word for me to arrange the material side of your destiny, what would your wish be? Would you like to be a clerk in my bank, or a private secretary to a Minister who is about to acquire enormous influence over the destinies of France, in other words, M. de Vaize? He may become Minister of the Interior tomorrow."

"M. de Vaize, that peer of France who has such a gift for administration, and is such a hard worker?"

"Precisely," replied M. Leuwen, amused and wondering at the lofty virtue of his son's aims and the stupidity of his perceptive faculties.

"I am not fond enough of money to go into your bank," replied Lucien. "I don't think enough of the *yellow metal*. I have never felt keenly, or for any length of time, the lack of it. That terrible lack would not be constantly present to cure me of my aversion. I'm afraid I'd show a want of perseverance for the second time if I decided for the bank."

"But, after I'm gone, what if you should be left poor?"

"At least, to judge by my expenditures in Nancy, I am rich now; and why shouldn't that last?"

"Because sixty-five is not twenty-four."

"But that difference . . ." Lucien's voice quivered.

"No flowery phrases, sir! I call you to order! Politics and sentiment lead us from the subject which is the order of the day:

Is he to be a god, a table or a wash-basin?

The question under consideration, and for which we must find an answer, is *you*. The bank bores you and you prefer the private office of M. de Vaize?"

"Yes, father."

"Now we come to the great difficulty: are you enough of a rogue for such an occupation?"

Lucien gave a start. His father continued to look at him with the same half amused, half serious expression. After a silence, M. Leuwen went on:

"Yes, Sir Second-Lieutenant, will you be enough of a rogue? You will be in a position to observe a lot of little maneuverings; will you be a good subordinate and help the Minister in bringing them off, or will you obstruct him? Will you pull a long face like a young republican who believes he can reform Frenchmen and make angels out of them? *That is the question;* and you will have to give me the answer to it this very evening after the Opera for—and this is a secret—there might well be a ministerial crisis at any moment. Haven't Finance and War insulted each other again for the twentieth time? I have a finger in all this and tonight am able, and will be tomorrow, but perhaps not day after tomorrow, to feather your nest handsomely. I will not hide from you the fact that mothers with marriageable daughters will all have their eyes on you; in short, an *honorable* position, as imbeciles say; but will you be enough of a rogue to hold it? Think it over then: do you feel that you have the strength of mind to be a rogue, that is, to assist in petty rogueries; for during the last four years there has been no occasion to spill blood."

"At the most, to steal money," Lucien interrupted.

"From the *poor masses!*" interrupted M. Leuwen in his turn with a mock pathetic air. "Or to employ it somewhat differently from the way they would," he added in the same tone. "But the masses are pretty stupid and their Deputies pretty silly and not altogether disinterested. . . ."

"So, what do you want me to be?" asked Lucien with an ingenuous air.

"A rogue," replied his father, "I mean a politician, a Martignac, I won't go so far as to say a Talleyrand. That, at your age and in your newspapers, is called being a rogue. In ten years you will realize that Colbert, Sully, Cardinal Richelieu, in short, that any man who has been a politician, in other words *a leader of men,* has risen by means of that first step in roguery which I am asking you to take. You mustn't be like N—— who, when he was appointed General Secretary of Police, resigned because the job was too dirty. It is true that it was at the time they had Frotté shot by the gendarmes who were taking him to prison; and even before they started, the gendarmes knew that their prisoner would try to escape and that they would be obliged to shoot him."

"The devil!" cried Lucien.

"Yes. And C——, Prefect of Troyes, a friend of mine and a fine fellow whom you may remember at Plancy, a man six feet tall with gray hair . . ."

"I remember him very well. Mother used to give him the nice red damask room at the château."

"That's the one. Well, he lost his Prefecture in the North, at Caen or thereabouts, because he refused to be enough of a rogue, and I thoroughly approved. Someone else took care of the Frotté affair. Ah! *my young friend,* as stage-fathers say, *you stand amazed!*"

"*It would take less than that,* as the young juvenile often replies," said Lucien. "But I believed that only the Jesuits and the Restoration . . ."

"Believe only what you see, my friend, and you will be all the wiser for it. . . . But now, because of that cursed freedom of the press," he said, laughing, "you can't treat people à la Frotté any longer. The worst that can happen to anyone at present is the loss of his money or position. . . ."

"Or a few months' imprisonment!"

"Very good. And so it's understood, an answer tonight, conclusive, clear, precise, above all, without any sentimental trimmings. Later, it may be, I can do *nothing for my son!*"

These last words were spoken with a tragic and sentimental air in the manner of the great actor Monvel.

"By the way," said M. Leuwen, turning as he reached the door, "you know, I suppose, that if it weren't for your father you would now be in the Abbaye. I wrote General D——, and told him that I had sent for you in haste because your mother was dangerously ill. I shall go to the Ministry of War to be sure that your furlough reaches the Colonel antedated. You must write to him and try to mollify him."

"I wanted to speak to you about the Abbaye. I thought of a couple of days in prison perhaps, and, after that, to settle the whole thing by resigning."

"Never resign, my friend. Only fools resign! I intend that all your life you shall be a young army officer of the greatest distinction attracted to politics, *a veritable loss to the army,* as the *Débats* would say."

CHAPTER TWO

THE FRANTIC DISTRACTION of deciding what the categorical, the decisive answer demanded by his father should be, was the first relief Lucien had known. During his trip from Nancy to Paris he had had no time for reflection. He was running away from his anguish, and physical action took the place of moral. Since his arrival, he was disgusted with himself and with life in general. To talk to anyone was a torture to him, and he even had difficulty mastering himself sufficiently to spend an hour chatting with his mother.

The minute he was alone, he was plunged either in a somber revery, or an endless sea of heart-rending emotions, or else, trying to reason with himself, he would say:

"I am an awful idiot, I am a perfect fool! I have held as worthy what was worthless: a woman's heart; and yearning for it passionately, was powerless to win it. Either I must correct myself fundamentally or quit life altogether."

At other moments, when a ridiculous tenderness got the upper hand:

"Perhaps I could have won her if it hadn't been for that inescapable confession: 'Another has loved me, and I am . . .' For there were days when she really loved me. . . . If it hadn't been for her embarrassing condition she would have said, 'Yes, it is true, I do love you!' But as it was, she would have had to add: 'My condition . . .' for she is honorable, of that I am sure. . . . She understood me badly. That admission would not have destroyed the strange sentiment I felt for her, a sentiment which—though I was always ashamed of it—dominated me completely.

"She has been weak, and I, am I perfect?" Then with a sad smile he would add: "But why deceive myself? Why try to reason? Even if I had discovered the most shocking things about her—what am I saying—even the most shameful vices, I would have been cruelly disillusioned, but I would not have been able to stop loving her. And what does life hold for me from now on? One long martyrdom. Where can I hope to find any happiness, or even a state exempt from pain?"

And before this melancholy sensation all others paled. He reviewed the possibilities life held for him—travel, living in Paris, great wealth, power. They aroused nothing but insuperable disgust. The last man he spoke to always seemed to him the most boring.

Only one thing could rouse him out of this profound lethargy, could stimulate his mind, and that was to live over again all that had happened to him in Nancy. When, by chance, he came upon the name of that little town on a map of France he would tremble; the name haunted him in the papers; all the regiments returning from Lunéville seemed to pass that way. The name of Nancy invariably recalled this idea:

"She could not bring herself to say: 'I have a terrible secret that I cannot tell you. . . . But if it weren't for that I should love you, and you only.' Often, it is true, I noticed that she was profoundly sad, and this seemed to me extraordinary, inexplicable at the time. . . . What if I went to Nancy and threw myself at her feet? . . ." "Yes," sneered his Mephistophelian side, "and ask her to forgive you for *her* having given *you* horns!"

After leaving his father's study, thoughts like these seemed to besiege Lucien's heart more fiercely than ever.

"And before tomorrow morning," he said to himself in terror, "I must make a decision, I must have *faith in myself*. . . . Is there anyone in the world whose judgment I trust less than my own?"

He was utterly miserable. At the bottom of all his reasoning was this mad idea:

"What is the use of choosing a calling for the third time? Since I didn't know enough to win Madame de Chasteller, what will I ever know? When one has a nature like mine, both weak and, at the same time, one that is never satisfied, the only thing to do is bury oneself in a Trappist monastery."

The ironical part of it was that all Madame Leuwen's friends were complimenting her on the fine poise her son had acquired. "He is now a man of parts," was heard on all sides, "a son to satisfy a mother's dearest ambitions."

In his disgust with men, Lucien was careful to keep them from divining his thoughts, and always answered them with well-turned commonplaces.

Tormented by the necessity of giving a final answer that very night, he went to dine by himself, for at home he would have been forced to be agreeable or else call down upon himself a rain of epigrams; nobody was ever spared.

After dinner, Lucien wandered along the boulevard and then through the more deserted little streets. He was afraid of meeting friends on the boulevard, for every minute was precious, any minute his answer might occur to him. He came to a reading room and entered mechanically. It was dimly lighted and he hoped to find not too many people. A servant was returning a book to the young librarian. To Lucien she seemed most attractively dressed and full of charm (Lucien was just back from the provinces).

He opened the book at random. It was by a boring moralist who divided his sermon into detached portraits after the manner of Vauvenargues: *Edgar, or the Parisian of Twenty.*

"What does a young man amount to who knows nothing of men, who has lived with genteel people only, or inferiors, or people whose interests he in no way endangers? To vouch for his merit, Edgar has only the magnificent promises he makes to himself. Edgar has received the most distinguished education possible. He can ride a horse, he manages his cabriolet admirably, he has, if you like, all the learning of a Lagrange, all the virtues of a Lafayette, and what of it? He has never experienced the effect of other people on himself. He is sure of nothing, knows nothing about other people and with all the more reason, nothing about himself. He is at best nothing but a brilliant *Perhaps*. What, after all, does he really know? He knows how to ride a horse because, if he didn't, his horse, having no manners, would throw him. The better his manners and the less like those of his horse, the less he is worth. If he lets his fleeting years between eighteen and thirty slip by without *coming to grips with necessity*, as Montaigne says, he is no longer even a *Perhaps*; public opinion dumps him in the same rut with ordinary people, pays no more attention to him, sees him as just another person like everybody else, important only because of the number of thousand-franc notes his stewards lay on his desk.

"Being a philosopher, I disregard the desk covered with bank notes, and look at the man counting them. I see in him only a sallow, worried individual reduced, by his own ineptitude, to becoming sometimes a fanatic of a party, sometimes a fanatic of the Bouffes and of Rossini, or a fanatic of the *Justemilieu*, rejoicing in the number of dead left on the quays of Lyons, or a fanatic of Henri V forever reiterating that the

Czar is going to lend them two hundred thousand men and four hundred million francs. What do I care, what does the world care? Edgar has let himself degenerate into nothing but a dolt!

"Provided he goes to Mass, provided he banishes all amusing conversation and pleasantries on all subjects, provided he gives, as of course he does, to charity, by the time he is fifty the charlatans of all kinds, those of the Institute and those of the Archbishopric, will proclaim that he has all the virtues, and will finally honor him by making him one of the dozen Mayors of Paris. He will end up founding a hospital. *Requiescat in pace.* Colas lived, Colas died."

Lucien read every word of this morality twice and three times; he studied its meaning and its bearing. His somberly meditative air made other readers lift their noses from the *Journal du Soir* to look at him. This annoyed him, he paid and left. For some time he paced up and down the Place de Beauvau in front of the reading room. Suddenly he made up his mind:

"*I will be a rogue!*" he cried, but spent another quarter of an hour deciding whether he really had the courage. Then he called a cab and was driven to the Opera.

"I was looking for you," said his father, as Lucien met him in the foyer. They went straight to M. Leuwen's box, where they found three young ladies of the ballet, and Raimonde in her *Sylphides* costume.

"They can't understand, so don't worry," said M. Leuwen, speaking English, whereupon Mademoiselle Raimonde rose and said:

"Gentlemen, I can read in your eyes that you have things to say to each other much too serious for us. We'll go backstage. Be happy—that is, as happy as you can be without us!"

"So you think you have the soul of a scoundrel and can

enter the race for honors?" M. Leuwen asked when they were alone.

"I shall be frank with you, father. Your excessive indulgence amazes me and increases my gratitude and my respect. Something has happened to me I can't even talk to my father about, and has disgusted me with myself and with life. How am I to choose one career in preference to another? Everything is a matter of indifference to me, odious, I might say. The only state that would really suit me is that of a man dying in the hospital, or that of a savage who has to hunt and fish for his food every day. It is not a very pretty state for a man of twenty-four, and no one in the world will have confidence . . ."

"What, not even your mother?"

"Her commiseration would only intensify my martyrdom. It would make her suffer too much to see me in this unhappy state. . . ." M. Leuwen's ego was flattered by this remark, which made him feel a little closer to his son. "He has secrets he keeps from his mother," he thought, "which are not secrets to me."

"Should external things ever begin to mean something to me again," Lucien pursued, "I shall most likely find myself strangely shocked by the demands of the career I have chosen. Whereas, the duties I should be called upon to perform at your bank are hardly calculated to scandalize anyone, and for that reason, perhaps, the bank should be my choice."

"There is another very important consideration I should mention," insisted M. Leuwen. "You would better serve my interests as a private secretary to the Minister of the Interior than as the head of the correspondence department of my banking house, where your social talents would be of no use to me."

For the first time since his *cuckolding* (that is the word he used with bitter irony, for, as an added torment to his soul, he looked upon himself as a deceived husband, and attributed to himself all the ridicule and antipathy that the theater and the world heaps upon that state, just as though such distinctions still counted), Lucien displayed tact. Principally out of curiosity, he had been about to decide in favor of the position in the Ministry. He was familiar with the bank but had not the slightest idea what the intimate life of a Ministry was like. He looked forward to meeting Comte de Vaize, that hard worker and foremost administrator of France, as the papers said, a man they compared to the Emperor's Comte Daru.

His father had hardly ceased speaking when Lucien exclaimed, with a duplicity that spoke well for the future:

"That decides me! I was rather inclined to the bank, but I now go over to the Ministry; but on one condition: that I shall not be involved in any assassinations like those of Marshal Ney, Colonel Caron, Frotté, etc. The most I'll commit myself to is a little crookedness in money matters; but, not being very sure of myself, I shall engage myself for one year only."

"The world would find that pretty short. People will say 'He can't stick to anything for more than six months.' It may be that the disgust you will perhaps feel in the beginning, in six months will change to indulgence for the foibles and knaveries of men. Out of friendship for me, will you promise not to leave the Ministry of the Rue de Grenelle for eighteen months?"

"Eighteen months then, I give you my word—provided always there's no assassination—for example, if my Minister should engage four or five officers to fight successive duels with an overly eloquent Deputy embarrassing to the Budget . . ."

"Ah, my friend," said M. Leuwen, laughing heartily, "where ever do you come from? Don't worry, there will never be any duels of the kind, and for a very good reason."

"That," continued Lucien very seriously, "would be a rehibitory case, and I should leave for England immediately."

"And who, O virtuous man, is to be the judge of such crimes?"

"You, father."

"But election machinations, lies and petty rogueries will not break our contract?"

"I won't write lying pamphlets. . . ."

"God forbid! That's the affair of the writing profession. You only direct the dirty work, you never do it yourself. The principle is this: every government, even that of the United States, lies always and about everything; when it can't lie on the main issue, it lies about the details. There are good lies and bad. *Good* ones are those that the public with incomes of from fifty louis to twelve or fifteen thousand francs, believes; *excellent* ones catch some of the carriage public; *execrable* ones are those nobody believes, and that only the most shameless Ministries dare repeat. Everybody knows this. It is one of the first *maxims of state,* and must never escape your memory—or your lips."

"I enter a cave of thieves, but all their secrets, great or small, are entrusted to my *honor!*"

"Sagely spoken! The government pilfers the rights and money of the masses while swearing every morning to protect them. You remember the red string that is always found at the center of all coils of rope, big or little, in the British navy; or rather, do you remember *Werther,* for I think it was there I read this admirable thing."

"Yes, very well."

"That is the image of a corporation, or a man, having a *fundamental* lie to uphold. No truth *pure and simple,* ever. There you have the *doctrinaires.*"

"Napoleon's duplicity was not so crude, not nearly," protested Lucien.

"In only two cases is hypocrisy impossible: winning a battle and being witty in conversation. Besides, you mustn't speak of Napoleon. Leave your moral sense at the door on entering the Ministry just as, in his day, one left one's love of country on joining his guard. Will you be a chess player for eighteen months, and not be repelled by any pecuniary transactions? Will you promise to be stopped by blood alone?"

"Yes, father."

"That's settled then."

And M. Leuwen fled. Lucien noticed that he walked like a man of twenty. As a matter of fact this conversation with a simpleton had exasperated him beyond endurance.

Astonished at having begun to take an interest in politics, Lucien surveyed the audience.

"Here I am in the midst of all that is most elegant in Paris. Here, before my eyes, lies spread out in profusion all that was lacking in Nancy."

As he pronounced the beloved word, Lucien looked at his watch.

"It is eleven o'clock. On those days of trusting intimacy or of light-hearted gaiety, I would sometimes stay with her until eleven o'clock."

A very cowardly idea, which several times he had already rejected, now presented itself with an insistence he could hardly resist:

"What if I just left the Ministry flat and went back to Nancy and the regiment? If I asked her to forgive me for knowing her secret, or rather (and that would be fairer) if I never even mentioned what I saw, why shouldn't she receive me again exactly as on the day before the fatal day? Looked at reasonably, why should I be offended? I am not her lover. Just because I discovered proof that she had had a lover before she knew me?

"But would my manner toward her be the same? Sooner or later she would guess the truth. I could not help telling her if she asked me, and then my very lack of vanity would make her despise me as a man devoid of feeling, as has happened several times before. Can I ever be at peace, feeling that if she understood me she would despise me?"

This grave question troubled Lucien's heart as his eyes rested with a sort of mechanical attention on the ladies of fashion in their boxes, one after the other. He recognized several of them; they seemed to him like provincial actresses.

"My God, I am literally going mad!" he said to himself when his opera-glass reached the end of the row of boxes. "I applied exactly the same words, *provincial actresses,* to the women who thronged the drawing rooms of Mesdames de Puylaurens and d'Hocquincourt. A man afflicted with a fever may even find the taste of sugared water bitter. The main thing is not to let anyone discover my madness. I must be careful to say only the most commonplace things and never anything that differs in the least from generally accepted ideas in any company in which I happen to find myself. Mornings, hard work at my office, if I have an office, or else long rides on horseback; evenings, I must display a passion for the theater, only natural after eight months of exile in the provinces; in the salons, when I cannot possibly avoid appearing, an inordinate appetite for écarté."

These reflections were interrupted by sudden darkness. They had turned out all the lamps.

"Well, well," he said to himself with a bitter smile, "the theater interests me so much that I am the last to leave."

A week after this interview at the Opera, the *Moniteur* carried the acceptance of the resignation of M. N——, Minister of the Interior; the nomination of M. le Comte de Vaize, Peer of France; similar announcements of four other Ministers, and much lower down, in an obscure corner of the paper:

"By decree, MM. N——, N——, and Lucien Leuwen have been named Masters of Petitions. M. Leuwen will be in charge of the private office of M. le Comte de Vaize."

CHAPTER THREE

WHILE LUCIEN was receiving his first lessons in common sense from his father, the following was happening in Nancy:

Two days after Lucien's sudden departure, when that great event became known to M. de Sanréal, Comte Roller, and the other conspirators who had dined together for the purpose of plotting a duel with him, they could hardly believe their ears. Their admiration for Dr. Du Poirier knew no bounds. How he had managed it, they could not imagine.

Acting on first impulse, which is always generous and dangerous, these gentlemen forgot their repugnance for that ill-mannered bourgeois, and went in a body to call on him. And, like all provincials, avid for anything that has an official air and that can relieve the monotony of their lives, they gravely climbed the stairs to the third floor where the doctor lived. Among a great many commonplaces, the following sentence made Du Poirier prick up his ears:

"If you are considering Louis-Philippe's Chamber of Deputies, and you see fit to stand for election, we promise you our votes and all those that are at our disposal."

When the discourse was finished, M. Ludwig Roller stepped awkwardly forward, and stood there in silent embarrassment. His lean fair face became covered with innumerable new wrinkles and finally, making a wry face, he said glumly:

"I am the only one perhaps who owes no thanks to Dr. Du Poirier. He has deprived me of the pleasure of punishing an impudent fellow, or of trying to, at least. However, I owe this sacrifice to His Majesty, Charles X, and although I am the injured party in this affair, I nevertheless make the same offer as these gentlemen. Yet, as a matter of fact, I am not sure, on account of the oath of allegiance to Louis-Philippe, that my conscience will permit me to assist at the elections."

In the end Dr. Du Poirier's arrogance and his mania for making speeches prevailed. It must be admitted that he spoke very well. He took good care not to explain to them why and how Lucien had left, but he was, nevertheless, able to move his listeners: Sanréal was actually in tears; even Ludwig Roller shook the doctor's hand most cordially on leaving.

As soon as the door closed, Dr. Du Poirier burst out laughing. He had talked for forty minutes, he had enjoyed an enormous success, he didn't care a rap for the gentlemen who had been listening to him—three essentials for the greatest enjoyment on the part of this singular rascal.

"So that's twenty or so votes I can count on, provided always they don't get wind of some of my methods between now and the elections. Well, it's worth thinking about. I hear on all sides that M. de Vassignies has not more than a hundred and twenty sure votes, and there will be three hundred electors present. The fanatics in his party will reproach him for the oath he would have to take to become a member of the Chamber of Deputies, considering his personal attachment to Henri V. I have the advantage of being only a plebeian. I live on the fourth floor and I don't keep a carriage. The friends of M. de Lafayette and the July Revolution, although hating us equally, are bound to prefer me to M. de Vassignies, a cousin to the Emperor of Austria, who has in his pocket the brevet of Gentleman of the Chamber (if ever there is a King's Chamber). I shall play the role of a liberal hero like Dupont de l'Eure, who is, since they buried M. de Lafayette, the one honest man of the party."

Another party leader, as honest as Du Poirier was not, but madder by far, since he exerted himself enormously without the least hope of making any money, M. Gauthier, the republican, was also astonished, but even more hurt, by Lucien's departure.

"Not to have said a word to me, and I so fond of him! Ah, these Parisians, all manners and no feeling! I thought he was a little different from the others, I thought I could detect both warmth of heart and enthusiasm in him."

The same sentiment, but raised to an infinitely greater degree of intensity, wrung the heart of Madame de Chasteller.

"To think that he did not even write to me, to *me* whom he swore he loved so much, and whose weakness he knew very well!"

The thought was too horrible. Madame de Chasteller finally persuaded herself that Lucien's letter had been intercepted.

"Have I received any answers from Madame de Constantin?" she thought. "And I have written her at least six times since my illness."

The reader must know that Madame Cunier, postmistress of Nancy, *thought right*. As soon as M. de Pontlevé saw that his daughter was too ill to leave the house, he hurried to Madame Cunier, a tiny bigot, hardly more than four and a half feet tall. After the preliminary courtesies, he had said with unction:

"You are too good a Christian, Madam, and too good a royalist not to realize what the authority of the King (id est Charles X), and of the Commissioners appointed by him in his absence, should be. The elections are about to take place—a crucial event! Prudence, it is evident, demands our taking certain precautions; that is as it should be, Prague before all! And, you may rest assured, a faithful reckoning is kept of all services, but . . . and it is my painful duty Madam, to tell you . . . anyone who fails to do everything to help us in these difficult times, is against us. . . ."

At the end of the dialogue between these two solemn individuals, endlessly long and infinitely cautious and even more boring to the reader if he had to read it (for today, after forty years of pure farce, who cannot imagine the result of a conversation between a selfish old Marquis and a professional bigot?), the following articles had been agreed upon:

1. *None of the letters of the Sub-Prefect, the Mayor, the Lieutenant of gendarmes, etc. shall ever be transmitted to M. le Marquis. Madame Cunier shall show him all letters written by M. Rey, the Grand Vicar, Abbé Olivier, etc. without letting them out of her possession.*

M. de Pontlevé had directed the conversation particularly to a discussion of this first article. For, by seeming to yield in these matters, he had obtained a complete triumph in regard to the ones that interested him.

2. *All letters addressed to Madame de Chasteller shall be given to M. de Pontlevé, who takes upon himself to deliver them to Madame de Chasteller, for the moment confined to her bed.*

3. *All letters written by Madame de Chasteller shall be shown to M. de Pontlevé.*

It was tacitly agreed that the Marquis could take the latter to have them delivered by a more economical means than the post. But in that case, as the government would lose some pennies by it, Madame Cunier, its representative in this affair, might naturally expect the gift of a basket of good Rhine wine of second quality.

Not more than two days after this conversation, Madame Cunier had a packet, wrapped by herself, delivered into the hands of the Marquis' valet, old Saint-Jean. In this packet was a tiny letter from Madame de Chasteller to Madame de Constantin. It was written in a sweet, affectionate vein; Madame de Chasteller would like to ask her friend's advice but could not explain more fully in a letter.

"Meaningless chatter," M. de Pontlevé had said to himself,

putting it away in his desk. And a quarter of an hour later the old valet could be seen carrying a basket of sixteen bottles of Rhine wine to Madame Cunier.

Gentleness and nonchalance were the leading traits of Madame de Chasteller's character. Nothing ordinarily troubled that sweet and noble soul. She loved her own thoughts and solitude. But, unhappily, not being at the moment in her normal state of mind, decisions cost her nothing: she sent her valet to Darney to mail a letter addressed to Madame de Constantin.

One hour after the departure of the valet what was her joy to see Madame de Constantin herself walk into her room. It was a precious moment for the two friends.

"What! dear Bathilde," cried Madame de Constantin when, after the first transports of joy, she was finally able to speak, "six weeks without a single word from you! And it was by the merest chance, from one of the agents employed by the Prefect for the elections, that I learned of your illness and that your condition caused some anxiety. . . ."

"I have written you at least eight letters."

"This, my dear, is too much! It has come to a point where goodness makes you a dupe. . . ."

"He means well. . . ."

This meant: "My father means well," for Madame de Chasteller's indulgence did not go so far as to blind her to what was going on. But the disgust inspired by all the little tricks she observed had only one effect—to increase her love of solitude. What she enjoyed in society were the pleasures afforded by the arts, the theater, a brilliant promenade, a crowded ballroom. When she saw six persons in a drawing room she shuddered, sure that something base or mean was going to offend her painfully. The fear of this disagreeable sensation made her dread any conversation between her and another person.

It was the diametrically opposite character of Madame de

Constantin that made her such an outstanding figure in society. A vivacious, enterprising disposition, not afraid of difficulties, and a taste for making fun of the absurdities of her enemies, made people look upon her as one of the most dangerous women to offend in the whole province. Her husband, a very handsome man and quite wealthy, undertook with enthusiasm anything she suggested. For example, during two years he had thought of nothing but a windmill he had had built on an old tower near his château, which brought him in forty per cent. But the windmill had been neglected for the last three months. He now thought of nothing but the Chamber of Deputies. Since he was without wit, had never offended anyone, and had the reputation of always acquitting himself cheerfully and faithfully of any little commissions entrusted to him, his chances were very good.

"We think we can count upon the election of M. de Constantin. The Prefect gives him only his second choice because he is afraid of the Marquis de Croisans, *our rival,* my dear. The ministerial candidate is sure to lose. He's a little scoundrel and sufficiently despised already, but, to make doubly sure, the day before the elections we are going to circulate three letters of his which prove clearly enough that he indulges in the noble calling of spy. That explains his Cross last May which so incensed the entire district of Beuvron. I'll tell you, dear Bathilde, but in the strictest confidence, that our trunks are already packed." And she added, laughing, "So it would be too ridiculous to lose! But if we win, the very next day, bright and early, we leave for Paris where we shall stay for six months. And *you* are coming with us."

At these words Madame de Chasteller blushed furiously.

"My God, darling," cried Madame de Constantin, looking at her, "whatever is the matter?"

Madame de Chasteller was crimson. She heartily wished that Madame de Constantin had received the letter her valet was at that moment mailing at Darney. In it were written the fatal words: "Someone you love has lost her heart."

Finally, with endless confusion, Madame de Chasteller said:

"Alas, dear friend, there is a man who must believe that I love him—and he is not wrong."

"What a little idiot you are!" said Madame de Constantin, laughing. "Really, if I leave you in Nancy another year or two, you will have the mentality of a nun. Great God, what harm is there if a young widow of twenty-four whose sole protector is an aged father of seventy-five who, through excess of affection for his daughter, intercepts her letters, thinks of choosing a husband, a helpmate, a protector? . . ."

"Alas, all those good reasons have nothing to do with it. I should be insincere if I admitted your praise. It so happens that he is rich and well-bred, but if he had been poor and the son of a farmer it would have made no difference."

Madame de Constantin demanded a full account; nothing interested her so much as stories of true love, and she was passionately fond of Madame de Chasteller.

"He began by falling off his horse twice, right under my windows. . . ."

Madame de Constantin burst out laughing and couldn't stop; Madame de Chasteller was hurt. Finally, wiping her eyes, Madame de Constantin succeeded in saying in little gasps:

"Well . . . my dear Bathilde . . . you can't apply . . . to this mighty conqueror of yours . . . that indispensable expression in the provinces: *he is a handsome cavalier!*"

This injustice to Lucien redoubled the enthusiasm with which Madame de Chasteller told her friend all that had happened in the last six months. But the sentimental aspects of her story failed to touch Madame de Constantin, she did not believe in these *grandes passions*. She grew thoughtful, nevertheless, toward the end of the recital, and when it was finished, remained silent.

"Your M. Leuwen," she said at length, "is he, I wonder, a terrible Don Juan for us poor females, or is he a child who lacks experience? There is nothing natural about his conduct."

"Say rather, there is nothing ordinary about it, nothing calculated in advance," replied Madame de Chasteller with a vivacity very rare in her. And she added with a sort of rapture:

"That is why he is so dear to me. He is not a simpleton who has read a lot of novels."

The discussion between the two friends on this subject was endless. Madame de Constantin had at first hoped for a perfectly proper little love affair that, if all requirements were met, could lead to an advantageous marriage, otherwise a trip to Italy or the distractions of a winter in Paris that would efface what remained of the ravages produced by three months of daily intercourse. Instead of that she found this gentle, timid, idle young woman whom nothing disturbed, quite out of her mind and ready for anything.

"My heart tells me," Madame de Chasteller kept saying, "that he has basely deserted me. Think of it, not even writing!"

"But of all the letters I wrote you, not a single one has reached you," Madame de Constantin replied, for she had a quality, very rare in this age: she was never insincere with her friend, even for her own good; lying, it seemed to her, would kill their friendship.

"Why couldn't he have said to a postilion," went on Madame de Chasteller with a very singular show of passion, "why couldn't he have said to a postilion ten leagues from here: 'My friend, here are a hundred francs, go to Nancy, Rue de la Pompe, and give this letter to Madame de Chasteller. Give the letter to her personally and to no one else.'

"And it is nine days since he left! I have never openly admitted my suspicions as to the fate of my letters, but he knows what I think about everything. My heart tells me he knows that my letters are opened."

CHAPTER FOUR

SUCH MISGIVINGS furnished Madame de Chasteller with a definite objection to Madame de Constantin's proposal that she should go with her to Paris, if Madame de Constantin's husband were elected Deputy.

"Wouldn't it look as though I were running after M. Leuwen?" she asked.

For the next two weeks this objection occupied all the most intimate conversations between the two friends.

Three days after Madame de Constantin's arrival, Mademoiselle Bérard, the companion, was handsomely paid, and dismissed. With her customary dispatch, Madame de Constantin questioned the estimable Mademoiselle Beaulieu and promptly dismissed Anne-Marie, Madame de Chasteller's other personal maid, as well.

The Marquis de Pontlevé, watching these little domestic arrangements with great attention, realized that he had an irresistible rival in his daughter's friend.

It was as Madame de Constantin had hoped: her bustling activity restored Madame de Chasteller to health. Madame de Constantin insisted on being taken into society constantly, and on this pretext forced her friend to appear almost every evening in the drawing rooms of Mesdames de Puylaurens, d'Hocquincourt, de Marcilly, de Serpierre, de Commercy, etc. Her object was to demonstrate to society that Madame de Chasteller was not inconsolable over the departure of Lucien.

"Without meaning to," she thought, "my little Bathilde

must have committed some indiscretion. And if we don't succeed in silencing malicious gossip, it can pursue us even to
Paris. Her eyes are so beautiful that they speak without her
consent,

E sotto l'usbergo del sentirsi pura

  they must have looked at that young officer with a
look that no explanation on earth could excuse."

One evening in the carriage, on their way to Madame de
Puylaurens', Madame de Constantin inquired:

"Among the young men here in Nancy, which one is the
most active, the most insolent, the most influential?"

"M. de Sanréal, without a doubt," replied Madame de Chasteller, smiling.

"Very well then, I am going to tackle this noble soul for
your sake . . . for my own too! Tell me, does he control any
votes?"

"There are his notaries, his agent, his stewards. Since he has
an income of at least forty thousand pounds, he is a popular
young man."

"What does he do?"

"He gets drunk morning, noon and night. And he has
horses."

"In short, he is bored. I will seduce him. Has any passable
woman ever tried to seduce him before?"

"I doubt it. She would first have to discover some way of
not dying of boredom listening to him."

On those days of profound melancholy when Madame de
Chasteller felt an irresistible aversion to going out, Madame
de Constantin would cry:

"I must go vote-hunting for my husband! In the vast field
of intrigue, nothing should be *neglected*. Four votes, three
votes, coming from the district of Nancy, might decide everything. Do you realize that I am dying to hear Rubini, and as

long as my stingy father-in-law lives, there is only one way in the world for me to get to Paris: via the Chamber of Deputies!"

It did not take long for Madame de Constantin to discover under Dr. Du Poirier's coarse and unprepossessing shell, his superior intelligence, and a real intimacy sprang up between them. This great bear had never known a pretty woman— unless she was ill—to address two consecutive words to him. Doctors in the provinces had not yet taken the place of priests.

"You must become our colleague, dear Doctor," she said to him. "We will vote together and make and unmake Ministers. . . . Our dinners will be every bit as good as theirs— you will give me your vote, won't you? If we always vote together, our twelve votes will make themselves felt. . . . Oh, but I am forgetting . . . you are a furious legitimist and we are moderate anti-republicans."

A few days later Madame de Constantin made a very useful discovery: Madame d'Hocquincourt was in despair over Lucien's departure. The ferocious silence of this usually gay and talkative young woman, formerly the life of Nancy society, saved Madame de Chasteller; hardly anyone thought of saying that Madame de Chasteller too had lost her *adorer*. Madame d'Hocquincourt never opened her lips except to talk of Paris and her plans for a little trip as soon as the elections were over.

One day when she spoke of going to Paris Madame de Serpierre maliciously said to her:

"Then you will see M. d'Antin again."

And much to the amusement of Madame de Constantin, Madame d'Hocquincourt stared at Madame de Serpierre with an expression of utter amazement. Madame d'Hocquincourt had forgotten the very existence of M. d'Antin, her former lover!

It was only in Madame de Serpierre's drawing room that

Madame de Constantin heard any remarks inimical to her friend.

"But how in the world," she cried, "could anyone expect to marry so painfully, so ridiculously ugly a daughter as Théodelinde de Serpierre to a rich young man from Paris, and especially as that young man had never given her a single word of encouragement? It is literally crazy. It would take millions to get a Parisian to enter a drawing room with such a fright on his arm."

"M. Leuwen is not like that, you don't know him! If he loved someone, he would scorn society's disapproval, or rather he wouldn't even notice it."

And for five minutes Madame de Chasteller enlarged upon Lucien's character. These explanations had the effect of making Madame de Constantin very thoughtful.

But Madame de Constantin had only to see Mademoiselle Théodelinde five or six times to be touched by the tender friendship the girl cherished for Lucien. It was not love, the poor girl would never have dared; she knew too well, and even exaggerated, all the disadvantages of her face and figure. It was her mother who had entertained expectations based on her belief that her noble Lorraine lineage would be too great an honor to be resisted by a simple plebeian.

Madame de Constantin was equally delighted with old M. de Serpierre. He had a heart overflowing with kindness, and spent his time defending inhuman doctrines.

"It reminds me," said Madame de Constantin to her friend, "how, at the Sacré Cœur, they insisted on our admiring the worthy Duc N—— because he would have his carriage call for him at seven in the morning in the middle of February, to go petitioning for the *amputated hand*. The law of sacrilege was under discussion in the Chamber of Deputies at the time, and the question of whether to make amputation of the right hand the penalty for thieves who stole holy vessels from the churches!"

Soon Madame de Constantin with her pretty face (a little commonplace perhaps), her vitality, her ingratiating courtesy, her unfailing wit, had made her friend's peace with the house of de Serpierre. It is true that the last time the delicate subject was broached, Madame de Serpierre had stubbornly insisted, in her unpleasant way:

"I have my own opinion."

"As you please, my dear," rejoined the kindly former King's Lieutenant, "but let's drop the subject, or else malicious tongues will say that we are husband-hunting."

It had been at least six years since M. de Serpierre had made a remark of such severity. It marked an epoch in the family, and the reputation of Lucien, who had figured as the faithless seducer of Mademoiselle Théodelinde, was restored.

Every day, for fear of meeting *electors* to whom they would have to be agreeable, the two friends took long walks in the woods near The Green Huntsman. Madame de Chasteller loved to revisit this charming coffee-house. It was there that the ultimatum on the trip to Paris was finally proclaimed.

"Even your conscience, no matter how finical, will not be able to apply the humiliating and vulgar expression, *running after a lover,* if you swear to yourself not to speak to him even if you see him in Paris."

"So be it then!" agreed Madame de Chasteller, eagerly grasping at the suggestion. "On those conditions I consent, my scruples vanish. If ever I meet him in the Bois de Boulogne, if he comes up and speaks to me, I swear I will not reply a single word until I have seen The Green Huntsman again."

Madame de Constantin looked at her in surprise.

"In this way, if I am tempted to speak to him," Madame de Chasteller explained, "I shall be obliged to leave for Nancy, and only after having been here again will I allow myself to reply."

There was a silence.

"That is a vow," Madame de Chasteller went on, with a seriousness that made Madame de Constantin smile, then threw her into a thoughtful mood.

Next day, as they were driving out to The Green Huntsman, Madame de Constantin noticed a framed picture in the carriage. It was a beautiful Saint Cecilia, engraved by Perfetti, that Lucien had once given Madame de Chasteller. She handed it to the proprietor of the café, asking him to hang it over the bar.

"*I may ask for it back again some day.* And," she added in lowered tone to Madame de Constantin as they moved away, "never will I be so weak as to utter a single word to M. Leuwen as long as that engraving hangs here. It was here that my *fatal* infatuation began."

"Ah, no! I protest the word *fatal!* Thank heaven love is not a *duty* but a pleasure, so don't take it so tragically. When your present age and mine add up to fifty, then we can be as sad, reasonable, and lugubrious as you please. We'll follow the lovely reasoning of my father-in-law: 'It's raining? So much the worse! It's a fine day? Still, so much the worse!' You have been bored to death while pretending to be angry with Paris, without being angry at all. A handsome young man appears . . ."

"But he isn't so very good looking . . ."

"A young man—no epithets—appears; you fall in love with him; your mind is occupied, boredom flies away, and you call that *fatal!*"

Now that the departure was settled, terrible scenes followed on the subject with M. de Pontlevé. Happily Madame de Constantin was there to bear the brunt of the discussions, and the Marquis had a deadly fear of her frequently ironic gaiety.

34

"That woman *says everything*; it isn't difficult to be amusing when there is nothing you dare not say," he complained to Madame de Puylaurens. "It isn't difficult to be witty when you allow yourself such liberties."

"Very well, my dear Marquis, try inviting Madame de Serpierre, who is right over there, to say anything she pleases, and see how amusing it will be!"

"Nothing but irony," said M. de Pontlevé peevishly. "Nothing is sacred to that woman!"

"No one on earth has ever had such wit as Madame de Constantin," cried M. de Sanréal, putting in his word with an air of importance, "and if she makes fun of people's ridiculous pretensions, whose fault is it?"

"Their pretentiousness, of course!" agreed Madame de Puylaurens, curious to see the two men sparring at each other.

"Yes," added Sanréal with a portentous air, "pretentiousness, tyranny!"

Happy to have had an idea, happier still to be approved by Madame de Puylaurens, something that had never happened to him before, M. de Sanréal kept turning his poor little idea upside down and inside out, as he held forth for a quarter of an hour

"Could anything be funnier," whispered Madame de Constantin to Madame de Puylaurens, "than a man without wit who encounters an idea? It's scandalous!" And the burst of laughter from the two ladies was taken by Sanréal as a mark of approbation.

Madame de Constantin accepted two or three magnificent dinners in her honor, attended by all the élite of Nancy. Whenever M. de Sanréal, trying his best to pay court to her, could find absolutely nothing to say, she would ask him for his vote for the hundredth time. She was sure of some bizarre protestation; he would swear that he was hers to command—himself, his agent, his notaries, and his intendants.

"And moreover, Madam, I am coming to Paris to see you."

"But in Paris I can only receive you once a week," she said, glancing at Madame de Puylaurens. "Here we all know each other, but in Paris you would compromise me—a young man like you, with your fortune, your horses, your position in the world! Once a week—what am I saying? Two calls a month at the most."

Never in his life had Sanréal enjoyed himself so much. If only he could have had all the amiable things Madame de Constantin said to him deposed before a notary—"that witty woman," as he repeated at least twenty times a day, and in stentorian tones that impressed people and made them believe him.

For her sake he quarreled with M. de Pontlevé, declaring that he intended to vote, and was ready to take the oath of allegiance to Louis-Philippe.

"Who believes in oaths in France today? Louis-Philippe doesn't even believe in his own. If I were held up by thieves in the woods, and they were three against one and insisted upon my taking an oath, would I refuse? Here the government is the thief who wants to rob me of my right, in common with all Frenchmen, to elect a deputy. The government has its Prefects, its police—am I going to fight them? No, egad! I'll pay it in the same coin in which it pays the partisans of the *Glorious Days.*"

In what pamphlet had M. de Sanréal read the last three sentences? For no one would ever accuse him of having thought them up himself. Madame de Constantin, who supplied him with ideas every evening, always took good care never to advance arguments that could shock the Prefect of the Department. This was the famous M. Dumoral, notorious renegade, who before 1830 had been a liberal orator, had even gone to prison, and never stopped talking of his eight months in Sainte-Pélagie under Charles X. As a matter of fact he was much less stupid now, having even acquired a certain amount of finesse since his change of religion, and Madame de Constantin would never have risked a really imprudent remark.

What M. Dumoral wanted was an administrative position of 40,000 francs and Paris, and for the sake of his ambition, he was obliged to swallow insults two or three times a day. Madame de Constantin knew that a man on such a diet is not very susceptible to the charms of a pretty woman. For the moment M. Dumoral was anxious to make a brilliant show at the elections and then to proceed to another Prefecture. The sarcasms of *L'Aurore* (M. Gauthier's paper), its eternal quotations of his former liberal opinions, had completely *demoralized* him (the local word for it) in the Department.

We will now suppress eight or ten pages on the sayings and doings of M. Dumoral preparing for the elections. All quite true, but true after the fashion of a morgue, and the sort of truth we willingly leave to the duodecimo novels for chambermaids. Let us now return to Paris and M. Dumoral's Minister. The machinations of men in power are somewhat less depressing in Paris than in the provinces.

CHAPTER FIVE

THE EVENING of the day Lucien's name figured so gloriously in the *Moniteur,* that Master of Petitions, dead with fatigue and disgust, was sitting in an obscure corner of his mother's drawing room looking like Molière's Misanthrope. Overwhelmed by the endless congratulations to which he had been exposed all day, the words *superb career, magnificent future, the first brilliant step* danced before his eyes and made his head ache. He was horribly weary of his replies—for the most part neither very gracious nor very felicitous—to so many compliments, all of them well-turned and even more gracefully spoken: a talent pre-eminently Parisian.

"So this is happiness!" he said to his mother when they were alone.

"My son," she replied, "there is no such thing as happiness when one is extremely tired, unless the mind is stimulated, or the imagination succeeds in painting a rosy picture of happiness to come. Compliments repeated over and over again are boring, and you are neither childish enough, nor old enough, nor ambitious enough, nor vain enough, to be dazzled by the uniform of a Master of Petitions."

M. Leuwen did not put in an appearance until after the Opera.

"Tomorrow morning at eight o'clock," he said to his son, "if you have nothing better to do, I will present you to your Minister."

Next morning at five minutes to eight, Lucien was in the little antechamber leading to his father's apartment.

Eight o'clock struck . . . eight-fifteen.

"Not for anything in the world," said Anselm, M. Leuwen's old valet, "would I go into Monsieur's room before he rings."

At last, at ten-thirty the bell was heard.

"I am sorry to have kept you waiting, my friend," M. Leuwen began amiably.

"It doesn't matter as far as I am concerned," Lucien hastened to reply, "but what about the Minister?"

"That is what the Minister is for, to wait for me if necessary. You may be sure he needs me more than I need him. He needs my bank, and is afraid of my salon. But, to impose two hours of boredom on you, my son, whom I love, *and whom I esteem,*" he added, laughing, "that is a different matter. I admit I heard eight o'clock strike, but as I was perspiring a bit

38

I thought I had better wait. At sixty-five life is a problem . . . and one should not complicate it with imaginary difficulties.

"But look at you!" he interrupted himself. "What a way to dress. You look very, very young! Go and put on something not quite so spick and span, a black waistcoat, comb your hair carelessly, cough now and then . . . try to appear at least twenty-eight or thirty. With imbeciles, the first impression counts for a lot and you must always treat a Minister as though he were an imbecile, he hasn't time to think. Remember, never dress too well as long as you are in the government."

After M. Leuwen had spent another full hour dressing, they left. M. de Vaize had not gone out and M. Leuwen's name produced an instant effect. He was introduced without delay.

"His Excellency was waiting for us," commented M. Leuwen as they crossed several rooms where petitioners were ranged according to merit and their rank in the world.

M. Leuwen and his son found the Minister very busy sorting three or four hundred letters. He was seated at a rosewood desk, covered with carvings in the worst possible taste.

"You find me in the midst of preparing my ministerial circular which will be torn to shreds by the *National,* the *Gazette,* etc., and these clerks of mine have kept me waiting here two hours for the circulars of my predecessors. I am curious to see how they got over the hurdle. I am sorry not to have it ready to show you. A man of your intelligence would immediately spot anything that might offer an opening to my critics."

His Excellency continued in the same vein for the next twenty minutes. During this time Lucien studied him carefully. M. de Vaize appeared to be about fifty years of age. He was tall, with quite a good figure. Nice hair turning gray, very regular features, a well poised head, all prepossessed a person in his favor. But this impression was of short duration. At second glance one noticed his low forehead, covered with wrinkles, that precluded all idea of thought. Lucien was shocked to find in this great executive a more than vulgar air, the aspect of a lackey. His long arms seemed to get in his way; and what was worse, Lucien thought he detected in His Excellency an evident desire to put on airs. He talked too loudly and listened to himself talk.

Practically interrupting this ministerial flow of eloquence, M. Leuwen finally succeeded in getting in the classic words: "I have the honor of presenting my son to Your Excellency."

"I shall make a friend of him, I hope," replied the Minister graciously. "He will be my first aide-de-camp. There is plenty of work ahead. I shall have to cram into my head the different characters of all my eighty-six Prefects, stimulate the phlegmatic, restrain exaggerated zeal that only adds the auxiliary of anger to the interests of the opposing party, enlighten those of limited intelligence. That poor N—— (his predecessor) has left everything in complete disorder, and the clerks I have inherited, instead of replying to my questions with facts, wax rhetorical.

"You see me seated at the desk of that poor Corbière. When, in the Chamber of Peers, I used to combat his little voice of a cat being skinned alive, who would have thought that I should one day be sitting in his chair? He had a shallow mind and was short-sighted, but within the limited range of his vision he was not lacking in common sense. He did possess discernment, but it was at the antipodes of eloquence; besides, he had that look of an angry cat which made everyone want to contradict him. M. de Villèle would have done better to get someone more eloquent as his assistant, Martignac for example."

Here followed a dissertation on M. de Villèle's system. After that M. de Vaize proved that justice was the primary need of society. From there he went on to explain how good faith is the foundation of credit. He then told his visitors that a biased and unjust government *commits suicide* with its own hands, etc., etc.

The presence of M. Leuwen had somewhat subdued his style in the beginning, but soon, drunk with his own words, he forgot that he was talking to a man whose epigrams were repeated from one end of Paris to the other. He assumed an air of importance and ended up with a eulogy on the probity of his predecessor, who, as was generally believed, had tucked away eight hundred thousand francs in the one year he had been Minister.

"All this is far too magnanimous for me, my dear Count," said M. Leuwen, as he made his escape.

But now M. de Vaize was in a talking vein. He proved to his private secretary at great length that without probity one cannot be a great Minister. Lucien, sole object of his eloquence, found him decidedly vulgar.

At last His Excellency installed Lucien at a magnificent desk only a step or two from his own private quarters. Lucien was surprised to find that the windows of his office looked out over a lovely garden, and it struck him as a curious contrast to the barrenness of his recent sensations. He gazed tenderly down upon the trees.

As he seated himself he saw powder on the back of the armchair.

"My predecessor," he said to himself, laughing, "was not burdened with such thoughts."

A little later, reading this predecessor's sober handwriting, very large and very well formed, he had an overwhelming sensation of the superannuated past.

"This office reeks of meaningless eloquence and empty bombast."

He took down several engravings of the French School: Ulysses halting Penelope's chariot by M. Fragonard or M. Le Barbier . . . and sent them to other offices. (Later he hung some engravings of Anderloni and Morghen in their place.)

In an hour the Minister returned and gave Lucien a list of twenty-five persons who were to receive invitations for the next day.

"I have arranged that when the clock of the Ministry strikes the hour, the porter shall bring you all the letters that have arrived for me. You will promptly give me those from the Tuileries or the Ministries, you will then open the rest and make me a résumé of their contents—a line or two at the most: my time is precious."

Hardly had the Minister left when eight or ten clerks came to make the acquaintance of the Master of Petitions whose cold and resolute manner, it seemed to them, boded ill for the future.

During the whole day, filled almost exclusively with prescribed and flagrantly absurd formalities, Lucien maintained an air that was even colder and more ironic than in the regiment. He seemed to be separated by at least ten years from that deplorable ordeal of his arrival at Nancy, when he had adopted a cold demeanor in order to avoid a witticism that might have led to a duel. Often in those days he had had all the difficulty in the world to repress his natural exuberance; and was often tempted to risk all the coarse pleasantries and all the duels on earth, in order to join his comrades of the Twenty-seventh in their sports. Today his only effort was to hide the profound disgust that all his fellow men inspired. His former coldness seemed to him the blithe sulkiness of a boy of fifteen. Now he had a sensation of swimming in mud. While he replied to the greetings of all the clerks who came to see him, he was thinking to himself:

"In Nancy I was a dupe because I wasn't skeptical enough. I had the simplicity and gullibility of an honest heart, I was not enough of a rogue. Oh, how very wise was my father's question: *Are you enough of a rogue?* I should either join the Trappists in a hurry, or else make myself as sincere as all these head clerks and deputy head clerks who come to welcome the honorable Master of Petitions. . . . But with the Trappists, who lead an innocent life whose worst crime consists in imposing a bit on a few peasants in the neighborhood or a few novices, would my unsatisfied vanity give me a moment's peace? How could I bear the idea of being mentally inferior to all my contemporaries? . . . So let's learn then, if not to steal, at least to *connive at the thefts of His Excellency,* like all these clerks I have met today."

Such ideas gave Lucien an air that was hardly calculated to inspire easy and polished conversation with people who were meeting him for the first time. After his first day at the Ministry, Lucien's misanthropy took this form: he never gave his fellow men a thought when he was not with them, but their presence for any length of time seemed importunate and finally insupportable.

The last straw was finding his father in a very gay mood when he got back home.

"Here are two little summonses," cried the latter, "which are the natural sequel to your new dignities of this morning."

They were two subscription cards to the Opera and the Bouffes.

"Ah, but these pleasures terrify me, dear father."

"For my sake, you agreed to maintain a certain position in the world for eighteen months instead of one year. To complete this gracious favor, promise me that you will spend half an hour every evening in these *temples of pleasure,* especially when the pleasure is about over, toward eleven o'clock."

"I promise. But am I not then to have even one poor little peaceful hour out of my entire day?"

"And what about Sunday?"

The second day the Minister said to Lucien:

"I am going to entrust to you the making of appointments with the crowds of people that always flock around a new Minister. Get rid of the Parisian intriguer who is mixed up with women of doubtful virtue—such people are capable of anything, even of quite sinister things. Be nice to the poor provincial devil obsessed by some crazy idea. The petitioner who wears a shabby suit with extreme elegance is a rascal; he lives in Paris; if he mattered at all, I would have met him in some drawing room, or he would find someone to present him and to recommend him."

A few days later Lucien, by mistake, invited to dinner at the Minister's a painter who was very witty and whose name, Lacroix, was the same as that of a Prefect dismissed by M. de Polignac. And this was a dinner to which only Prefects were to be invited.

That evening when the Comte de Vaize was alone in his drawing room with his wife and Lucien, he laughed with great glee over the discomfiture of all the assembled Prefects who, assuming the painter to be a candidate for a Prefecture and destined to replace one of them, had viewed him with jaundiced eye.

"And to complete the misunderstanding," said the Minister, "a dozen times during dinner, I turned to Lacroix and talked to him earnestly on matters pertaining to administrative policies."

"So that explains why he looked so bored and so boring," exclaimed little Comtesse de Vaize in her soft timid voice. "He was hardly recognizable; I observed his clever little face above the flowers of the centerpiece, and couldn't imagine what had happened to him. He will revile your dinner."

"No one reviles a Minister's dinner," retorted the Comte de Vaize.

"The lion's paw," thought Lucien.

Madame de Vaize, who was very sensitive to such savage slaps, looked crestfallen.

"This little Leuwen," the Minister said to himself, "will make me cut a sorry figure with his father."

"So, Lacroix wants patronage for his paintings, does he?" he went on gaily. "And, egad, on your recommendation, he shall have it. I notice he manages to come here twice a week."

"You are serious? You promise me that for him, and without his asking?"

"My word on it!"

"In that case, I'll make of him a real friend of the house."

"So, Madam, you will have two clever men: Messieurs Lacroix and Leuwen."

From this gracious remark the Minister proceeded to banter Lucien relentlessly on his blunder in inviting the historical painter to the dinner of Prefects. This acted as a spur to Lucien, who replied to His Excellency in a tone of perfect equality, thereby shocking the latter exceedingly. Perceiving this, Lucien continued to talk with an ease that amazed and amused him.

He enjoyed being with Madame de Vaize—pretty, kind, and very shy. When she was talking to him she entirely forgot that she was a young woman and he a young man, an arrangement which suited our hero perfectly.

"Here I am," he thought, "on terms of intimacy with two people whose faces I had never set eyes on a week ago, one of whom amuses me when he attacks me, and the other of whom pleases me."

Lucien gave his work the closest attention; it seemed to him that the Minister wanted to make the most of his blunder as an excuse for attributing to him the amiable heedlessness of extreme youth.

"You are a very great administrator, *M. le Comte*," he said to himself, "for which I respect you, but *epigram in hand* I

45

am your equal and, considering your honorific position, I prefer to risk being a bit too firm to letting you infringe upon my dignity. It will show you, besides, that I don't give a rap for my office, whereas you adore yours."

At the end of one week of ministerial life, Lucien was back on earth again. He had surmounted the state of demoralization he had been in ever since that last evening in Nancy. His first pang of remorse came at the thought of Gauthier, to whom he had never written. He at once sent him an interminable and, it must be admitted, a rather imprudent letter. He signed the first name that came into his head and sent it to the Prefect of Strasbourg, asking him to forward it for him.

"Coming from Strasbourg," he thought, "it may escape Madame Cunier and that renegade Dumoral's Chief of Police."

He was amused to read, in the different departments, the correspondence of M. Dumoral, Prefect of Nancy, which seemed to give M. de Vaize so much concern. All France at that moment was in the fever of the elections and of the Spanish question. M. Dumoral's letters about Nancy entertained Lucien no end: M. de Vassignies was represented as a very dangerous man, Du Poirier as someone less to be feared and who could be had with a Cross and a tobacco shop for his sister. These poor Prefects trembling for fear of losing their elections, and exaggerating their difficulties to their Ministers, had the gift of making Lucien forget his melancholy.

Such was Lucien's life: six hours at the office in the Rue de Grenelle every day, at least one hour at the Opera every evening. Without, of course, admitting as much, his father had seen to it that every minute of his time was occupied.

"It is the best guarantee against a bullet," he said to Madame Leuwen, "though I very much doubt if we have reached such an extremity. His virtue, which is so awfully boring, would be enough to keep him from leaving us forever. Besides he has

46

a natural love of life and a great curiosity to come to grips with the world."

For the sake of his wife M. Leuwen had given himself up whole-heartedly to this problem.

"You cannot live without your son," he said; "I cannot live without you. And I confess that since I have been observing him closely he no longer seems to me so dull. He sometimes even finds a ready rejoinder to his Minister's epigrams, and Madame de Vaize admires him. Everything considered, Lucien's somewhat callow repartee is really worth more than the old, pointless witticisms of de Vaize. . . . It is still to be seen how he will take His Excellency's first piece of rascality."

"Lucien still has the highest regard for M. de Vaize's talents."

"That is our only hope. It is an admiration we must carefully cultivate. It is our capital. After I have denied as well as I can the first flagrant blow to honesty, my only recourse will be to say: 'Is a Minister of such talent overpaid at forty thousand francs a year?' Thereupon I will prove that Sully was a thief. Three or four days later I'll bring up my reserves—which are superb: In 1796, in Italy, General Bonaparte stole. Would you have preferred an honest man like Moreau, letting himself be beaten in 1799 at Cassano, at Novi, and so on? Moreau cost the Treasury perhaps two hundred thousand francs, Bonaparte three million. . . . I trust Lucien will not be able to find an answer, and I'll guarantee that he will stay in Paris as long as he admires M. de Vaize."

"If we can just get through to the end of the year, he will have forgotten Madame de Chasteller."

"I am not so sure! You have endowed him with such a constant heart! In spite of my abominable conduct you have never been able to get over loving me. For a heart all of a piece such as you have given your son, a new interest is necessary. I am

47

waiting for a favorable occasion to present him to Madame Grandet."

"She is certainly very pretty, very young, and very brilliant."

"And, besides, is absolutely bent on having a *grande passion.*"

"But if Lucien senses affectation he will take to his heels. . . ."

One very sunny day, towards two-thirty in the afternoon, the Minister entered Lucien's office, flushed, wild-eyed, and quite beside himself.

"You must go to your father at once. . . . But first copy this telegraphic dispatch. . . . Be good enough also to make a copy of this note I am sending to the *Journal de Paris.* . . . You perceive the full importance of the thing and its confidential nature . . ." and while Lucien was busy copying, the Minister added:

"For very good reasons I should advise your not taking the cabriolet of the Ministry. Get a cab across the street, give the driver six francs in advance, and for God's sake find your father before the Bourse closes. It closes at half-past-three, as you know."

Seeing him enter, Lucien thought he had come to tell him that he was putting someone else in his place, but at the word *telegraph* Lucien understood. The Minister fled, but came rushing back again to say:

"You will bring me back the two copies you have just made, sir, to me and to no one else, and on your life, don't show it to a soul but your father!"

Having said this he again disappeared.

"What a rude, what a ridiculous tone to use," said Lucien to himself. "Such an offensive tone inclines one to think of too easy a revenge."

"And so," he thought, as he went to find a cab, "all my suspicions are confirmed. His Excellency is certainly playing the market, and I am purely and simply an accomplice in a rascally practice."

Lucien had great difficulty finding his father. Finally, as it was pleasantly cold with still a little sunshine, he thought of looking for him on the boulevard, and at last found him in contemplation before a huge fish displayed at the corner of the Rue de Choiseul.

M. Leuwen was not pleased to see him, and refused to get into the cab.

"Devil take your old rattletrap! All the stock markets on earth can close without me before I'll ride in anything but my own carriage!"

Lucien hurried to get his father's carriage, which was waiting for him at the corner of the Rue de la Paix. At last, at a quarter-past-three as the Bourse was about to close, M. Leuwen arrived.

He did not return home until six o'clock.

"Go back to your Minister and give him this note. You may be surprised at your reception."

Lucien went off extremely vexed at having to take part in shady transactions, "Minister or no Minister I shall take a firm tone with him."

He found the Minister surrounded by twenty Generals. "All the more reason for firmness," he said to himself. Dinner had been announced and Marshal N—— had already given Madame de Vaize his arm. The Minister was standing in the middle of the drawing room perorating, but as soon as he caught sight of Lucien he stopped short in the middle of a sentence and dashed out of the room, beckoning Lucien to follow him. When they were in his study he quickly locked the door and began poring over M. Leuwen's letter. He was almost mad with joy, took Lucien in his arms and hugged him over and over again. . . . With his black jacket buttoned up to his chin Lucien stood and surveyed him with disgust.

"So this is a thief," he said to himself, "and a thief at work! And no matter whether he is elated or worried his gestures are always those of a lackey."

The Minister had quite forgotten his dinner party; this was his first operation on the Bourse, and he was beside himself with joy at having made a few thousand francs. The thing that was most amusing was that he seemed to be proud of himself, as though now he were truly a Minister in every sense of the word.

"This is marvelous, my friend," he said to Lucien as they went back to the dining room. . . . "And tomorrow we shall have to see about re-selling."

Everyone was seated at the table, but out of deference to His Excellency they had not dared to begin to eat. Poor Madame de Vaize was flushed and perspiring with anxiety. The twenty-five guests, sitting in silence and well aware that they should be talking, could find nothing to say. They presented a ridiculous spectacle in their embarrassed silence, interrupted from time to time by Madame de Vaize's timid and hardly audible voice as she offered a plate of soup to the Marshal sitting on her right. The attention of the whole company became centered on his refusal. It was altogether comical.

So wrought-up was the Minister that he had completely lost that famous poise of his, so much vaunted by the newspapers. Still in a flurry he seated himself at the table murmuring: "A dispatch from the Tuileries . . ."

The soup was cold, and a chill hung over the whole company. Everyone was ill at ease, and the silence so complete that Lucien caught a whispered remark of a Colonel sitting next to him to a General on his other side.

"He seems very much upset. Could he have fallen from grace?"

"I should say that joy was uppermost," replied the old, white-haired General in the same tone.

That evening at the Opera all Lucien's attention was taken up by the grievous thought:

"My father is a party to this maneuver. . . . One could, I suppose, retort that it is simply a function of his calling as banker. He has some information and profits by it, he does not betray his oath of office. . . . Yet without a fence there would be no thieves."

This reply did nothing to restore his peace of mind. All the charms of Mademoiselle Raimonde, who came to the box as soon as she saw him, failed to draw a word out of him. His *former self* had got the upper hand.

"Mornings with thieves, evenings with wenches!" he thought bitterly. "But what does public opinion amount to? It will respect me for my mornings and despise me for my evenings spent with this poor girl. Beautiful ladies are very much like the Academy in its treatment of romanticism: they are both litigants and judge. . . . Ah! if I could only talk of all these things with . . ."

He stopped just as he was about to pronounce the name— Bathilde!

The next day M. de Vaize came rushing into Lucien's office. He closed and locked the door. There was a queer expression in his eyes.

"God, how ugly vice is!" thought Lucien.

"My friend, go to your father as quickly as you can," said the Minister in a tremulous voice. "I must speak to him . . . *without fail.* . . . Do everything under heaven to bring him to the Ministry, for after all, I cannot very well be seen at the banking house of MM. Van Peters and Leuwen."

Lucien examined him attentively.

"He has not the least shame in speaking to me of his theft!"

Lucien was wrong. M. de Vaize was simply so consumed with cupidity (it was a matter of realizing a profit of seventeen thousand francs) that he forgot all the trepidation he usually felt when speaking to Lucien, not for any moral reason, but because he thought him a man of wit like his father, and dreaded some disagreeable sally. The Minister's tone was at the moment that of a master speaking to his valet. In any case, the difference would certainly never occur to him. A Minister, according to him, conferred so great an honor on anyone he spoke to that he could not possibly be impolite. And then, besides, whenever money was involved, excitement prevented him from noticing anything at all.

M. Leuwen laughed when he heard the message his son had been charged with.

"Ah!" he said, "because he is a Minister he thinks he can make me trot? Tell him for me that I am not going to his Ministry and that I urgently advise him not to come to me. Yesterday's transaction is terminated; today I am engaged in others."

As Lucien made haste to leave:

"Don't be in such a hurry," said his father. "Your Minister has a genius for administration, but one should never spoil a great man, otherwise he becomes negligent. . . . You say that he assumes a rude and too familiar a tone with you— *with you* is superfluous. Except when the man is perorating in his drawing room like a Prefect accustomed to being the only one who talks, he is rude to everyone. It is because all his life has been spent studying the great art of handling men and leading them to happiness along the path of virtue."

M. Leuwen glanced at his son to see if he would let this pass. Lucien did not even notice the sarcasm.

"How far he still is from listening to his interlocutor and from knowing how to take advantage of his mistakes!" thought M. Leuwen. "This son of mine is an artist. His art requires an embroidered coat and a carriage, as the art of Ingres and Prudhon call for brushes and an easel."

"Which would you prefer," he asked, "a perfectly polished,

graceful artist with finished manners who painted daubs, or a man who, entirely preoccupied with the essence of things and not their appearance, produced masterpieces? If, after two years as Minister, M. de Vaize can point to twenty Departments where agriculture has advanced one step, thirty others in which public morals have improved, won't you forgive him his somewhat incorrect and rude way of speaking to his first aide-de-camp, a young man he likes and who is, moreover, necessary to him? You must forgive him that ridiculous tone he adopts without knowing it. It is because he was born ridiculous and pompous. What you should do is to remind him of the courtesy due you by a firm manner and a few timely and telling words."

M. Leuwen went on talking for a long time without eliciting any response from Lucien. He did not like this pensive air.

"I saw three or four brokers waiting in the first reception room," Lucien said, getting up to return to the Rue de Grenelle.

"My friend," said his father, "you who have such good eyes, I wish you would read me a little from the *Débats,* the *Quotidienne* and the *National."*

Lucien began reading, and could not help smiling to think of the stock brokers. "Waiting is their job, and mine is reading newspapers aloud!"

M. de Vaize was almost out of his mind when at three o'clock Lucien finally returned. He was in Lucien's office and had, as the office boy said with bated breath and an air of profound respect, been back and forth at least ten times before.

"Well, sir?" said the Minister with haggard eyes.

"Nothing new," replied Lucien with the most perfect calm. "I have just left my father who kept me until now. He will not come, and urgently advises you not to come to him. Yesterday's transaction is terminated, and he is engaged on others today."

M. de Vaize turned purple and hastily left his secretary's office.

Completely dazzled by his new dignity which he had worshiped in anticipation for the last thirty years, M. de Vaize now perceived for the first time that M. Leuwen was equally proud of the position he had made for himself in the world.

"I see the logic of this young man's insolence," M. de Vaize said to himself as he paced up and down the room. "A Minister is made by royal decree, but a decree cannot make a man like M. Leuwen. That's what comes of the government leaving us in office for only a year or two. Would a banker have refused to come if Colbert had sent for him?"

After this discreet comparison, the angry Minister fell into a profound meditation.

"Couldn't I possibly get along without this insolent individual? But his honesty is famous, almost as famous as his malice. He is a pleasure lover, a *rake,* who for twenty years has been making fun of everything that is most respected: the King, religion . . . He is the Talleyrand of the Bourse. In that world his epigrams are law and, since the July revolt, *that world* is coming nearer every day to the aristocratic world, the only one that should, by rights, have influence. People with money have succeeded to the place and privileges of the great families of the Faubourg Saint-Germain. . . . His salon brings together all the cleverest men of the business world. . . . He is on friendly terms with all the diplomats who frequent the Opera. . . . Villèle used to consult him."

At that name, M. de Vaize almost bowed. Although his tone was overbearing, and he sometimes carried assurance to the point where it is known by another name, he was by a strange contradiction subject to fits of unbelievable timidity. For example, it would have been very painful and almost impossible for him to make overtures to any other banking house. He combined a violent love of money with the fantastic idea that the public looked upon him as spotlessly honest; this came from having been preceded in office by a thief.

After a full hour of pacing the floor and after having very energetically sent to the devil his usher when the latter came to announce the department heads, and even one of the King's aides-de-camp, he felt that the effort of getting another banker was beyond his powers. His Excellency had a holy fear of the newspapers. His vanity having bowed before the epigrammatic indolence of a man of pleasure, he now proceeded to conciliate his vanity.

"After all, I knew him before I was Minister. . . . I am not compromising my dignity by allowing this caustic old man to continue the same tone of equality he was accustomed to use toward me in the past."

M. Leuwen had foreseen this reaction. That evening he said to his son:

"Your Minister has written me a letter full of pinpricks, like a lover to his mistress. I was obliged to reply. What a bore! I am like you, the *yellow metal* does not interest me enough. You really should learn to play the market. Nothing could be simpler for a great mathematician, a former student of the École Polytechnique. There is only one principle involved: the stupidity of the petty speculator is an infinite quantity. My clerk, M. Metral, will give you lessons, not in stupidity but in the art of profiting by it." (Lucien looked severe.) "You will do me a great personal service if you will make yourself competent to act as intermediary between M. de Vaize and me. The natural arrogance of this great administrator has to contend with the natural impassivity of my character. He keeps dancing around me, but since our last operation I refuse to do anything but jest. Yesterday evening his vanity was fairly seething, he tried his best to reduce me to seriousness. It was most amusing. If he cannot humble you within the next week, he will begin to court you. How will you receive the advances of a Minister and a man of merit? Do you realize, my dear son, the advantages of having a father? In Paris, a very useful article."

"On that score I should have much too much to say, and you are not fond of provincial sentimentality. As to His Excellency, why shouldn't I be as natural with him as I am with everybody else?"

"The expedient of laziness. Shame on you!"

"I mean I shall be distant and respectful, while always showing, even quite plainly, my desire to terminate the interview with so great a personage."

"Would you have the spunk to risk a light and somewhat chaffing remark? He would then say to himself: Worthy son of such a father!"

"Unfortunately the clever rejoinder that occurs to you on the spur of the moment, only enters my head two minutes later."

"Bravo! You always see the useful side of things and, what is worse, the honest side. All that is perfectly ridiculous and out of place in France. Take your Saint-Simonism! There was some good in it, and yet for the first and second floors it remains odious and unintelligible, and even for the third; only in the garret does it meet with some consideration. But the French Church, so eminently reasonable—just look at the fortune it makes! This country will not attain the level of reason before 1900. Until then one should instinctively see the amusing side of things, and only perceive the *useful* and the *honest* by an effort of will. Before your trip to Nancy I should never have thought of going into all these details with you, but now it is a pleasure to talk with you. Have you ever heard of a plant that is said to thrive all the better for being trampled on? I should like to have some of them for you, if they exist. I'd ask my friend Thouin to send you a large bouquet to serve as a model for your conduct toward M. de Vaize."

"But, my dear father, what about gratitude? . . ."

"But, my dear son, he's a clown! Is it his fault if chance has thrown the gift of administration into his lap? He is not like us. He is not a man who appreciates gracious behavior, a lasting friendship that makes one feel free to indulge in delicate exchanges: he would consider it a weakness. He is like a Prefect, insolent after dinner, but every morning for twenty years shaking in his boots for fear of reading his dismissal in the *Moniteur;* he's another of those heartless and soulless provincial prosecutors, but endowed, on the other hand, with the restless, timid and violent temper of a child. As insolent as a Prefect in high favor every morning, and every evening as nervous as a courtier who finds himself *de trop* in a drawing room. But the scales have not yet fallen from your eyes; believe no one blindly—not even me. In one year you'll see all this for yourself. As for gratitude, I advise you to eliminate the word from your vocabulary. An agreement, a bilateral contract was made between M. de Vaize and myself after your return to Paris (your mother seemed to think she would die if you went to America). He pledged himself: first, to arrange your desertion from your regiment with his colleague in the War Ministry; second, to appoint you Master of Petitions and his private secretary, with the Cross at the end of the year. On my part I have pledged myself and my salon to play up his reputation, his talents, his virtue and especially his honesty. I succeeded in obtaining his appointment to the Ministry as well as his nomination to the Bourse, and I have promised that on the Bourse all operations based on telegraphic dispatches shall be divided equally. Now he insists that I am pledged as well for all operations based on the deliberations of the Council of Ministers, but that is not true. On the Council I have M. N——, Minister of —— who hasn't the faintest notion of administration but who can *divine* and read faces. N—— can foretell the King's intentions a week in advance, but poor de Vaize can't foresee them even an hour in advance. Already he has been defeated at two Cabinet meetings and he has been Minister barely a month. You must always remember that M. de Vaize cannot get along without my son. If I were to become an imbecile, if I gave up my salon, if I stopped going to the Opera, it might possibly occur to him to make arrangements with some other banking house, but I don't really think he has that much gumption. He may give you the cold shoulder for five or six days, after which there will be an explosion of confidence. That is the moment which causes me some uneasiness. If you give the impression of being overjoyed and grateful like a clerk earning a hundred louis, such worthy sentiments will class you forever among the dupes who can be loaded with work, compromised and humiliated without pity or protest—as the Third Estate was formerly taxed, and for that are only the more grateful."

"I shall regard the effusions of His Excellency as mere childishness combined with deceit."

"Will you have sense enough to observe such a program?"

During the days that followed this paternal lesson, the Minister always spoke to Lucien with the absent-minded air of a man overwhelmed by affairs of the greatest importance. Lucien made his replies as brief as possible and paid court to Madame de Vaize.

One morning the Minister arrived in Lucien's office followed by an office boy carrying an enormous portfolio. When the boy had left them, the Minister himself locked the door and, sitting down familiarly beside Lucien, said:

"That poor N——, my predecessor, was no doubt a most honest fellow; but the public holds strange notions about him. They insist that he speculated. Here, for example, is the portfolio of the Administration of ——.* It is a matter of seven to ten million. Can I very well ask the department head who has had charge of all this for ten years, whether there has been any abuse of power? I can only try to guess; M. Crapart (Chief of Police of the Ministry) does say that the wife of this same department head spends fifteen or twenty thousand francs a year, and her husband's salary is only twelve; they also own two or three little estates about which I am waiting for information. But all that is remote, very vague, not very conclusive. What I need is facts. To pin him down, I asked M. N—— for a general and a thorough report. Here it is with corroborative documents. I want you, my dear fellow, to lock yourself in, compare the documents with the report, and give me your opinion."

Lucien was amazed at the Minister's manner: it was courteous, reasonable and not in the least supercilious. Lucien went to work in earnest. Three hours later he sent the following note to the Minister:

"This report is not thorough. It is nothing but words. M. N—— does not frankly admit any fact; I have not found a

---

* It has seemed preferable to leave a little obscurity and reserve in the description, than to run the risk of having one of the characters turn this epic into a satire. Imagine any administration—Post Office, Public Works, Foundlings, . . .

The gentlemen recently appointed Ministers are so well known for their intelligence, their probity, and their strength of character, that I have been at no great pains to avoid the reproach of *indulging in personalities.* Nothing easier than to attempt the portrait of these gentlemen, but such a portrait would seem very boring at the end of a year or two when Frenchmen will have agreed on the two or three lines to be accorded each of them by history. Having, through repugnance, avoided personalities, I have tried to strike an average of all the Ministers of the period just past, and this is not the portrait of any one of them; I have been careful to strike out any witticism or personal remark against any of their Excellencies. [STENDHAL] single statement that does not dodge the issue. M. N—— does not *commit* himself in any way. It is a well written dissertation, abounding in the humanities; it is a newspaper article, without facts or figures—the author seems to have had a falling-out with Barrême!"

A few minutes later the Minister burst into Lucien's office. It was an eruption of affection. Embracing his secretary, he cried:

"How happy I am to have such a captain as you in my regiment!"

Lucien had anticipated great difficulty in being hypocritical. Now he assumed the air of a man anxious for this effusion to come to an end without the least effort, because this second entrance of M. de Vaize made him think of a cheap country actor who shamelessly overacts his part. M. de Vaize was almost as lacking in dignity as Colonel Malher, Lucien's martinet superior in Nancy, but his duplicity was more apparent.

Lucien's manner was so icy as he listened to the Minister's praises, and, without knowing it, he too so overacted his part that the disconcerted Minister began abusing the department head, N——. One thing struck Lucien: the Minister had not read N——'s report. "The devil, I'm going to tell him so," he decided. "What's the harm?"

"Your Excellency is so overwhelmed by important Cabinet discussions and the preparation of the budget of his department that he has naturally not had time to read this report of M. N—— which he so justly censures."

The Minister could not restrain a movement of violent anger. To attack his aptitude for work, to doubt those fourteen hours which, either by day or night, he said he spent at his desk, was to attack his palladium.

"Egad, sir, you will have to prove that," he said, flushing hotly. "My turn," thought Lucien and, with moderation, lucidity and respectful courtesy, proceeded to win the day. He proved clearly that the Minister had not read the report of the poor man he had so abused. Two or three times M. de Vaize endeavored to end the discussion by confusing the issue.

"You and I, my dear friend, *between us,* have read it all."

"Your Excellency will permit me to remark that if I should read too carelessly or too hastily any document Your Excellency deigns to entrust to me, I who am a mere novice in this career, who have nothing else to do, I should be altogether unworthy of his confidence. There is here in paragraph five . . ."

After bringing the question back to the point three times, Lucien obtained a success which would have been fatal for anyone else in his position. His Excellency left the office in a rage and Lucien could hear him abusing the poor department head whom the usher, hearing the Minister return, had introduced into his office. The Minister's formidable voice penetrated to the reception room and through the hidden door leading into Lucien's office. An old servant who had been placed there by the Minister of the Interior, and whom Lucien suspected of being a spy, hurried into M. de Vaize's office without being summoned.

"Does His Excellency wish anything?"

"Not His Excellency but I, *I* wish to beg you never to come in unless I ring!"

Such was the outcome of Lucien's first battle.

CHAPTER SIX

ONE THING Lucien had to be thankful for was not to have found his cousin, Ernest Dévelroy, future member of the Academy of Moral and Political Sciences, in Paris on his return. One of the Moral Academicians who occasionally gave bad dinners and had three votes, besides his own, at his disposal, had been obliged to go to Vichy to drink the waters, and M. Dévelroy had taken upon himself to play the part of nurse. This sacrifice of two or three months had produced the happiest effect in the Moral Academy.

"He is a man one is pleased to sit next to," said M. Bonneau, one of the leaders of that society.

"Ernest's campaign at Vichy," remarked M. Leuwen, "will get him into the Institute four years sooner."

"Wouldn't it be better for you, father, to have a son like that?" said Lucien almost compassionately.

"Troppo aiuto a sant' Antonio," M. Leuwen rejoined, "I like you better in spite of your virtue. I am certainly not worried about Ernest's getting ahead; it won't take long before he has positions bringing him thirty thousand francs like the philosopher Victor Cousin. But I should as soon have M. de Talleyrand for a son."

In one of the ministerial departments, there was a certain M. Desbacs whose social position was rather similar to Lucien's. He was wealthy and M. de Vaize called him *my cousin,* but he did not boast an accredited salon, nor a celebrated dinner once a week to give him prestige in the world. He felt this difference keenly and decided to attach himself to Lucien.

M. Desbacs had the same character as Blifil (in *Tom Jones*)

62

and, unfortunately, this was plainly visible on his extremely pale and pock-marked countenance which had no expression other than that of forced politeness and an amiability reminiscent of Tartuffe. His jet-black hair and his very white face made people stare at him. With this disadvantage, which was by no means negligible, and because he always said the correct thing and never anything out of the way, M. Desbacs had made very rapid progress in the drawing rooms of Paris. He had been dismissed as Sub-Prefect by M. de Martignac who had found him too much of a Jesuit, and he was now one of the brightest clerks in the Ministry of the Interior.

Like all tender souls in despair, Lucien was indifferent to everything. He did not choose his acquaintances but took up with anyone who presented himself: Desbacs presented himself most gracefully.

Lucien did not even notice that Desbacs was trying to ingratiate himself. Seeing that Lucien really wanted to learn and to work, Desbacs offered his services in getting information for him, not only from the various offices of the Ministry of the Interior, but from all the other Ministries of Paris. There is nothing that is more helpful or that so greatly curtails such work.

In return, Desbacs never missed one of the weekly dinners that Madame Leuwen had instituted for any of the clerks of the Ministry of the Interior with whom her son should become friendly.

"You are getting us mixed up with a queer lot," said her husband; "subaltern spies perhaps."

"Or else people of worth not yet recognized," his wife rejoined. "Béranger was once a clerk at eighteen hundred francs. But at all events, it is only too evident from Lucien's behavior that men bore and irritate him. This is the sort of misanthropy that is the least easily forgiven."

"And you want to silence his colleagues of the Interior. But at least try to keep them from coming to our Tuesdays."

M. Leuwen's chief aim at present was to prevent his son from having even a quarter of an hour of solitude. And he felt that Lucien's one hour at the theater every night was not sufficient.

One evening he ran into his son in the foyer of the Bouffes. "How would you like me to take you to Madame Grandet's later?" he proposed. "She is dazzling tonight and certainly the prettiest woman in the audience. But I don't want to sell you a pig in a poke. I'll first take you to Duvernoy's box next to Madame Grandet's."

"I should be so happy not to talk to anyone but you tonight!"

"Your face must be known to people as long as I have a salon."

M. Leuwen had already tried several times to take Lucien to a dozen houses of the *Juste-milieu*, altogether suitable for the private secretary of the Minister of the Interior. Lucien had always found some excuse for not going.

"I am too stupid. Let me first cure myself of absent-mindedness. I should only commit some blunder that would cling to my name and discredit me forever. . . . The first impression is all-important."

But since a soul in despair is without resistance, that evening he let himself be dragged to the box of M. Duvernoy, Collector General, and then, an hour later, to the salon of M. Grandet, a retired manufacturer, formidably rich and furiously *Juste-milieu*. His house seemed to Lucien charming, the drawing room magnificent, but M. Grandet himself too preposterously absurd.

"He is a Guizot minus the intelligence," Lucien decided, "and with no aversion to blood—an infraction of our contract, my dear father!"

At the dinner which followed Lucien's presentation, M.

Grandet, in the presence of at least thirty persons, had loudly expressed the hope that M. N—— of the opposition would die of the wound he had received in a notorious duel.

The famous beauty of Madame Grandet could not compensate for the disgust inspired by her husband. She was a young woman of about twenty-three or -four, and more regular features could not be imagined. Hers was a delicate and flawless beauty, a face carved in ivory, one might have thought. She sang very well, having studied with Rubini. Her gift for painting in water colors was famous, and her husband sometimes paid her the compliment of stealing one of her pictures and sending it to be sold; it brought three hundred francs.

But not satisfied with the distinction of being an excellent water colorist, she was an irrepressible talker. Woe to the conversation if anyone happened to mention the fatal words: happiness, religion, civilization, legitimate power, marriage . . .

"I believe, God forgive me, that she is trying to ape Madame de Staël," thought Lucien after one of these disquisitions. "She can never let anything pass without giving her opinion. It is generally right, but platitudinous to a deadly degree, although invariably delicately and nobly expressed. I am willing to wager that she gets her provision of wit out of the three franc manuals."

In spite of his complete distaste for the classical beauty and imitative attractions of Madame Grandet, Lucien was faithful to his promise and twice a week appeared in the most agreeable salon of the *Juste-milieu.*

One evening when Lucien came home at midnight and said, in reply to his mother's inquiry, that he had been at the Grandets', his father asked:

"And what did you do to shine above all others in Madame Grandet's eyes?"

"I imitated the talent that makes her so seductive: I painted a water color."

"And what subject did your gallantry select?" asked Madame Leuwen.

"A Spanish monk mounted on a donkey whom Rodil is having hanged."

"How horrible!" Madame Leuwen exclaimed. "You will give yourself a terrible reputation in that house. And it isn't even true. You will have all the inconveniences without the advantages. My son, an executioner!"

"Your son, a hero!" replied Lucien. "That is what Madame Grandet will see in punishments ruthlessly meted out to those who do not think as she does. A young woman with any delicacy or intelligence, who saw things as they are, in short, someone lucky enough to be a little like you, would think me a very wicked person, a ministerial fanatic who wants to be a Prefect and is anxious for another *Rue Transnonain*. But all Madame Grandet is looking for is geniuses, a *grande passion* and master-minds. For a poor little woman endowed simply with common sense, and that of the commonest kind, a monk sent to his death in a superstitious country and by a *Juste-milieu* general, is sublime. My water color is a Michael Angelo."

"So you're assuming the dismal character of a Don Juan?" Madame Leuwen said with a deep sigh.

M. Leuwen burst out laughing.

"Ah! That is really good. Lucien a Don Juan! But, my angel, you must love him to distraction: you are raving. I congratulate you. Happy those who rave because of some passion. A thousand times happy those who rave out of love in an age when no one raves except out of mental impotence and mediocrity! Poor Lucien will always be the dupe of the women he loves. I see in that heart the makings of a dupe up to the age of fifty . . ."

"At least," Madame Leuwen said, turning to Lucien with a smile of contentment, "you saw that the horrible and the banal

were, for that poor little Madame Grandet, the sublime of a
Michael Angelo."

"I'll bet you never had any such ideas when you were painting your monk."

"True. I was thinking of M. Grandet who, this evening,
merely wanted to hang all the journalists of the opposition. At
first my monk on the donkey resembled M. Grandet."

"Have you guessed yet who the lady's lover is?"

"She has such a callous heart I thought she must be virtuous."

"But without a lover her household arrangements would not
be complete. The choice has fallen on M. Crapart."

"What! My Ministry's Chief of Police?"

"The same, and the person who can spy on your mistress at
the expense of the State."

At these words Lucien grew suddenly very silent; his mother
guessed the reason.

"You are looking pale, my dear. Take your candle, and for
pity's sake, do try to get to bed before one o'clock."

"If I had had M. Crapart in Nancy," Lucien said to himself, "I should have known without being a witness, what was
happening to Madame de Chasteller. And what would have
happened if I had known a month earlier? I should simply
have lost the best days of my life that much sooner. I should
have been condemned one month sooner to live all morning
with a rascally Excellency, and all evening with a little bag-
gage who is the most sought-after woman of Paris."

It can be seen from the exaggerated bitterness of his judgments how much Lucien was still suffering. Nothing makes
people so spiteful as unhappiness. Look at prudes!

CHAPTER SEVEN

C OMING BACK from the Tuileries one evening at five o'clock, Lucien was summoned to the Minister's office. Our hero found him looking as pale as death.

"A terrible business, my dear Leuwen! Here is a mission of the utmost delicacy for you . . ."

Unconsciously Lucien assumed a haughty air of refusal, and the Minister hastened to add:

". . . and highly honorable."

These words failed to soften Lucien's cold disdainful attitude. He did not have a very high opinion of the honor that can be acquired on a salary of nine hundred francs.

His Excellency continued:

"You know that we have the good fortune to live under the protection of five police forces . . . but you know it only as the public knows it and not as you should in order to act effectively. Pray forget all that you think you know on the subject. To get people to read their papers, the opposition poisons everything. Be careful not to confuse what the public believes to be true and what I shall tell you, otherwise you will certainly do the wrong thing. Above all, my dear Leuwen, never forget that even the lowest rascal has vanity and a sense of honor of his own. If he suspects contempt on your part, he becomes intractable. . . . Forgive me all these details, my friend, but I am so anxious for you to succeed . . ."

"Ah!" Lucien said to himself, "I too have my vanity like the lowest rascal. Those two sentences were suspiciously close together. . . . He must really be upset."

The Minister no longer thought of trying to cajole Lucien;

he was too completely absorbed by his anguish. His haggard eyes stood out in relief against the deathly pallor of his face; everything about him betrayed his distress.

"That devil of a General Rumigny," he went on, "thinks of nothing but being made a Lieutenant General. He is, as you know, Chief of Police of the Château. And that's not all: he wants to be Minister of War to show how clever he is in a difficult post. As a matter of fact," the great administrator added with scorn, "the only difficult thing connected with that poor Ministry is to keep soldiers and civilians from getting too friendly, and at the same time to limit the number of fatal duels between them to not more than six a month."

Lucien looked at him narrowly.

"For the whole of France," the Minister continued, "that is the rate fixed upon by the Council of Ministers. Until now, General Rumigny has been satisfied to spread rumors in the soldiers' barracks of assaults by working men on isolated soldiers. But *sweet equality* still keeps bringing the two classes together; they respect each other; and to excite their hostility takes the constant vigilance of the military police. General Rumigny is always plaguing me to have exact accounts inserted in *my papers* of all the fights in all the taverns, all the brutalities of the guard, and all the drunken brawls which are reported to him by his spies disguised as sergeants. Those gentlemen are supposed merely to observe the drunkenness of others without ever being tempted themselves. Such accounts are the despair of our writers. How, they say, can you expect a distinctive phrase or a subtle touch of irony to be effective after such vulgarity? What does polite society care about tavern victories, endlessly repeated? The revelation of such villainies simply makes the reader with the slightest literary taste fling down his newspaper and give vent to some scornful sarcasm on the subject of salaried writers. And you can't very well blame him.

"You must admit," continued the Minister with a laugh, "that no matter how cleverly these literary gentlemen present them, the public no longer bother to read their endless stories of those strange quarrels in which two masons would have assassinated three grenadiers (armed with their sabers) if it hadn't been for the miraculous intervention from the nearby guardhouse. Even the soldiers make fun of this section of our papers, which we are at such pains to have distributed in their barracks. And with things in this state, that devil Rumigny, dissatisfied with the two stars on his epaulets, decides to get at the facts. Now, my dear friend," the Minister added, lowering his voice, "you must know that the Kortis affair, so emphatically denied in our papers yesterday morning, is only too true. Kortis, one of General Rumigny's most trusted agents, who gets three hundred francs a month, last Wednesday tried to disarm a stupid-looking young soldier he had had his eye on for the last week. At midnight this soldier was stationed on guard duty right in the middle of the Austerlitz Bridge. Kortis comes along pretending to be drunk. Then, suddenly, he flings himself at the soldier and tries to pull away his gun. But the confounded soldier, who looks like such a simpleton, and chosen for that very reason, backs away a couple of steps and lodges a bullet in Kortis' belly. The soldier happens to be a hunter from the Dauphiné mountains. So there is our Kortis mortally wounded, but not dead—and that's the devil of it!

"Such is the situation. Now, since Kortis knows that he hasn't more than three or four days to live, the problem is, how can we make sure he won't talk?

"A certain person (id est the King) was furious with General Rumigny and made a terrible scene. Unfortunately I happened to be present and the *certain person* insisted that I was the only one who had the necessary tact to bring the affair to a happy conclusion. If I were less well known, I would go myself to see Kortis—he is in the —— Hospital—and study everyone who comes near him. But my presence would be enough to make the affair a hundred times worse.

"General Rumigny pays the men of his police more than I pay mine. It's only natural: the blackguards they have to deal with are more dangerous than the ruffians who are the ordinary fare of the police of the Ministry of the Interior. Not a month ago General Rumigny stole two of my men. With us they were paid a hundred francs, with an occasional five francs, here and there, when they happened to bring in good reports. Now they get two hundred and fifty francs a month. But I didn't dare do more than refer jokingly to his absurd recruiting practices. He must be furious about the scene this morning, and the praises of which I was the recipient, made in his presence and almost at his expense. A clever man like you can guess the rest: if my agents accomplish anything worthwhile at Kortis' bedside, they'll take good care to put their report on my desk five minutes *after* they see me leave the Ministry, and General Rumigny will already have questioned them an hour before at his leisure.

"Now, my dear Leuwen, will you get me out of a serious predicament?"

After a little silence, Lucien replied:

"Very well, sir."

But the expression of his face was infinitely less reassuring. He continued icily:

"I am not to approach the surgeon, I suppose?"

"Splendid, my friend, splendid; you have grasped the crux of the matter," the Minister hastened to reply. "General Rumigny has already done enough and more than enough. This surgeon is a sort of giant named Monod, who reads nothing but the *Courrier Français* at the café near the hospital and who, at the third mention of a Cross by Rumigny's confidential agent, answered his offer with a punch in the jaw which considerably cooled the man's ardor and, in addition, caused a scandal in the hospital.

" 'There's a cool customer for you,' Monod cried, 'he merely proposes poisoning the wounded man in 13 with opium!' "

The Minister, whose tone until now had been energetic, terse and sincere, thought it incumbent on him to add two or three eloquent remarks in the style of the *Journal de Paris,* to the effect that he himself would never have dreamed of approaching the surgeon.

The Minister ceased speaking. Lucien was violently upset. After an alarming silence, he finally said to the Minister:

"I do not want to be a perfectly useless person. If I have His Excellency's consent to my treating Kortis as tenderly as would his own family, I accept the mission."

"You insult me by such a condition," the Minister cried with an air of affectionate reproach. And it was perfectly true that the idea of poisoning or even of opium was horrible to him.

When the question of opium to relieve poor Kortis' suffering was brought up at the Cabinet meeting, he had turned pale.

"We should remember," he had insisted, "all the criticism against General Bonaparte for the use of opium before the walls of Jaffa. We must not expose ourselves to the calumnies of the republican press for the rest of our lives, and what is worse still, of the legitimist papers which get into the salons. . . ."

This sincere and virtuous recoil of the Minister slightly calmed Lucien's horrible anguish. He said to himself:

"This is much worse than anything I could have met with in the regiment. There it was a question, as at ——, of slashing or even shooting a poor misguided, or even innocent, workman; here I find myself mixed up in a frightful story of poisoning. What difference does the kind of danger matter so long as I show courage?"

Finally, in a firm tone, he said:

"I will second you, Monsieur le Comte. It may be that for the rest of my life I shall regret not having fallen ill on the instant and gone to bed for a week. In that case on coming back to the Ministry, if I found you too greatly changed, I could have handed in my resignation. His Excellency is too fair a man (*too involved with my father* is what he thought) to persecute me with the long arm of his power, but I am tired of recoiling in the face of danger." (This was said with restrained warmth.) "Since life in the Nineteenth Century, under any circumstances, is so painful, I shall not bother changing my calling for the third time. To what calumny I am exposing my whole future life I am perfectly well aware. I know how M. Caulaincourt died. I shall therefore act with the prospect in view of having later to justify my conduct in a printed statement. Perhaps it would have been better, even for you, Monsieur le Comte, to have left these measures to an agent protected by epaulets: Frenchmen will forgive a uniform almost anything . . ."

The Minister seemed about to protest, and Lucien added:

"I don't mean to give you unsolicited advice, sir,—moreover, a trifle late—and even less to insult you. As I hated to ask you for an hour to think it over, I have simply been thinking out loud."

This was said in so natural yet, at the same time, in so manly a tone that the Minister revised his whole opinion of Lucien's character.

"He is a man!" he thought, "and a man of decision. So much the better! It will help make up for his father's appalling indolence. Our telegraphic transactions are safely buried forever, and I can, with a clear conscience, silence the son with a Prefecture. It will be a way of paying my debt to the father (unless he dies of indigestion first) and of *binding* his salon to me."

These reflections were made in less time than it takes to read them.

The Minister tried to assume as manly and magnanimous a tone as he could. The day before he had seen Corneille's tragedy, *Horace,* very well acted.

"I must remember," he thought, "the intonations of Horace and Curiace talking together after Flavian has announced their future combat."

Whereupon the Minister, taking advantage of his position, began pacing up and down his office reciting:

> "By Albe, now appointed, I no longer know you."
> "But *I* know you still, and that is what kills me. . . ."

Lucien had made up his mind.

"Any delay," he said to himself, "is a proof of uncertainty; and any show of cowardice might win me another enemy tongue."

As he made this grim observation, he turned toward the Minister:

"I am ready, sir. Has the Ministry of the Interior made any move in this affair yet?"

"To tell the truth, I don't know."

"Then I'll just find out how matters stand, and be back directly."

Lucien hurried to M. Desbacs' office and, without betraying his real object, sent him to the different departments for information. In a very short time he was back in the Minister's office.

"Here is a letter," said the Minister, "that will place everyone in the hospital at your disposal, and here is money."

Lucien went over to the table to write out a receipt.

"What are you doing, my dear fellow? A receipt between us?" the Minister exclaimed with forced lightness.

"Everything we do here may one day be printed, sir," Lucien answered with all the solemnity of a man defending his head from the scaffold.

Seeing Lucien's expression, all His Excellency's nonchalance vanished.

"Do you think you are going to find a representative of the *National* or the *Tribune* at Kortis' bedside? Mind you—no imprudence, no duels with these gentlemen! You must certainly feel what an immense advantage that would give them, and how General Rumigny would gloat over my poor Ministry."

"I promise you there will be no duels, at least as long as Kortis still lives."

"This business takes precedence for the day. As soon as you have done everything possible, you must find me no matter where I happen to be. This is my itinerary: in one hour I shall go to the Ministry of Finance, from there to ——, then to ——. You will greatly oblige me by keeping me posted on every move you make."

"Has His Excellency acquainted me with everything he has done?" Lucien asked pointedly.

"On my honor," the Minister assured him, "I have not said a word to Crapart. As far as I am concerned, I turn over to you a perfectly virginal affair."

"Your Excellency will permit me to say, with all due respect, that in case I see anyone connected with the police, I withdraw. Such company is not to my taste."

"None of my police, my dear aide-de-camp. But you can't hold me responsible for the stupidities of the other Ministries! I have no wish to keep anything from you, nor could I. But who can guarantee that right after my departure *a certain person* did not give the same commission to another Ministry?

The anxiety at the Château is intense. The article in the *National* is atrocious in its moderation; there is a subtlety, an arrogance in its scorn. . . . It will be read from beginning to end in the salons. Much worse than the *Tribune*. Ah! Why did Guizot fail to make M. Carrel a Councilor of State!"

"Carrel would have refused a thousand times, it seems to me. It is better to be candidate for the Presidency of the Republic than Councilor of State. A Councilor of State receives twelve thousand francs while Carrel gets thirty-six for saying what he thinks. Besides, his name is on every tongue. But even if I find *him* at Kortis' bedside there will be no duel."

This truly youthful digression, spoken with great warmth, did not appear to please His Excellency inordinately.

"Good-by, my dear boy! Good-by and good luck! You have unlimited credit, and be sure to keep me informed. If I am not here please be so good as to look for me."

Lucien returned to his office with all the resolution of a man marching to the assault of a battery. There was one little difference, however: instead of thinking of glory, he looked forward to nothing but infamy.

He found Desbacs in his office.

"Kortis' wife has written," he informed Lucien. "Here is the letter." Lucien took it and read:

"My poor husband is not being looked after in the hospital as he ought to be, and how can I lavish on him all the tender care I owe him unless someone takes my place here to care for his poor, orphaned little ones? . . . Death has stricken my husband on the very steps of the throne and of the altar. . . . All I ask of Your Excellency is justice. . . ."

"Excellency be damned!" thought Lucien. "But I can't very well say this letter is addressed to me."

"What time is it?" he asked Desbacs. He wanted to have an irrefutable witness.

"Quarter-to-six. There's not a soul left in the place."

Lucien noted the hour on a piece of paper. He called the office boy, who was a spy:

"If anyone enquires for me this evening, kindly say that I left at six o'clock."

Lucien noticed that Desbacs, usually so discreet, was burning with curiosity and a desire to put in his oar.

"Ah, my friend," thought Lucien, "you may very well be a thorough rogue, or even one of General Rumigny's spies."

"You see," he went on indifferently, "I have promised to go to dine in the country. They will think that I am playing the nobleman, and willfully keeping them waiting."

He looked straight into Desbacs' eyes, which instantly lost their fire.

CHAPTER EIGHT

LUCIEN flew to the hospital. He asked the porter to take him to the surgeon on duty. Crossing the courtyard he met two doctors and, giving them his name and titles, asked them to accompany him. He made his request with so much graciousness that it never occurred to these gentlemen to refuse.

"Good," thought Lucien. "I have not been alone with anyone for an instant; that's the great point."

"What time is it, if you please?" he asked the porter who was walking in front of them.

"Half-past-six."

"So, it only took me eighteen minutes to come from the Ministry to the hospital, and I can prove it."

When he reached the surgeon on call, he gave him the Minister's letter.

"Gentlemen," he said to the three doctors present, "aspersions have been cast on the Minister of the Interior in regard to one of your patients, a wounded man named Kortis who belongs, it is said, to the republican party. . . . The word *opium* has been pronounced. For the sake of your hospital's reputation and, as employees of the government, everything that happens at the bedside of the wounded man, Kortis, must be given the greatest publicity. They may possibly send agents. Don't you think, gentlemen, that it would be well to call the head physician and the head surgeon?"

Two internes were sent to fetch those gentlemen.

"Would it not be advisable to assign two male nurses at once to remain on duty at Kortis' bedside, sensible men, incapable of lying?"

These last words were understood by the oldest doctor present in the sense that used to be given to them four years earlier. He designated two male nurses who had formerly belonged to the Congrégation and who were thorough scamps. One of the doctors went off to install them without delay.

Physicians and surgeons quickly thronged into the staff house. Profound silence reigned; everyone looked mournful. As soon as Lucien saw that there were seven doctors assembled, he addressed them:

"In the name of His Excellency, the Minister of the Interior, whose order I have here in my pocket, I propose that Kortis be treated as though he belonged to the wealthiest class. I believe that this arrangement will prove satisfactory to everyone."

There was a general, if somewhat suspicious, assent.

"Don't you think, gentlemen, that it would be a good thing for *all of us together* to go to see Kortis and afterwards to have a consultation? I am going to have a written report of all that is said drawn up for His Excellency, the Minister of the Interior."

Lucien's determined manner overawed the worthy doctors

who had been counting on spending their evening in a rather more amusing fashion, or at least more profitably.

"But I examined Kortis this morning," one of them, with a dried-up avaricious little face, protested. "He's a dead man. What's the use of a consultation?"

"I shall have your observation placed at the head of the report, sir."

"But I didn't say that with the intention of having it broadcast."

"*Broadcast,* sir; you forget yourself! I beg to assure you on my word of honor, that everything that is said here will be faithfully set down in the report, your remark, sir, as well as my reply."

The lines of Lucien's role were not too bad, but he flushed hotly as he said them, and that threatened to aggravate matters.

"All of us certainly desire only the recovery of the wounded man," hastily intervened the eldest doctor, to put an end to the quarrel. He opened the door and, as they started through the hospital courtyards, was careful to keep the captious doctor separated from Lucien. Three or four other persons joined the procession. Finally, as they were about to open the door into the ward where Kortis was, the head surgeon arrived. He and Lucien went into the porter's room next door.

Lucien took the head surgeon over to the lighted lamp, showed him the Minister's letter, and in two or three words told him what had been done since his arrival at the hospital. This head surgeon was a very honest man and, in spite of his rather pompous bourgeois manner, was not lacking in tact. He sensed the importance of the affair.

"Let us do nothing without Dr. Monod," he said to Lucien. "He lives only a step away from the hospital."

"Ah!" thought Lucien. "That is the surgeon who combated the suggestion of opium with his fists."

In a few moments Dr. Monod arrived, grumbling; they had interrupted his dinner, and besides, he was a bit uneasy about the consequences of the blow he had administered that morning. As soon as he learned how matters stood, he said to Lucien and the head surgeon:

"Well, gentlemen, the man's as good as dead, that's clear. It is a miracle he's still alive, with a bullet in his belly, and not only the bullet, but bits of cloth, the gun wad, and I don't know what else! You can understand why I didn't probe for the bullet in a wound like that. The skin was burned by the shirt that had caught fire."

As he was talking, they reached Kortis' bed. Lucien thought the wounded man had a resolute and not too knavish look, less knavish than Desbacs.

"Sir," began Lucien, "this letter has come from Madame Kortis. . . ."

"Madame! Madame!" cried Kortis. "A funny kind of a Madame who will be begging her bread in a few days. . . ."

"For the Minister, no matter what party you belong to, sir, *res sacra miser,* you are simply a suffering human being. I am told that you have been in the service. . . . I am Second-Lieutenant in the Twenty-seventh Lancers. As a comrade-in-arms, allow me to offer you some slight temporary assistance. . . ."

And he placed two napoleons in the hand the sick man had taken out from under the covers, and held out to him. The hand was burning hot to the touch. Lucien felt sick at the contact.

"That's what I call talking," said the wounded man. "This morning a gentleman came and mouthed something about the hope of a pension. . . . It's easy to promise . . . but no cash in hand. With you, Lieutenant, it's different, *to you I'll talk. . . .*"

Lucien hastened to interrupt the sick man, and turning toward the physicians and surgeons present, seven in all, he said to the head surgeon:

"I think, sir, that the chairmanship of this consultation belongs to you."

"I suppose so," the head surgeon rejoined, "if these gentlemen have no objection. . . ."

"In that case, as it is my duty to ask one of these gentlemen to draw up a detailed report of everything we do, will you kindly indicate the one who will be good enough to write the report. . . ."

But, the doctors having begun talking among themselves in terms not altogether flattering to the government, Lucien added with the greatest possible suavity:

"It would, I think, be preferable for each of us to speak in turn."

This courteous firmness on Lucien's part had a salutary effect. The wounded man was examined and questioned in an orderly manner. Dr. Monod, the surgeon of the ward and of bed number 13, made a concise report. After that they left the wounded man's bedside and, in a private room, held a consultation which Dr. Monod took down in writing. A young doctor, well known in the medical world, wrote out the minutes of the meeting, dictated by Lucien. Of the seven physicians and surgeons, five agreed that death might occur at any moment but certainly within two or three days. One of the seven proposed opium.

"Ah!" Lucien thought. "So here's the scamp bought over by General Rumigny."

He was an extremely elegant gentleman with beautiful blond hair, and wore two enormous ribbons in his buttonhole.

Lucien read his own thought in the eyes of several of the others. The proposition was quickly dismissed:

"The man is not suffering excessive pain," said the old doctor.

Another proposed an abundant bleeding of the foot to prevent an internal hemorrhage. Lucien could see nothing of a political nature in such a measure, until Dr. Monod remarked gruffly, and with a significant air:

"Bleeding would have only one effect, that's certain: it would remove the wounded man's power of speech."

"I violently object to that," said the surgeon who was an honest man.

"So do I."

"And I."

"And I."

"That seems to make a majority," said Lucien with all too evident excitement.

"I ought to remain impassive," he thought. "But how can I contain myself?"

The consultation and the minutes were signed at quarter-past-ten. All the doctors and surgeons, saying they had patients to visit, left as soon as they had finished signing. Lucien remained alone with the giant Monod.

"I am going back to see the wounded man," Lucien said.

"And I am going back to my dinner. You will find him dead perhaps: he might go off like a sick chicken."

Lucien returned to the ward. He was shocked by the odor and the darkness. Now and then feeble groans assailed his ears. Our hero had never seen anything like it. Death had certainly always seemed to him terrible, but clean and mannerly. He invariably imagined himself dying on the grass with his back against a tree, like Bayard. In all his duels that is how he had envisaged death.

He looked at his watch.

"In another hour I'll be at the Opera. . . . But never, as long as I live, shall I forget this evening. . . . Let's get it over!" And he drew near the sick man's bed.

The two nurses were lolling on their chairs, their feet

stretched out on the night-stool. They were half asleep, and seemed to be half drunk as well.

Lucien went around to the other side of the bed. The wounded man's eyes were wide open.

"The principal organs of the body are not affected," Lucien began, "or you would have died the first night. You are much less dangerously wounded than you think."

"Bah!" said the man impatiently, as though the idea of hope was absurd.

"My dear comrade-in-arms, either you will die or you will live," Lucien went on in a manly, resolute and almost affectionate tone. He found this wounded man less disgusting than the handsome gentleman with his two ribbons. "You will live or you will die."

"There's no *or* about it, Lieutenant. I'm done for."

"In any case, please look upon me as your Minister of Finance."

"What? Will the Minister of Finance give me a pension? When I say *me* . . . I mean my poor wife!"

"Yes, my friend, *if you don't blab.*"

The eyes of the dying man lighted up and he looked at Lucien with a strange expression.

"Do you understand me, comrade?"

"Yes, but on condition that I am not poisoned. . . . I'm going to croak, I'm done for. . . . All the same I have a notion that they give me . . ."

"You're mistaken. But if you feel that way, don't eat anything that is furnished by the hospital. You have money. . . ."

"The minute I am asleep those damn buggers will steal it."

"Would you like me to send your wife to you, comrade?"

"Damn it all, Lieutenant, you're all right. I'll give my two napoleons to my wife."

"Just don't swallow a thing your wife doesn't give you her-

83

self. Now that's talking, isn't it? Besides, I give you my word of honor that there is nothing to worry about. . . ."

"Will you bring your ear a little closer, Lieutenant? Not wishing to give you orders! . . . but hell! my belly kills me every time I move!"

"You can count on me," Lucien said, bending over the bed.

"What is your name?"

"Lucien Leuwen, Second-Lieutenant of the Twenty-seventh Lancers."

"Why aren't you in uniform?"

"I am on leave in Paris, detailed to the service of the Minister of the Interior."

"Where do you live? Excuse me . . . but you see . . ."

"13 Rue de Londres."

"Ah! you're the son of the rich banking house of Van Peters and Leuwen?"

"Precisely."

After a little silence:

"All right, I believe you. This morning I fainted while they were dressing my wound, but I heard somebody asking that big hulk of a surgeon to give me *opium*. The surgeon started cursing, and then they went away. I opened my eyes but everything was blurred, loss of blood I guess. . . . But the point is, did the surgeon fall for the proposition or didn't he? That's what I'd like to know!"

"Are you really sure?" said Lucien, very much embarrassed. "I didn't think the republican party was as vigilant as all that."

The sick man looked at him.

"Saving your grace, Lieutenant, you know as well as I do where it comes from."

"I detest such horrors, I abhor and despise the men who may have thought of them," Lucien cried, almost forgetting his role. "You can count on me! Haven't I brought you seven doctors in consultation? Do you think so many would dare condone any unethical practice? You have money; send for your wife or a relative, drink nothing that has not been brought in by your wife. . . ."

Lucien was very much wrought up; the sick man watched him fixedly. His head remained motionless, but his eyes followed Lucien's slightest movement.

"Hell," he said. "I was 3rd line corporal at Montmirail; I know a bloke's got to croak sometime, but no one likes to be poisoned. . . . I'm not ashamed . . . and," he added, his expression changing, "shame's something you can't afford *in my job*. If he had any guts, after what he's had me do for him, and dozens of times, General Rumigny would be here in your place. Are you his aide-de-camp?"

"I have never seen him in my life."

"The name of his aide-de-camp is Saint-Vincent, not Leuwen," the sick man said as if to himself. . . . "There's something I'd like even better than money."

"What is that?"

"Well, if it wouldn't be making too bold—I won't let them dress my wound except in your presence. . . . The son of M. Leuwen, the rich banker who keeps Mademoiselle Des Brins of the Opera . . . For it's simple, Lieutenant, when they see I won't drink their opium . . . while they're dressing my wound, zip! . . . a little stroke of the lancet in the belly is soon done. Oh! it hurts, it hurts! . . . It can't last much longer. . . . Will you give the order tomorrow, because you seem to be in command around here. . . . And why? You're not even in uniform! . . . Having it dressed before your eyes, at least . . . And that big, husky surgeon, did he say yes or no? That's the thing."

His mind was growing confused.

"You mustn't blab," said Lucien, "and I will take you under my protection. I am going to send your wife to you."

"You're a good sort. . . . The rich banker Leuwen with Mademoiselle Des Brins, that doesn't cheat. . . . But what about General Rumigny?"

"Of course I don't cheat. And, incidentally, never mention General Rumigny to me or to anyone else, and here are your ten napoleons."

"Count them out in my hand, will you? It hurts my belly too much if I lift my head."

Lucien counted out the napoleons in a low voice, pressing each one down on the man's palm so that he could feel them.

"Mum's the word," said the wounded man.

"Mum's the word all right. If you talk they will steal your napoleons. Talk only to me and only when we are by ourselves. I shall come to see you every day until you are better."

He stayed on a few moments longer with the sick man whose mind was beginning to wander. Then he hastened to the Rue de Braque where Madame Kortis lived. He found her surrounded by the goodwives of the neighborhood, whom he had some difficulty getting rid of.

The woman began to weep, insisted on showing Lucien her children who were peacefully sleeping.

"She is half sincere, half acting a part," Lucien thought. "I'll have to let her talk herself out."

After twenty minutes of a rambling monologue full of endless oratorical circumlocutions—for the poor people of Paris have one thing in common with the gentry, a holy horror of presenting an idea straight—Madame Kortis spoke of opium.

"Yes," Lucien answered carelessly, "it has been rumored that the republicans tried to give your husband opium. But the King's government keeps watch over all its citizens. No sooner had I received your letter than I brought seven doctors to your husband's bedside. And here is their consultation." Lucien handed the paper to Madame Kortis.

He noticed that she was hardly able to read.

"Who would dare to give your husband opium after that? Yet your husband still can't get the idea out of his head, and that will have a bad effect on his condition. . . ."

"He's as good as done for," said the woman coolly.

"No, Madam, since gangrene did not set in within twenty-four hours, there is still hope. General Michaud had exactly the same wound. However, it is better not to mention opium. It will only make for more political bitterness. Kortis must not blab. Therefore, Madam, you must get some woman to look after your children. You can offer her forty sous a day— here is a week in advance. In that way you will be able to stay with your husband in the hospital."

At this all Madame Kortis' eloquence seemed to desert her, and her pathetic expression vanished. Lucien continued: "Your husband must drink nothing, must eat nothing that you have not prepared with your own hands. . . ."

"Oh, but it's such a disgusting place, a hospital, sir. . . . Besides, my poor babes, my little orphans, without their mother's watchful eye, how do you think they're going to be looked after?"

"As you like, Madam. You are a very good mother! . . . What worries me is that someone may steal his money. . . ."

"Whose money?"

"Your husband's."

"Not likely! I took the twenty-two francs and seven sous he had on him. I filled his snuff box, the poor man, and I gave the nurse ten sous. . . ."

"Well done! Nothing could have been wiser. . . . But, with the understanding that he won't talk politics, that he won't mention opium, and that you won't either, I gave M. Kortis twelve napoleons. . . ."

"Gold napoleons?" Madame Kortis interrupted sharply.

"Yes, Madam, two hundred and forty francs," Lucien answered with a great show of indifference.

"And he isn't to blab?"

"If I am satisfied with him and with you, I will give you a napoleon a day."

"That's twenty francs?" said Madame Kortis, her eyes popping out of her head.

"Yes, twenty francs if you don't mention opium. As a matter of fact, I, myself, was given opium for a wound, and no one wanted to kill me. All these ideas are nonsense. However, if you talk, or if it appears in any paper that Kortis was in fear of opium, or that he spoke of being shot and of his quarrel with the soldier on the Austerlitz Bridge, no more twenty francs; in other words, *if neither of you blabs,* twenty francs a day."

"Starting when?"

"Tomorrow."

"You're such a kind gentleman, couldn't you start tonight, and before midnight? Then I'll go to the hospital. The poor dear man, there's no one can keep him from blabbing but me. . . . Madame Morin! Madame Morin!"

Madame Morin was the neighbor who would look after the children while their mother was away. Lucien gave her fourteen francs for a week, and forty sous to Madame Kortis for a cab to take her to the hospital.

CHAPTER NINE

A T LAST, as the clock of Saint-Gervais was striking the quarter before midnight, Lucien got back to his office. Suddenly he realized that he was dying of hunger. He had not dined and had talked almost without stopping.

"But first I must find my Minister."

He was not at the Ministry. Lucien left a note, changed horse and driver of his cabriolet, and drove off to the Ministry of Finance. M. de Vaize had left some time ago.

"That's enough zeal for the moment," he said to himself, and stopped at a café to have dinner. A few moments later he got into his carriage again and did two unnecessary errands in the Chaussée d'Antin. As he was passing the Ministry of Foreign Affairs it occurred to him to try there. The porter replied that the Minister of the Interior was with His Excellency.

Unwilling to interrupt the conference of the two Ministers, the footman refused to announce him. But as Lucien knew of a secret entrance, he was afraid that his Minister might escape him. He was tired of running around and had no desire to return to the Rue de Grenelle. He became insistent and the footman continued haughtily to refuse. Finally Lucien lost his temper.

"Damn it, sir, let me repeat, I am here at the express order of His Excellency, the Minister of the Interior. I insist on entering. Call the guard if you like, but I will enter by force if necessary. I have the honor of repeating that I am M. Leuwen, Master of Petitions. . . ."

Several servants had appeared in haste, and stood in a group at the drawing room door. Lucien saw that he would have to fight all these scoundrels; he was in a very tight place and very angry. He thought of taking hold of the bell-rope and pulling it hard enough to rip it out of the wall.

A sudden obsequiousness in the lackeys' manner made him aware of the entrance of the Comte de Beausobre, Minister of Foreign Affairs, into the drawing room.

"M. le Comte, my name is Lucien Leuwen, Master of Petitions. I have a thousand excuses to offer Your Excellency. But I have been looking for M. le Comte de Vaize for the last two hours on his express order. I must speak to him about an affair that is both important and urgent."

"What . . . *urgent* . . . affair?" said the Minister with unparalleled fatuity, straightening his tiny stature.

"By gad," thought Lucien, "I'll make you change that tone." And with perfect composure and significant emphasis he added:

"The Kortis affair, M. le Comte, the man who was wounded on the Austerlitz Bridge by a soldier he was trying to disarm."

"You may go," said the Minister, addressing his servants. But, as one of them still lingered: "Didn't you hear me? Get out!"

When the footman had left, he turned again to Lucien:

"The word Kortis, sir, would have been sufficient without explanations." His tone and manner were unbelievably insolent.

"M. le Comte, I am a novice in the affairs of state," Lucien said with marked emphasis. "In my father's circle I am not accustomed to a reception such as you have given me tonight. I wanted to bring to an end as quickly as possible a situation that was both painful and improper."

"What do you mean, sir, *improper?*" said the Minister in a

pinched nasal tone, lifting his head still higher, and more insolent than ever. "You had best weigh your words, sir."

"And if you add one more in that tone, M. le Comte, we will
measure swords. Impertinence, sir, has never impressed me."

M. de Vaize now appeared from a remote study to see what
was going on. He overheard the last words spoken by Lucien
and realized that he himself must be the indirect cause of the
altercation.

"Please, my friend, please!" he said to Lucien. "My dear
colleague, this is the young officer I was telling you about. Let
us go no further."

"There is only one way not to go further," Lucien rejoined
with a composure that struck the two Ministers dumb. "There
is absolutely only one way," he repeated icily, "and that is not
to say another word about the incident, and to assume that
the footman announced me to Your Excellencies."

"Sir . . ." exclaimed the Minister of Foreign Affairs, drawing himself up angrily.

"I beg Your Excellency a thousand pardons; but if you say
another word, I shall hand in my resignation to M. de Vaize
and I shall insult you in such a way, sir, that you will be
forced to demand satisfaction."

"Come, let us be going," cried M. de Vaize, very much upset, taking Lucien by the arm. The latter listened for a word
from M. de Beausobre. He heard nothing.

When they were in the carriage, as M. de Vaize was beginning a discourse in paternal vein, Lucien asked to be allowed
first of all to give him an account of the Kortis affair. His account was long. At the outset he had spoken of the signed
minutes and consultation of doctors. As soon as he had finished his report, the Minister asked to see the documents.

"I find I have forgotten to bring them with me," Lucien replied, saying to himself: "If the Comte de Beausobre wants
to make trouble, these documents will prove that I was right in

insisting on seeing the Minister of the Interior at once and that I was not a petitioner forcing myself into his house."

Before reaching the Rue de Grenelle, they had finished with poor Kortis, and M. de Vaize tried once more to adopt an unctuous and fatherly tone.

"M. le Comte," Lucien interrupted, "I have been working for Your Excellency since five o'clock this afternoon. It is now one o'clock. Permit me to get back into my cabriolet which is following your carriage. I am dead tired."

M. de Vaize made one last attempt to be fatherly.

"Not another word about the incident," said Lucien. "The least little word will spoil everything."

At this the Minister let him go. Lucien got into his cabriolet. He told the servant to take the reins. He was too tired to drive himself. As they were crossing the Louis XV Bridge, his servant said:

"There goes the Minister."

"Ah," thought Lucien, "in spite of the lateness of the hour he is going back to his colleague's and I am quite certain that I shall be the subject of their conversation. I don't care about my post but, I swear, if he has me removed I shall force him to use his sword! These gentlemen can be as insolent as they please but they should know whom to pick. With the Desbacs, who are bent on making their fortunes at any price, it's all very well, but not with me."

When he got home he found his father, with a lighted candle in his hand, going upstairs to bed. Although Lucien longed passionately to have the advice of a man of such intelligence, he hesitated.

"Unhappily he is old and I must not keep him from his sleep. Politics will have to wait until tomorrow."

The next morning at ten o'clock he gave his father a detailed account of the whole affair. His father laughed.

"Now M. de Vaize will take you to dine at his colleague's.

But, believe me, there have been enough duels in your life as it is. At this stage they would do you more harm than good. Between them, these gentlemen have it all settled—you will be removed in two months or be made Prefect of Briançon or Pondichéry. Now, if the distant post they select does not suit you any more than it suits me, I will frighten them and will prevent your disgrace . . . or at least I'll try, and with some chance of success."

The dinner with His Excellency, the Minister of Foreign Affairs, did not take place until two days later, and in the interval Lucien, still very busy with the Kortis affair, refused to allow M. de Vaize to mention the *incident*.

The day before the dinner, M. Leuwen recounted the anecdote to three or four diplomats. He withheld only the name of Kortis and the nature of the urgent affair that had forced Lucien to look for his Minister at one o'clock in the morning.

"All I can say about the untoward hour is that the affair had nothing to do with the telegraph," he remarked to the Russian Ambassador.

Two weeks later M. Leuwen became aware of a vague rumor going the rounds to the effect that his son was a Saint-Simonian. Whereupon, without his son's knowledge, he asked M. de Vaize to take him to call on his colleague, the Minister of Foreign Affairs.

"And why, my dear friend?"

"Do let me have the pleasure of surprising Your Excellency."

And all the way to the Ministry, M. Leuwen never stopped teasing his friend on his curiosity.

He began the interview accorded him by His Excellency, the Minister of Foreign Affairs, in a very serious tone.

"There is no one, M. le Comte, who appreciates more than I do Your Excellency's talents; but you must admit that they are admirably seconded! Forty eminent personages covered with titles and decorations, whom I will name if you like, five or six great ladies belonging to the highest nobility and fairly opulent, thanks to Your Excellency's generosity, do my son the honor of occupying themselves with him. Nothing simpler than for these respectable personages discreetly to spread the rumor that he is a Saint-Simonian. They could just as easily insinuate that on a certain crucial occasion he was lacking in courage. Better still, two or three of the estimable personages I have mentioned who, being still young, will take on anything, and are hotheads besides, can be counted on to pick quarrels with him; or, if they wanted to be kind and show some consideration for my gray hairs, these gentlemen, such as M. le Comte de ——, M. de ——, M. le Baron de —— (who has an income of forty thousand francs), M. le Marquis de ——, would confine themselves to saying that young Leuwen invariably wins at écarté. Your Excellency, I have come to you in your capacity of Minister of Foreign Affairs to offer you—peace or war."

M. Leuwen took a malicious pleasure in prolonging the interview thus begun as long as possible. When he left the Ministry of Foreign Affairs, he went to see the King, with whom he had obtained an audience. He repeated verbatim the conversation he had just had with the Minister of Foreign Affairs.

"Now," he said to his son on arriving home, "let me repeat for the second time the conversation I had the honor of having with the Ministers to whom you failed to show proper respect. But so that I won't be liable to a third repetition, let's go and find your mother."

At the end of this conference in his mother's apartments, our hero thought he would hazard a word of thanks to his father.

"Now, my friend, you are becoming banal. You have never amused me so much as you have in the last month. I have you to thank for the *youthful* zeal with which, for the last two weeks, I've been watching things on the Bourse, for I have to

94

be prepared to play a trick or two on my two Ministers if they should allow themselves any impertinence in your regard. I really love you at last! For, as your mother will tell you, to borrow a phrase from the mystics, I have simply loved *her in you*. But you will have to reward my affection by accepting certain obligations."

"And what is it I have to do?"

"Come with me and I shall tell you."

When they were in his study, M. Leuwen said:

"First of all it is of prime importance to clear yourself of the imputation of Saint-Simonism. Your serious, I might even say, imposing air, might give it credence."

"Nothing could be simpler—with a good sword . . ."

"Yes, to give you the reputation of an inveterate duellist, which is almost as dismal. No, please, no more duels under any pretext!"

"Then what *do* you want?"

"A notorious love affair."

Lucien turned pale.

"Nothing less," his father continued. "You must seduce Madame Grandet—or (which would be more costly but perhaps less boring) ruin yourself for Mademoiselle Gosselin, and spend four hours with her every day. I will pay all the costs of this great passion."

"But I thought, dear father, I had the honor of being in love with Mademoiselle Raimonde?"

"She is not well enough known. Take a sample dialogue: 'Young Leuwen is certainly keeping Mademoiselle Raimonde.' . . . 'And who is Mademoiselle Raimonde? . . .' Now this is the way it should run: 'Young Leuwen is at present with Mademoiselle Gosselin.' . . . 'Egad! is he really? And is he her official lover?' 'He is mad about her, jealous . . . wants to be the only one.' . . . After that I shall have to introduce you into at least ten houses where they will fathom the mystery of your Saint-Simonian sadness."

This alternative between Madame Grandet and Mademoiselle Gosselin greatly embarrassed Lucien.

The Kortis affair had been brought to a happy conclusion. M. de Vaize had even congratulated him. The too zealous agent had not died for a week and he had not talked.

Lucien now asked the Minister for a week's leave of absence to wind up some business affairs in Nancy. For some time he had felt a mad desire to see the little window with the parrot-green shutters. Having obtained his leave from the Minister, he spoke to his parents. They had no objection to this little trip to "Strasbourg," for Lucien would never have had the courage to pronounce the name Nancy.

"To make your absence seem less long to him, every day at two o'clock I shall look in on your Minister," said M. Leuwen.

Lucien was still ten leagues from Nancy when his heart began pounding uncomfortably. He could no longer breathe normally. As he thought it expedient to enter Nancy after nightfall and to avoid being seen by anyone, he stopped at a village situated about a league away. Even at this distance he was not master of his emotions. He could not hear a cart passing on the highroad without thinking he recognized the sound of Madame de Chasteller's carriage. . . .*

* [*Stendhal never wrote the account of this brief visit of Lucien's to Nancy. He left seventeen blank pages and the following note: "The trip will occupy the blank pages of this notebook. While I am not in the right mood, I'll do Madame Grandet." According to another note Lucien remained "incognito" during his stay in Nancy.*]

CHAPTER TEN

W HILE YOU were away your Minister's telegraph has made me a lot of money," said M. Leuwen to his son on his return from Nancy, "and your presence was never more needed."

At dinner, Lucien found his friend Ernest Dévelroy. His cousin was most downcast because his moral savant, who had promised him four votes in the Academy of Moral and Political Sciences, had died at Vichy; and, after duly burying him, Ernest perceived that he had just wasted four boring months as a nurse, and had won nothing but ridicule.

"For, one simply has to succeed," he said to Lucien. "And, by gad, the next time I devote myself to a member of the Institute, I'll choose a healthy one!"

Lucien marveled at his cousin's disposition. Ernest was depressed for no more than a week; by that time he had thought of a new plan, and proceeded to plunge into it with renewed energy. In the salons he would explain: "I owed a few days of infinite sorrow to the memory of our learned Descors. The friendship of that excellent man and his loss will mark a new era in my life—he has taught me how to die! I saw a sage on his deathbed, surrounded by all the consolations of Christianity. It is at the bedside of a dying man that one learns to appreciate religion. . . ."

A few days after Lucien's return, Ernest said to him:

"I hear that you are head over heels in love." (Lucien turned pale.) "By gad, you're a lucky fellow, everybody's talking about you! And now their chief occupation is trying to guess the name of the object of your passion. I ask nothing, but I shall soon tell you whose are the lovely eyes that have stolen all your gaiety. Lucky Lucien, you have caught the public's attention! God, how fortunate you are to have been born of a father who gives dinners, frequents M. Pozzo di Borgo and is a friend of high diplomacy! If I had such a father I'd be a hero this winter, pointed out as a model of devoted friendship; and Descors dying in my arms would perhaps be more useful to me than Descors alive. For want of a father like yours, I perform miracles to no avail, or only to give me the reputation of being a schemer."

In the more modest salons of three old ladies, who were friends of his mother, Lucien came upon the same gossip.

Young Desbacs, whom he encouraged to talk about things besides ministerial matters, admitted that the best-informed persons spoke of him as a young man destined for great things but checked by a fatal passion. "Egad, there's no end of what that will do for you. Such a whitewashing will make you impermeable to ridicule for a long time."

Lucien defended himself as best he could, but thought:

"It is my unfortunate trip to Nancy that has given everything away."

He was far from suspecting that he owed this famous passion of his to his father who, since Lucien's encounter with the Minister of Foreign Affairs, had conceived a real fondness for his son, even to the extent of going to the Bourse himself—and on cold damp days, too—a thing which, since his sixtieth birthday, nothing else could have induced him to do.

"Lucien will end up by detesting me," he remarked to Madame Leuwen, "if I interfere with him too much or keep talking to him about his private affairs. I must be careful not to play the heavy father, so boring for a son if the father is bored or too fond of him."

Madame Leuwen's tender reticence was staunchly opposed

to saddling her son with a great love affair; she saw in this gossip a source of danger.

"What I should like for him," she said, "is a peaceful rather than a brilliant life."

"Impossible," M. Leuwen replied. "In all fairness, I couldn't wish him that. He must be suffering from a fatal passion. Otherwise his seriousness, which you so greatly prize, will do him an ill turn. He will become nothing but a dreary Saint-Simonian and (who knows?) perhaps later, say at thirty, the inventor of a new religion. All I can do is to leave him the choice of the fatal beauty for whom he will have this great, this profound infatuation. Is it to be Madame de Chasteller, Madame Grandet, Mademoiselle Gosselin, or that wretched little Raimonde—an actress with a salary of only six thousand francs?" (He failed to add what really rankled—"and who all day long has the impudence to be witty at my expense!"—for Mademoiselle Raimonde was much cleverer than Mademoiselle Des Brins, with whom she spent a great deal of her time.)

"Ah!" cried Madame Leuwen, "don't mention Madame de Chasteller. You will drive him to commit some real folly."

M. Leuwen now bethought him of his two old friends, Mesdames de Thémines and Toniel, whom he had known for twenty years and who were both great friends of Madame Grandet. For many years he had looked after M. de Thémines' business interests—a very great service in Paris, and one for which gratitude knows no bounds, for in the general rout of titles and the old nobility of birth, money is the only thing left, and income without anxiety is the most beautiful of all beautiful things. M. Leuwen went to see them to enquire into the state of Madame Grandet's heart.

We shall trim their replies of much of their long circumlocution, and even combine the information gathered from each of the ladies, who lived in the same house, shared the same carriage, but did not always tell each other *everything*. Madame Toniel was endowed with a very strong character but also with a certain asperity; she was Madame Grandet's mentor in all the momentous events of the latter's life. As for Madame de Thémines, she possessed infinite sweetness, a nice sense of fitness, and was the sovereign arbiter of what was or was not correct. Her lorgnette did not see very far, but within its range, it saw to perfection. Born into the highest society, she had made certain mistakes which she had subsequently been able to retrieve, and for the last forty years had never been wrong in her judgments on what the effect of any happenings in the salons of Paris would be. Her serenity had been a trifle ruffled during the last four years by two calamities: one, the appearance in society of names which never should have been found there or which never should have been heard announced by the lackeys of the best houses; and the other, the sorrow of no longer seeing places reserved in the regiments for all the young men of the best families who had formerly been friends of her grandsons whom she had long since lost.

M. Leuwen, who met Madame de Thémines once a week either at his house or hers, thought it incumbent on himself to take his role of father seriously for her benefit. He went even further and decided that, considering her age, he could risk frankly deceiving her about his son's amatory career and suppress the name of Madame de Chasteller. He made a very pretty story of Lucien's adventures and, after entertaining her during the entire latter half of the evening, ended by confessing his present grave concern on his account; for, ever since Lucien had been taken to Madame Grandet's drawing room, three weeks ago, he had been a prey to the blackest despondency. M. Leuwen said that he very much feared a serious infatuation which would interfere with his own paternal projects for his cherished son. For, naturally, he had to think of a suitable marriage. . . .

"What is most singular," Madame de Thémines rejoined thoughtfully, "is that, since her return from England, Madame Grandet seems also to have some anxiety on her mind."

But to take things in order. Here follows a résumé of what M. Leuwen learned from Mesdames de Thémines and Toniel (seen separately and then together), as well as additional particulars we have gleaned from certain secret memoirs about this celebrated woman.

Madame Grandet was just about the prettiest woman in Paris, or at least one could not name the six prettiest women without including her among them. What was particularly alluring about her was her tall, lithe and charming figure. She had the loveliest blond hair in the world, and on horseback displayed not only the greatest possible grace but also daring. She had the tall blond beauty of the young Venetian women of Paul Veronese. Though pretty, her features were not very distinguished. As for her heart, it was the direct opposite of what the Italian heart is generally reputed to be. Hers was entirely alien to what are called the tender emotions and to all enthusiasm, yet she spent her life aping these sentiments. A dozen times Lucien found her weeping over the fate of some missionary priest preaching the Gospel in China, or over the hardships of some provincial family—*one of the very best families!* But in her heart of hearts, nothing seemed to her more ridiculous, in other words more bourgeois, than to be really moved. It was for her the surest sign of an inferior nature. She liked to read the *Mémoires* of Cardinal de Retz. They had for her the charm she vainly sought in novels. The political role played by Madame de Longueville and Madame de Chevreuse was for her what sentimental and dangerous adventures are to a young man of eighteen.

"What wonderful lives theirs were, if only they had been able to guard against those errors of conduct which expose us to public censure!"

Even love in its realest, sincerest aspects seemed to her nothing but a nuisance and a bore. Perhaps it was to this extraordinarily placid disposition that she owed her extraordinarily
fresh complexion, which could safely vie with that of the
most beautiful German women, and gave her that air of dewy
youth and health which was a joy to the eye. She even liked
to be seen at nine o'clock in the morning when she first got
out of bed. At that moment, above all others, she was incomparable and, in spite of the triteness of the phrase, one could
hardly refrain from likening her to the dawn. Not one of her
rivals could compare with her insofar as complexion was concerned. Consequently she took great delight in prolonging the
balls she gave till morning and having breakfast served to her
guests in the full light of the morning sun with all the blinds
wide open. If pretty women, never suspecting the treachery
of this maneuver and carried away by the pleasure of the
dance, thoughtlessly stayed on, Madame Grandet triumphed.
It was the only moment when her soul really soared and her
beauty seemed to her made expressly for the humiliation of
her rivals. Music, painting, love were inanities to her, invented
by and for petty souls. And she spent her life at the Bouffes
enjoying serious entertainment for, as she was careful to explain, she preferred that theater because Italian singers are not
excommunicated. Mornings she would paint water colors with
a really distinguished talent. This seemed to her as necessary
to a woman of society as an embroidery frame, and much less
boring. The one thing that proved that she lacked real nobility
was her habit, amounting almost to a necessity, of always comparing herself to something or someone in order to appraise
and to judge herself, as, for example, to the noble ladies of
the Faubourg Saint-Germain.

She had induced her husband to take her to England so
that she might satisfy herself on two points: first, whether any
English blond could boast as lovely a complexion as hers, and

second, whether she would be frightened on horseback. At the stately country seats to which she was invited, she experienced a vast deal of boredom but no cause for anxiety on either count.

At the time Lucien was first presented to her, she had just returned from England, where her stay had greatly aggravated her feeling of admiration for hereditary nobility. In England Madame Grandet had been merely the wife of one of the men of the July *Juste-milieu* who had been most highly honored by Louis-Philippe, and at every turn she had been made to feel that she was nothing but a *merchant's wife*. Her income, which in Paris gave her such an advantage, was fairly looked down upon in England as just another vulgarity. She came back from England with this preoccupation: not to remain merely a merchant's wife, but to become a Montmorency.

As her husband, a tall robust man of forty, enjoyed excellent health, widowhood was hardly to be hoped for. In fact no such idea had ever entered her head. Early in life her enormous fortune—and her pride too—had eliminated any temptations of a dubious nature, and she despised anything approaching crime. The point was to become a true Montmorency without stooping to anything she would ever be unable to acknowledge. It was like the diplomacy of Louis XIV when he was successful.

Her husband, a Colonel in the National Guard, had indeed taken the place, politically speaking, of the Rohans and the Montmorencys, but as far as she was personally concerned she had yet "to make her fortune."

What would a Montmorency, hardly twenty years old and possessing an enormous fortune, do with all this felicity?

Besides, there was more to it than that.

Wasn't there something more she must do to succeed in being looked up to in society as a Montmorency would have been?

A lofty, sublime piety perhaps, or the wit of a Madame de Staël; or else an illustrious friendship, becoming, for example, the intimate friend of the Queen or of Madame Adelaide, a sort of Madame de Polignac of 1785, and thus the foremost woman of the Court, giving suppers to the Queen; or, if all that was perhaps too much to expect, at least an illustrious friendship in the Faubourg Saint-Germain.

All these possibilities, all these different expedients, occupied her thoughts one after the other, and quite exhausted her, for she had more perseverance and courage than brains. Nor did she know how to ask for advice. There were her two friends Mesdames de Thémines and Toniel, it is true, but to them she confided only a part of those projects which kept her awake nights. Several of the ideas of which we have spoken, and even more brilliant ones whose unlimited possibilities had presented themselves to her ambition, were quite outside the realm of probability.

The night Lucien was presented to Madame Grandet, he had found her playing Madame de Staël, and hence his disgust, already mentioned, for her terrifying prattle on every imaginable subject.

A short time before Lucien's trip to Nancy, Madame Grandet, since nothing had occurred to bring about the realization of her grand projects, had said to herself:

"Will I not be neglecting my actual advantages, and losing an opportunity of winning a great distinction, if I fail to inspire a hopeless passion which my lover's despair will make famous? In any case, wouldn't it be an admirable thing to have a distinguished young man go to America in order to forget me, the woman who would not accord him the slightest favor?"

This grave question had been maturely weighed without the least shred of feminine weakness, and all the more precisely weighed since it had always been the pitfall of the very women whose destiny, whose way of life, she never ceased to envy. She particularly coveted the niche they had made for themselves in history.

"I should be neglecting an actual and very fleeting advantage," she said to herself, "if I failed to inspire a hopeless passion; but the choice is difficult. What would I not have given to win even the friendship of a man of noble birth? Physical attractions, youth and, above all, money have never meant anything to me; all I have ever desired was noble blood and a stainless name. But no man belonging to the ancient nobility of the Court has thought fit to accept that role. How can I hope to find one for the part of the despairing lover, in short, of the adorer of the wife of a merchant who has made a huge fortune?"

Thus Madame Grandet would argue with herself. She had strength of character and did not mince words in judging herself, but she lacked imagination and real intelligence. In her mind she reviewed all the endless maneuvers, the even abject devices she had stooped to, to induce two or three gentlemen of this caliber, who had by chance appeared in her drawing room, to come to call on her more frequently. All in vain. These noble gentlemen had attended for two or three months but gradually their visits became more and more rare.

All this was undoubtedly true, but it was nonetheless desirable to inspire a hopeless passion! While she was harboring these secret thoughts (unknown of course to M. Leuwen) Madame de Thémines came one morning to spend an hour with her young friend for the purpose of finding out if, by chance, her heart was occupied with our hero. After taking into account her vanity, or rather ambition, and exercising all possible tact, Madame de Thémines said to her:

"You are breaking hearts, my beauty, and you choose very well."

"Choose?" replied Madame Grandet very seriously. "But I

am so far from choosing that I don't even know the name of the unhappy knight. Is he a man of distinction?"

"He lacks nothing but noble birth."

"Are really good manners to be found without noble birth?" she replied, with a sort of discouragement.

"How I love the perfect tact that distinguishes you!" cried Madame de Thémines. "In spite of the groveling admiration for that acid-eaten etching, the mind, that vitriol which bites into everything, corrodes everything, you do not look upon it as a compensation for good manners. Ah! you are really one of us! But I must say that your new victim has most distinguished manners. Of course it is not easy to judge at the moment because of the state of melancholy he has been in ever since he met you. After all, it is a man's gaiety, the character of his quips and his manner of expressing them that stamp him in society. And yet, if the man you have made miserable belonged to an old family, he would indubitably be placed in the front rank."

"Ah! it is M. Leuwen, Master of Petitions."

"Well, my dear, you are driving him to his grave."

"He doesn't seem unhappy to me," said Madame Grandet, "only bored."

Little more was said on the subject. Madame de Thémines turned the conversation to politics, remarking à propos of something:

"What is utterly shocking—what decides everything today is the Bourse, where your husband does not go."

"It is almost two years at least since he set foot there," Madame Grandet was quick to rejoin.

"The men you receive in your house are the ones who make and unmake Ministers."

"But I don't receive such gentlemen exclusively by any means!" (In the same piqued tone.)

"You must not give up your splendid position, my dear!

And just between us," lowering her voice and assuming a confidential tone, "in estimating it you must not adopt the opinion of the enemies of that position. Once before, under Louis XIV, as that wicked Duc de Saint-Simon you're so fond of never tires repeating, the bourgeoisie took over the Ministry. What were Colbert and Séguier? In fact, Ministers can make the fortune of anyone they please. But who makes Ministers today? The Rothschilds, the ——, the ——, the Leuwens. By the way, wasn't it M. di Borgo who said the other day that M. Leuwen made a scene at the Ministry of Foreign Affairs about his son, or else it was the son who, in the middle of the night, went to make a scene at the Minister's?"

Madame Grandet told her old friend what she had heard. It was approximately the truth, but told to the advantage of the Leuwens. Even so, she betrayed not the slightest trace of interest or intimacy, but rather a certain pique because of Lucien's air of boredom.

That evening, Madame de Thémines felt that she could reassure M. Leuwen. She told him that neither love nor intrigue existed between his son and the beautiful Madame Grandet.

CHAPTER ELEVEN

M. LEUWEN was a man of stout build and florid complexion, with twinkling eyes and thick curly gray hair. His suits and waistcoats were models of quiet elegance suitable to a man of his years. Everything about him was brisk and decided. From his keen black eyes and the quickly changing expression of his mobile features one might have fancied him a painter, a great artist (such as are no longer to be found), rather than a famous banker. He put in an appearance in many drawing rooms, but spent most of his time with clever diplomats (he abhorred solemnity) and with the respectable corps-de-ballet of the Opera. He was their providence in all their little money matters. Every evening he could be found in the foyer of the Opera. He had little use for the society called "high." The impudence and charlatanism, without which no one could succeed, exasperated him, were too blatant. Just two things in the world he feared: dampness and bores. To escape these two pests he did things which would have made anyone else ridiculous, yet up to his sixty-fifth year (his present age) he it was who had always made others ridiculous and never the other way round. When strolling on the Boulevard, his lackey would hand him a topcoat whenever he passed by the Chaussée d'Antin. He changed his clothes at least five or six times a day, as the wind changed, and for that purpose kept quarters all over Paris. The turn of his mind was natural, vivacious and engagingly indiscreet, rather than marked by lofty ideals. At times he would forget himself, and had to be careful not to give way to a somewhat daring and indecorous propensity.

"If you hadn't made your fortune in speculation," his wife, who adored him, used to say, "you would never have succeeded in any other career. You tell a story in all innocence and never notice that you have trodden on two or three toes with fatal effect."

"I have guarded against this disadvantage: any man who is solvent is always sure of a thousand francs graciously at his disposal at my bank. Besides, for the last ten years nobody has thought of discussing me. I am accepted."

M. Leuwen told the truth to no one but his wife, and to her he told the whole truth. She acted for him as a second memory in which he had more confidence than in his own. At first he had tried to maintain a certain reserve when in the presence of his son, but the restraint nettled him and spoiled all his pleasure in the conversation, and Madame Leuwen refused to be deprived of her son's company; deciding that Lucien's discretion could be trusted, he ended by saying everything in front of him.

This man, now well along in years, and whose tongue was the terror of everybody, was of a naturally cheerful disposition. But at this particular time he had for several days seemed dejected and worried. Evenings he gambled recklessly, he even allowed himself to speculate on the Bourse. Mademoiselle Des Brins gave two dances at which he did the honors.

One night at two o'clock, coming home from one of these evenings, he found his son warming himself in front of the fire in the drawing room, and all his pent-up vexation exploded:

"Go and bolt that door!" And, as Lucien came back to the fire, he exclaimed irritably, "Do you know how ridiculous I have become?"

"Have you, father? I hadn't noticed it."

"I love you, and consequently you make me unhappy; for of all cheats, love is the worst." He was growing more and more excited, and spoke in a serious tone his son had never heard before. "In my long life I have known but one exception, and that is unique: I love your mother. She is necessary to my life, and she has never given me an iota of distress. I decided that instead of looking upon you as a rival in her affections, I would love you. It is a ridiculous state that I always swore I would never fall into—you actually *keep me from sleeping at night!*"

At this Lucien grew really alarmed. His father never exaggerated, and Lucien understood that he was about to witness an access of real anger.

M. Leuwen was all the more irritated because for the past

two weeks he had been swearing that he would not say a single word to his son of what tormented him.

Suddenly, M. Leuwen left the room, saying:

"Kindly wait for me here."

He soon returned with a little wallet of Russian leather.

"Here are twelve thousand francs. If you refuse to take them I think we are going to quarrel."

"That would be something new in the way of quarrels," Lucien rejoined, smiling. "The roles would be reversed. . . ."

"Yes, that's not bad. Mildly witty. Well then, not to waste any more words, I insist that you fall madly in love with Mademoiselle Gosselin. And you're not just to give her your money and then fly away on your horse into the Meudon woods, or the devil knows where, as usual. The point is to spend all your evenings with her, to give her every moment of your time—in a word, to be completely mad."

"Mad about Mademoiselle Gosselin!"

"Devil take you! Mad about Mademoiselle Gosselin or anybody else, it doesn't matter. But the public must know that you have a mistress."

"And the reason for this stern command?"

"You know it very well! Don't be a hypocrite with your father, especially when he has your best interests at heart. The devil take you, and when he has taken you, may he never bring you back! I am sure if I stayed two months without seeing you I wouldn't think about you in this idiotic fashion any longer. Why couldn't you have stayed in your Nancy? It suited you very well, you would have become the worthy hero of two or three virtuous prudes."

Lucien flushed crimson.

"But in the position I have made for you, your infernally solemn air—downright doleful it is—so much admired in the provinces where it is only an exaggeration of the local fashion, gives you the ridiculous air of an infernal Saint-Simonian."

"But I am no Saint-Simonian. I think I have proved that to you."

"Well, you can be a Saint-Simonian, or anything a thousand times more idiotic, if you choose, but don't show it!"

"My dear father, I promise you I'll be more talkative, more cheerful, and I'll spend two hours instead of one at the Opera."

"Can a leopard change his spots? Will you ever be wild and frivolous? And all your life, unless I put some order into it, and do it within the next two weeks, your seriousness will be taken, not for a sign of intelligence, bad consequence of a good thing, but for everything that is most objectionable in the eyes of society. And in Paris, once you have turned society against you, you can expect a dozen pinpricks a day, for which the best remedy is to blow out your brains or, if you haven't the courage, to bury yourself in a Trappist monastery. And that's the pass you were in two months ago, while I was killing myself trying to make everyone believe you were ruining me by your youthful follies! And in this fine state of affairs, with that infernal intelligence written all over your face, you go and make an enemy of the Comte de Beausobre, an old fox who will never forgive you, for if you succeeded in cutting some sort of figure in the world and should decide to talk, sooner or later you two would have to cut each others' throats—which wouldn't suit him at all! In spite of that infernal intelligence of yours (which heaven confound!) you don't know it, but you have always at your heels eight or ten clever men, smooth-spoken, extremely virtuous, very well received in society, in addition to being spies of the Minister of Foreign Affairs. Do you think you can kill them all off in duels? And if you are killed, what will become of your mother—for the devil if I should think of you twice a month if I didn't see you. And for your sake, all during the last three months, I've been running the risk of an attack of the gout that could very well carry me off. I spend my whole life at the damned Bourse which is damper than ever since they installed stoves. For your sake, I refuse myself the pleasure of gambling my whole fortune, double or nothing—something that would amuse me very much. Now then, will you make up your mind to fall madly in love with Mademoiselle Gosselin?"

"So this is the way you declare war on those few little quarter-hours of freedom that were left me! I don't want to reproach you, but you have taken every minute of my time. There is no poor ambition-ridden man who works more than I do, for I count as work—and the hardest kind of work—the time I spend at the Opera and in drawing rooms where I wouldn't be seen once in a fortnight if I followed my own inclinations. Ernest aspires to a seat in the Academy, that little scamp of a Desbacs wants to become a Councilor of State, their ambition sustains them. But in my case, the only interest I have in all this is to prove my gratitude to you. Happiness for me would be, or at least so I believe, to live on an income of six or eight thousand francs either in Europe or America, wandering from one city to another, stopping for a month or for a year according to my fancy. The charlatanism, so indispensable in Paris, seems absurd to me, and yet I get angry when I find it succeeding. Here, even if one is rich, one has to be an actor always on the alert for fear of making oneself ridiculous. But my happiness doesn't depend on what people think of me. It would consist in coming to Paris for six or seven months a year to see whatever is new in painting, plays, inventions or pretty dancers. If I led a life like that, society would forget all about me, I should live here in Paris like a Russian or an Englishman. Instead of making me the happy lover of Mademoiselle Gosselin, why don't you allow me to take a trip of six months somewhere, anywhere—Kamchatka, for example, or Canton, or South America?"

"When you returned at the end of six months, you would

find your reputation completely ruined. Your odious vices would have been proved by irrefutable facts, and completely forgotten. And that is the worst thing that can happen to a reputation. Calumny would be delighted if it could force you to run away. Then you would be obliged to catch the public's attention all over again, and re-open the wound in order to cure it. Do you follow me?"

"Only too well, alas! I see plainly that you will not accept either six months of traveling, or six months of prison, in exchange for Mademoiselle Gosselin."

"Ah! heaven be praised, you're growing sensible! But I don't want you to think me capricious. Let's look at this thing together. M. de Beausobre has twenty, thirty, perhaps forty diplomatic spies who belong to good society, several in the most exclusive circles; he has voluntary spies like de Perte, who has an income of forty thousand francs. Madame la Princesse de Vaudemont used to be at his beck and call. These people do not lack tact, most of them have served under ten or a dozen Ministers, and the person they watch most closely, with the greatest care, is their Minister himself. I used to surprise them gathered together in conference on the subject. I have even been consulted by two or three of them who are indebted to me in financial matters. Four or five of them (M. N—— for example, whom you have seen here), when they get a sure tip, want to speculate on the market and haven't enough security. I help them out, now and then, for small sums. Well, two weeks ago, I'd have you know, I made them admit that Beausobre entertains an insane spite against you. He has the reputation of being ruthless—except when there is some chance of a grand cordon. Perhaps he is ashamed of having shown himself weak in your presence. The wherefore of his hate I don't know, but the fact is he does you the honor of hating you.

"But of one thing I am sure: the current gossip to the effect that you are a Saint-Simonian and that only your fondness for me keeps you in society, has been deliberately circulated. When I die, it is being said, you will openly profess Saint-Simonism, or found a new religion.

"If Beausobre's anger lasts, I wouldn't guarantee that one of his spies won't serve him as the followers of Henry II served their King against Becket. In spite of their fine cabriolets, several of these gentlemen are often in pressing need of a favor of fifty louis, and would be only too happy to find such a sum by means of a duel. This is why I have had the weakness to talk to you on the subject. You young scoundrel, you have made me do something that hasn't happened to me for at least fifteen years, you have made me break a promise I made to myself. It is this question of a gratuity of a hundred louis as the price of sending you *ad patres* that made it impossible for me to speak to you in the presence of your mother. If she lost you she would die, and I could then commit all the follies in the world, nothing would ever console me for her loss; and," he added dramatically, "our family would be erased from the face of the earth."

"I'm afraid you are making fun of me," Lucien said, and his voice seemed to falter as he spoke. "You know that whenever you contrive an epigram about me, it always strikes me as so pat that for days I keep repeating it to myself against myself. The devil of doubt gets the better of the man of action in me. Don't tease me and I shall have the courage to be frank with you; don't joke about something which I am sure you know, but which I have never admitted to a living soul."

"The devil! It's news in that case. I shall never mention it."

"I am resolved," Lucien added in a quick curt tone, looking down at the floor, "to be faithful to a mistress I have never possessed. My relations with Mademoiselle Raimonde, involving no moral considerations, give me scarcely any remorse, and yet . . . (you are going to make fun of me) I do feel remorse sometimes . . . whenever I find myself liking her. But when I'm not making love to her . . . I am so depressed I can't help thinking of suicide, for nothing interests me. The only moment of diversion I have known was at the bedside of that poor devil Kortis . . . and then at what a price! Fairly courting disgrace. . . . But you must be laughing at me," he said, stealthily raising his eyes for a moment.

"Not at all! Happy the man who has a great passion, even if it is only a passion for a diamond—like that Spaniard whose story is told by Tallemant des Réaux. Old age is nothing but the absence of madness, the loss of illusion and passion. And I put absence of madness far above the decline of physical powers. I should like to be in love if it were only with the ugliest cook in Paris and know that she reciprocated with the same ardor. I should say with Saint Augustine: *Credo quia absurdum.* The more absurd a passion is the more I envy it."

"But please be merciful, and on the subject of my touch of madness, never make even an indirect allusion, although no one would understand it but myself."

"Never!" cried M. Leuwen, and his face took on an expression of solemnity Lucien had never seen before. For M. Leuwen was never absolutely serious; when there was no one else to laugh at he laughed at himself, often without even Madame Leuwen's being aware of it. This change of physiognomy delighted our hero and encouraged his weakness.

"So you see," Lucien went on in a more assured voice, "if I make love to Mademoiselle Gosselin, or any other notorious young lady, it is inevitable that, sooner or later, she would make me a happy man, and that is what horrifies me. If it's all the same to you, I'd rather choose a virtuous woman."

At this M. Leuwen burst out laughing.

"Don't be angry," he said, choking with laughter. "I am not being unfaithful to our agreement. . . . I am not laughing at the forbidden subject. . . . But where the devil are you going to find your virtuous woman? . . . Ah! my God" [tears of merriment filled his eyes], "and when one fine day your virtuous woman finally confesses that your passion is reciprocated, when the happy hour arrives . . . then what will you do?"

"I shall gravely reproach her for her want of virtue," Lucien calmly replied. "Wouldn't that be in keeping with this moral age?"

"But to make it a really good joke this mistress must be chosen in the Faubourg Saint-Germain."

"Unfortunately, you are not a Duke and I could never be witty and gay if I had to respect some of their preposterous prejudices which we laugh at even in our *Juste-milieu* drawing rooms—stupid enough themselves, God knows!"

While he was speaking Lucien began to realize just what he was thoughtlessly promising. He immediately grew sad and said, in spite of himself:

"But just think what you are asking! A great passion with all its demands, constancy and the monopoly of every second!"

"Precisely."

"Pater meus, transeat a me calix iste!"

"But you can understand my reasons.

Make your arrest yourself, and choose your own punishment.

"Of course the joke would be better with a virtuous lady of exalted piety and special privileges, but you are not what such ladies require. Moreover, power, a very pleasant thing, has passed from those people to us. Very well, among us of the new nobility, gained by crushing or circumventing the July Revolution. . . ."

"Oh! I see what you are leading up to!"

"And where," M. Leuwen went on with an air of the most perfect candor, "where could you do better? Isn't Madame Grandet's virtue *patterned after* the Faubourg Saint-Germain?"

"Just as Dangeau was not a great nobleman but only *patterned after* a great nobleman. No! to me she is really too ridiculous. I could never accustom myself to being desperately in love with Madame Grandet. God! What a deluge of words! What pretentiousness!"

"But at Mademoiselle Gosselin's you would have to meet impossible people without taste. Besides, the more your mistress differs from the woman you love, the less infidelity is involved."

M. Leuwen suddenly crossed to the other end of the drawing room. He was angry with himself for this last allusion.

"I have broken our agreement," he thought, "that is bad, very bad. But, damn it all, can't I be permitted to think aloud with my own son?"

"My dear boy," he said, going back to Lucien, "my last remark was wretched, and I shall do better in the future. But there—the clock is striking three. If you make this sacrifice it is solely for my sake. I shan't point out that, like the prophet, you have been living in a cloud for the last three months, and that when you come out of your cloud you will be astonished at the new aspect everything will have for you. . . . Naturally you believe your own feelings rather than my arguments. So, all my affection dares ask of you is the sacrifice of six months of your life. The only really bitter one will be the first; after that you will get used to the ways of Madame Grandet's famous drawing room, frequented by a few passably amusing men—provided, of course, you are not driven out by her terrible virtue, in which case we'll look for another virtue. Do you feel brave enough to sign a contract for six months?"

Lucien paced the drawing room without replying.

"If you are going to sign the contract, I wish you would sign it right away and let me have a good night's sleep, for" [with a smile] "because of you, I haven't slept for two weeks."

Lucien stopped short, looked at his father and threw himself into his arms. M. Leuwen was very much touched by this embrace: he was sixty-five!

Still in each other's arms, Lucien asked his father:

"Will this be the last sacrifice you ask of me?"

"Yes, my boy, I swear it. You have made me very happy. Good night!"

Lucien remained standing in the drawing room lost in thought. The unquestionably sincere emotion of so undemonstrative a man and that touching *you have made me very happy,* still echoed in his heart.

But, on the other hand, a love affair with Madame Grandet seemed a monstrous thing—a perfect hydra of disgust, boredom and wretchedness.

"My fate was not unhappy enough already," he said to himself. "To give up all that is most beautiful, most moving, most sublime in the world was not enough; I must now spend my life with something utterly low, utterly insipid, putting up with a constant affectation which represents everything that is most vapid, vulgar and detestable in the general trend of the world today! Ah, my fate is unendurable!"

Then all at once he thought: "But let's see what reason would say. Even if I had none of the feelings I ought naturally to have for my father, I should still in strict justice owe him obedience, for what Ernest says is true: I have proved myself incapable of earning eighty-five francs a month. If my father didn't give me what it takes to live in Paris, wouldn't it be much worse to have to earn enough than to make love to Madame Grandet? No! a thousand times, no! Why deceive myself?

"Of course in that salon I can always think my own thoughts; I may meet some curious phenomena, famous men. Whereas, as the slave of an agency of some Amsterdam or London merchant, correspondent of the bank, my thoughts would have to be constantly on what I was writing for fear of making mistakes. I'd rather go back to garrison life: drill all morning, billiard rooms all evening. With an allowance of a hundred louis I could live very well. But who is to give me the hundred louis? My mother? And if she didn't have them, could I live on what my present possessions would bring, plus my soldier's pay of ninety-five francs a month?"

Lucien lingered a long time over this question, to put off facing one much more terrible:

"What am I going to do tomorrow to show Madame Grandet that I adore her?"

The last words stirred profound and tender memories of Madame de Chasteller. And he felt such an irresistible charm in these thoughts that he said to himself:

"Tomorrow is time enough for business. . . ."

That *tomorrow* can hardly be taken literally, for when at last he blew out his candle the melancholy sounds of a winter morning already filled the street.

He had a great deal of work that morning both at the Ministry and at the Bourse. Until two o'clock he studied the articles of a long ordinance relative to the National Guard. The duties of the Guard throughout France had to be made more and more boring, for after all, it was certainly not with the aid of the National Guard that the government intended to keep order! For the last few days the Minister had been in the habit of sending to Lucien (for his conscientious examination) all the reports of the division heads that required intelligence and honesty rather than a profound knowledge of the forty-four thousand laws, orders and circulars which govern the Ministry of the Interior. The Minister called Lucien's reports *brief summaries;* these *brief summaries* were often ten or fifteen pages long. Since Lucien had been very busy with telegraphic business, and found himself several *brief summaries* in arrears, the Minister authorized him to take two clerks to assist him; he even sacrificed half of his own inner office. But, as by this arrangement the clerks would be separated only by a thin partition (muted with mattresses, to be sure) from all the momentous affairs of state, the difficulty was to find someone absolutely discreet and with a sense of honor who would be incapable of furnishing articles, even anonymous articles, to the abhorred *National*.

After searching in vain through all the departments, Lucien suddenly remembered a former student of the École Polytechnique, an extremely taciturn youth who had decided to be a tradesman and who, because he had superior attainments, thought them inferior. This new clerk, named Coffe, the most silent man at the École Polytechnique, cost the Ministry eighty louis, for Lucien had found him in the prison of Sainte-Pélagie, and could only get him out by paying his creditors something on account. But Coffe agreed to work for only ten louis and—most important—one could talk in front of him with impunity. This assistant made it possible for Lucien occasionally to get away from his office for a quarter of an hour at a time.

Coffe was a little man, nervous, skinny, alert, active and almost completely bald. He was twenty-five years old and looked thirty-six. Wretchedly poor and equally honest, discontent was written all over his face, which never brightened except when he was engaged in some strenuous activity. Coffe had been famous at the École Polytechnique for his almost unbroken silence; but, without his realizing it, his little gray eyes that were never at rest spoke for him. In his contempt for the present age, Coffe was sure that there was nothing worth getting excited about. But, in spite of himself, injustice and absurdity roused his anger; afterwards he would be furious with himself for having been angry and for having taken an interest in that absurd and rascally mass of humanity comprising the vast majority of mankind. A degree from the École Polytechnique was his sole fortune. After being expelled, he had turned everything he possessed into cash and with a capital of three thousand francs had set up a little business. He soon went bankrupt and was sent to Sainte-Pélagie, where he would have spent five years, only to find at the end of them the same poverty awaiting him in the outside world, had not Lucien come to his rescue. He planned, if ever he could get together an income of four hundred francs, to go to Provence and there live in solitude.

A week later, the Comte de Vaize received five or six anonymous denunciations of M. Coffe. But as soon as Coffe left Sainte-Pélagie, Lucien, unknown to him, had taken the precaution of placing him under the surveillance of M. Crapart, the Ministry's Chief of Police. It was thus proved that M. Coffe had no connection with the liberal newspapers; as for his having any relations with the political committee of Henri V, even the Minister joked with him about it.

"Get their few louis out of them if you can. I don't mind," he said to Coffe, who was very much shocked at the proposal, for he happened to be an honest man.

To Coffe's exclamations, the Minister replied:

"I understand! You want some mark of favor that will stop these anonymous letters from supernumeraries jealous of this post M. Leuwen has obtained for you. Very well," he said, turning to Lucien, "make out an order for me to sign authorizing M. Coffe to have copies made, in any of the departments, of documents needed in duplicate by my private staff—and without any delays."

At this moment the Minister was interrupted by the announcement of a telegraphic dispatch from Spain. This dispatch quickly took Lucien's thoughts away from all these bureaucratic arrangements and had him jumping into a cabriolet and speeding swiftly toward his father's bank, and from there to the Bourse. As usual he carefully avoided going in himself, but, while awaiting news from his agents, went to look over the latest pamphlets in a nearby reading room.

Here he was discovered by three of his father's employees who had all been looking for him everywhere. He was handed a note of two lines from his father:

"Rush to the Bourse, go in yourself, stop all operations. Sell even at a loss, then come to me at once."

This order astonished him. He hastened to carry it out, had some difficulty, but finally arrived at his father's office.

"Well, did you succeed?"

"Completely. But why? It seemed an excellent thing."

"It is by far the best we've ever handled. There was a three thousand franc profit to be realized."

"Then why sell out?" asked Lucien, looking puzzled.

"Egad, and I don't know why," M. Leuwen mysteriously replied. "You will find that out from your Minister if you know how to question him. You'd better hurry back now and reassure him. He is insane with anxiety."

M. Leuwen's attitude only intensified Lucien's curiosity. He hastened to the Ministry and found M. de Vaize pacing the floor of his bedroom with the door double-locked, and in a state of profound agitation.

"He is really the most timorous of men," thought Lucien.

"Well, my friend, have you succeeded in getting rid of everything?"

"Absolutely everything except for a matter of some ten thousand francs. I haven't been able to find Rouillon who has orders to buy."

"Ah, my friend, I would give fifty francs, I would give a hundred francs to get back that scrap too, and not to seem to have made the slightest profit on the cursed telegram. Will you go and get back those ten thousand francs?"

The Minister's whole air said, "Hurry!"

"I'll never know the inside of this affair if I don't get it out of him while he is still in such a state."

"The truth is, I wouldn't know where to go," Lucien said

with the air of a man who has no desire to get into a cabriolet again. "M. Rouillon is dining out. I could perhaps look for him at home in another two hours, and then explore the neighborhood around Tortoni's. But, would Your Excellency care to tell me the why and wherefore of all this trouble I have gone to, and which is going to take up my whole evening?"

"I really shouldn't tell you," His Excellency replied, looking very much worried, "but I am sure, and have been for a long time, of your perfect discretion. *Certain persons* are reserving this little venture for themselves; and," he added with a look of terror, "it is a miracle, one of those strokes of luck, that I discovered it in time. That reminds me—will you be good enough to buy a very pretty watch—a lady's watch?"

The Minister went to his desk and took out two thousand francs.

"Here are two thousand francs. I want it done handsomely; if necessary go as high as three thousand. Can you get something presentable for that?"

"I think so."

"Well then, this pretty watch with a gold chain and with one volume of Balzac's novels bearing an uneven number, say, 1, 3 or 5, must be taken, by someone absolutely trustworthy, to Madame Lavernaye, 90 Rue Sainte-Anne. Now that you know everything, my friend, do me one last favor, don't leave the thing half done. Get me back those ten thousand francs, so that it can never be said, or at least proved, that I ever made one penny on that telegram."

"Your Excellency need have no further worry in this matter, it is as good as done!" Lucien replied, taking his leave with every mark of respect.

Lucien had no difficulty in finding M. Rouillon who was peacefully dining with his wife and children in their third-floor apartment. And with the promise of paying him the difference that very evening at the Café Tortoni, which might amount to fifty or a hundred francs, all trace of the transaction was now obliterated, and so he informed the Minister in a brief note.

Lucien did not arrive home until the end of dinner. He was jubilant all the way from the Place des Victoires, where M. Rouillon lived, to his father's house on the Rue de Londres. His herculean task for the evening in Madame Grandet's drawing room now seemed to him a simple matter. So true is it that people whose imaginations are their worst enemy should always start action as soon as possible when they have anything painful to accomplish and never give themselves time to think about it beforehand.

"I shall talk *ab hoc et ab hac,*" Lucien said to himself, "and say anything that comes into my head, good, bad, or indifferent. I suppose that is the way to appear brilliant in the eyes of that sublime woman, Madame Grandet. For one must be brilliant before being tender. The gift is despised if the object presented is not of great price."

CHAPTER TWELVE

"FORGIVE ME, mother, all the trite things I shall be guilty of tonight," said Lucien, as he took leave of his mother at nine o'clock.

When he arrived at the Grandet mansion he examined his surroundings with new curiosity—the porter, the courtyard, the great stairway—for it was in the midst of all these things that his campaign was about to begin. Everything was magnificent, costly and new. In the antechamber, however, a blue velvet screen, studded with gold nails and a trifle worn, might have been saying to those who passed: "You see, our wealth is not of recent date . . ."; but to a Grandet a screen was an investment and not what it has to say to people passing through the antechamber.

Lucien found Madame Grandet surrounded by a small group of her more intimate friends. There were seven or eight persons in the elegant rotunda where she always received at this hour. It was early—much too early to arrive at Madame Grandet's. Lucien was well aware of this fact, but he wanted to play the *lovesick adorer*. In the light of candles placed successively at all vantage points, Madame Grandet was examining a bust of Cleopatra by Tenerani, which the King's Ambassador at Rome had just sent her. The expression of the Egyptian queen was simple and noble. The company gave vent to its admiration in high-sounding phrases.

"She is illuminating their vulgarity," Lucien said to himself. "All these smug faces and graying hair seem to be saying: 'Oh! How prosperous I am!'"

A Deputy of the Center, and an intimate of the house, proposed making up a pool at billiards. Lucien recognized the booming voice as that of the Deputy whose duty it was in the Chamber to laugh whenever, by chance, some generous measure was proposed.

Madame Grandet hastened to ring and order the billiard room lighted. For Lucien everything now took on a new aspect.

"There is some good in having a plan, no matter how ridiculous it may be. She has a charming figure and playing billiards provides hundreds of occasions to show it in alluring postures. It is surprising that the religious proprieties of the Faubourg Saint-Germain have not yet thought of forbidding this game!"

Over the billiard table Lucien began talking almost incessantly. His gaiety increased as the success of his heavy commonplaces made him quite forget the embarrassing necessity of paying court, by paternal order, to Madame Grandet.

At first his sallies were really too hackneyed, and he amused himself making fun of his own words. It was barber-shop wit —anecdotes repeated everywhere, stories from the newspapers . . .

"She is a mass of absurdities," he thought, "but she is, nevertheless, accustomed to a certain standard of wit. Anecdotes are all right, but preferably ones that are a little less trite, heavy commentaries but on delicate subjects—on the tenderness of Racine as compared to Virgil, on the Italian tales from which Shakespeare took his plots; never any quick, pointed remarks: they would pass unnoticed. But the same rule does not hold true for glances, especially when one is very much in love." And he contemplated with barely disguised admiration Madame Grandet's charming attitudes.

"God! What would Madame de Chasteller say if she could see one of these glances of mine?

But I must forget her to be happy here,"

he murmured to himself. And he brushed aside this fatal thought, but not before emotion had darkened his eyes.

Madame Grandet herself looked at him in a very special fashion, not tenderly, it is true, but in pleasant surprise. She remembered vividly all that Madame de Thémines had told her a few days before of Lucien's passion for her. It now seemed to her strange that she had thought Madame de Thémines' revelations so ridiculous.

"Really he is quite presentable," she said to herself, "he has great distinction."

Lucien had drawn ball number 6. A tall silent young man, apparently a mute adorer of the mistress of the house, had number 5 and Madame Grandet number 4. Lucien tried to kill the 5, succeeded, and thereby found himself in a position to play on Madame Grandet's ball and make her lose the game, a proceeding he avoided with considerable skill. He attempted only the most difficult shots, and had the misfortune of never hitting Madame Grandet's ball and of almost always placing her in an advantageous position. Madame Grandet was overjoyed.

"Can the hope of winning a pool of twenty francs," Lucien thought, "really excite her chambermaid soul, tenant of such a lovely body? The game is nearly over, let's see if my conjecture is correct."

Lucien let himself be killed; it was now the turn of number 7 to play on Madame Grandet. This number belonged to a Prefect on leave, a great braggart with all the conceit in the world, including that of being a good billiard player. This fatuous puppy kept boasting in the worst possible taste of all the points he was going to make, and threatening Madame Grandet with killing her ball or putting her in a disadvantageous position.

Seeing her fate reversed by the *death* of Lucien, Madame Grandet began to be very ill-tempered, and bit her lovely fresh lips, now tightly compressed.

"So that's the way she looks when she is piqued!" thought Lucien.

At the third hit from the pitiless Prefect, Madame Grandet glanced ruefully at Lucien, and Lucien had the temerity to respond by watching amorously all her charming postures, which, in spite of her despair, she did not neglect. Lucien, *dead* though he was, was very active around the table, following Madame Grandet's ball with apparently all the anxiety of keenest interest. With affected and somewhat ridiculous alacrity, he took her part in her unjustified resentment against the conceited Prefect who remained *alone* with her and who was determined to win.

Soon Madame Grandet lost the pool, but Lucien had advanced so considerably in her estimation that she thought fit to make him a little dissertation, geometrical and profound, on the angles formed by the billiard balls striking the cushions of the table. Lucien raised some objections.

"Ah," Madame Grandet rejoined, "it is true, you are a student of the École Polytechnique. But being an expelled student you are probably not very well up on geometry."

Lucien suggested experimenting. They measured distances on the table. The experiments elicited from Madame Grandet charming exclamations of surprise and delightful little cries, also another opportunity for displaying those alluring postures, so provocative indeed that at one time Lucien thought:

"I could not have asked more of Mademoiselle Gosselin!"

From that moment he was in wonderful form. Madame Grandet abandoned the scientific experiments to propose their playing a game. She found Lucien interesting because he surprised her. "I can't get over it," she said to herself, "how stupid shyness can make even the most agreeable men!"

About ten o'clock a good many people began to arrive. Everyone was in the habit of bringing any notable persons passing through Paris to meet Madame Grandet. Only the really famous artists and great noblemen of the highest rank were missing from her collection. And their presence in Paris, invariably heralded in all the newspapers, never failed to throw her into a very bad humor; she would even indulge, at times, in semi-republican remarks at their expense, which very much annoyed her husband. At half-past-ten this husband, all puffed up with the favor shown him by the King of his choice, came in with a Minister and, on their heels, three or four Deputies very influential in the Chamber. Five or six scholars who were present began to pay court to the Ministers and even to the Deputies. Soon they had as rivals two or three celebrated writers who were a little less servile in manner but perhaps more slavish at heart, hiding their sycophancy under the perfect urbanity of their style. They would begin in a rhetorical tone softened by indirect compliments of an admirable delicacy. They reduced the conceited Prefect, terrified by this language, to silence.

"These are the people we make such fun of at home," thought Lucien. "Here they are admired."

Most of the well-known figures of Paris appeared one after the other.

"The only clever men missing are those who have the bad taste to belong to the opposition. How can anyone have respect enough left for the filthy bit of matter called man to belong to an opposition? . . . In the midst of so many celebrities my reign must surely be over."

At that moment Madame Grandet crossed the length of the drawing room to speak to him.

"What audacity!" he said to himself, laughing. "Why the devil this special attention? Can she really afford such behavior? I must be a duke without knowing it!"

There was an abundance of Deputies in the drawing room. Lucien noticed that they were all talking in loud voices, and were trying to make themselves conspicuous. They held their grizzled heads as high as possible, and took care to make their gestures brusque and emphatic.

One of them set his gold box down on the table where he was playing cards, in such a way as to rouse the envy of two or three of his neighbors; another, settling himself in his chair, kept scraping it on the floor with no regard for neighboring ears.

"They all have the look of a big landowner who has just renewed a profitable lease," Lucien thought.

The one who had been scraping his chair on the floor so unpleasantly came into the billiard room a few minutes later, and asked Lucien if he might look at the *Gazette de France* which Lucien was reading. He *begged* this little favor with

such a humble air that our hero was touched because it reminded him of Nancy. And suddenly Lucien's eyes stared
unseeingly, and his mouth lost its expression of urbanity. He
was roused from his reverie by bursts of laughter next to him.
A famous writer was telling an amusing anecdote about the
Abbé Barthélemy, author of the *Voyage d'Anacharsis.* Then
followed an anecdote about Marmontel, and still a third about
the Abbé Delille.

"All this merriment is at bottom dry-as-dust and dreary.
These Academicians live solely on the absurdities of their
predecessors, but will themselves die bankrupt and leave nothing for their successors, being too timid to commit absurdities.
Here is none of that heedless fun there used to be at Madame
d'Hocquincourt's once M. d'Antin got us started."

When a fourth anecdote began on the absurdity of Antoine-
Léonard Thomas, Lucien could endure no more and went
back to the large drawing room through a gallery orna-
mented with busts. He came upon Madame Grandet standing
in one of the doorways, and again she hailed him.

"It would be ungrateful of me not to join her group in case
she takes a notion to play Madame de Staël."

Lucien had not long to wait. That evening a painfully thin
young German scholar, with a mass of blond hair parted in
the middle, had been presented to Madame Grandet. She was
talking to him about all the learned discoveries made by Germans: Homer had perhaps written only one of the famous
"Homeric hymns" whose masterly treatment, the fruit of
chance, is so admired by pedants. Madame Grandet spoke very
well of the Alexandrian School. A large group had gathered
around her. The subject of Christian antiquities was brought
up and Madame Grandet immediately looked serious and
gave the corners of her mouth a downward twist.

Then, of all things, what did this newly presented German
do, but attack the Catholic Mass to a bourgeois woman of the

court of Louis-Philippe? These Germans are the very kings of tactlessness!

"The Mass in the Fifth Century," he explained, "was nothing but a social gathering at which bread was broken in memory of Jesus Christ. It was a sort of tea party for the faithful. It never occurred to them that they were doing anything solemn or out of the ordinary, and much less that a miracle was taking place, the incarnation of the bread and wine into the body and blood of the Saviour. Then we see this tea party of the early Christians gradually growing in importance and taking its present form."

"Good God! Where ever did you find all that, my dear sir?" cried Madame Grandet, horrified. "In some of your German authors, most likely, although they are usually so sympathetic to sublime and mystical ideas, and for that very reason are cherished by all right-thinking people. A few must have gone astray, and as your language is, unfortunately, so little known to my frivolous compatriots, they have been saved from all refutation."

"No, Madam. The French too have very great scholars," replied the young German dialectician, who had apparently learned polite forms of address in order to have the pleasure of spinning out discussions interminably. "But as French literature, Madam, is so rich and the French have so many treasures, they are like people with enormous wealth, ignorant of half the treasures they possess. This whole authentic story of the Mass I found in old Father Mabillon, who has just given his name to one of the streets of your brilliant capital. To be exact, it is not in Mabillon's text—the poor monk would hardly have dared—but in his notes. Your Mass, Madam, is a recent invention; it is like your Paris which did not yet exist in the Fifth Century."

All along Madame Grandet had been replying in hesitant and ineffectual phrases, which the German, adjusting his glasses, would invariably answer with facts, or, if these were contested, with textual citations. The monster had an astonishing memory.

Madame Grandet was exceedingly vexed.

"How wonderful Madame de Staël would have been in a moment like this," she thought, "surrounded by such a large attentive audience! I see at least thirty people listening to us and here I am, incapable of finding a word to reply, and it is too late to become indignant!"

As she was counting the listeners who, after laughing at the strange appearance of the German, were beginning to admire him precisely because of his peculiar gawkiness and his novel way of adjusting his glasses, Madame Grandet's eye caught Lucien's. In her panic they almost begged for sympathy. She had just made the discovery that her most bewitching glances had no effect on the young German who, completely absorbed in listening to himself, was blind to them.

Lucien deciphered Madame Grandet's suppliant look as an appeal to his chivalry; he made his way through the listening circle and took his place beside the young German dialectician.

"But, sir . . . . " *

It turned out that the German was not overly awed by French wit and irony. Lucien had counted too much on this means of escape, and, as he did not know the first thing about the question, did not even know in what language Mabillon had written, he was defeated.

At one o'clock Lucien left the Grandet mansion where every effort had been made to please him. His soul was dried up. He loathed everything he had heard—the anecdotes of the

* Stendhal left this sentence blank with a marginal reminder to consult his acquaintance, Ampère, son of the great French physicist, for some plausible objection, or, as Stendhal puts it in his inimitable English: "To ask objection, the less bad, to Mr J. J. Ampère."

famous writers, the learned discussion, all the admirably correct manners. It was with delight that he gave himself up to an hour's tête-à-tête with the memory of Madame de Chasteller. Such men as he had seen tonight, and he had seen the flower of their kind, almost made him doubt the possibility of the existence of beings like Madame de Chasteller. Joyfully he recaptured the beloved image, and it had something of the charm of novelty, the one thing usually lacking in the memory of love.

The writers, scholars, Deputies whom he had just met at Madame Grandet's, took good care not to appear in Madame Leuwen's caustic drawing room; they would have been made fun of pitilessly. There everybody made fun of everybody else. So much the worse for fools and hypocrites who did not have an infinite store of wit. The titles of Duke, Peer of France, Colonel of the National Guard (as M. Grandet had discovered) saved no one from the most sprightly irony.

"I have no favor to ask of any man, either the governing or the governed," M. Leuwen would sometimes remark in his drawing room. "I address myself exclusively to their purses. Mornings in my office, it is for me to prove that their interest is the same as mine. Outside my office I have only one interest, to relax and to laugh at fools, whether they are on the throne or in the gutter. And so, my friends, laugh at me if you can."

The next day Lucien spent his entire morning trying to understand a denunciation of the Algerian policy by M. Gandin. The King had asked M. de Vaize for a well-founded opinion on the subject. This was most flattering inasmuch as it was properly an affair for the Minister of War. M. de Vaize had spent the whole night over it and had done an excellent piece of work. He had then sent for Lucien.

"My friend, I want you to criticize this ruthlessly," he said, as he gave Lucien his much corrected copybook. "Try to find objections. I would rather be criticized by my aide-de-camp in private than by my colleagues in the middle of a Cabinet meeting. As you finish with each page have it copied by some *discreet* clerk—the writing doesn't matter. What a pity yours is so frightful! You never bother to form your letters. Couldn't you try to reform?"

"Can a bad habit be reformed? If that were possible how many two-million-franc thieves would become honest men!"

"This Gandin insists that the General tried to silence him with fifteen hundred louis. . . . All this, both your criticism and a fair copy of my report, I must have within eight hours. I want to put it in my portfolio. But I ask you to be unsparing in your criticism. If we could be sure your father wouldn't make one of his epigrams on the treasures of the Bey's citadel, I would give anything to have his advice on the question."

Lucien glanced through the Minister's rough draft, which was twelve pages long.

"Nothing in the world could persuade my father to read a report of such length, and, in addition, the documents will have to be verified."

Lucien found that this problem was as difficult, at least, as the origin of the Mass. At seven-thirty he sent M. de Vaize the result of his labors, which was quite as long as the Minister's report, together with a fair copy of the report. His mother had managed to delay dinner so that they were still at table when he got home.

"What makes you so late?" M. Leuwen asked him.

"His affection for me," replied his mother, "for it would certainly have been more convenient for him to eat at a tavern. And what can I do to show my gratitude?"

"Persuade my father to give me his advice on a little opuscule of my fashioning that I have here in my pocket."

And they discussed Algiers, the forty-eight million in the

Bey's treasury, and a stolen thirteen million, until half-past-nine.

"And Madame Grandet?" M. Leuwen enquired.

"I had completely forgotten her. . . ."

CHAPTER THIRTEEN

THERE WAS NOTHING but business for Lucien that day from the beginning to the end; for he hastened to Madame Grandet's in the evening as he would have gone to his office to keep a belated appointment. Lightly he crossed the courtyard, mounted the stairs, went through the antechamber, smiling all the time at the simplicity of the venture he was about to engage in. He knew the same pleasure he might have felt at recovering some document that had disappeared at the moment he wanted to attach it to a report for the King.

He found Madame Grandet surrounded by her faithful admirers, and suddenly distaste extinguished his youthful smile. The gentlemen were arguing: a M. Greslin, who was Referendary at the Court of Accounts (thanks to twelve thousand francs presented to the cousin of the mistress of the Comte de Vaize), questioned whether the corner grocer, M. Béranville, who was purveyor to the General Staff of the National Guard, would dare displease such *good customers* by voting in accordance with his newspaper. One of the other gentlemen, a Jesuit before 1830 and now a Lieutenant of Grenadiers, and decorated, had just offered the information that one of Béranville's clerks subscribed to the *National,* a thing he certainly would never have dared to do if his employer had had a proper horror of that rhapsodical and disruptive republican sheet.

With each word, Madame Grandet's beauty perceptibly faded in Lucien's estimation. And the worst of it was that she was taking a very active part in a discussion which would not have been out of place in a porter's lodge. She voted that the grocer be indirectly threatened with loss of patronage by the Drum-Major of the company of Grenadiers, whom she knew very well.

"Instead of enjoying their enviable position," Lucien thought, "these people waste their time *being afraid,* like my friends, the nobles of Nancy, and, furthermore, they make me sick at my stomach."

Lucien was leagues away from that youthful smile with which he had entered the magnificent drawing room, now transformed into a porter's lodge.

"I am sure that the conversation of the young ladies of the Opera is less vulgar. What a curious age! These Frenchmen who are normally so brave, as soon as they become rich spend their lives being afraid. But perhaps these noble souls of the *Juste-milieu* are incapable of serenity as long as any possibility of danger exists in the world."

And he stopped listening to them. It was only then that he noticed that Madame Grandet was receiving him very coolly; this amused him.

"I thought," he said to himself, "that I would remain in favor for at least a couple of weeks. But it doesn't take that long for this featherbrain to tire of an idea."

This brisk and breezy reasoning of Lucien's would have seemed pretty ridiculous to any politician. It was he who was the featherbrain: he had failed to divine Madame Grandet's character. This woman, so fresh, so young, and apparently so taken up with the frescoes of her summer gallery, copies of those of Pompeii, was almost constantly engrossed in the most profound political calculations. She was as rich as a Rothschild and longed to be a Montmorency!

"This young Leuwen, Master of Petitions, is not bad. If half of his real merit could be exchanged for an inherited position in the world, a position no one could dispute, he would be good for something in society. Just as he is, with that simplicity amounting almost to naïveté, yet not lacking in nobility by any means, he would suit to perfection one of those little women who look for gallantry, and not for a distinguished position in society."

And she was quite horrified by this vulgar way of thinking.

"He has no name. He is an insignificant young man, the son of a rich banker who has acquired the reputation of being clever because he has a malicious tongue. But his father is nothing but a beginner in the career in which M. Grandet has advanced so far. He is without a name or a family solidly established in society. It is not in his power to add anything to my position. Every time he is invited to the Tuileries I shall also be invited, and before he is. He has never yet had the honor of being invited to dance with the Princesses."

Such were Madame Grandet's thoughts as she studied Lucien, who all the time believed her to be entirely engrossed by the question of the crimes of the corner grocer and the means of punishing him by withdrawing the patronage of the General Staff of the National Guard.

Suddenly Madame Grandet laughed to herself, something very unusual for her.

"If, as Madame de Thémines so generously believes, he has such a passion for me, the thing to do is to drive him completely mad. And I believe, to begin with, harsh treatment would best suit this handsome young man, and it will certainly suit me very well."

At the end of half an hour, seeing that he was really being treated with marked coolness, Lucien found himself, in regard to the beautiful Madame Grandet, in the same position as a connoisseur who is bargaining for a mediocre painting;

as long as he thinks he can have it for a few louis he exaggerates its beauties; but if the salesman sets an exorbitant value on it, the painting begins to seem absurd to him, he finds nothing but flaws in it and thinks only of ridiculing it.

"I am here," Lucien admonished himself, "to make plain to fools that I am hopelessly in love. Let's see, what does one do when one is consumed by such a passion and has been badly received by so pretty a woman? Naturally one sinks into a melancholy silence."

And he didn't utter another word.

"How well the world understands passion!" he thought, smiling to himself and becoming really melancholy. "When I was actually in the state I am now assuming, no one was noisier than I at the Café Charpentier!"

Lucien remained seated on his chair in the most praiseworthy immobility. Unhappily he could not shut his ears.

About ten o'clock M. de Torpet, an ex-Deputy, a very handsome young man, and the eloquent editor of a government newspaper, arrived.

"Have you read the *Messager,* Madam?" he said, coming up to the mistress of the house with a vulgar and almost familiar air, as though showing off his intimacy with this young society woman who was so much talked about. "Have you read the *Messager?* They won't be able to find a reply to those few lines I launched this morning on the latest crazy idea of the reformists. In a few brief words I dealt with the question of the increase in the number of voters. England has eight hundred thousand, and we have a hundred eighty thousand. But if I take a quick glance at England, what is it that strikes me first of all, what pre-eminently and startlingly meets my eye? A powerful and respected aristocracy, an aristocracy which has its roots deep in the customs of that supremely serious people; serious because they are a Biblical people. And on this side of the Channel what do I see? People who have wealth and nothing more! Perhaps in two years the heirs to their wealth and to their names will be in Sainte-Pélagie. . . ."

Addressed to a rich bourgeois woman whose grandfather had certainly not kept a carriage, this discourse amused Lucien for a while. Unfortunately, M. de Torpet did not have the wit to be witty in a few words, he required endless periods.

"This impudent Gascon thinks it incumbent on him to talk like M. de Chateaubriand's books," thought Lucien impatiently. He put in two or three little remarks himself, which, had they been carefully explained to this audience, might have been considered amusing. But he quickly cut himself short. "I am forgetting that I am hopelessly in love. Silence and sadness are the only fitting attitudes to assume, after the reception Madame Grandet has given me tonight."

Reduced to silence, Lucien heard so many stupidities and, above all, witnessed the proud display of so many base sentiments that he had the feeling that he was in his father's servants' hall.

"When my mother finds her lackeys talking like M. de Torpet, she dismisses them."

He began to feel a distinct dislike for all the elegant appointments of Madame Grandet's little oval drawing room. He was wrong: nothing could have been more charming and less theatrical; if it had not been for the oval form and some of the gay ornaments skillfully placed there by the architect, this delicious little drawing room would have been a perfect temple; artists would have agreed, "It borders on the solemn." But the impudence of M. de Torpet spoiled everything for Lucien. The youth, the freshness of the mistress of the house, although somewhat enhanced for him by her cool reception, seemed that of a chambermaid.

Lucien continued to think of himself as a philosopher, and failed to see that it was simply a question of not being able to stand effrontery. This attribute, so indispensable to success and carried to the extreme by M. de Torpet, filled him with a loathing that came very near to anger. This loathing for so necessary an attribute was the symptom which alarmed M. Leuwen about his son.

"He is not made for this age," Lucien's father used to say to himself, "and will never be anything but an insignificant man of merit."

When the inevitable pool at billiards was suggested, Lucien saw that M. de Torpet was disposed to take a ball. Lucien's ears were really offended by the loud voice of this handsome man. His disgust was so great that he felt incapable of dancing attendance at the billiard table and silently took his leave, but remembering to walk with dragging steps as befitted his sorrow.

"It is only eleven o'clock," he said with delight, and for the first time that season hastened toward the Opera with pleasure at the thought of arriving.

He found Mademoiselle Raimonde in his father's latticed box. She had been alone for the last quarter of an hour and was dying to talk to someone. Lucien listened to her with unmistakable pleasure which surprised her. He was altogether charming to her.

"She has real wit," he said to himself in his state of infatuation. "What a contrast to the slow, monotonous pomposity of the Grandet drawing room!"

"You are charming, my lovely Raimonde, or at least I am charmed. Now tell me all about the dispute between Madame —— and her husband, and about the duel."

While Raimonde's soft little voice, that was as clear as a bell, went flitting from one detail of her story to another, Lucien's thoughts were still occupied with the scene he had just left.

"How heavy and sad those people are, exchanging their specious arguments which both listener and speaker know to be false! But it would shock all the proprieties of that confraternity not to exchange this counterfeit money of theirs. One has to swallow I don't know how many imbecilities, but never laugh at the fundamental verities of their religion, or all is lost." He then surprised his companion by interrupting her chatter to say:

"In your company, my lovely Raimonde, a Torpet would be impossible."

"Where have you come from?" she asked.

"With your impetuous, fearless disposition, it wouldn't take you long to make a fool of him, you would tear his grandiloquence to tatters. . . . What a pity I can't have you both to lunch together! My father would deserve to be present at such a luncheon. Never could your lively spirit endure that man's long pompous periods, which are in perfect keeping with the manners of the provinces."

Our hero fell silent.

"Perhaps," he thought, "I should transfer my consuming passion from Madame Grandet to Mademoiselle Elssler or Mademoiselle Gosselin? They, too, are very famous; neither Mademoiselle Elssler nor Mademoiselle Gosselin has the wit nor the unexpectedness of Mademoiselle Raimonde, but at least at Mademoiselle Gosselin's, a Torpet would be impossible. And that is why society in France has fallen into decadence. We have reached the age of Seneca; we no longer dare act or speak as in the time of Madame de Sévigné and the great Condé. Spontaneity has taken refuge in the corps-de-ballet. I wonder which would be less troublesome as the object of my hopeless passion, Madame Grandet or Mademoiselle Gosselin? Am I really to be condemned to write inanities all morning and to listen to them all evening?"

In the midst of this self-examination, while Lucien half-listened to Mademoiselle Raimonde's foolish chatter, the door of the box burst open, giving entrance to no less a personage than His Excellency, M. le Comte de Vaize.

"I have been looking for you," he said to Lucien in a solemn tone, not without a touch of self-importance. "I must talk to you! But . . . this young lady . . . can she be trusted?"

Although he had lowered his voice, Mademoiselle Raimonde caught his words.

"That is a question no one has ever asked without regretting it," she cried. "And since I can't ask Your Excellency to get out, I'll postpone my revenge till the next session of the Chamber." And she disappeared.

"Not bad," said Lucien, laughing. "Really not bad at all."

"But how can anyone be so frivolous, engaged, as you are, in affairs of such importance?" the Minister exclaimed with the ill humor of a man beset by grave difficulties who sees himself put off with a jest.

"I have sold myself body and soul to Your Excellency during the day, but it is now eleven o'clock at night and, by gad, my evenings are my own. But," he continued jokingly, "what am I offered for them?"

"I will make you a Lieutenant instead of a Second-Lieutenant."

"Alas! A very pretty offer, but I wouldn't know what to do with it."

"There will come a time when you will appreciate its full value. Can you lock this box?"

"Nothing could be easier," replied Lucien, bolting the door.

Meanwhile the Minister looked to see if people in the adjoining box could hear them. It was empty. His Excellency was careful to hide behind a column.

"Entirely through your own merit you have become my aide-de-camp," he began with an air of gravity. "The office you hold was nothing, and my only reason for placing you there was to please your father. You have created the office yourself, it is at present not without importance, and I have just spoken of you to the King."

He paused, expecting this last declaration to have a great effect. He looked at Lucien intently and found nothing but a somewhat listless attention.

"Unhappy monarchy!" he thought. "The name *King* has been shorn of all its magical effect. It is really impossible to govern with all these little newspapers demolishing everything. We have to pay everything in cash or preferments. . . . And it is ruining us: the Treasury is not infinite, nor preferments either."

There followed a little silence of ten seconds during which the Minister's face took on a somber expression. In his early youth at Coblentz, the four letters K I N G had still produced an effect.

"Is he about to make some proposition like the Caron affair?" Lucien wondered. "In that case, the army will never have a Lieutenant by the name of Leuwen."

"My friend," said the Minister finally, "the King approves my sending you on this double electoral mission."

("Elections again!" thought Lucien. "Tonight I am like M. de Pourceaugnac.")

"Your Excellency," he rejoined firmly, "is not ignorant of the fact that such missions are not looked upon by a disabused public as altogether honorable."

"That is what I am far from admitting," the Minister replied. "And, allow me to add, I have had more experience than you."

This last was said with an air of self-complacency in the worst possible taste, nor was the retort slow in coming:

"And I, M. le Comte, have less interest in power, and beg Your Excellency to confide such missions to someone more worthy than myself."

"But, my friend," the Minister replied, trying to restrain

his ministerial vanity, "it is one of the duties of your office, that office which you have succeeded in making something of . . ."

"In that case I have a second request to add to my first, that of asking you to accept my resignation, together with my thanks for all your kindness to me."

"Unhappy monarchical principle!" the Minister said almost to himself.

As it did not suit him to part either with Lucien or his father he added in the most courteous tone:

"Permit me to say, my dear sir, that the question of your resignation can only be discussed with M. Leuwen, your father."

"I should be happy not always to have recourse to my father's talents. If Your Excellency would be good enough to explain these missions to me, and if there is no danger of a Rue Transnonain at the end of the affair, I might accept them."

"I deplore no less than you the terrible accidents that can happen in the precipitate use of even perfectly legitimate force. But you must surely feel that an accident, deplored and rectified as far as was possible, proves nothing against a system. Is a man who shoots his friend while hunting, a murderer?"

"M. de Torpet talked to us for an endless half hour this evening about such misadventures, exaggerated by a wicked press."

"Torpet is a fool, and it is because we haven't a Leuwen, and the others are wanting in flexibility, that we are forced to use a Torpet. For, after all, the machine must function. The arguments and torrents of eloquence, for which these gentlemen are paid, are not intended for intelligences such as yours. But in a large army you cannot expect all the soldiers to be marvels of delicacy."

144

"But who will guarantee that another Minister will not employ in my honor the same terms Your Excellency has used in your panegyric of M. de Torpet?"

"Really, my friend, you *are* intractable!"

This was said so naturally and so good-naturedly, and Lucien was still so young, that this tone brought a response:

"No, M. le Comte. Indeed, in order not to disappoint my father, I am ready to accept your missions provided there is no bloodshed at the end of them."

"But do you really suppose we have the power to shed blood?" the Minister exclaimed in a very different tone of voice and with something like reproach, and even regret.

This remark coming from the heart struck Lucien.

"What a perfect inquisitor," he thought.

"The object of your mission is twofold," the Minister continued, assuming an altogether official tone, and at the same time thinking to himself: "I shall have to watch my words so as not to offend our young Leuwen. And this is what we are reduced to with *our inferiors* today. If we find one who is deferential he is untrustworthy, ready to sell us to the *National* or to Henri V."

"As I say, your mission is twofold, my dear aide-de-camp," he continued out loud. "First of all you must put in an appearance at Champagnier in the Cher, where your father has large estates, talk to your father's agents and, with their assistance, try to find out what makes M. Blondeau's nomination so uncertain. The Prefect, M. de Riquebourg, is a worthy man, pious and completely devoted, but he seems to me to be an imbecile. You will have letters to him. You will have money to distribute on the banks of the Loire and, in addition, three tobacco concessions. I think there will also be two post-office directorships. The Minister of Finance has not yet replied on the subject, but I shall inform you later by telegraph. In addition you may remove from office just about anyone you choose. You are intelligent and will make use of all your powers with discretion. Conciliate the ancient nobility and the clergy: the life of a child is all that stands between them and us. No mercy for the republicans, especially for those young men who have received a good education and who do not have one penny to their names. Not all of them are in Mont-Saint-Michel. You know how my departments are honeycombed with spies, so you will address all important communications to your father.

"But Champagnier does not worry me inordinately. M. Malot, the liberal rival of Blondeau, is a braggart, a swaggerer, but no longer young, and he has had himself painted in the uniform of a Captain of the National Guard complete with bearskin on his head. He is not a man on the stern and energetic side. To play a good joke on him, I suppressed his Guard a week after he was made Captain. Such a man cannot be indifferent to a red ribbon that will make a fine effect in the portrait. In any case, he is an imprudent, fatuous boaster who, in the Chamber, would do his party more harm than good. You must study the means of winning Malot over, in the event of the failure of the faithful Blondeau.

"The crucial point, however, is Caen in the Calvados. You will give a day or two to the business of Champagnier, and then get on to Caen with all possible dispatch. At any cost, M. Mairobert must not be elected. He has both intelligence and wit. With a dozen or more heads like that, the Chamber would become unmanageable. I give you practically carte blanche in the matter of money, as well as offices to be given and taken away. Only, in the latter case, there might be some objections from two Peers belonging to us who are great landowners in that region. In any case, the Chamber of Peers is not troublesome, but I don't want M. Mairobert under any consideration. He is rich, he has no poor relations, and he already has the Cross. So there is no way of getting at him.

"The Prefect of Caen, M. Boucaut de Séranville, is rabid with all the zeal you lack. He himself has written a pamphlet against M. Mairobert, and has been rash enough to have it printed down there, right in the county-seat of his Prefecture. I have just issued an order to be sent to him by tomorrow's telegraph, not to distribute a single copy. Since M. Mairobert has public opinion in his favor, it is through that means we must attack him. M. de Torpet has also written a pamphlet. You will take three hundred copies with you in your carriage. Two more pamphlets by our regular writers, MM. D——— and F———, will be ready at midnight. All this is of very little value but costs a great deal. M. D———'s pamphlet, which is insulting and sarcastic, cost me six hundred francs; the other, which, according to the author, is subtle, ingenious and in good taste, cost me fifty louis. You will distribute either one or both of these pamphlets according to circumstances. The Normans are very canny. In short, you are at liberty to distribute or not to distribute them. If you care to write one yourself, either an entirely new one or adapted from the others, you would be doing me a great service. In a word, do anything on earth to prevent the election of M. Mairobert. Write me twice a day, and I give you my word that I will read your letters to the King."

Lucien smiled.

"An anachronism, M. le Comte. We are no longer living in the days of Samuel Bernard. What can the King do for me in a concrete way? As for distinctions, M. de Torpet dines once or twice a week with Their Majesties. No, really, your monarchy is lacking in rewards, bribes and means of seduction."

"Not so lacking as you think. If, in spite of your good and loyal services, M. Mairobert is elected, you will be made a Lieutenant. If he is not elected you will be made a Lieutenant of the General Staff, with the ribbon."

"M. de Torpet did not neglect to inform us this evening that he had been made an Officer of the Legion of Honor a week ago, apparently because of his long article on the houses demolished by cannon-fire at Lyons. Moreover, I remember the advice given by Marshal Bournonville to the King of Spain, Ferdinand VII. It is now midnight; I shall leave at two o'clock in the morning."

"Bravo, bravo, my friend! Write out your instructions in the way I have suggested and your letters to the Prefects and Generals. I will sign everything at one-thirty before going to bed. I shall probably have to be up the whole night again because of these infernal elections. So don't be afraid of disturbing me. Then, too, you will always have the telegraph."

"Does that mean that I can send you messages without showing them to the Prefects?"

"To be sure! In any case, they will always be kept informed by the telegraph operator. But it would be wise not to offend the Prefects. If they are good sorts tell them only as much as you see fit. If they seem inclined to view your mission with a jealous eye, try not to provoke them: we must not divide our army on the eve of battle."

"I shall try to act with all prudence," Lucien said, "but, in plain words, am I to telegraph Your Excellency without communicating my dispatch to the Prefect?"

"Yes, I agree, but don't quarrel with the Prefects. I wish you were fifty years old instead of twenty-four."

"Your Excellency is certainly free to choose a man of fifty who would be less susceptible, perhaps, to the insults of the press."

"You shall have all the money you need. If your pride will allow me the satisfaction, you shall have that and more. In a word, we must succeed. My private opinion is that it is better to spend five hundred thousand francs than to be faced with Mairobert in the Chamber. He is tenacious, wise, respected—

a terrible man. He despises money, of which he has a great deal. In short, we couldn't have anyone worse."

"I shall do my best to save you from him," Lucien coldly replied.

The Minister rose and, followed by Lucien, left the box. He had to return at least fifty bows and shake eight or nine hands before reaching his carriage. He invited Lucien to get in with him.

"Handle this as well as you did the Kortis affair," he said to Lucien, whom he insisted on taking to the Place de la Madeleine, "and I shall tell the King that his government has no subject superior to you. And you are not yet twenty-five. There is nothing you cannot aspire to. I see only two obstacles: will you have the courage to speak before four hundred Deputies of whom three hundred are imbeciles? And can you control that first impulse which in you is so terrible? Above all, let it be understood, and make the Prefects understand, that you must never appeal to those so-called magnanimous sentiments so closely allied to mass insurrection."

"Ah!" Lucien painfully ejaculated.

"What is the trouble?"

"It doesn't sound very alluring."

"Remember that your Napoleon, even in 1814 when the enemy had crossed the Rhine, would have none of them."

"May I take M. Coffe with me? He has enough sang-froid for two."

"But then I should be left with no one!"

"With only four hundred clerks! What about M. Desbacs, for example?"

"He's a little schemer, far too ingratiating, who will betray more than one Minister before he gets to be a Councilor of State. And I shall do my best not to be one of those Ministers. That is why, despite all your asperity, I call upon your aid. Desbacs is your exact opposite. . . . However, take with you whomever you please, even M. Coffe. No Mairobert at any price! I shall expect you within an hour and a half. Ah! youth, with all its activity! What a happy time!"

CHAPTER FOURTEEN

LUCIEN went to say good-by to his mother. He was given the traveling calash of his father's banking house, which was always in readiness, and at three o'clock in the morning was on his way toward the Department of the Cher.

The carriage was piled high with election pamphlets. They were everywhere, even on the roof; there was scarcely any room left for Lucien and Coffe. At six o'clock in the evening they reached Blois, and stopped for dinner. While they were eating they heard a terrific commotion in front of the inn.

"Apparently someone is being hooted," Lucien remarked.

"To hell with them!" returned Coffe coolly.

The host came in looking deathly pale.

"You must fly, sirs! They are going to rifle your carriage."

"And what for?"

"Ah, you ought to know that better than I."

"What do you mean?" cried Lucien, furious. Quickly he left the inn parlor, which was on the ground floor, followed by Coffe. He was greeted by deafening shouts of:

"Down with the spy! Down with the police informer!"

Crimson with fury, Lucien decided not to answer them, and went straight to his carriage. The crowd gave way a little. As he opened the door an enormous handful of mud hit him in the face and splashed over his cravat. Some even went into his mouth, for he was speaking to Coffe at the moment.

150

A burly lackey with red side-whiskers, supposed to look after the travelers at the inn, was calmly smoking on a first-story balcony directly overlooking the scene. He shouted down to the mob:

"Look how dirty he is! You've put his soul on his face."

This remark was greeted with a little silence, followed by a great shout of laughter that spread along the street with a deafening roar, and lasted for fully five minutes.

Lucien turned brusquely, and looking up at the balcony tried to make out, among all those jeering faces, the insolent fellow who had insulted him. Two gendarmes came galloping down upon the crowd. The balcony emptied in the twinkling of an eye, and the crowd scattered down all the side streets. Beside himself with anger, Lucien started to enter the inn to find the man who had insulted him, but the innkeeper had barricaded all the doors, and it was in vain that our hero pounded on them furiously with fists and boots. During these frantic efforts the Brigadier of the gendarmes was standing behind him.

"You'd better be off, and in a hurry," this functionary said, laughing openly at the sad state of Lucien's waistcoat and cravat. "I have only three men, and that mob may come back with stones."

In all haste the horses were brought out and put into the shafts. Wild with rage, Lucien kept talking to Coffe who did not reply but, with the aid of a large kitchen knife, went on scraping off some of the foul mud that covered his sleeves.

"I must find that lout who insulted me," repeated Lucien for the fifth or sixth time.

"In the trade we follow, you and I," Coffe said at length with perfect composure, "there's nothing we can do but shake our ears and go on."

The innkeeper came up to them. He had left the inn by a

back door, and refused to give Lucien the name of the man who had insulted him.

"You'd do well just to pay me what you owe me. It's forty-two francs."

"Are you joking? A dinner for two, forty-two francs!"

"I advise you to be off," the Brigadier put in. "They will soon be back with rotten cabbages."

And Lucien noticed that the innkeeper threw the officer a grateful look.

"But how can you have the audacity . . . !" Lucien cried.

"All right then, go to the Justice of the Peace if you think you're the injured party," the innkeeper said with all the insolent assurance of a man of his class. "All my guests have been terrorized. There's an Englishman inside with his wife who has taken half of my first floor for two months. He says if I am going to receive in my house such . . ."

The innkeeper stopped short.

"Such what?" Lucien cried, pale with anger and starting toward his carriage for his sword.

"You understand me, don't you? The Englishman has threatened to leave."

"Let's go," said Coffe. "Look, they're coming back."

Lucien tossed the innkeeper forty-two francs, and the carriage started.

"I shall wait for you outside the city limits," he said to the Brigadier. "I order you to join me there."

"Ah, I understand," the Brigadier said, smiling scornfully, "our emissary is frightened."

"I order you to take a different street from the one we take and to wait for me outside the city gate. And you," he said to the postilion, "I order you to go through the crowd at a walk."

People began to gather again at the end of the street. When he got to within twenty feet of them, the postilion put his horses to a gallop in spite of Lucien's furious protestations.

Mud and cabbages came flying into the calash from all directions, and despite the hullabaloo, our gentlemen had the pleasure of hearing all the filthy insults shouted after them.

Nearing the city gate, the horses had to slow down to cross a narrow bridge. There were eight or ten brawlers standing right under the vault of the double gate.

"Duck him! Duck him!" they shouted.

"Why, that's Lieutenant Leuwen," said a man in a torn green military coat—apparently a discharged Lancer.

"Leuwen, Leuwen, let's duck Leuwen!" they started yelling in chorus.

They kept on yelling as the calash passed under the gateway not two steps away from them, and their cries redoubled as soon as the calash was six paces outside the gate. Two hundred paces farther along everything was calm. The Brigadier soon arrived.

"I congratulate you, gentlemen," he said to the travelers. "You had a narrow escape."

His jeering manner put the finishing touch to Lucien's anger. He was beside himself. He told the gendarme to examine his passport.

"What is the meaning of all this?" he asked.

"Eh, my dear sir, you know that better than I do. You are the Police Commissioner down for the elections. All those printed papers of yours fell off the roof of your carriage as you were coming into town just opposite the Café Ramblin—it is the Café *National*. They read your papers, you were recognized, and it's a mighty lucky thing for you that there weren't any loose stones lying about."

M. Coffe quietly climbed onto the front seat of the calash.

"It's true, there's nothing left," he said, peering over the roof of the carriage.

"And this lost package of pamphlets—was it the one for the Cher or the one on M. Mairobert?" Lucien asked him.

"It was the attack on M. Mairobert," Coffe answered. "It was Torpet's masterpiece."

The gendarme's expression during this conversation infuriated Lucien. He gave him twenty francs and dismissed him. The Brigadier was profuse in his thanks.

"Gentlemen," he added, "the inhabitants of Blois are hotheaded. Generally gentlemen like you go through the town at night."

"Will you be gone!" Lucien cried; then, turning to the postilion, "Make your horses gallop as fast as they can go!"

"Oh, you needn't be afraid," the latter replied, grinning. "There's no one on the road."

After galloping for five minutes:

"Well, Coffe?" Lucien said, turning to his companion.

"Well!" coldly replied Coffe. "The Minister takes your arm when you leave the Opera, all the other Masters of Petitions, the Prefects on leave, the Deputies with their tobacco concessions, envy you. This is the other side of the medal. It's very simple."

"Your coolness will drive me mad," Lucien cried, drunk with anger. "All these indignities! That atrocious remark: 'His soul is on his face!' That mud!"

"That mud," Coffe replied, "is for us the noble dust of the field of honor; that public hooting will count in your favor. They are shining deeds in the career you have chosen and in which my poverty and my gratitude have caused me to follow you."

"You mean that if you had an income of twelve hundred francs you would not be here."

"If I had an income of three hundred francs I would not work for a Ministry that holds thousands of poor devils in the horrible dungeons of Mont-Saint-Michel and Clairvaux."

A profound silence followed this too candid reply, and lasted for the next three leagues. About six hundred paces outside a village whose steeple could be seen rising above a barren treeless hill, Lucien called to the postilion to stop.

"There will be twenty francs for you," he said to him, "if you don't mention what has happened."

"Twenty francs! Well, well, that's fine, and I thank you. But you know, Master, with that face of yours still so pale from fright, and your beautiful English calash all covered with mud, people are bound to think it funny and begin to gossip. But it won't be me that does the talking."

"Say that our carriage was overturned, and tell the people at the post that there are twenty francs for them if they change horses in three minutes. Say that we are merchants in a great hurry because of a bankruptcy." And turning to Coffe: "To think that we should be forced to dissimulate like this!"

"Do you want to be recognized, or don't you?"

"I'd like to be a hundred feet under the ground, or else to have your imperturbability."

Lucien did not say another word while the horses were being changed. He sat motionless in the back of the calash, one hand on his pistols, dying, it was quite plain, of rage and shame.

When they were five hundred yards away from the next relay:

"What do you advise me to do, Coffe?" he asked, turning to his taciturn companion with tears in his eyes. "I want to send in my resignation and transfer my mission to you, or if that doesn't suit you, I shall send for M. Desbacs. I'll wait eight days and then go back to look for that insolent lout at Blois."

"I advise you," Coffe coldly rejoined, "to have your carriage washed at the next post, to go on as if nothing had happened, and never to breathe a word of this affair to a soul, for everybody would laugh."

"What!" cried Lucien. "You want me, for the rest of my

life, to put up with the idea that someone has insulted me with impunity?"

"If you are too thin-skinned to stomach contempt, why did you leave Paris?"

"I shall never forget that quarter of an hour we spent outside the inn! For the rest of my life that quarter of an hour will be a red-hot brand on my breast."

"What makes the adventure particularly galling," Coffe remarked, "is that there was never for a moment the slightest danger. We had ample time to relish the crowd's contempt to the full. The street had plenty of mud but was perfectly paved, not a single loose stone available. It is the first time I've known what it feels like to be despised. When I was arrested and about to be taken to Sainte-Pélagie, only three or four people saw what was going on. As I got into the cab, with some little assistance, one of them said with sympathy and pity: *Poor devil!*"

Lucien did not reply, and Coffe continued to think aloud with cruel frankness.

"But back there at the inn—that was unmitigated scorn. It made me think of the old saying: You swallow scorn but you don't chew it."

Coffe's coolness drove Lucien wild. If he hadn't been restrained by the thought of his mother, he would have deserted then and there on the highroad and would have had himself driven to Rochefort. From there it would be a simple matter to embark, under an assumed name, for America.

"At the end of two years I can come back to Blois and insult the most prominent young man of the town."

This temptation was too strong in him: he had to talk about it.

"My friend," he said to Coffe, "I trust you never to laugh at my anguish with anyone."

"You saved me from Sainte-Pélagie where I would have

had to do my five years—besides, we've known each other a good long time."

"Well, my heart is overflowing, I have to talk, and I shall confide in you if you will promise eternal silence."

"I'll promise you that."

Lucien explained his whole scheme of desertion and finished by bursting into tears.

"I've managed my whole life badly," he kept repeating. "I'm in an inextricable mess."

"That may be," Coffe answered him, "but no matter what your reasons are, you can't desert in the middle of the battle, like the Saxons at Leipzig. It would be odious, and afterwards you'd be filled with remorse, or at least, I'm afraid you would. Try to forget the whole thing and, above all, not a word to M. de Riquebourg, the Prefect of Champagnier."

After this fine bit of consolation, a silence followed that lasted for two hours. There was a stage of six leagues to be covered. It was cold. It was raining. The calash had to be closed. It was beginning to get dark. They were driving through a flat and barren country without a single tree. During the last part of this endless relay of six leagues total darkness fell. Coffe could feel Lucien changing his position every five minutes.

"He is writhing like Saint Lawrence on his bed of coals. . . . It's too bad he can't find some way out for himself . . ." and a half hour later he added: "A man in that state is not very polite. . . ." Then after another half hour of cogitations and mathematical deductions he continued to himself: "Nevertheless, I owe him my gratitude for having got me out of that cell at Sainte-Pélagie which was about as big as this calash. . . . So, let's risk an angry retort. He wasn't any too civil in our preceding conversation but anyway let's endure the boredom of talking, and talking to an unhappy man and, even worse, to a handsome son of Paris unhappy through his own fault, unhappy despite health, wealth and youth to spare. What a fool! How I could hate him! But he saved me from Sainte-Pélagie! At Polytechnique what a puppy, and above all what a wind-bag: talk, talk, talk, nothing but talk! . . . Still, and it's a famous point *in his favor,* never an offensive word when he took the notion of getting me out of Sainte-Pélagie. . . . Yes, but only to make an executioner's apprentice of me. A real hangman is less objectionable. . . . People's horror of executioners is pure childishness, due to their usual stupidity. After all, he does a job . . . a necessary job . . . indispensable. . . . But what of us? We who are on the road to all the honors that society can offer, we are also on the way to commit infamy . . . *pernicious* infamies. The people, who are usually wrong, by some chance were right this time. . . . In this handsome and very comfortable English calash they discover two infamous wretches . . . and say to us: 'You are infamous wretches!' Quite true," thought Coffe, smiling. "But wait a moment, they didn't say to Leuwen: 'You are an infamous wretch,' but they said to both of us: 'You are infamous wretches!' "

And Coffe weighed their words on his own account. At that moment, Lucien gave a half audible sigh.

"There he is, suffering because of his absurd assumption: he actually believed he could combine the advantages of the Ministry with the delicate susceptibilities of a man of honor. What could be stupider! Eh! my friend, when you put on that embroidered coat you should have got yourself a thicker skin impervious to insults. . . . However, it must be said in his favor that there isn't another of the Minister's rascally agents who suffers in the least from the workings of the governmental machine. That somewhat absolves him. . . . The others know perfectly well what kind of missions they'll be employed in before soliciting office. . . . It would be a good thing if he could only discover the solution for himself. His pride and joy at the discovery would somewhat attenuate the sharp pain of the conclusion as it penetrates his mind. . . . But rich and spoiled as he is by all the delights of an enviable position, the idea of a solution will never occur to him by himself . . . if solution there be. For the devil take me if I can get to the bottom of his situation. . . . That's where the devil's always to be found. That jackanapes of a Minister treats him with astonishing consideration; perhaps the Minister has a daughter, legitimate or bastard, he wants to palm off on him. . . . Or perhaps Leuwen is ambitious. He's just the man to get a Prefecture, a Cross, and to go strutting under the lindens—a red ribbon on a new dress-coat. . . ."

"Oh, God!" murmured Lucien.

"He's on the rack of public scorn . . . like me during those first days at Sainte-Pélagie when I was sure all the neighbors around my shop thought I was a fraudulent bankrupt. . . ."

The memory of that moment of bitter suffering was powerful enough to make him break the silence.

"We won't reach Caen until eleven o'clock. Do you want to go directly to the hotel or to the Prefect's?"

"If he is still up, let's see the Prefect at once."

Lucien had the weakness of thinking aloud in front of Coffe. He was beyond shame now, since he had wept.

"I couldn't feel any worse than I do now," he said. "And so, as a last resort, let's do our duty."

"You are right," Coffe replied coldly. "In extreme misfortune, particularly the worst of all misfortunes, one caused by contempt for oneself, to do one's duty is, indeed, the only resource left. *Experto crede Roberto:* my life has not been a bed of roses. If you take my advice you will just shake your ears and try to forget the outrage at Blois. You are still far from the worst that can befall a man: you have no reason to despise yourself. The most severe judge would find nothing more than imprudence in your case. You gauged the life of members of the Ministry by what you saw in Paris, where Ministers and everyone connected with them enjoy all the pleasures society has to offer. It is only in the provinces that they are made to feel the contempt so liberally accorded them by the great majority of Frenchmen. You are not thick-skinned enough not to feel the public's scorn. But one gets used to it. All you have to do is to transfer your vanity elsewhere. Look at M. de Talleyrand. As in the case of that celebrated man—when scorn gets too commonplace it's only fools that bother giving voice to it. Thus the fools among us spoil everything, even scorn."

"That's strange consolation you offer me," retorted Lucien somewhat curtly.

"The only kind for you, it seems to me. When one undertakes the thankless task of consoling a brave man, one must first of all speak the truth. I am a surgeon, cruel only in appearance. I probe the wound deeply, but in order to cure it. You remember that story of Cardinal de Retz, a man of such intrepid spirit, and of all Frenchmen the one who has perhaps displayed the greatest courage, a man comparable to the ancients. In a moment of irritation he gave his equerry a kick in his posterior for some out-and-out stupidity, and the fellow —who happened to be stronger than he—turned on him and, with the Cardinal's own cane, gave him a very proper trouncing! Well, that is certainly more humiliating than to have mud thrown at you by a mob that believes you to be the author of the abominable pamphlet you were carrying into Normandy. Look at it the right way and you will realize that they were really throwing mud at that fatuous fool of a Torpet. If you were an Englishman this little incident would have left you quite cold. The Duke of Wellington went through the same thing four or five times in his life."

"Ah, but in the matter of honor the English are not such subtle or delicate judges as the French. The English workman is nothing but a machine; ours may not make the heads of pins so perfectly, but he is often a sort of philosopher, and his scorn is a terrible thing to encounter."

Lucien went on talking for some time with all the weakness of a man reduced to the last degree of wretchedness. Coffe took his hand, and Lucien wept for the second time.

"And that Lancer who recognized me! They shouted: *Down with Leuwen!*"

"The soldier was simply informing the people of Blois who, as he imagined, was the author of Torpet's infamous pamphlet."

"But how can I ever get rid of the mud I'm covered with, morally as well as physically?" Lucien cried with the utmost bitterness. "Always, even as a child," he continued after a moment, "I have tried to do what I could to be useful and to merit the esteem of my fellow men. I worked ten hours a day for three years to enter the École Polytechnique. You were received with a number 4, I with a number 7. At the École, more work still, with no time for amusement. Then, indignant at the government's infamous action, we appeared on the streets. . . ."

"Ridiculous miscalculation, especially for mathematicians: we were two hundred and fifty youths, the government met us with twelve hundred peasants incapable of reasoning, but having in their veins the hot blood of Frenchmen that quickens at the first sign of danger and makes them such good soldiers. We made the same mistake as those poor Russian noblemen in 1826. . . ."

The taciturn Coffe chatted on, trying to divert Lucien's thoughts, but noticed that his companion was not listening.

"Because I was disgusted at being idle and worthless, I entered the army. I left it for private reasons, but sooner or later I should have left it anyway so as not to be forced to turn my saber against workmen. Would you have wanted me to become the hero of another Rue Transnonain? It's all right for a soldier who sees in the inhabitants of the house Russians defending an enemy battery; but for me! an officer who knows . . ."

"Well, that's a lot worse, isn't it, than having mud thrown at you by the people of Blois who, at the time of the partial elections a year ago, were duped in the most flagrant fashion by their Prefect, M. de Nontour? You remember, he stationed on the bridge over the Loire gendarmes who asked all the people from the surrounding districts coming to vote in town for their passports; and as none of them had passports they were forbidden to cross. Those people at Blois saw a chance of being revenged on M. de Nontour in your person, and you must admit they were justified."

"While the calling of soldier leads to an outrage like the Rue Transnonain! Should an unhappy officer who is waiting in his regiment for a war, resign in the midst of the bullets of a riot?"

"Of course, and you were quite right to leave when you did."

"Now I am in the administration. You know that I work conscientiously from nine o'clock until four. I dispatch at least twenty affairs a day, and often very important ones. If at dinner I happen to think of something urgent I may have forgotten, instead of staying peacefully by the fire with my mother, I return to the office where I get cursed by the night watchman who doesn't expect me at such an hour. Not to disappoint my father, and also a little because of my fear of getting into an argument with him, I have let myself be involved in this execrable mission. Here I am, engaged in slandering an honest man, M. Mairobert, with all the means a government has at its disposal; I get covered with mud and am told that my dirty soul is now on my face! Oh . . ."

And Lucien writhed on his seat as he stretched his legs in the carriage.

"What am I going to do? Spend the money my father has earned, do nothing, be good for nothing? Wait around for old age, despising myself and crying: 'How happy I am to have a father who is worth more than I am'? What am I to do? What calling am I to adopt?"

"When one has the misfortune," replied Coffe, "to live under a knavish government, as well as the misfortune of thinking clearly and perceiving the truth, one sees that, under such a government, essentially unscrupulous and even worse than those of the Bourbons or Napoleon, for it is constantly betraying its word, husbandry and trade are the only independent callings. But reminding myself that husbandry would drag me fifty leagues from Paris and keep me in the middle of fields surrounded by our peasants who are still only brutes, I preferred to go into trade. It is true that in trade, due to the total lack of the commonest decency, one has to put up with and share certain frightful and sordid practices established by the barbarism of the Eighteenth Century, aided and abetted today by a set of avaricious and contemptible old men who are the plague of business. These practices are like the cruelties of the Middle Ages which were not cruelties at that time, and have become such only because of the progress of humanity. But, in spite of that, these sordid practices, even if one ends by accepting them as normal, are better than cutting the throats of peaceful citizens in the Rue Transnonain or, what is worse and even more base, justifying such things in pamphlets like these we are peddling."

"So, I suppose, I ought to change callings for the third time!"

"You still have a month to decide that. For, to desert in the middle of a battle, to embark for America at Rochefort, as you suggest, would stain your reputation with the taint of cowardly folly which you could never live down. The question is, are you a man who can despise the opinion of the society into which he was born? Lord Byron did not have strength enough,

Cardinal Richelieu himself did not have it, Napoleon, who thought himself so superior, trembled before the opinion of the Faubourg Saint-Germain. In the situation in which you find yourself, one false step might lead to suicide. Remember what you told me a month ago of the hatred and the cunning of the Minister of Foreign Affairs with his forty society spies."

After having made the effort of talking for such a long time, Coffe fell silent, and a few moments later they arrived at the county seat of the Department of the Cher.

CHAPTER FIFTEEN

M DE RIQUEBOURG, the Prefect, was alone in his study, wearing a cotton nightcap and engaged in eating an omelette at a little round table, when Lucien and Coffe were introduced.

He summoned his cook Marion, and with her discussed the contents of the larder and what could most quickly be prepared for the travelers' supper.

"These gentlemen have nineteen leagues in their bellies," he said, alluding to the distance the travelers had come since their dinner at Blois.

When the cook left, he explained:

"You see, gentlemen, it is I who attend to all our domestic arrangements with Marion. In that way my wife has only the youngsters to look after and I, by letting the girl chatter, learn everything that is going on. My conversations are entirely at the service of the police, a wise precaution, for I am surrounded by enemies. You have no idea, gentlemen, all the trouble I take. Just to give you an example: for myself I have a barber who is a liberal, and for my wife, the hairdresser of the legitimist ladies. Naturally I could just as well shave myself. I keep two little lawsuits going simply to provide both the public prosecutor, M. Clapier, one of the craftiest liberals we have, and the advocate, M. Le Beau, an eloquent, moderate and pious individual like the great landowners he serves, with an excuse for coming to the Prefecture. My position, gentlemen, hangs by a thread. Without His Excellency's patronage I should be the most miserable of men. My first-line enemy is Monseigneur, the Bishop; he is the most dangerous. He seems to be tied up with someone who is pretty close to the ear of Her Majesty the Queen. Monseigneur's letters never go by the post. The nobility do not deign to come to my drawing room, but keep plaguing me with their Henri V and their universal suffrage. Finally I have those miserable republicans to cope with; they are only a handful, but they make noise enough for a thousand. Will you believe me, gentlemen, the sons of the wealthiest families, by the time they are eighteen, are not ashamed to side with that party. Recently, to pay a fine of a thousand francs I had imposed on the republicans' insolent paper for having seemed to approve the charivari inflicted on the worthy substitute Receiver General, the young men of the nobility gave sixty-seven francs, and the wealthy young men not of the nobility gave eighty-nine francs. Shocking, isn't it? When they ought to be thankful to us for saving their property from the republicans!"

Bored by these endless details, at a quarter-before-midnight, Lucien said somewhat brusquely:

"Would you be good enough, sir, to read this letter from the Minister of the Interior?"

Taking his time, the Prefect read the letter through twice. The two young travelers exchanged glances.

"It's the very devil of a thing, these elections," the Prefect remarked after he had finished reading the letter for the second time. "They've kept me awake every night for the last three weeks—though, God be praised, I'm usually asleep before my second slipper touches the floor. Why, if ever, in my zeal for the King's government, I allow myself to adopt some measure perhaps a trifle too severe for the good people under my jurisdiction, I lose all peace of mind. Just as I am about to fall asleep, suddenly remorse pricks me awake again, or, at least, a painful doubt in my own mind as to whether I should feel remorse or not. You don't yet know what it is, Monsieur le Commissaire." (This was the title the worthy M. de Rique-bourg conferred on Lucien, thinking to honor him by treating him as the Commissioner of Elections.) "Your heart is young, sir, the cares of administration have never disturbed the tranquillity it enjoys. You have never found yourself in opposition to an entire population. Ah, sir, what trying moments! Afterwards one asks oneself: has my conduct been absolutely disinterested? Has my devotion to King and country been my sole guide? You, sir, have never known these painful uncertainties. For you life is still rose-colored; riding from post to post you can still be diverted by the curious shape of a cloud. . . ."

"Ah, sir, I . . ." began Lucien, forgetting all caution, all decorum, tortured by his conscience.

"Your unspoiled and tranquil youth cannot even conceive of such dangers, the mere mention of them horrifies you. And permit me to say, my young collaborator, I respect you all the more for it. Ah! keep while you can the peace of an honest heart. In office never allow yourself any act in the least questionable, I will not say in the eyes of the strictest honor, but questionable in your own eyes."

Supper had been served and our travelers were now at table.

" 'You have killed sleep,' as the great English dramatist says in *Macbeth*."

"Ah! Infamy," cried Lucien to himself, "was I born to be tortured by you forever!" And although he was dying of hunger he felt such a contraction of the diaphragm he could not swallow a morsel.

"But you aren't eating, Monsieur le Commissaire," exclaimed the Prefect. "You should follow the example of this gentleman, your assistant."

"*Secretary* only, sir," said Coffe, continuing to guzzle like a famished wolf.

This word, so emphatically spoken, seemed very cruel to Lucien. He could not help turning toward Coffe with a look that said, "So, you refuse to share with me the infamy of my mission?"

Coffe failed to understand. He was a man of intelligence but without delicacy. He despised delicacy as an excuse that weak people use to avoid doing the sensible thing or that which is their duty.

"Do eat, Monsieur le Commissaire. . . ."

"Master of Petitions, if you please, sir," Coffe quickly corrected him, knowing how the wretched title of Commissioner shocked Lucien, "and private secretary to His Excellency, the Minister of the Interior."

"Ah! Master of Petitions!" the Prefect exclaimed in surprise. "That, you know, is the height of ambition for us little provincial Prefects, after we've brought off two or three successful elections."

"Is this imbecile naïveté or is it malice?" Lucien wondered, little disposed to be indulgent.

"You must eat, my dear sir. If you are to grant me only thirty-six hours, as the Minister says in his letter, there are quantities of things I must tell you, all sorts of detail you should know, certain measures to be submitted—and all before tomorrow afternoon, the time set for your departure. Tomorrow my plan is to ask you to receive fifty or more persons, fifty or more doubtful or timorous officials and some undeclared enemies, or perhaps only timorous, too. Everyone's convictions will, I am sure, be stimulated by this opportunity of talking with an official who himself talks with the Minister. Moreover this audience that you grant them, and that the whole town is certain to talk about, will be for them a solemn pledge. To be able to talk with the Minister, what an advantage, what a splendid prerogative! What can we expect from our cold dispatches which to be clear must necessarily be long? What are they compared to the vivid and interesting accounts of someone who can say: *I have seen?*"

At one o'clock in the morning these fatuous phrases were still going on. . . . Coffe, who was dying for lack of sleep, had gone to see about their beds, and the Prefect asked Lucien if he could speak freely in front of his secretary.

"Certainly, sir. M. Coffe works in the Minister's private office and, as far as these elections are concerned, has His Excellency's entire confidence."

When Coffe returned, M. de Riquebourg felt obliged to repeat all the considerations he had already laid before Lucien, now adding certain proper names. But these names, all equally unknown to our travelers, served only to make the system M. de Riquebourg proposed for influencing votes, all the more confused in their minds. Coffe, terribly annoyed at not being able to go to bed, wanted at least to get some serious work done, and with the approval of the Master of Petitions, began to ply M. de Riquebourg with questions.

This worthy Prefect, so very moral and so careful not to provide regrets for himself later on, finally admitted that the Department was most unfavorably disposed because eight Peers of France, of whom two were large landowners, had had a considerable number of petty officials appointed, who now enjoyed their protection.

"These people, sir, receive my circulars and answer me with evasions. If you had arrived two weeks sooner we could have arranged three or four salutary removals."

"But didn't you write to the Minister along these lines? I believe there was some question of the removal of a postmistress."

"Madame Durand, the sister-in-law of M. Duchadeau? Eh! poor woman! She thinks all wrong, it is true; and, if it happens in time, her removal will frighten two or three officials of the district of Tourville, one of whom is her son-in-law and the other two her cousins. But it is not there that my greatest trouble lies. It is at Mélan where, as I have had the honor of showing you on my electoral chart, we have a majority of twenty-seven votes against us."

"But, sir, I have here in my portfolio copies of your letters. If I am not mistaken, you never mentioned the district of Mélan to the Minister."

"Eh! my dear sir, how can I be expected to write such things? Doesn't M. le Comte d'Allevard, Peer of France, see your Minister every day? Aren't his letters to his notary, old Rufle, full of the things he has heard discussed the day before, or the day before that; when he has the honor of dining with His Excellency, le Comte de Vaize? These dinners, it seems, are of frequent occurrence. One doesn't put such things in writing, my dear sir. After all I am the head of a family. To-morrow I shall have the honor of introducing Madame de Riquebourg and our four daughters. Four daughters to be married off! And my son, who has been a sergeant with the Eighty-sixth for two years, must be made a Second-Lieutenant. To be perfectly frank, I confess—and under the seal of confession—that one word from M. d'Allevard would ruin me. And M. d'Allevard, who wants the course of the public road that now passes through his park diverted, is the protector of everybody in the district of Mélan. For me, sir, even the semi-disgrace of being transferred to another Prefecture would be my ruin. Three marriages which Madame de Riquebourg has in prospect for our daughters would no longer be possible, and my interests here are enormous."

It was only toward two o'clock in the morning that the urgent (to use no stronger word) questions of the inflexible M. Coffe, forced the Prefect finally to reveal the grand scheme to which he had kept referring.

"It is my last resource, gentlemen, and if it is known in advance, if it is even suspected a day before the elections, all is lost! For, gentlemen, this is one of the worst Departments in France: twenty-seven subscriptions to the *National* and only eight to the *Tribune!* But to you, gentlemen, who have the Minister's ear, I can conceal nothing. So then, I must tell you that I shall wait to launch my great electoral maneuver, to spring the mine, until I see that the nomination of the chairman is almost decided; for if it is launched too soon, two hours would be enough to ruin everything: the election as well as the position of your very humble servant. Let us assume that we put up as our government candidate, M. Jean-Pierre Blondeau, an iron-master of Champagnier; and that, as our rival candidate, we shall probably—unfortunately more than probably—have M. Malot, an ex-Battalion Head and an ex-National Guardsman of Champagnier. I say *ex,* although the National Guard is only suspended, but it will be a fine day when it is re-established! M. Blondeau is a friend of the government, for he has a holy terror of a reduction of the duty on imported iron. Malot is a cloth merchant as well as a dealer in lumber and fire-wood. Malot has large accounts at Nantes. Two hours before the ballots for the nomination of chairman are counted, a business messenger, who has *actually* come from Nantes, will arrive with the alarming news that two merchants of Nantes, whom I know very well and who control a large part of Malot's fortune, are on the verge of bankruptcy, and are already transferring their property to their friends by means of antedated deeds of sale. Our Malot will straightway lose his head and depart for Nantes, of that I am sure. He will throw up all the elections in the world. . . ."

"But how will you manage to have a real messenger from Nantes arrive at just the right moment?"

"Through the kind offices of that admirable M. Chauveau, General Secretary of Nantes and an intimate friend of mine. You see, the Nantes telegraph line is only two leagues from here, and Chauveau knows that my election begins the evening of the 23rd. He will be waiting for a word from me the evening of the 23rd or the morning of the 24th. Once the rumor reaches M. Malot about his Nantes accounts, I shall take my stand in full regalia near the Ursulines Hall where the voting is to be held. With Malot absent, I shall not hesitate to address the peasant voters and," continued M. de Riquebourg, lowering his voice almost to a whisper, "if the chairman of the electoral college is an official, even if he is a liberal, I shall launch bulletins for the benefit of my clodhopper voters on which will appear in huge letters: *Jean-Pierre Blondeau, Iron-Master.* I'll gain at least ten votes in this way. The voters, knowing that Malot is on the verge of bankruptcy . . ."

"What! Malot on the verge of bankruptcy?" said Lucien, frowning.

"Eh! after all," M. de Riquebourg replied, looking more benign than ever, "can I keep gossips in the town from exaggerating everything as usual, or from believing that, if M. Malot's correspondents are ruined, he himself will be obliged to suspend payments here? For," he continued in a firmer tone, "with what could he pay except the profits he gets for the wood he sends to Nantes?"

Coffe smiled, and could hardly keep from bursting out laughing.

"But this breach once made in M. Malot's credit by alarming those persons who have money invested with him, couldn't it *actually* force a suspension of payments?"

"Well! So much the better, by gad!" exclaimed the Prefect, completely forgetting himself. "Then I wouldn't have him on my hands at the re-election of the National Guard, should that occur."

Coffe was in the seventh heaven.

"Such success might, perhaps, shock my sensibilities . . ." he offered.

"Eh, my dear sir, republicanism rises like a flood. The dam against this torrent, which would carry off our heads and set fire to our houses, is our King. We must strengthen authority! When a city is on fire, so much the worse for the house that has to be destroyed to save all the rest! For my part, gentlemen, when the King's interest is at stake, nothing else—absolutely nothing—matters."

"Bravo, Monsieur le Préfet, a thousand times bravo! *Sic itur astra,* that is to say, on to the Council of State!"

"As for that, my dear sir, I am not sufficiently rich: twelve thousand francs and Paris would ruin me with my numerous family. The Prefecture of Bordeaux perhaps, or Marseilles, or Lyons, with a good little secret fund. Lyons for example must be really excellent. But let us return to our subject, it is getting late. So then, we count on ten votes at least that I have personally secured. My terrible Bishop has a little Grand Vicar, a sly dog with a rare taste for hard cash. If His Excellency should think fit to make some outlay, I could give twenty-five louis to M. Crochard, that is the Grand Vicar, to distribute charitably among his poor priests. You may say, sir, that to give money to the Jesuit party is to give aid to the enemy. A thing to be carefully weighed. Those twenty-five louis would give me the ten or more votes which are at M. Crochard's disposal, and twelve sooner than ten."

"This M. Crochard would take your money and then laugh at you," Lucien replied. "At the last moment his electors' consciences would prevent their voting."

"Ah! Not at all! One does not *laugh* at a Prefect," said M. de Riquebourg haughtily, very much offended by the word. "We have certain information in our files, together with seven original letters of our friend Crochard. It all has to do with a young girl in the convent of Saint-Denis-Sambuci. I swore to him that I had destroyed these letters after a little favor he had obtained for me from his Bishop at the time of the —— affair . . . but our friend Crochard does not really believe it."

"Twelve votes, or at least ten?" Lucien repeated.

"That's right, sir," said the Prefect in surprise.

"I shall give you twenty-five louis."

He went over to the table and wrote out an order for six hundred francs on the Minister's Treasurer.

M. de Riquebourg's lower jaw dropped slowly and his consideration for Lucien rose with a bound. Coffe could not quite suppress a little gurgle of the glottis, as the worthy Prefect added:

"By gad, sir, that is certainly doing things up brown! Besides my general resources: circulars, traveling agents, verbal threats, with which I won't weary you, for you can't think me so incompetent as not to have pushed things already as far as possible (and I can prove all this, sir, by letters of the enemy intercepted at the post office, three of them addressed to the *National* and as detailed as official minutes, which, I assure you, ought to please the King) besides these general resources, as I say, besides the removal of M. Malot at the opening of the battle, besides M. Crochard's Jesuit votes, I have still another means of persuasion in behalf of Blondeau. This excellent man will never set the world on fire, but he sometimes knows how to follow good advice and to make timely sacrifices. He has a nephew in Paris, a lawyer and a man of letters, who has written an article for the *Ambigu.* This nephew is by no means stupid, he has received a thousand écus from his uncle

173

with the understanding that he will take the necessary steps to insure the continuation of the duty on iron imports. He writes articles for the papers; also, he dines with the Minister of Finance. Certain persons from here, now settled in Paris, have written him. By the first post after the departure of Malot, I shall receive a letter containing the announcement that M. Blondeau's nephew has been appointed General Secretary to the Minister of Finance. For the past week I have received a letter to that effect by every post. Now, the seventeen liberal electors (I am sure of my figures) are directly interested in the Ministry of Finance, and M. Blondeau will tell them plainly that if they vote against him his nephew will resent it.

"And will Your Excellency be good enough to glance at this memorandum of votes:

Registered electors	613
Present in the electoral college, at the most	400
Constitutional votes I can count on	178
Electors for Malot I can personally win over	10
Jesuit votes secretly controlled by M. Crochard, 12 or at least	10
Total	198

I am short two votes, but the nomination of M. Blondeau's nephew, Aristide Blondeau, to the Ministry of Finance, will give me at least six more. Majority: four votes. Moreover, my dear sir, if you will authorize me, in an emergency, to promise four removals I can assure the Minister (on my word of honor backed by a guarantee of a thousand francs deposited with a third party) a majority, not of four miserable votes, but of twelve or even eighteen. I am fortunate in that M. Blondeau is an idiot who has never offended anybody in his life. Every day he tells me that he can guarantee personally a dozen votes, but I wouldn't count on that too much. Naturally, all this comes high, and, as the head of a family, I cannot carry on the war wholly at my own expense. In his dispatch of the 5th, marked *private,* the Minister opened a credit for me of twelve hundred francs and I have already spent over nineteen hundred. I am sure that His Excellency is too fair a man to leave me seven hundred francs out of pocket."

"If you succeed, there is no doubt about it," Lucien said. "In case of failure, however, I must tell you, sir, that my instructions do not cover such an eventuality."

M. de Riquebourg was toying absent-mindedly with the order for six hundred francs. All at once he noticed that the writing was the same as that of the letter stamped *private,* of which he had out of discretion read them only a part. From this moment his respect for the Commissioner of Elections knew no bounds.

"Not two months ago," M. de Riquebourg continued, flushing with emotion to find himself actually talking to a favorite of the Minister, "His Excellency condescended to write me a letter with his own hand on the N—— affair, to which the King attaches the greatest importance."

The Prefect opened a secret compartment of an enormous roll-top desk and took out the Minister's letter which he read aloud, afterwards handing it to his visitors.

"This," remarked Coffe, "is in Cromier's handwriting."

"What! It isn't His Excellency's?" cried the Prefect, aghast. "I have some knowledge of handwriting, gentlemen!"

And as M. de Riquebourg was not thinking about his voice, it had taken on a very sharp and sarcastic tone, half-reproachful, half-threatening.

"The true Prefect tone," Lucien thought. "There is no calling like it to ruin a man's voice. Three-quarters of the rudeness of M. de Vaize comes from his having for ten years held forth alone in the drawing room of his Prefecture."

"M. de Riquebourg," said Coffe, who, no longer sleepy, from

time to time poured himself a generous glass of white Saumur wine, "is indeed a connoisseur of handwriting. Nothing could be more like His Excellency's hand than that of young Cromier, especially when he is trying to copy it."

The Prefect offered a few objections; he felt humiliated, for these letters from His Excellency's own hand were the cornerstone of his vanity and of his hopes of advancement. He was finally convinced by Coffe who, thinking of the bankruptcy in store for the wool and wood merchant, M. Malot, had no pity for this honorable Amphytrion. The Prefect remained stunned, having been so certain that the letter was in the Minister's own hand.

"Four o'clock is striking," Coffe said. "If we prolong this session we shall never be up at nine o'clock, as Monsieur le Préfet wishes."

M. de Riquebourg took *wishes* as a reproach.

"Gentlemen," he said, rising and bowing almost to the ground, "I shall have the persons I have asked you to receive, convoked for nine-thirty. And I myself will come to your rooms promptly at ten o'clock. Until you see me appear, sleep soundly on both ears."

Despite all their protests, M. de Riquebourg insisted on personally conducting them to their rooms, which were separated by a small parlor. He even went so far in his attentions as to look under their beds.

"This man isn't so stupid after all," Coffe remarked when the Prefect had finally left them. "Look!"

And, pointing to a table on which a cold chicken, a roasted hare, wine and fruits were invitingly laid out, he began a second supper with very good appetite.

The two travelers did not separate until five o'clock in the morning.

"Leuwen seems to have forgotten the incident of Blois," Coffe thought. And indeed, like a conscientious employee, Lucien was entirely occupied with the election of M. Blondeau, and before going to bed, once more read over the memorandum of votes M. de Riquebourg had given him at his request.

At ten o'clock sharp, M. de Riquebourg entered Lucien's bedroom, followed by the faithful Marion bearing a tray with café-au-lait, followed by a little page with another tray laden with tea, butter and a kettle of hot water.

"The water is good and hot," said the Prefect. "Jacques will light your fire. Now take your time! Have some tea or some coffee. Luncheon will be served at eleven o'clock, and a dinner for forty persons at six. Your arrival has had the happiest effect. The General is as susceptible as a fool, the Bishop is choleric and fanatical. If it meets with your approval my carriage will be waiting for you, and you can give these functionaries each ten minutes. But don't hurry: the fourteen persons whom I have summoned for your first audience have only been waiting since half-past-nine. . . ."

"I am terribly sorry," said Lucien.

"Bah!" said the Prefect. "They belong to us, they all live off the Budget. Waiting is what they were made for."

Lucien had a horror of anything that might seem to be an incivility. He dressed hurriedly, and made all haste to receive the fourteen officials. He was stunned by their ponderous stupidity and their reverential attitude toward himself.

"Were I the Prince Royal they couldn't have bowed any lower."

He was amazed when Coffe said to him later:

"You disappointed them. They think you are arrogant."

"Arrogant?"

"Naturally. You had ideas. They didn't understand you. You were much too clever for animals like them. *You spread your nets too high*. At luncheon be prepared to see some strange faces! You are going to meet the Mesdemoiselles de Riquebourg."

The reality far surpassed all expectations. Lucien had time to whisper to Coffe:

"They are grisettes who have just won forty thousand francs in the lottery."

One of them was even uglier than her sisters but not quite so impressed by the grandeur of her family. She looked a little like Théodelinde de Serpierre. This recollection had a potent effect on Lucien. As soon as he noticed the resemblance he began talking to Mademoiselle Augustine with great interest; and Madame de Riquebourg had visions of a brilliant marriage for her daughter.

The Prefect reminded Lucien of the calls he was scheduled to pay on the General and the Bishop. Madame de Riquebourg gave her husband a glance full of scornful annoyance, and, in the end, the luncheon lasted until one o'clock. Indeed, before Lucien drove away there were already four or five groups of more or less sure friends of the government installed, and carefully guarded, in different offices of the Prefecture.

Coffe had preferred not to go with his old comrade, counting on taking a stroll about town to see what it was like, but instead, he was forced to receive the official visit of Monsieur the private secretary of Messieurs the clerks of the Prefecture.

"I shall help peddle our nostrum," he said to himself. And with his withering sang-froid he succeeded in giving these clerks a lofty idea of the mission on which he was engaged.

At the end of ten minutes he dismissed them coldly, and was just escaping, in a second attempt to take a look at the town, when M. de Riquebourg, who had been lying in wait for him, pounced upon him as he passed, and forced him to listen to all the letters from the Comte de Vaize on the subject of the elections.

"They are third-rate newspaper articles," Coffe thought indignantly. "Our *Journal de Paris* wouldn't pay twelve francs an article for them. The man's conversation is a hundred times better than his correspondence."

Just as Coffe was trying to think up an excuse to get away from M. de Riquebourg, Lucien returned, followed by the General, Comte de Beauvoir. The General was a dandy, with a fair rotund face of rare insignificance, otherwise still a good-looking man, very polite, very elegant, but who literally never understood one word of what was being said. The elections seemed to have addled his wits completely. In and out of season he kept saying: "That is a matter for the administrative authorities." From his conversation, Coffe saw that he was still mystified as to the object of Lucien's mission, in spite of the fact that the evening before the latter had sent him a letter from the Minister which could not have been more explicit.

The audiences before dinner were more and more absurd. Lucien had made the mistake of exerting himself at the morning interviews so that by two o'clock in the afternoon he was dead tired, and did not have an idea left in his head. He now became admirably correct and the Prefect began to have a very high opinion of him. During the four or five last audiences accorded to the most important personages one at a time, he was perfect, and displayed the most commendable insignificance. The Prefect insisted on Lucien's seeing the Grand Vicar, M. Crochard, a puny individual with the face of a *Penitent,* and judging by his conversation Lucien decided that he was just the man to receive twenty-five louis and to make a dozen electors vote as he directed.

All went well until dinner. At six o'clock forty-three personages, the élite of the town, assembled in the drawing room of the Prefecture. Then the great double doors opened and the Prefect was stunned to see Lucien appear without his uniform. The Prefect himself, the General and the Colonels were all in full dress uniform. Lucien, who was dying with fatigue and boredom, had been seated on Madame de Riquebourg's right hand, making the General sulk in consequence. The government's logs had not been spared. It became insufferably hot in the room and before the dinner was half over (it lasted seven quarters of an hour) Lucien really thought he was going to faint and create a scene.

After dinner he asked permission to take a turn in the garden of the Prefecture with M. Coffe. To get rid of the Prefect, who insisted on following him, he was obliged to say:

"I have to give M. Coffe instructions about letters which I must sign before the post leaves. It is not enough to take wise measures, one must also record them."

"What a day!" the travelers exclaimed when they found themselves alone.

After a twenty-minute respite they were obliged to return to the drawing room so that Lucien might grant five or six more private interviews in the embrasures of the windows to important men—friends of the government, to be sure, but hesitant because of the hopeless nonenity of M. Blondeau, who, at table, had succeeded in exasperating even the patience of government officials of a provincial town by his eternal harping on the subject of iron and the justice of prohibiting the importation of English iron into France. Several of them, moreover, thought it ridiculous that the *Tribune* was now at its hundred and fourth lawsuit, and that so many poor young men were being held on suspicion without trial. Lucien had to consecrate his whole evening to combatting these heresies. With great eloquence he cited the case of the Greeks of the Byzantine Empire who were quarreling over the question of *increate light* on Mount Tabor while the ferocious Turks were scaling the walls of Constantinople.

Seeing the effect produced by this stroke of erudition, Lucien deserted the drawing room of the Prefecture and beckoned Coffe to follow him.

"Let's have a look at the town," these poor young men proposed. A quarter of an hour later they were engaged in trying to puzzle out the architecture of a more or less Gothic church, when they were joined by M. de Riquebourg.

"I've been looking for you everywhere, gentlemen. . . ."

Lucien's patience was about exhausted.

"The courier, Monsieur le Préfet, does not go till midnight."

"Between midnight and one o'clock."

"Well, M. Coffe, you see, has such an astonishing memory that I can dictate my dispatches to him right here just as we are. He remembers everything marvelously, even corrects my repetitions and other little errors. I have so much on my mind! You have no idea of all my difficulties!"

By means of such remarks and others even more ridiculous, Lucien and Coffe finally succeeded, with great difficulty, in getting rid of M. de Riquebourg.

The two friends returned to the Prefecture at eleven o'clock and wrote the Minister a letter of twenty lines. This letter, addressed to M. Leuwen, was promptly taken to the post by Coffe.

The Prefect was very much astonished when, at a quarter-to-twelve, his messenger came to tell him that he had been given no dispatches for Paris. His astonishment was considerably increased when the postmaster later informed him that no dispatch addressed to the Minister had been mailed. This plunged him into the deepest dismay.

At seven o'clock the next morning, the Prefect sent to ask Lucien for an audience in order to present him with his report on the removals he requested. M. de Riquebourg asked for seven, which Lucien with much effort finally persuaded him to reduce to four.

For the first time the Prefect, who until then had been humble to the point of servility, took on an intransigeant tone and began talking of Lucien's responsibility. To which Lucien replied with the greatest impertinence, and ended by declining

M. de Riquebourg's invitation to a dinner for intimate friends (not more than seventeen persons) arranged for two o'clock. Lucien went to pay his respects to Madame de Riquebourg and left at noon, exactly according to the instructions which he had drawn up for himself, and without permitting the Prefect to bring up the subject again.

Happily for the travelers, their road ran over a series of hills, and, much to the horror of the postilion, they did two leagues on foot.

The frightful activity of the past thirty-six hours had succeeded in blurring the memory of the mud and the hisses of Blois. Since then the carriage had twice been washed and brushed. But on opening one of the pockets to take out M. de Vaize's itinerary, Lucien found it full of mud that was still damp, and the book ruined.

CHAPTER SIXTEEN

OUR YOUNG GENTLEMEN made a detour of six leagues in order to visit the ruins of the celebrated Abbey of N——. They found them admirable and, like true students of the École Polytechnique, could not resist a desire to measure certain parts.

This was a most refreshing diversion for the travelers. All the vulgarity and platitude that had been encumbering their brains were swept away in a discussion on the suitability of Gothic art for a religion that dooms fifty-one out of every hundred children that are born to eternal damnation.

"Nothing could be stupider than our Madeleine, the church all the newspapers are so proud of. Imagine a Greek temple, made for joy and gaiety, harboring the terrible mysteries of a religion of fear! Even St. Peter's at Rome is nothing but a brilliant absurdity today; but in 1500 when Raphael and Michael Angelo were at work there, St. Peter's was not absurd: the religion of Leo X was gay, and it was he, the Pope himself, who ordered Raphael to paint, among the decorations of his favorite gallery, the amours of Leda and the swan, repeated twenty times. St. Peter's has become absurd since Pascal's Jansenism frowned on the pleasure of loving one's sister, and since Voltaire's witticisms have resulted in a stricter observance of religious practices."

Resuming their trip, Coffe said to Lucien:

"You treat the Minister too much as a man of intelligence. You act *for his best interests,* as we say in business. But a letter of twenty lines will hardly satisfy him. In all probability he takes his entire correspondence to the King, and if your letter should be seen it would be found adequate only if it were signed Carnot or Turenne. But permit me to say, Honorable Commissioner of Elections, your name does not yet call to mind a quantity of acts of high prudence."

"Very well then, let us demonstrate just such prudence to the Minister."

So the travelers stopped off for four hours in a little town, and wrote forty pages on the subject of MM. Malot, Blondeau and de Riquebourg. The conclusion was that even without removals, M. Blondeau would have a majority of from four to eighteen votes. The decisive expedient of the bankruptcy at Nantes, invented by M. de Riquebourg, the nomination of M. Aristide Blondeau as General Secretary at the Ministry of Finance, and, finally, the Grand Vicar's twenty-five louis were all reserved for another letter to the Minister, addressed to M. M——, Rue du Cherche Midi, No. 8, whose function it was to receive such letters, and to write the ones that His Excellency desired to appear to have been written by his own hand.

"We have now proved that we are true administrators, as

that word is understood in Paris," Coffe said to his companion as they got back into their carriage.

Two hours later, in the middle of the night, they met the courier, and requested him to stop. The courier began by getting angry and insolent, but was soon begging the Special Commissioner's pardon after Coffe had acquainted him with the name of the personage transmitting the dispatches to him. All this had to be set down in an official report.

The third day at noon the travelers saw on the horizon the spires of Caen, county seat of the Department of Calvados, where the election of M. Mairobert was so much feared by the government.

"There is Caen," said Coffe.

Lucien's gaiety straightway vanished, and turning to his companion with a deep sigh: "With you, my dear Coffe, I think aloud. I have drunk the cup of humiliation to the dregs; you have seen me weep. . . . What new infamy will I be guilty of here?"

"Just keep in the background; be satisfied with seconding the Prefect's measures; don't work at the thing so seriously."

"It was a mistake to stay at the Prefecture."

"Undoubtedly, but that is just another instance of the seriousness with which you set to work, and the terrible zeal with which you press forward toward your goal."

As they approached Caen, the travelers noticed many gendarmes on the road, and certain civilians in frock coats, striding along very straight and carrying thick cudgels.

"If I am not mistaken those are the bludgeoners of the Bourse," Coffe said.

"But is it true that they really did bludgeon people at the Bourse? Wasn't it all an invention of the *Tribune*?"

"I can vouch for it, having been struck myself five or six times, and it would have ended badly for me if I hadn't happened to have a pair of large compasses which I flourished as though I meant to eviscerate the gentlemen. Their worthy chief, M. N——, who wasn't more than ten paces away at a mezzanine window, shouted: 'Look out—that little bald man is an agitator!' I made my escape through the Rue des Colonnes."

When they reached the gates of Caen they were held up for a good ten minutes while their passports were being examined, and as Lucien was about to lose his temper, a man well past middle age, tall and broad-shouldered, who was pacing up and down under the gateway swinging a huge cudgel, told him quite plainly to go and f . . . himself.

"Sir, my name is Leuwen, Master of Petitions, and to me you are a nobody. Give me your name if you dare."

"My name is *Lustucru*," the man with the cudgel replied jeeringly, as he strutted around the carriage. "Give my name to your King's Prosecutor, Mr. Daredevil. And," lowering his voice, he added, "if ever we meet in Switzerland you'll get all the slaps in the face and marks of contempt you could ask to curry favor with your chiefs."

"Never pronounce the word honor, you spy in disguise!"

"Gad," said Coffe, almost laughing, "I'd like to have seen you insulted as I was at the Bourse."

"Instead of a pair of compasses, I have my pistols."

"You can kill this disguised gendarme with impunity. He has orders not to lose his temper. Yet, perhaps at Montmirail or Waterloo, he was a brave soldier. Today we're all in the same regiment," Coffe added with a bitter laugh. "Let's not fight."

"You are cruel," said Lucien.

"I speak the truth when I am asked, take it or leave it."

Tears filled Lucien's eyes.

The carriage was now allowed to enter the city. On reaching the inn, Lucien seized Coffe's hand:

"I am a child," he said.

"Not at all, you are simply one of the privileged class of this age, as the preachers say, and you have never had any disagreeable work to do."

The innkeeper's reception of them was most mysterious: first, there were rooms available, then, there were no rooms to be had.

The fact was that the innkeeper had sent to advise the Prefect of their arrival. The inns, which feared provocations by the gendarmes or secret police agents, had been ordered not to have any rooms for the partisans of M. Mairobert.

Finally the Prefect, M. Boucaut de Séranville, duly authorized the innkeeper to lodge MM. Leuwen and Coffe. They had hardly reached their rooms when a very young man, exceedingly well dressed but evidently armed with pistols, appeared and, without a word, handed Lucien two copies of a little octodecimo pamphlet covered in red paper and very badly printed. It was a collection of all the ultra-liberal articles that M. Boucaut de Séranville had published in the *National,* the *Globe,* the *Courrier,* and other liberal papers in 1829.

"Not bad," said Lucien. "He writes well."

"What pomposity!" objected Coffe. "What a lifeless, vapid imitation of M. de Chateaubriand! The words are constantly being twisted out of their natural meaning, their common acceptation."

The gentlemen were again interrupted by a secret agent who, with a hypocritical smile and many questions, presented them with two more pamphlets in octavo.

"What magnificence! This is certainly taxpayers' money," said Coffe. "I'd be willing to wager they are government pamphlets."

"By gad, they're ours," cried Lucien, "the ones we lost at Blois. This is pure Torpet."

Then he turned again to the liberal articles which had formerly made the name of M. Boucaut de Séranville famous in the *Globe.*

"Come, let's go and see this renegade," Lucien proposed.

"I am not in agreement on the subject of his talents," persisted Coffe. "He no more believed in the liberal doctrines in 1829 than he believes today in the maxims of order, tranquillity, stability. Under Napoleon he would have got himself killed to be a Captain. The only advantage of the hypocrisy of those days over that of today (that of 1809 over that of 1834) is that anyone who practiced it under Napoleon could not get along without courage, which is a quality that, in wartime, does not admit of hypocrisy."

"The goal was noble and grand."

"That was only because of Napoleon. Put a Richelieu on the throne of France and de Séranville's scurviness, the zeal with which he disguises his gendarmes, would perhaps serve some useful purpose. The misfortune of these Prefects is that their profession today calls for nothing more than the qualities of a pettifogging Norman public prosecutor."

"And a pettifogging prosecutor was given sovereign power, and he sold it to his cronies."

It was in this lofty and really philosophic mood, viewing Frenchmen of the Nineteenth Century without either hate or love, and solely as the tools wielded by the possessor of the Budget, that Lucien and Coffe entered the Prefecture of Caen.

A footman dressed with a spruceness rare in the provinces, showed them into a very elegant drawing room. The walls were hung with portraits done in oil of all the members of the royal family. They would not have been out of place in the most elegant houses of Paris.

"This renegade," said Coffe, "is going to keep us waiting ten minutes. Considering your rank, his rank and his important occupations, it is mandatory."

"It so happens," rejoined Lucien, "I brought along the pamphlet made up of his liberal articles. If he keeps us waiting for more than five minutes he will find me plunged in the perusal of his works."

The gentlemen were warming themselves in front of the fire when Lucien saw by the clock that the five minutes that any man can keep another waiting without affectation, were up. He settled himself in an armchair with his back to the door and, continuing his conversation, held the red pamphlet conspicuously in his hand.

They heard a slight noise, and Lucien became suddenly engrossed in his articles. A door opened, and Coffe, whose back was turned to the fireplace, and who was very much amused to be a witness to this meeting of two coxcombs, saw in the doorway a diminutive creature, very short, very thin and exceedingly elegant. Although it was still morning, he was already arrayed in skintight black breeches that molded perhaps the skinniest legs in the Department. At sight of the pamphlet, which Lucien returned to his pocket only four or five mortal seconds after the entrance of M. de Séranville, the latter's face took on a dark red hue, the color of wine. Coffe saw his lips contract.

Coffe found Lucien's tone cold, simple, military and a trifle quizzical.

"It's funny," thought Coffe, "what a little time it takes for a uniform to become part and parcel of the character of the Frenchman who wears it. Look at this fundamentally good-natured fellow who has been a soldier (but what a soldier!) for only ten months and now all his life his leg, and his arm, will say: 'I am a military man!' It is not surprising that the Gauls were the bravest people of antiquity. The pleasure the French take in wearing any mark of the military caste quite unsettles them, but also inspires in them two or three never-failing virtues."

During these philosophic and perhaps slightly envious reflections, for Coffe was poor and that thought was often on his mind, Lucien and the Prefect plunged into the elections.

The little Prefect spoke slowly and with an extreme affectation of elegance. But it was evident that he was controlling himself with difficulty. When he mentioned his political adversaries his lips became pinched and his little eyes blazed.

"Unless I am very much mistaken," Coffe said to himself, "he has a murderous look. This is particularly amusing when he pronounces the word *Monsieur*—in saying *Monsieur* Mairobert, which he does every two seconds. It is highly possible that we have a little fanatic on our hands. He looks to me capable of having M. Mairobert shot if only he had him up before a nice court martial, like that of Colonel Caron. It is also possible that the sight of the red pamphlet has deeply troubled his *political* soul." (The Prefect had just said: *If I am ever a politician*.) "A fatuous fool," Coffe thought, "to be a politician. If the Cossack doesn't conquer France, our politicians will be Tom Joneses like Fox, or Blifils like Peel, and M. de Séranville will be, at most, Grand Chamberlain or Grand Referendary of the Chamber of Peers."

It was apparent that M. de Séranville was treating Lucien very coldly.

"He looks upon him as a rival," Coffe thought. "Yet this diminutive coxcomb must be at least thirty-two or -three years old. Our little Leuwen is not doing badly: admirably cold, with a tendency to a polite irony in excellent form; and the care he takes to keep his manner sufficiently distant and to avoid all fashionable sprightliness in no way distracts his attention from the ideas he has in mind."

"Would you care to let me see your election list?"

M. de Séranville plainly hesitated, and finally replied:

"I know it by heart but I have not written it down."

"Monsieur Coffe, my associate in this mission . . ."

Once more Lucien enumerated Coffe's qualities, for it

seemed to him that the Prefect accorded him too little attention.

". . . M. Coffe has perhaps a pencil about him and, with your permission, will take down the figures if you are kind enough to confide them to us."

The irony of these last words was not lost on M. de Séranville. He looked really upset as Coffe, with the most provoking coolness, unscrewed the inkwell in the Russian leather case of the honorable Master of Petitions.

"Between us we have him on the rack. It's my business to keep him there as long as possible."

Arranging the writing case and then the table took at least a minute and a half. During this time Lucien maintained an admirably frigid silence.

"The military coxcomb outdoes the civil coxcomb!" thought Coffe to himself.

When at last he was comfortably settled for writing, he turned to M. de Séranville:

"If you care to communicate your list to us, we can now take it down."

"Certainly, certainly," said the diminutive Prefect.

"Superfluous repetition," thought the inexorable Coffe.

And the Prefect began to speak, but did not dictate.

"There are all the earmarks of the diplomat in that shade of difference," Lucien thought to himself. "He is less bourgeois than Riquebourg, but is he as apt to succeed? He spends so much thought on the figure he will cut in a drawing room, I wonder if he has any left for his job of Prefect and Director of Elections? In that narrow skull and low forehead are there brains enough for so much fatuity and work as well? I doubt it. *Videmus infra.*"

Lucien began to feel satisfied that he was adopting the correct manner with this captious little Prefect, and that he took sufficiently into account the rascality of the business in which he had consented to take part. It was the first pleasure his mission had afforded him, the first compensation for his atrocious suffering over the mud-throwing of Blois.

Coffe wrote while the Prefect, sitting stiffly opposite Lucien, his knees pressed tightly together, recited:

Registered electors	1280
Probable number present	900
M. Gonin, constitutional candidate	400
M. Mairobert	500

He added nothing to the evidence of those lump figures: four hundred and five hundred, and Lucien did not deem it proper to ask him for further details.

M. de Séranville apologized for not lodging them at the Prefecture. As he had workmen in the house at the moment he was unable to offer them suitable rooms. He did invite them to dinner, but only for the following day.

The three gentlemen parted with a coolness that could not have been greater without being pointed.

Gaily, Lucien remarked to Coffe as soon as they were on the street:

"At least he's less boring than Riquebourg."

The consciousness of having played his part well relegated the incident of Blois to the background for the first time.

"And you behaved much more like a statesman," Coffe rejoined. "That is to say, insignificant and given to elegant and empty commonplaces."

"On the other hand, how much less we know about the elections of Caen after a whole hour than we did about M. de Riquebourg's in fifteen minutes—that is, when you had finally got him away from his infernal generalities by your incisive questions. M. de Séranville never would admit of a comparison between himself and the worthy bourgeois Riquebourg who held forth to us on the subject of his cook's accounts. M. de

Séranville is far more correct, is not at all ridiculous and, as my father would say, is *pickled* in suspicion and meanness. But I'll wager he isn't as good at his job as the Prefect of Cher."

"The animal certainly makes a better appearance than Riquebourg," Coffe admitted, "but it is very possible that he is worth much less."

"I noticed in his face, especially when he mentioned M. Mairobert, that same asperity which alone gives some life to the literary gems of the red pamphlet."

"Is he, by chance, a dismal fanatic who feels the need to be constantly active and plotting, making men feel the weight of his power? Has he turned this need of his for hurting people to the service of his ambition, as formerly he used it in his criticisms of the literary works of his rivals?"

"I think he has more of the sophist who likes to talk and cavil because he rather fancies himself as a profound reasoner. This man would exert a powerful influence in the Chamber of Deputies; he would be a Mirabeau for country notaries."

Leaving the Prefecture, they learned that the Paris courier did not leave until evening. Whereupon they merrily set out to take a look at the town. Some extraordinary event, it was evident, had roused these bourgeois provincials out of their habitual apathy.

"These people have not that listless air which is normal to them," Lucien remarked.

"You'll see, after thirty or forty years of elections, the provinces are going to be less stupid."

They went to inspect a collection of antiquities which had been discovered at Lillebonne, and wasted a great deal of time arguing with the custodian about the antiquity of an Etruscan chimera completely covered with verdigris. The custodian, on the authority of the librarian, had just fixed its age at twenty-seven hundred years, when our travelers were accosted by an extremely courteous individual.

"Will the gentlemen kindly pardon my addressing them without being known to them? I am General Fari's valet. The General has been waiting for an hour at the inn for the gentlemen, and begs that they will excuse his sending to inform them of the fact. General Fari has charged me to repeat his exact words: *There is no time to lose*."

"We'll follow you," Lucien said to the General's man, and turning to Coffe, "that is a valet who fills me with envy."

"Let's see whether we can say: Like man, like master. As a matter of fact it was a bit childish of us to go looking at antiquities when we are charged with the mission of forging the present. Perhaps our conduct is just the natural result of our resentment at the administrative fatuity of Séranville. But, I must say, if you'll excuse the word, your military fatuity quite outdid his."

They found the entrance to the inn cluttered with gendarmes and in their sitting room, waiting for them, a ruddy-faced man of about fifty years. He looked rather like a peasant, but his eyes were gentle and vivacious, and his manners did not belie the promise of his eyes. This was General Fari, the Division Commander. In spite of his rather crude ways (he had been a simple Dragoon for five years), it would have been difficult to find anyone with greater courtesy or, as they were soon to discover, a better grasp of the situation. Coffe was astonished to notice that he was without the least sign of military fatuity. His arms and his legs moved exactly like those of any ordinary mortal. The zeal with which he was trying to get M. Gonin, the government's candidate elected, and to defeat M. Mairobert, had not the least taint of meanness, nor even of animosity. He spoke of M. Mairobert as he would have spoken of a Prussian General commanding a city he was besieging. Indeed, General Fari invariably spoke with great consideration of everyone, even of the Prefect; though it was evident that he was no exception to the rule that makes Generals the natural and instinctive enemies of Prefects who are all-powerful in their Departments, whereas the Generals have only a dozen higher officers to bully.

The General told Lucien that he had started looking for him the minute he received the Minister's letter, which Lucien had sent him on arriving.

"But you were at the Prefecture. I admit, gentlemen, that I tremble for our election. M. Mairobert's five hundred and fifty electors are energetic and filled with conviction. They can make converts. Our four hundred electors are gloomy and silent. I shall speak plainly to you, gentlemen—we are on the eve of battle and any vain beating about the bush might compromise our affair—our electors are ashamed of their role. That devil of a Mairobert is the most honest of men, rich and obliging. He has been angry but once in his life, and that was when he was goaded into a positive frenzy by the black pamphlet. . . ."

"What pamphlet?" asked Lucien.

"Do you mean, sir, that M. de Séranville did not give you a pamphlet bound in funereal wrappers?"

"This is the first I have heard of it, and I should be much obliged if you would get me a copy."

"I have one right here."

"Why, this is impossible! It is the Prefect's own pamphlet. But, didn't he get the order by telegraph that he was not to let a single copy leave the printers?"

"M. de Séranville," replied the General, "took it upon himself to ignore that order. The pamphlet is really pretty violent and it has been in circulation since the day before yesterday. I will not try to conceal from you that it has had a most deplorable effect. At least, that is how it strikes me."

Lucien, who had only seen it in manuscript in the Minister's office, now glanced rapidly through it. But, as a manuscript is always difficult to read, the barbed and even slanderous satire against M. Mairobert now seen in print seemed to him a hundred times worse.

"Great God," exclaimed Lucien as he read it, and his tone was rather that of an honest man who is painfully shocked, than a Commissioner of Elections worried over a false move. "And the election is day after tomorrow! And M. Mairobert is universally respected! This is just the thing to rouse honest but indolent people to action, and even the timorous."

"Yes," said the General, "I am very much afraid that this pamphlet will win M. Mairobert at least forty votes of that sort. For, it can't be denied, if he were not opposed by the King's government, M. Mairobert would have every vote except his own and those of a dozen or more rabid Jesuits."

"But at least he must be stubborn—niggardly?" Lucien insisted. "Here he is accused of winning lawsuits by giving dinners to the Judges of the Lower Court."

"He is the most generous man in the world. Naturally he has lawsuits. After all we are in Normandy!" said the General, smiling. "He wins them because he is a man of resolute character, but it is well known throughout the Department that, out of charity, he returned to a widow whose husband had begun an unjust suit against him, the entire sum she had been sentenced to pay him. M. Mairobert has an income of over sixty thousand pounds and every year he inherits twelve or fifteen thousand more. He has seven or eight uncles, all rich and unmarried. Unlike most openhanded men he is no fool. He doubles the revenues of perhaps forty farmers around here. If a farmer can prove to M. Mairobert that, after deducting the living expenses of his children, his wife and himself, he has made five hundred francs that year, M. Mairobert hands him an equal sum of five hundred francs, payable in ten years without interest. It is to accustom farmers, he says, to keep books like business men, otherwise there can be no agriculture. To perhaps a hundred small manufacturers, he gives a sum equal to a third of their profits. In 1814, as Counselor of the provisory Prefecture, he directed the affairs of the Prefecture and took charge of everything during the occupation. He once defied an insolent Colonel, and even chased him out of the Prefecture at pistol point. In a word, he is a finished specimen of a man."

"M. de Séranville never breathed a word to me of all this," said Lucien. He read a few more sentences of the black pamphlet.

"My God! This pamphlet is our ruin!" he said hopelessly. "You are right, General, we are at the beginning of a battle that may well turn into a rout. Though M. Coffe and I have not the honor of being known to you, I am going to ask you to accord us your full confidence for the three days still remaining before the final ballot which will decide between M. Mairobert and the government. I have a hundred thousand pounds at my disposal; I have seven or eight posts to distribute; by telegraph I can ask for at least as many removals. Here are my private instructions which I drew up for myself, and which I entrust to you alone."

General Fari read them slowly and with marked attention.

"M. Leuwen," he then said, "in what concerns these elections I shall have no secrets from you, as you have kept none from me, and I say: *It is too late*! If you had come two months ago, if M. de Séranville had consented to write less and talk more, perhaps we might have succeeded in winning over the timorous. All the wealthy people here, although they do not properly appreciate the King's government, have a terror of the Republic. Nero, Caligula, the devil himself might be King and they would support him out of fear of a Republic which, instead of governing us according to our natural bent, has the intention of remolding us; and they know very well that such a refashioning of the French character would require another Carrier or a Joseph Le Bon. So then, we are sure of three hundred votes. We would have three hundred and fifty except for the fact that we must discount thirty Jesuits and fifteen or twenty landowners—the pious old men or the young men with weak lungs—who will vote as directed by Monseigneur the Bishop, acting in concert with the Henri V committee. We have in the Department thirty-three or -four out-and-out republicans. If it were a question of choosing between the Monarchy and the Republic we could count on eight hundred and sixty of the nine hundred votes, as against forty. But one could wish that the *Tribune* was not at its hundred and fortieth lawsuit; above all, that the King's government did not humiliate the nation in the eyes of foreigners. Hence the five hundred votes that the Mairobert party is counting on. Two months ago I didn't think M. Mairobert would have more than three hundred and fifty to eighty unquestionable votes. I felt sure that the Prefect would win at least a hundred on his electoral tour. But he hasn't the least personal appeal. He talks too well and lacks the gift of specious cordiality; he can't expect to win over a Norman in a conversation of half an hour. Even with his Police Commissioners he is terrible. But they grovel to him for all that. Realizing finally that he couldn't influence people personally, he has resorted to circulars and letters to the Mayors. It seems to me (of course I have never been an executive myself, all I have done is to command, and I bow to the judgment of those who are better qualified than I am), but, as I say, it seems to me that M. de Séranville, who writes very well, has overdone the administrative letter. I know more than forty Mayors (I can furnish the Minister with a list) who are up in arms over his continual threats. 'What can happen anyway,' they say. 'His election will miss fire. Well, and so much the better! He'll be removed and we'll be rid of him. They can't send us anybody worse.' M. Bordier, the timorous Mayor of the big Commune of N——, which has nine electors, was so terrified by the Prefect's letters and the nature of the information demanded of him, that he feigned an attack of gout. He let it be known that he was in bed and didn't leave his house for five days. But Sunday at six o'clock in the morning he went to Mass.

"In short, M. de Séranville by his electoral tour frightened away fifteen or twenty timorous electors and riled at least a hundred. These, added to the three hundred and sixty I regard as unshakable because they want a King Log who will stick to the Charter verbatim, make up a total of four hundred and sixty. That is M. Mairobert's count—an extremely small majority—only ten."

The General, Lucien, and Coffe discussed these figures at length, juggling them in every possible way. They invariably came out with at least four hundred and fifty votes for M. Mairobert, only one more making a majority in an Electoral College of "nine hundred."

"But Monseigneur the Bishop must surely have a favorite Grand Vicar," Lucien remarked. "What if this favorite Grand Vicar were to be offered ten thousand francs?"

"He is quite comfortably off and would like to become a Bishop," replied the General. "Besides, it is barely possible he's an honest man. It has been known to happen."

CHAPTER SEVENTEEN

"WELL," said Lucien to Coffe as soon as General Fari had left them, "the sun is shining, it is only half-past-one, and I feel like sending a telegraphic dispatch to the Minister. It is better for him to know the truth."

"You do him a service and yourself a disservice. It's no way to curry favor with him. This truth is unpalatable. And if M. Mairobert should not be elected after all, what will they think of you at Court?"

"Isn't it bad enough to be a rogue in reality, without acting like one?"

Lucien wrote out his dispatch. After making him strike out three words and substitute a single one in their place, Coffe gave his approval, and Lucien left for the Prefecture.

Going up to the telegraph office, he showed his credentials to M. Lamorte, the director, and asked him to transmit his dispatch without delay. The man seemed very much embarrassed and began temporizing. Fearing the mists of a winter day, Lucien kept glancing at his watch and finally spoke without mincing matters. The clerk intimated that it would be advisable for Lucien to consult the Prefect.

M. de Séranville was plainly annoyed. He read over Lucien's credentials several times and, on the whole, behaved exactly like his employee, M. Lamorte. Exasperated at having lost three-quarters of an hour already, Lucien said finally:

"At least, sir, deign to give me a clear, straightforward answer."

"I endeavor, sir, always to make myself clear."

"Then, sir, are you or are you not willing to have my dispatch sent?"

"It seems to me, sir, that I might see that dispatch. . . ."

"You avoid, sir, that clarity which you just led me to expect, after three-quarters of an hour already wasted."

"Your objection, sir, might, it seems to me, be couched in a tone rather more . . ."

Lucien interrupted the Prefect, who was by now pale with rage:

"I cannot admit further quibbling. It is getting late. To defer your answer is to give it in the negative without daring to admit as much."

"*Daring,* sir!"

"Will you or will you not allow my dispatch to go through?"

"Very well, sir! For the moment I am still the Prefect of Calvados and my answer is: *No.*"

This *no* was spoken with all the fury of an outraged martinet.

"Sir," replied Lucien, "I shall have the honor of making my request in writing. I trust that you will dare to make your reply in writing as well, and I shall immediately send a courier to the Minister."

"A courier! A courier! You will have neither horses, nor courier, nor passport. Are you aware, sir, that at the —— Bridge there is an order signed by me to let no one through without a passport, and a passport bearing a certain distinguishing mark?"

"Very well, Monsieur le Préfet!" and Lucien paused deliberately between each word, "from the moment you refuse to obey the instructions of the Minister of the Interior, there is no longer any government. I have orders for General Fari, and I shall ask him to arrest you."

"Arrest *me,* damn you!"

And the little Prefect hurled himself at Lucien who, picking up a chair, warded him off.

"With such behavior, sir, you will first be well thrashed and then arrested. Perhaps that will satisfy you."

"You are an insolent puppy, sir. I demand satisfaction."

"For the present I am obliged to confine myself to telling you that my contempt for you is unbounded; but I will do you the honor of crossing swords with you the day after the election of M. Mairobert. I shall now make it my business to write to you, sir, and, at the same time, to acquaint the General with my instructions."

At these last words the Prefect seemed beside himself with rage.

"If the General obeys the orders of the Minister of War," continued Lucien, "as I have no doubt he will, you will be arrested and I shall automatically assume control of the telegraph. In case the General is unwilling to use force, I shall give you, sir, the sole honor of getting M. Mairobert elected and shall leave for Paris. I shall pass the —— Bridge, I assure you. Moreover, whether here or in Paris, I shall always be ready to reaffirm the contempt I entertain for your abilities and for your character. Good-day, sir."

Just as Lucien was about to leave the room there came a loud knock on the door which M. de Séranville had bolted as soon as their conversation became a little too heated. Now Lucien unlocked it.

"A telegraphic dispatch," announced M. Lamorte, the man who had made Lucien lose half an hour.

"Give it to me," said the Prefect with an arrogance that lacked the barest politeness.

The poor man stood petrified. He knew only too well the violence and vindictiveness of the Prefect.

"By God, sir, will you give me that dispatch?"

"It is for M. Leuwen," said the poor fellow in a scarcely audible voice.

"Well, M. Leuwen, you seem to be Prefect here!" cried M. de Séranville, baring his teeth in a bitter sneer. "I relinquish my place to you." And he went out, slamming the door so that the room shook.

"He looks like a wild beast," Lucien thought to himself.

"Will you kindly hand me that terrible dispatch, sir?"

"Here it is. But Monsieur le Préfet will report me! I hope you'll stand by me, sir."

Lucien read:

"M. Leuwen will take complete charge of the elections. Suppress the pamphlet without fail. M. Leuwen will reply immediately."

"And here is my reply!" cried Lucien as he wrote:

"Things could not be worse. M. Mairobert has a majority of at least 10 votes. Have quarreled with the Prefect."

Handing the waiting employee these three sentences, Lucien said:

"Send this off at once. I regret to say that the situation is grave. Without wishing to offend you, sir, in your own interest I must warn you that if this dispatch fails to reach Paris, or if a living soul here gets wind of it, I shall request your removal by the telegraph tomorrow."

"Ah, sir, my devotion and my discretion . . ."

"We'll judge of that tomorrow. Be off, sir. And lose no time."

M. Lamorte departed. Lucien looked around the room and, after a moment, burst out laughing. He found himself standing alone in front of the Prefect's table. There lay the Prefect's handkerchief, his open snuffbox, his scattered papers.

"I feel exactly like a thief," he said to himself. "Without false modesty I may say that I have more sang-froid than that little martinet."

He went to the door, called the usher, and had him stand in the doorway. Then sitting down at the Prefect's desk, at the side furthest from the fireplace so as not to appear to be reading the Prefect's scattered papers, he began to write. First, addressing M. de Séranville personally:

If you will take my advice, sir, until the day after the elections you will act as though what happened an hour ago were null and void. For my part, I shall not let anyone in the city know of the unpleasant incident.

I am, etc.

Leuwen.

He then took a large official sheet of paper:

Monsieur le Préfet,

In two hours, at seven o'clock this evening, I am sending a courier to His Excellency, the Minister of the Interior. I have the honor of asking you for a passport, and I beg that you will send it to me before half-past-six. It is desirable that you should affix the distinguishing marks you mentioned, so that my courier will not be delayed at the —— Bridge. After leaving me with my letters, my courier will stop at the Prefecture to pick up yours, and will proceed at top speed to Paris.

Leuwen.

After sealing the two letters, Lucien called to the usher who, pale as death, was standing at the door.

"Take both these letters to Monsieur le Préfet."

"Is M. de Séranville still Prefect?" asked the usher.

"I said to give these letters to Monsieur le Préfet."

Then, coldly and with great dignity, Lucien left the Prefecture.

"You've behaved just like a child," Coffe said, when Lucien told him of his threat to arrest the Prefect.

"I don't think so. In the first place, I was not really angry, and was able to consider what I was going to do. If there is one thing in the world that can prevent M. Mairobert's election it is the departure of M. de Séranville and the temporary substitution of one of the Prefecture Councilors. The Minister told me that he would give 500,000 francs not to have M. Mairobert opposing him in the Chamber. Weigh that remark! Money is now the key to the whole question."

The General arrived.

"I have come to make my report."

"My dear General, won't you share my tavern dinner? I am about to send a courier to Paris and should be most grateful if you would look over and correct what I say about the general state of public opinion. It is better, it seems to me, that the Minister should know the truth."

The General looked at Lucien with an air of astonishment which seemed to say:

"You must be young indeed, or else you are gambling your future most recklessly."

But all he said was:

"You will find, sir, that in Paris they do not want to face the truth."

"Here," said Lucien, "is a dispatch I have just received by telegraph, to which I replied: 'M. Mairobert has a majority of ten votes. Things could not be worse.' "

Dinner was served. M. Coffe excused himself, saying that with the dispatches on his mind it was impossible for him to eat, and that he preferred to write his letters first and dine afterwards.

"We still have time enough before your courier leaves," said the General, "to hear the reports of two Police Commissioners and the Captain who is my second in everything concerning the elections. I don't want you to see things only through my eyes. I might be mistaken."

At that moment Presiding Judge Donis d'Angel was announced.

"What kind of a man is he?" asked Lucien.

"An insufferable chatterbox, explaining at length everything that is not of the slightest importance and carefully side-stepping any difficult question. Besides, he's always on the fence. He has extensive connections among the priests who, in this Department, are very hostile. He'll only make you waste a lot of precious time. It takes twenty-seven hours for your courier to get from here to Paris. It seems to me that you cannot get him started too soon, that is if you really wish to send him—a step I am very far from advising. But one thing I do emphatically advise: put off the Honorable Donis d'Angel until later this evening, or tomorrow morning."

And so it was done. Notwithstanding the sincerity and

probity of these two companions, their dinner was gloomy, dull and short. At dessert the two Police Commissioners arrived, and after them, a little Captain named Ménière. The latter was quite as sharp as the other two. He was looking forward to acquiring a Cross by this election.

"And that," said the General to Lucien, "is the sum of our brilliant achievements."

Finally, at half-past-seven, the courier galloped off, bearing with him Coffe's memorandum on the elections and thirty pages of explanations for M. de Vaize. In a separate letter Lucien gave the Minister a detailed account of his dispute with the Prefect. He reported the dialogue with absolute precision as though written by a stenographer.

At nine o'clock, the General returned to Lucien's inn, bringing fresh reports from the district of Risset. He also told Lucien that at six o'clock the Prefect had sent a courier to Paris. This gave him a half-hour start on their man. The General insinuated that the latter was not too anxious to overtake his comrade.

"Would it suit you, General, to go with me tomorrow morning on a round of visits to fifty of Caen's most respected citizens? This may attract some ridicule, but if it wins us ten votes it is worth it."

"For me it would be a pleasure to accompany you anywhere," the General replied, "but what of the Prefect? . . ."

After discussing at length the means to be employed to spare the morbid vanity of that eminent functionary, it was decided that the General and Lucien should each write to him. General Fari's zeal was both candid and prompt. They wrote their letters without delay, and the General's valet took them to the Prefecture. M. de Séranville received the valet and questioned him at length. This association of Lucien and General Fari drove the poor man nearly out of his mind. To both letters he replied in writing that he was indisposed and confined to his bed.

When the calls for the next day had been agreed upon, a list of the persons to be visited was drawn up, and little Captain Ménière, summoned once more, was sent into the next room to dictate to Coffe a few words of explanation about them. Pacing silently up and down, Lucien and the General racked their brains to try to find some way out of their dilemma.

"The Minister can no longer be of the least help; it is too late."

And the silence continued.

"General," Lucien said at length, "in the army, I am sure, you often risked a charge, even after the battle was three-quarters lost. According to last reports from the district of Risset, there is no further hope. More than twenty of our supporters will vote for M. Mairobert simply to get rid of de Séranville. Under these desperate circumstances what if we could find some way of approaching M. Le Canu, leader of the legitimist party?"

The General stopped short in the middle of the room. Lucien went on:

"I would say to him: 'Choose any one of your electors and I will have him nominated and turn the government's four hundred votes over to him. Can you, and will you send messengers with instructions to one hundred of your country gentry? With these votes added to ours we can defeat M. Mairobert.' After all, General, what can one more legitimist in the Chamber matter to us? In the first place, it's a hundred to one that he'll be some imbecile who will never open his mouth, or a bore whom nobody will listen to. Even if he has the eloquence of M. Berryer, the party is not dangerous. It represents only itself—that is, one hundred or, at the most, one hundred and fifty thousand wealthy Frenchmen. If I have understood the Minister correctly, better ten legitimists than one

Mairobert representing every small landowner in the four Departments of Normandy."

The General paced the floor for a long time before replying.

"It is an idea," he said at length, "but a very dangerous one for you. The Minister, who is some eighty leagues away from the field of battle, will blame you. When unsuccessful, a Minister is only too happy to find a scapegoat and have some actual performance to attack. I don't ask you what terms you are on with M. de Vaize . . . but, after all, sir, I am sixty-one and could be your father. . . . Let me tell you frankly what I think. . . . Even if you were the Minister's own son, this extreme measure you propose would be dangerous for you. As far as I am concerned, sir, this is not a military engagement and my role is to remain in the second or even third line.

"I am not the son of a Minister," the General added, smiling, "and I should be grateful if you would avoid mentioning that you have spoken to me about this project of joining forces with the legitimists. Should this election turn out badly, someone is going to be severely blamed, and I'd as soon remain in the background."

Suddenly, a thought occurred to Lucien: "Instead of drawing up his instructions for me himself, the Minister, who has been Prefect of two or three Departments, who has himself directed elections, who, in short, knows what is happening in the provinces as well as the will of the Château, said to me, 'Draw up your own instructions,'—to me who am the veriest novice in this business of politics. Was he afraid of compromising himself? Or did he want to compromise me?"

"I give you my word," continued Lucien aloud, "that no one shall know that I have ever spoken to you about this idea, and, to prove as much, I shall have the honor of giving you a letter before you leave. In regard to the interest you are good enough to show in my youth, my thanks are as sincere as your kindness, but I must confess that I am seeking nothing more than the success of the election. All personal considerations are secondary. I should prefer not to make use of the unsavory expedient of removals; I do not want to use any infamous weapons; however I will sacrifice everything to our success. Unhappily I have been here in Caen for only ten hours, I don't know a soul here, and the Prefect treats me as a rival instead of an ally. If M. de Vaize is just, he will take all this into consideration. But, I should never forgive myself if I let fear of his censure serve as an excuse for doing nothing. I should look upon such a course as beneath contempt.

"This being understood, General, and you remaining entirely ignorant of the singular measure I propose under desperate circumstances (as shall be proved by a letter I shall have the honor of addressing to you) will you, knowing the country as you do, consent to give me the benefit of your advice, or will you force me to rely solely on those two Police Commissioners who'd be quite ready, for a consideration, to sell me to either party—legitimist or republican?"

To this General Fari replied:

"Your plan of campaign being drawn up without my participation, if you explain to me that you want to join forces with the legitimist party because your Minister prefers to have a fanatical or even a clever legitimist in the Chamber rather than M. Mairobert, I say neither yes nor no, inasmuch as no act of war or rebellion is involved. I do not point out the terrible effect of such a move on the adjoining Department of the Vendée, where the least of the petty nobles refuses to admit the highest government official into his drawing room. This being understood and agreed, you might say to me, 'General, I am a stranger here, will you guide me?' Is that what you will be good enough to put in your letter to me?"

"Exactly. That is how I look at it."

"Then, sir, my answer is: 'As far as its execution is concerned, I can have no opinion on the measure you wish to adopt. The responsibility rests entirely with you. But, if you wish to ask me any questions, I am ready to reply.' "

"I am going to write down the dialogue that has just taken place between us, General, and give it to you duly signed."

"We'll make two copies, as for the provisions of a capitulation."

"Agreed. Now then, how am I to put my plan into execution? How can I reach M. Le Canu without alarming him?"

General Fari thought for a few moments.

"You must send for that merciless chatterbox, Donis d'Angel, who would see his own father hanged if it would get him the Cross. But he'll be back, you won't have to send for him! I advise you to have him read your instructions. It will impress him to know that the Minister has such confidence in you that he let you draw them up yourself. Although suspicious by nature, once Donis d'Angel is convinced that you are in favor with the Minister, there is nothing he will refuse you. He showed that plainly enough in the lawsuit over press violations, when his bad faith was so flagrant that he was even hooted on the street by all the ragamuffins of the town. Besides, it's a small thing you are asking of him—merely to put you in touch with his uncle, Abbé Donis-Disjonval, a serene, discreet old gentleman and not too foolish for his age. If the Judge approaches his uncle in the right way, the latter will obtain an audience for you with M. Le Canu. But where and how, I cannot say. Beware of a trap. Will Le Canu wish to see you? That also I cannot tell you."

"Hasn't the legitimist party a deputy leader?" Lucien asked.

"Certainly—the Marquis de Bron. But he takes care never to do anything of importance without the approval of M. Le Canu. You will see for yourself—Le Canu is a blond, beardless little man of about sixty-six or -seven who, rightly or wrongly, has the reputation of being the shrewdest man in all Normandy. In 1792 he was a rabid patriot. Consequently he is a turncoat, and that makes the worst kind of rascal. Such men think they can never do enough to prove their zeal. He has the gentlest manners in the world—in other words, Machiavelli in person! One day he even asked me if he could be my confessor! He claimed that through the Queen he could have me made Officer of the Legion of Honor."

"Well," returned Lucien, "he shall be mine. I'll confess to him. I'll be entirely frank."

After discussing MM. Donis-Disjonval and Le Canu at length, General Fari asked:

"And the Prefect? What are we going to do about him? How can you give the government's votes to M. Le Canu?"

"I'll get an order by telegraph and I'll persuade the Prefect. If I obtain neither my order nor the Prefect's assent, then I shall leave Caen, and when I get back to Paris I shall send my two intermediaries some money for Masses."

"It is dangerous."

"But at present our defeat is certain."

Lucien had the General repeat in detail everything it was important for him to know. In ten hours' time he had seen three hundred proper names pass under his eyes; he had insulted a man he had never seen before and assured him of his contempt; he was now making another man he had never seen before his intimate confidant, and the following morning he was probably going to negotiate with the shrewdest man in Normandy. Coffe kept saying to him: "You're sure to get these people all mixed up."

Presiding Judge Donis d'Angel was announced. A lean man with a square face, beautiful black eyes, rather scanty white hair, white side-whiskers, and enormous gold buckles on his shoes, he would have been personable enough if he hadn't insisted on smiling all the time with a great show of frankness —certainly the most irritating form of hypocrisy! Lucien exercised all his self-restraint:

"I am in Normandy for a reason," he said to himself. "This man's father, I'd be willing to wager, was a simple peasant."

"Your Honor," Lucien began, "I should like first of all to make you fully acquainted with my instructions."

After that he spoke of his standing with the Minister, of his father's millions. Then, acting on the General's advice, he let the Judge talk without interruption for three interminable quarters of an hour.

"After all," he thought, "there is nothing more I can do this evening."

When the Honorable Donis d'Angel had quite exhausted himself, having insinuated in five or six different ways that the Cross was his rightful due, and that the government was really doing itself and not him an injustice by failing to confer on him an honor which it bestowed on young Surrogate Judges who had not worn the gown three years, Lucien spoke in his turn:

"The Minister knows all about you—your rights are recognized. What I require at this moment is that, at seven o'clock tomorrow morning, you introduce me to your uncle, Abbé Donis-Disjonval. I want M. Donis-Disjonval to arrange for me an interview with M. Le Canu."

At this strange intelligence, the Judge grew extremely pale.

"His cheeks are almost as white as his whiskers," thought Lucien.

"Moreover," Lucien continued, "I am instructed to recompense the friends of the government liberally for any trouble I may occasion them. But there is so little time. I'd give a hundred louis to see M. Le Canu an hour sooner."

"Being lavish with money like this," thought Lucien, "I shall give this man a high idea of the confidence the Minister deigns to repose in me."

We herewith skip twenty pages of the original narrative, and spare our reader all the sly waggishness of a provincial

Judge inspired by his desire for the Cross. We are afraid of causing the same sensations which M. Donis d'Angel's protestations of zeal and devotion produced in Lucien, whose moral disgust almost amounted to physical nausea.

"Unhappy France," he thought. "I never dreamed that Judges had come to this. The man hasn't even any qualms of conscience. What barefaced rascality! There is nothing he wouldn't stoop to."

An idea suddenly occurred to him:

"Lately, Your Honor, I believe that all the lawsuits in your court have been decided in favor of anarchists and republicans. . . ."

"Alas!" cried the magistrate, interrupting Lucien with tears in his eyes and in a woebegone tone. "I know it only too well. His Excellency, the Minister of Justice has written complaining to me on the subject."

Lucien could scarcely contain himself.

"Great God!" he thought, sighing like a man sunk in despair. "I'll hand in my resignation! I'll go to America! This final stage of my journey marks a milestone in my life! It is even more crucial than all the taunts and the mud of Blois."

Lucien suddenly became aware that, plunged as he had been in his own thoughts, for the last five minutes he had not heard a word of what Judge Donis was saying. His ears now became conscious of the sound of the worthy magistrate's words but at first failed to understand them.

With interminable details, none of which sounded entirely candid, His Honor was explaining all the efforts he had made to ensure the anarchists losing their suits. He complained bitterly of the courts. Juries, according to him, were detestable; the jury system was an English institution which it behooved us to get rid of as quickly as possible.

"Professional jealousy," thought Lucien.

"I have the faction of the cautious, sir," he complained, "the faction of the cautious. They will be the ruin of the government and of France. Judge Ducros, when I reproached him for voting in favor of a cousin of M. Léfèvre, the liberal journalist of Honfleur and an out-and-out anarchist, had the effrontery to reply: 'Your Honor, I was named Surrogate Judge by the Directory, to which I swore allegiance, Judge of the Lower Court by Bonaparte, to whom I swore allegiance, Presiding Judge of the same court by Louis XVIII in 1814, confirmed by Napoleon during the Hundred Days, called to a more advantageous position by Louis XVIII on his return from Ghent, named Judge of the Court of Appeals by Charles X, and I intend to die a Judge. Well, if the Republic comes into power this time, we won't be immovable. And who would be the first to seek revenge but these gentlemen of the press? The wisest thing to do is to pardon. Just look at what happened to the Peers who condemned Marshal Ney. In other words, being now fifty years old, if you can give me the assurance that you will last another ten years, I will vote with you.' How shocking, sir, what selfishness! And this is the kind of infamous reasoning I see written in all eyes."

When Lucien recovered from his amazement, he said with the coldest air he could summon:

"Sir, the equivocal conduct of the Court of Caen (to put it in the mildest terms) will be counterbalanced by that of Presiding Judge Donis if he procures for me the interview I have solicited with M. Le Canu, and if this transaction *remains buried in the deepest secrecy.*"

"It is a quarter-past-eleven," said the Judge, looking at his watch. "It is quite possible that my uncle has not yet returned from his game of whist. My carriage is downstairs. Would you care, sir, to risk a fruitless ride? The venerable Abbé Disjonval will be impressed by the untowardness of the hour and all the more ready because of it to come to our assistance. Besides, at this hour, the spies of the anarchist party will not see us; night marches are always the safest."

As Lucien followed the Honorable Donis d'Angel to his carriage, the latter kept on talking, harping on the danger of being too lavish with Crosses. According to him the government could accomplish wonders with Crosses.

"This man is at any rate obliging," thought Lucien, looking out at the city through the carriage window while the Judge talked on.

"The city seems to be extraordinarily lively for such an hour," he observed.

"It's these miserable elections! You have no idea, my dear sir, the harm they do. If the Chamber were elected only every ten years it would be far better—and more constitutional. . . ."

Suddenly he put his head out of the window and in a low voice ordered the coachman to stop.

"There is my uncle just coming home," he announced. At the same moment Lucien saw, walking slowly toward them, an old servant carrying a lighted candle in a round tin lantern protected by panes of glass a foot in diameter. With a remarkably firm step the venerable Abbé followed.

"He is just going into his house," the nephew explained. "He disapproves of my keeping a carriage so we'll wait here till he's in the house before getting out."

This they did. Then, after ringing for a long time at the entrance door, supplied with a wicket through which visitors were scrutinized, they were finally admitted to the presence of the Abbé.

"I come to you, my dear uncle, on the King's business, and in the King's service there is no untimely hour. Allow me to present, M. Leuwen, Master of Petitions."

The old gentleman looked stupefied, almost stupid. At the end of five or six minutes he invited them to be seated, and it was only after at least a quarter of an hour that he apparently began to understand what it was all about.

"Invariably," Lucien thought to himself, "the Judge says simply *the King*. I'd be willing to wager a hundred to one that the worthy old gentleman thinks he is speaking of Charles X."

After making his nephew repeat all over again what he had been explaining for the last twenty minutes, Abbé Donis-Disjonval finally said:

"Tomorrow morning I am officiating at Sainte-Gudule. At half-past-eight, after benediction, I shall go to the Rue des Carmes and try to see the estimable Le Canu. With all his occupations, so numerous and so important, besides his religious duties, I cannot promise you that he will be able to receive me as he used to twenty years ago, before he had such a multitude of affairs on his shoulders. We were younger then, things could be done more quickly, these elections were unheard of. Tonight the city seems to be in a state of insurrection—just like 1786. . . ."

Lucien noticed that Donis d'Angel was not nearly so talkative in the presence of his uncle. He seemed to know how to handle the old gentleman, who was at least seventy years old. The Abbé's little head was entirely concealed by an enormous nightcap.

When they had left Abbé Disjonval, his nephew said to Lucien:

"As soon as I have seen my uncle tomorrow morning at about eight-thirty, I shall have the honor of calling upon you. Or, perhaps it might be better, since you have the advantage of being unknown to our agents of disorder on the streets, and will be taken for a young elector—almost all the young are liberals—if you would be so good as to meet me at my cousin Maillet's at 9 Rue des Clercs."

Next day at eight-forty-five, Lucien, leaving the General in his carriage in the Cour Napoléon, hurried over to M. Maillet's. M. Donis d'Angel arrived almost at the same moment.

"Good news," he cried. "M. Le Canu grants your interview, either at this very instant or, if you prefer, at five o'clock this afternoon."

"I should rather go at once."

"M. Le Canu is taking his chocolate at Madame Blanchet's, 7 Rue des Carmes. Despite the fact that that is a rather deserted street, it is better, I assure you, that I should not accompany you. M. Le Canu is a great advocate of secrecy and does not care for what he calls useless publicity."

"I shall go to see him alone."

"7 Rue des Carmes, second floor rear. You must give two knocks on the door, followed by five. Two and five: Henri *V* is our *second* King, you see, Charles X being our first."

Lucien was completely dominated by his sense of duty. He felt like a General, a Commander-in-Chief who sees that he is going to lose the battle. Although thoroughly amused by all these details we have reported, he would not allow himself to be distracted by them.

"All this is too late," he said to himself as he looked for 7 Rue des Carmes. "We are going to lose the battle. Am I doing everything possible to be ready to take advantage of some lucky chance?"

There must have been someone listening at Madame Blanchet's door, for he had hardly knocked twice and then five times, when he heard whispering within.

After a short pause, the door was opened. Lucien was received in a dark room, as dismal as a prison warden's office, with its white-painted woodwork and smoky window panes, by a sickly looking man with a sallow face and drawn features. This was the Abbé Le Canu. The Abbé motioned with his hand to a high-backed chair. In place of a mirror over the mantelpiece hung a large black crucifix.

"What do you wish to see me about, sir?"

"Louis-Philippe, the King my master, has sent me here to Caen to prevent the election of M. Mairobert. M. Mairobert's election is, however, almost certain, inasmuch as he has four hundred and ten indubitable votes out of a probable total of nine hundred. The King, my master, commands three hundred and ten. If you care to have one of your friends elected, I am here to offer you our votes. Add to these the hundred and sixty of your country gentry, and you will have a man of your party in the Chamber. I make only one stipulation: he must be an elector, and a native of Caen."

"Ah! So you are afraid of M. Berryer!"

"I am afraid of nothing but the triumph of the opposition, which, by the way, would reduce the episcopal sees to the number fixed by the Concordat of 1802," replied Lucien, while thinking to himself:

"The man's tone is that of an old country Prosecutor." And he relaxed his cautious vigilance considerably. Thanks to the works of M. de Chateaubriand and the lofty idea generally entertained of the Jesuits, Lucien had conjured up in his still youthful imagination a wily dissembler, as artful as Cardinal Mazarin, combined with the aristocratic manners of M. de Narbonne, whom he had once glimpsed as a boy. The coarseness of M. Le Canu's manner as well as his tone of voice quickly gave Lucien his cue. "I am a young man who is bargaining for a piece of land worth a hundred thousand francs that a wily old pettifogger prefers not to sell me because he has been promised a hundred louis by a neighbor to reserve it for him."

"May I venture, sir, to ask for your credentials?"

"Here they are," replied Lucien, not hesitating to hand Le Canu the letter of the Minister of the Interior addressed to the Prefect. It is true he could have wished that certain sentences had not been there, but there was no time to lose.

"If only the Prefect had been willing to handle this transaction himself," thought Lucien, "we could have avoided letting Le Canu see the Minister's letter. But, even if his vanity hadn't been piqued, that captious little perfumed Prefect would never have agreed to any measure which he had not himself originated."

The look of vulgar anger, trying to mask itself as contemptuous disdain, with which the Abbé read the Minister's letter to the Prefect, succeeded in completely restoring Lucien's sense of reality and dispelling forever those lofty notions which M. de Chateaubriand's elegant periods had imposed on the world. The exaggerated wrath displayed by the leader of the church party at certain of the Minister's expressions, made Lucien smile.

"The man is trying to impress me by his indignation. I must not lose my temper and spoil everything. Let's see if, despite my youth, I can succeed in my role."

Lucien took a letter out of his pocket and began reading it attentively. From his expression one might have thought he was before a court martial. Abbé Le Canu stole a glance at him out of the corner of his eye. Seeing that he was not being observed, the Abbé's perusal of the ministerial letter became less affected. He re-read it carefully with the absorbed expression of a surly business man.

"Your powers are very extensive, sir. They are such as to give anyone a high idea of the missions with which, young as you are, you have been entrusted. May I venture to ask if you were already in government service under our legitimate Kings—before the fatal . . ."

"Permit me to interrupt you, sir. I should be loath to be obliged to use not very agreeable epithets in speaking of the adherents of your cause. As far as I am concerned, sir, it is my habit to respect any opinion professed by an honest man, and for that reason I am disposed to honor yours. Let me point out, sir, that I shall make no attempt, directly or indirectly, to try to influence or alter in any way your point of view on any subject. Such an attempt would ill befit my age, as well as my personal respect for you. But it is my duty to request you to forget my age and all the respectful attention that, in any other circumstances, I should be prepared to give to your wise counsels. I come to you, sir, simply to propose a measure that seems to me advantageous both to my master and to yours. You have very few Deputies in the Chamber; one more spokesman is something scarcely to be scorned by your side. As for ours, we are afraid of the extreme measures M. Mairobert is likely to propose—among others, that of allowing the faithful to pay the doctor of their souls as they pay the doctor of their bodies. We are sure of defeating the measure at this session. However, if it won an imposing minority vote, we should perhaps find ourselves obliged to permit the reduction of the number of episcopal sees by tacit agreement, to prevent the Chamber from doing it by law."

The ensuing arguments were endless, as Lucien had expected.

"My age is against me," he thought. "I am like a cavalry General who in a lost battle, forgetting his own interests, tries the expedient of dismounting his men and having them fight on as infantry. If he fails, all the imbeciles will laugh at him, especially the cavalry Generals. But if he is a man of spirit, his consciousness of having, for the sake of victory, had the courage to do something regarded as impossible, will be sufficient consolation."

Seven times in succession (Lucien counted them) Abbé Le Canu tried either to avoid answering Lucien or to outwit his young antagonist.

"Before giving me his answer, he evidently wants to put me to the test."

Seven times Lucien succeeded in bringing Abbé Le Canu

back to the question in hand, but always in the most courteous terms, that implied his great respect for the Abbé's venerable age, which he seemed to hold entirely distinct from the Abbé's political views and the pretensions of his party. Once Lucien let his adversary gain a slight advantage. But he quickly repaired his slip without losing his equanimity.

"I must be just as much on my guard as in a duel with swords."

After a discussion of fifty minutes, Abbé Le Canu finally assumed an extremely haughty, insolent air.

"My man is about to reach a conclusion," Lucien decided. He was right.

"It is too late," said the Abbé.

But instead of breaking off the conference, he set about trying to convert Lucien.

"Now I am on the defensive," thought Lucien, feeling perfectly at ease. "This is the moment to introduce the idea of money and personal benefits."

Lucien did not defend his cause too obstinately. He spoke casually of his father's millions, and had the satisfaction of noticing that it was the one and only thing which made the least impression on the Abbé.

"You are young, my son—permit me the appellation which carries with it the expression of much esteem. Consider your future. You are, I should judge, not more than twenty-four."

"I am almost twenty-five."

"Well then, my son, without wishing to speak ill of the banner under which you are fighting, and limiting myself to what is absolutely essential for the expression of my thought (charged, moreover, with the greatest good will toward your interests in this world and the next), let me ask you this question: do you think that banner will still be floating, as it is today, fourteen years hence? You will then have reached the age of forty, that age of maturity which a wise man keeps ever before his mind's eye as the crucial point in every man's career. For it is at that age, and rarely before, that a man begins to play an important part in the great affairs of the world.

"Until that age the ordinary run of men think only of making money. You are above such considerations. Observe that I do not speak of your soul's interests—so far above all mundane concerns. If you should deign to come to see an old man again, my door will always be open to you. I should lay everything aside to bring back to the fold a young man of your high repute in the world, and who, while still so young, has developed such mature gifts. For the less I share your illusions on the subject of a King raised to power by the revolution, the more I am in a position to appreciate the talent you have shown in trying to bring about a truly singular co-operation: David allied to the Amalekite! I beg you sometimes to stop and ask yourself the question: 'Who is going to be in power in France when I am forty?' Religion does not forbid a legitimate ambition."

The interview ended in a kind of sermon, but Lucien had been practically invited to come to see the Abbé again.

He was not discouraged.

CHAPTER EIGHTEEN

LUCIEN went to General Fari's to give him an account of his interview. Reports kept coming in from all sides and prevented the General from leaving his hotel. Lucien's idea of sending a telegraphic dispatch was thoroughly approved by General Fari, and afterwards by Coffe, who merely remarked:

"You are trying bloodletting on a man who is going to die

in two hours anyway. And all the fools can then say that you killed him."

Going to the telegraph office, Lucien sent the following message:

The nomination of M. Mairobert is considered certain. Would you care to spend a hundred thousand francs to have a legitimist elected rather than M. Mairobert? In that case, send the Receiver General a dispatch authorizing him to put a hundred thousand francs at the disposal of General Fari and myself. . . . The election starts in nineteen hours.

After leaving the telegraph office, Lucien decided to return to the Abbé Disjonval's. The difficulty was to find the house again. He succeeded in losing himself in Caen's maze of streets, but, finally, going into a church he found a sort of beadle to whom he gave five francs to conduct him to the Abbé's house. Leaving the church, the man led him through two or three different passageways separating several blocks of houses, and in four minutes Lucien found himself face to face with the Abbé Disjonval.

The Abbé had just finished an early luncheon, and a bottle of white wine still stood on the table. The man, whose face had been so completely devoid of expression yesterday, was now transformed.

After an introductory preamble of not more than ten minutes, Lucien was able, without appearing too indecent, to make the Abbé Disjonval understand that he was prepared to give a hundred thousand francs to keep M. Mairobert from being elected. The idea was not rejected too energetically. After a few moments, the Abbé laughingly asked Lucien:

"Have you those hundred thousand francs about you, by chance?"

"No," Lucien rejoined, "but a telegraphic dispatch which may arrive this evening, and which will certainly arrive before noon tomorrow, will give me credit to the amount of a hundred thousand francs on the Receiver General who will pay me the money in bank notes."

"Bank notes are looked upon with suspicion here."

This remark opened Lucien's eyes.

"Great God! Can I possibly succeed?" he asked himself.

"Would a bill of exchange, accepted by the first merchants of the city, be agreeable? Or, if you prefer, I can get gold or écus, as I choose."

Lucien intentionally prolonged this enumeration during which he saw his host's expression undergo an instant transformation. In spite of the prelate's recent meal, his face turned pale.

"Ah!" thought Lucien. "If only I had forty-eight hours ahead of me, the election would be mine."

Lucien made full use of his advantage and, to his unbounded satisfaction, the Abbé himself voiced, in a rather roundabout way to be sure, the thought Lucien had been mulling over for the last three-quarters of an hour: "Without the credit of a hundred thousand francs which the telegraph is to bring you, your negotiations can advance no further."

"It is to be hoped," said the Abbé Disjonval, "that the Abbé Le Canu and his friends have considered what an advantage it will be to have another spokesman in the Chamber, especially if the government has the weakness to allow the fatal discussion on a reduction of episcopal sees to be brought up once more. . . . Till tomorrow then at seven o'clock or, by two o'clock at the latest if nothing comes before. . . . The election of the President of the Electoral College begins at nine o'clock, the balloting will be closed at three."

"It is essential that your friends should not vote until after I have the honor of seeing you at two o'clock."

"That is no small thing you ask of me. We'll have to collect them in one room and lock them up."

223

Coffe was waiting for Lucien on the street. They hurried back to the inn to write a letter to the Minister.

"I fully realize the risks I run in mixing so actively in a hopeless affair. If the Minister wished to put all the blame on me, nothing would be simpler; but it is more than I can bear to see a battle being lost before my very eyes without bringing out my troops. The resources at my disposal are ridiculously inadequate, and rendered ineffectual by the stranglehold of time. At eight-forty-five I saw the cousin of Judge Donis; at nine o'clock I had an interview with the Abbé Le Canu, leader of the legitimist party, and was with him until eleven o'clock. At eleven-fifteen I went to see the Abbé Donis again, and at noon I was at General Fari's. At half-past-twelve I sent you my second telegraphic dispatch. Now, at one o'clock I am writing to you. At two o'clock, just to oil the wheels, I shall pay a call on Monseigneur, the Bishop. It is now too late for me to receive a reply to this letter. By the time Your Excellency reads it, all will be over. The chances are ten to one that M. Mairobert will be elected. But, up to the last moment, I shall offer my hundred thousand francs—provided you have decided that M. Mairobert's absence from the Chamber is worth that much. I shall regard it as a very happy chance if your telegraphic dispatch, in reply to my second dispatch, arrives before two o'clock tomorrow, the 17th. The election of the chairman of the Electoral College will begin at nine o'clock. The Abbé Disjonval seems disposed to delay the vote of his friends until two o'clock. The ballot will not, I hope, be closed until four."

Lucien hurried off to pay his diplomatic call on the Bishop. He was received with a haughtiness, contempt and arrogance that amused him. "We will lay that at the foot of the cross," he said, laughing, as he travestied to himself the prelate's favorite remark.

He carefully avoided all mention of business. "This is just a drop of oil in the machinery."

At half-past-one, he went to lunch at the General's, with whom he then continued the visits which had been decided upon the day before. At five o'clock he was completely exhausted. It had been the busiest day of his life. There still remained the most onerous duty of all, the Prefect's dinner. That disgruntled functionary was not likely to be very civil. Lucien had been informed by young Captain Ménière that the Prefect had set his two best spies to dog Lucien's footsteps.

Lucien felt a sense of profound satisfaction. He knew he had given all that was in him to this cause, whose justice, if the truth were told, seemed somewhat dubious. This little flaw in his contentment was offset by the consciousness of having had the courage recklessly to jeopardize the consideration he was beginning to enjoy at the Ministry of the Interior. More than once Coffe had said to him—or words to this effect:

"In the eyes of our old chief clerks and department heads, your conduct, even if crowned by the defeat of M. Mairobert, will be regarded merely as a rather splendid blunder. Have you forgotten what you once called them? As they sat in their mahogany armchairs during the discussion on the subject of foundlings, you said they were nothing but 'armchairs incarnate,' and they will certainly seize this opportunity to take their revenge."

"What should I have done then?"

"Nothing! Except to have composed three or four letters of six pages each. That is what, in ministerial departments, is called having administrative ability. They will always look upon you as mad, because of the way you risked your career. And then, to ask a hundred thousand francs for bribery at your age! They will spread the report that you put at least a third of it into your own pocket."

"That," replied Lucien, "was my first thought. A second has

just occurred to me: When you work in the interest of Ministers, it is not the adversary you have to fear but the men you are working for. That is how things were done at Constantinople in the Byzantine Empire. But even if I had done nothing, and written all those fine letters, I should still have the mud of Blois on my conscience. And you have been a witness of my weakness."

"A good reason for your hating me and having me removed from the Ministry," rejoined Coffe. "I have thought of that."

"On the contrary, it is a great comfort to me now to be able to tell you everything, and I beg you not to spare me."

"I shall take you at your word. That little carping Prefect must be bursting with rage against you. After all, you have been exercising his functions for the last two days while he writes hundreds of letters and, of course, does nothing. From all this we may safely conclude that he will be praised in Paris and you will be blamed. But tonight, no matter what he does, don't lose your temper. If we were living in the Middle Ages I should be afraid of poison for you. I can see that this little sophist suffers from the same sort of fury as an author whose play has been hissed."

The carriage stopped in front of the Prefecture. There were eight or ten gendarmes stationed outside on the first and second landings of the broad flight of stairs.

"In the Middle Ages these people would have been ready to assassinate you."

The gendarmes rose as Lucien passed.

"Ah, so your mission is known—the gendarmes are polite! Just think of de Séranville's fury."

That functionary was extremely pale and received the two gentlemen with constrained politeness which was certainly not made more cordial by the eager reception accorded Lucien by everyone else present.

The dinner was stiff and dismal. All these ministerial supporters foresaw defeat on the following day. Each one was saying to himself: "The Prefect will be removed or sent elsewhere. I shall say that he deserves all the blame. This young whippersnapper is the son of the Minister's banker, and already a Master of Petitions. He may well be a successor in embryo."

Lucien ate ravenously; he was very gay.

"And I," said M. de Séranville to himself, "I send my plate away untouched, I can't swallow a mouthful."

As both Lucien and Coffe talked a great deal, little by little the conversation of the entire company, the District Collector of Direct Taxes, the Controller of Public Lands, and other high officials, was entirely addressed to the newcomers.

"And I am ignored," thought the Prefect. "Already I am a stranger in my own house, my removal is certain, and, in addition, I am forced to do the honors of the Prefecture for my successor—a thing that has certainly never happened before."

Toward the middle of the second course, Coffe, whom nothing escaped, noticed that the Prefect kept wiping his forehead.

Suddenly a great commotion was heard outside. The courier had just arrived from Paris. The man burst noisily into the room, and the District Collector of Indirect Taxes, who was sitting near the door, said to him:

"That is Monsieur le Préfet over there."

"I don't want Prefect de Séranville," the courier said with a coarsely insulting emphasis. "I want M. Leuwen, Master of Petitions."

"What humiliation!" thought M. de Séranville. "I am no longer Prefect." And he fell back on his chair. Then leaning forward over the table he buried his head in his arms.

"M. de Séranville has fainted," cried the Secretary General glancing apologetically at Lucien, as though to ask his pardon for this gesture of humanity which called attention to the

Prefect. That functionary had, in truth, fainted. They carried him over to a window which had been thrown open.

During this time, Lucien was surprised to notice the total lack of interest in the dispatch the courier had brought. It was a long letter from the Minister all about Lucien's conduct at Blois. M. de Vaize had added, in his own hand, that the authors of the riot would be found and punished, that he had read Lucien's letter aloud to the King and the Council, and that it had been highly approved.

"But not a word of the present election," thought Lucien. "It was hardly worthwhile to send a courier just for that."

He went over to the window where they were engaged in rubbing the Prefect's forehead with eau de Cologne, and endlessly repeating: "It's the fatigue of the elections." Lucien made some suitable remark and then asked permission to retire with M. Coffe for a moment.

"Think of sending a courier for a letter like that," Lucien said, handing the Minister's letter to Coffe.

He now opened a letter from his mother brought by the same courier. As he read it his expression changed. He became serious: Madame Leuwen expressed alarm for her son's life. "And for *such a filthy cause,*" she added. "Drop everything and come home. . . . I am alone. Your father has taken a notion to be ambitious, and has gone to the Department of Aveyron, two hundred leagues from Paris, to get himself elected Deputy."

Lucien acquainted Coffe with the news.

"It was your mother's letter that made them send a courier. Madame Leuwen must have insisted on her letter reaching you quickly. On the whole, there is nothing in it to change your plans. At this moment, it seems to me, your place is in there with that little Jesuit who is dying of suppressed hate. And I am now about to finish him off with my air of importance!"

Coffe was indeed perfection as he re-entered the dining

room. He had taken eight or ten election reports out of his pocket and stuck them in the dispatch which he carried as though it were the *holy sacrament*. M. de Séranville had regained consciousness, he had vomited, and now looked up at Lucien and Coffe in his anguish with a moribund air. The state of this spiteful little man touched Lucien; he saw in him simply a suffering human being.

"We must relieve him of our presence," Lucien thought. And after a few courteous words he and Coffe retired.

The courier ran down the stairs after them to ask for instructions.

Coffe answered him with admirable gravity:

"The Honorable Master of Petitions will send you back tomorrow with dispatches."

The next day, the 17th, was the day of the election.

At seven o'clock in the morning of this great day, Lucien was already at the Abbé Disjonval's. He was struck by the change in the venerable old gentleman's manner. The Abbé was now all eagerness; Lucien's most insignificant remark was not allowed to pass unanswered.

"Those hundred thousand francs are having their effect," Lucien said to himself.

Several times, however, the Abbé made it quite clear, but with a delicacy and courtesy which astonished Lucien, that anything he might say, in the absence of the principal condition, was contingent on the future.

"Precisely," said Lucien. "That is how I understand it. But, even if today, and in good time, the telegraph does not bring me a credit of a hundred thousand francs, I shall in any case have had the privilege of your acquaintance; I shall have had an interview with the Abbé Le Canu which has left a deep impression on my mind; and my esteem will have been redoubled for the men who believe that the welfare of our dear country lies along a different road from the one which to me seems the safest to follow, and . . ."

But we shall spare our reader all the fine phrases inspired by the necessity of persuading the Abbé and his friends to be patient until the arrival of the diplomatic dispatch. The unaccustomed turmoil in the street which was occasioned by the great event of the day, and which reached Lucien even at the rear of the house where the Abbé's apartment was situated, seemed to strike an answering chord in his own breast. What would he not have given for the election to be put off for another day!

At nine o'clock he returned to his inn, where Coffe had prepared two enormous narrative and explanatory letters.

"What a strange style!" remarked Lucien as he signed them.

"Pompous and vapid, and never, above all, simple and straightforward—that is what the ministerial departments like."

The courier was now sent for.

"Sir," said the courier, "would you be so good as to permit me to take charge of the Prefect's—that is to say, M. de Séranville's—dispatches. I won't try to hide from you, sir, that he has promised me quite a nice little gift if I would take his letters. But after all, you're the one that's sending me. . . . I know what's proper."

"You may go to the Prefect on my behalf, and ask him for his letters and packets—wait half an hour if necessary. The Prefect is the first representative of the government in the Department. . . ."

"Catch me telling the Prefect he sent me," the courier said to himself. "What about my tip if I did? They say he's an old skinflint."

CHAPTER NINETEEN

GENERAL FARI, through his young aide-de-camp, had rented a second floor apartment opposite the Hall of the Ursulines where the election was to take place. There, with Lucien, he took up his headquarters at ten o'clock in the morning. News was brought to them at fifteen minute intervals by the General's agents. Even some of the Prefect's agents, having learned of the dispatches of the day before, and seeing in Lucien their future Prefect, sent him cards marked with red pencil every quarter of an hour. The information on these cards turned out to be exact.

The electoral proceedings followed the usual course. The chairman by seniority was a man devoted to the Prefect. The latter had seen to it that the heavy berlin of M. Marconnes, who was older, was held up at the city gates so that it did not arrive until eleven o'clock. Thirty ministerial supporters who had breakfasted at the Prefecture were hooted as they entered the election hall.

A little printed broadside had been plentifully distributed among the electors. It read:

Honest people of all parties who desire the welfare of the country in which you were born, rid yourselves of the Prefect, M. de Séranville. If M. Mairobert is elected Deputy, M. de Séranville will be removed or sent elsewhere. What difference does it make who is elected Deputy so long as we get rid of a mean, mischief-making, lying Prefect? Is there one of you to whom he has not broken his word?

Toward noon, the election of the permanent chairman was going badly. All the electors from the district of —— arrived early and voted for M. Mairobert.

"It is to be feared," observed the General, "that if Mairobert is made chairman, fifteen or twenty of our ministerial supporters, the timorous ones, and ten or fifteen imbecile country electors, seeing him in the most conspicuous position, will hardly dare put any other name on their ballots."

Every fifteen minutes Lucien sent Coffe to observe the telegraph. He was on tenterhooks waiting for the reply to his second dispatch.

"The Prefect is perfectly capable of delaying the reply," said the General. "It would be just like him to have sent one of his clerks to the telegraph station four leagues from here on the other side of the hill, to stop everything. It is by such feats he imagines he will become another Cardinal Mazarin—for he is well up on the history of France, our little Prefect."

And the worthy General hoped by this remark to show that he too was up on history! Young Captain Ménière offered to get on his horse and ride posthaste to the top of the hill from which the second telegraph station could be observed. But Coffe, borrowing the Captain's horse, galloped off in his stead.

There were at least a thousand people gathered in front of the Hall of the Ursulines. Wishing to get an idea of the tenor of popular opinion, Lucien went down to the square to listen to what people were saying. He was recognized. With true mob courage the crowd became insolent:

"Look! Look! That's the little fop of a Police Commissioner they've sent down from Paris to spy on the Prefect!"

Lucien was now almost impervious to such remarks.

Two o'clock struck . . . half-past-two. The telegraph did not budge.

Lucien was dying with impatience. He went to see the Abbé Disjonval who, Lucien thought, showed marked signs of resentment.

"I could not put off my friends' voting any longer," said the Abbé. Yet Lucien felt sure that he had, in reality, put them off.

"This man thinks I have been playing with him, while he has dealt squarely with me. I'd be willing to swear he has kept his not very numerous following from voting."

As Lucien was trying to prove in the warmest terms that he had had no intention of deceiving the Abbé, Coffe arrived quite out of breath.

"The telegraph is moving!"

"Be so kind as to wait for me here a few moments longer, sir," said Lucien, addressing the Abbé Disjonval. "I'll run over to the telegraph office and be with you again in a quarter of an hour."

Twenty minutes later Lucien came rushing back.

"Here is the dispatch," he said, handing it to the Abbé:

The Minister of Finance to the Receiver General:
Remit one hundred thousand francs to General Fari and M. Leuwen.

"The telegraph is still moving," Lucien added.

The Abbé Disjonval appeared satisfied.

"I shall go at once and see what I can do about the election of the chairman. We shall put up M. de Cremieux. After that I shall make all haste to see M. Le Canu, and I advise you to go to him without delay."

The door of the Abbé Le Canu's apartment was open. There was a crowd of people waiting in the anteroom as Lucien and Coffe hurried through.

"This, sir," said Lucien, "is the dispatch."

After reading it, the Abbé glanced at the clock.

"It is ten minutes past three. . . . I trust that you have no objection to M. de Cremieux: fifty-five years of age, an income of twenty thousand francs, subscribes to the *Débats,* did not emigrate."

"General Fari and I approve M. de Cremieux. If he is elected instead of M. Mairobert, the General and I will remit to you one hundred thousand francs. But while awaiting the outcome, to whom do you wish the hundred thousand francs to be entrusted?"

"Calumny, sir, is ever on the alert. It is already a great deal that four persons, no matter how honorable, know a secret which slander might so readily pervert to its own advantage. There is this gentleman," and the Abbé indicated Coffe, "yourself, the Abbé Disjonval, and myself. Why must this detail be divulged to General Fari, worthy though he be of every regard?"

Lucien was charmed by these words which were *ad rem.*

"Sir," he replied, "I am too young to take upon myself the sole responsibility of such a considerable secret expense. . . ."

Lucien finally persuaded M. Le Canu to consent to the General's intervention.

"But," said the Abbé, "I formally insist, I even make it a condition *sine qua non,* that the Prefect be entirely left out of the affair."

"A nice recompense," thought Lucien, "for all the poor man's assiduous attendance at Mass."

It was agreed at last that the sum of a hundred thousand francs should be deposited in a little coffer to which General Fari and a friend of M. Le Canu, M. Ledoyen, should each have a key.

On his return to their headquarters opposite the election hall, Lucien found General Fari looking unusually flushed. The moment was approaching when the General had decided to cast his vote and, as he confessed, he dreaded the thought of being hissed. In spite of this private apprehension, he was much pleased to learn of the *ad rem* character the Abbé Le Canu's replies had acquired.

Lucien received a note from the Abbé Disjonval asking him to send Coffe to him. When Coffe returned half an hour later, Lucien sent for the General, and Coffe gave them his report.

"I saw, actually saw with my own eyes, fifteen men mounted on horseback ready to scour the country to make sure that a hundred and fifty legitimist electors should arrive this evening or tomorrow morning. The Abbé Disjonval is like a young man—nobody would think he was more than forty. Three times, at least, he said to me: 'If only we had time to have four articles in the *Gazette de France!*' I really believe they are going about it in good earnest."

The director of the telegraph office sent a second telegraphic dispatch to headquarters, addressed to Lucien personally:

"I approve your projects. Distribute a hundred thousand francs. Any legitimist, no matter whom, even Berryer or Fitz-James, rather than Hampden."

"I don't understand," said the General. "Who is Hampden?"

"Hampden stands for Mairobert. It is the name agreed on with the Minister."

"But I must be off now," cried the General in a state of great agitation. "It is time," and taking up the tunic of his uniform he left their post of observation to cast his vote across the street. The crowd made way for him as he walked the dozen or more steps to the election hall. He entered, and as he crossed the hall to the table, all the Mairobert electors broke into applause.

"He's not a contemptible rogue like the Prefect," could be heard on all sides. "He has nothing but his pay to live on, and he has a family to support."

Lucien now sent the following dispatch—his third:

Caen, four o'clock.
Legitimist leaders seem to be acting in good faith. Military observers stationed at the gates have seen nineteen or twenty agents leaving to round up a hundred and sixty legitimist electors. If eighty or a hundred arrive before three o'clock the 18th, Hampden will

not be elected. At this moment, Hampden has a majority for the chairmanship. Ballots will be counted at five o'clock.

The results of the count were as follows:

Electors present	873
Majority	437
M. Mairobert	451
M. Gonin, the Prefect's candidate	389
M. de Cremieux (candidate of M. Le Canu after accepting the hundred thousand francs)	19
Scattered votes	14

Those nineteen votes for M. de Cremieux pleased Lucien and the General immensely. It was part proof that M. Le Canu was not deceiving them.

At six o'clock securities above reproach to the amount of a hundred thousand francs were remitted by the Receiver General himself into the hands of General Fari and Lucien, who gave him a receipt.

M. Ledoyen arrived. A very wealthy landowner, he was universally respected. The ceremony of the coffer was accomplished, word of honor exchanged that the coffer and its contents would be handed over to M. Ledoyen should any candidate other than M. Mairobert be elected, and to General Fari if M. Mairobert were victorious.

When M. Ledoyen left them, dinner was served.

"The important thing now is the Prefect," said the General in an unusually gay mood. "Let's muster our courage and open the attack! There will undoubtedly be 900 voters tomorrow. Today M. Gonin had 389, M. de Cremieux 19, which makes a total of 408. So we have 408 votes out of 873. Supposing that 27 votes come in tomorrow morning, giving 17 to Mairobert and 10 to us: Cremieux, 418; Mairobert, 468. Then M. Le Canu's 51 votes will give M. de Cremieux the advantage."

These figures were twisted and turned in a hundred different ways by the General, Lucien, Coffe and the General's aide-de-camp, assembled around the table.

"Let's call in our two best agents," the General suggested.

Those gentlemen presented themselves and, after a fairly long discussion, arrived independently at the conclusion that sixty legitimist votes would settle the matter.

"And now," cried the General, "on to the Prefecture!"

"If you don't find my request indiscreet, General, may I ask you to do the talking? The poor man can't endure me."

"Isn't that contrary to our agreement? My role was to be an entirely secondary one. However, if you like, I will, as they say in England, *open the debate*."

General Fari was always trying to show that he was a highly lettered man. But, as a matter of fact, he was much better than that: he was blessed with rare common sense and natural goodness.

Hardly had the General explained to the Prefect that they had come to ask him to turn over the votes he had had at his disposal yesterday for the election of the chairman to M. de Cremieux who, in turn, would do everything in his power to assemble sixty legitimist votes—perhaps even eighty—than the Prefect interrupted him:

"I might have expected this! After all those telegraphic dispatches. However, gentlemen, there is one vote you won't get. I have not yet been removed, and M. Leuwen is not yet the Prefect of Caen."

All that rage could put into the mouth of a conniving little sophist was now discharged upon the General and Lucien. The scene lasted five hours. Only toward the very end did the General begin to lose patience. Never wavering in his refusal, M. de Séranville kept changing his reasons for refusing.

"But looking at it, sir," said the General, "from a purely selfish point of view! Your election is patently lost. It is to your advantage to let it die in M. Leuwen's hands. He then, like the doctors who are called in too late, will get all the blame for the death of the patient."

"He will get what he likes or what he can, but, until my removal, he will not get the Prefecture of Caen."

At this reply of M. de Séranville's, Lucien had to restrain the General.

"A man who desired to betray his government," cried the General, "could do no more than you are doing! And that, sir, is what I shall write to the Ministers. Good-night, sir."

Leaving the Prefecture at half an hour after midnight, Lucien said to the General:

"I shall write M. Le Canu of this charming result."

"If you take my advice you will wait and see what these doubtful allies are going to do. Let's do nothing until tomorrow morning after your telegraphic dispatch. Besides, that confounded little Prefect might change his mind."

Five o'clock the next morning found Lucien waiting for daylight in the telegraph office. The moment it was light enough to see clearly, the following dispatch, the fourth, was sent:

Last night the Prefect refused to give his 389 votes to M. de Cremieux. The 70 or 80 votes, obtained by General Fari and M. Leuwen from the legitimists, are now useless, and M. Hampden will be elected.

After thinking it over, Lucien, instead of writing, went himself to see MM. Disjonval and Le Canu. He explained the new disaster with such simplicity and evident sincerity that these gentlemen, who knew the Prefect's character, were in the end convinced that Lucien had not been setting a trap for them.

"The mind of this little Prefect of the *Glorious Days*," said M. Le Canu, "is like the horns of the billy goats where I come from: black, hard and twisted."

Poor Lucien was so obsessed by his determination not to pass for a rogue that he begged M. Disjonval to accept his purse as reimbursement for the expense of messengers and other things, which the extraordinary convocation of legitimist electors must have entailed. M. Disjonval refused, but before leaving the city, through the intermediary of the Abbé's nephew, Judge Donis d'Angel, Lucien sent him five hundred francs.

At ten o'clock on the morning of the election five letters arrived from Paris containing the startling information that an indictment had been signed against M. Mairobert as instigator of the great republican insurrectional movement that was being talked about everywhere at that time. Instantly twelve of the wealthiest merchants of Caen declared that they would not vote for Mairobert.

"This is something really worthy of the Prefect," General Fari remarked to Lucien. They were once more in their observation post opposite the Hall of the Ursulines. "Funny if that little sophist succeeded after all. In that case," the General added with all the gay and generous kindliness of a man of feeling, "if the Minister has the least resentment toward you, and needs a scapegoat, you will certainly be given that charming role."

"I would do the same thing all over again a thousand times. Although the battle seemed lost, I engaged my regiment!"

"What a good fellow you are!" cried the General, but quickly added, "If you will permit me so familiar an expression." He was afraid of having failed in the amenities which for him were like a foreign language learned late in life. Lucien pressed his hand and let his heart speak for him.

At eleven o'clock it was estimated that there were 948 electors present.

Judge Donis, arriving at the same moment as the General's messenger with the above information, attempted to force his way into their office against orders, but without success.

"We might receive him for a moment," Lucien proposed.

"Ah, no! It could be used as a basis for calumny on the part of the Prefect, of M. Le Canu, or of those poor republicans who are even madder than they are malicious. Go out and see the worthy Judge, but don't let yourself be betrayed by your natural honesty."

Returning, Lucien explained:

"He just came to let us know that, in spite of the counter-orders of this morning, there are forty-nine legitimists in the Hall of the Ursulines, as well as eleven of the Prefect's supporters who have been won over to M. de Cremieux."

The election pursued a peaceful course. The figures were less promising than the day before. The Prefect's false news of the indictment against M. Mairobert had put that gentleman, who had never been known to lose his temper, into a towering rage, as well as all his followers. Two or three times there was danger of an outburst. They wanted to send three agents to Paris at once to question the five persons who had sent down the false news of the indictment. But finally a brother-in-law of M. Mairobert, jumping upon a wagon stationed a hundred feet from the hall, addressed the excited crowd:

"Let us put off our vengeance for forty-eight hours after the election, otherwise it will simply be foiled by the majority which is sold to the Chamber of Deputies."

Soon twenty thousand copies of this brief address were printed. Someone had even had the idea of setting up the press right on the square next to the election hall. The Prefect's police were afraid to go near the press, or to do anything to prevent the distribution of the circular. All this made a great impression on the indignant throngs, and did much to quiet them.

Lucien wandered boldly about among the crowds and was not insulted that day. He noticed that this mob was fully conscious of its power. Unless fired on from a distance, no display of force was likely to daunt it.

"This is truly the rule of the People," he thought to himself.

From time to time he would return to headquarters. In the opinion of Captain Ménière no one would win a majority that day.

At four o'clock the Prefect received a dispatch from Paris ordering him to turn over his votes to the legitimist candidate designated by General Fari and Lucien. The Prefect failed to have Lucien or the General informed of this order. At four-fifteen Lucien received a similar dispatch. Whereupon Coffe recited the line from *Polyeucte:*

A shade less good fortune but sooner encountered . . .

The General was delighted with this quotation and asked Coffe to repeat it.

At that moment they were deafened by a general earsplitting cheer.

"Is it joy or revolt?" cried the General, hurrying over to the window.

"It is joy," he announced with a sigh. "We are f . . . ed."

It was true. At that moment a messenger, his coat torn from his struggles to break through the crowds, arrived with the election returns.

Electors present	948
Majority	475
M. Mairobert	475
M. Gonin, the Prefect's candidate	401
M. de Cremieux	61
M. Sauvage, republican (whose ambition was to change French character by means of Draconian laws)	9
Scattered votes	2

That evening the whole city was illuminated.

"But which are the windows of the Prefect's 401 supporters?" Lucien asked Coffe.

The answer was a terrific noise of broken glass. They were smashing the windows of Judge Donis d'Angel.

The next day Lucien woke at eleven o'clock and went for a solitary walk through the city. A singular question had taken possession of his thoughts:

"What would Madame de Chasteller say if I were to tell her of my conduct?"

He spent at least an hour trying to find the answer to this question, and a very sweet hour it was indeed.

"Why shouldn't I write to her?" he finally asked himself. And this second question preoccupied him for a week.

As he was nearing Paris, he happened to think of the street on which Madame Grandet lived, and then of her. He burst out laughing.

"What's the matter?" asked Coffe.

"Nothing. Only I had quite forgotten the name of a lovely lady I am supposed to be madly in love with."

"I assumed you were thinking of the welcome you are about to receive from the Minister."

"The devil with him. . . . He will receive me coldly, will ask for a statement of my disbursements, and will find that it all came very high."

"It depends on the report the Minister's spies have given him of your mission. Your conduct has been wildly imprudent. You have indulged without restraint in that folly of early youth which is called zeal."

CHAPTER TWENTY

LUCIEN'S CONJECTURES proved to be fairly accurate. M. de Vaize received him with his customary politeness, but failed to ask him a single question about the elections, or to congratulate him on his trip; he treated him exactly as though he had seen him the day before.

"He has better manners than are natural to him. Since he became Minister he mixes in good company at the Château."

But after this flash of intelligence, Lucien became once more afflicted by that folly known as love of the truth—at least in the matter of details. He had summed up in a few sentences the useful observations made during his mission. It required great self-control not to tell the Minister frankly everything he had found patently evil, and which could so easily be ameliorated. He was certainly not governed by vanity. He knew exactly how the Minister would judge everything that, directly or indirectly, had the remotest relation to logic or straightforward narration. But because of his foolish love of truth, which is quite unpardonable in a man whose father keeps a carriage, Lucien was eager to correct three or four abuses—at least those which did not bring the Minister a penny. He was, however, sufficiently *civilized* to feel a mortal fear lest his love of truth should make him overstep the bounds which the Minister's tone seemed to set to their relations.

"How humiliated I should feel if, with a public official in a position so far above mine, while I talk about useful things, he should speak to me only of trifling details."

Lucien let the subject drop, and fled. He found his office occupied by young Desbacs who had taken his place while he was away. . . . This little person, who, before Lucien's trip, had danced obsequious attendance, was now extremely cool as he acquainted Lucien with the current state of affairs.

During that day Lucien had no occasion to speak to Coffe who was working in an adjoining room and who, for his part, had met with an even more significant welcome. At half-past-five Lucien called him and they went out to dinner. As soon as they were alone in a private room of the restaurant:

"Well?" said Lucien, laughing.

"Well," replied Coffe, "all the good and admirable things you did to try to save a lost cause constitute nothing but a glaring sin. You will indeed be fortunate if you escape the charge of Jacobinism or Carlism. In the office they are still looking for a name for your crime; they are in agreement only as to its enormity. Everybody is watching to see how the Minister is going to treat you. You have certainly cooked your goose."

"How lucky for France," rejoined Lucien gaily, "that these rascally Ministers don't know how to take advantage of that folly of youth called zeal. I should be curious to know whether a General-in-Chief would behave in the same way toward an officer if, in a retreat, his subaltern should make a regiment of Dragoons dismount in order to attack a battery barring the road and engaged in a horrible massacre?"

After endless repetition, Lucien finally convinced Coffe that neither had he any desire to marry a member of the Minister's family, nor any favor to ask.

"But then," asked Coffe in amazement, "why the marked partiality shown you by the Minister before your mission? And at present why, after M. de Séranville's letter, doesn't he wreck your career?"

"He is afraid of my father's drawing room. If I didn't have the most dreaded wit in Paris for a father, I should be in your boots. I should never have been able to live down that terrible disgrace of École Polytechnique republicanism. . . . But tell me, do you think that a republican government could be quite as absurd as this one?"

"It would be less absurd but more violent; it would frequently be a ravening wolf. Do you want me to give you a proof? It isn't hard to find. If tomorrow you were an omnipotent Minister of the Interior, what changes would you make in the Departments of M. de Riquebourg and M. de Séranville?"

"I would name M. Mairobert Prefect, and give General Fari command of the two Departments."

"Good. Now consider the consequences of such measures, think of the wild enthusiasm that would take possession of all the partisans of good sense and justice in both the Departments. M. Mairobert would be king of his Department. Then think of what would happen if that Department decided to have an opinion on what goes on in Paris. And, speaking of what we both know something about, what if it decided to turn a rational eye on the four hundred and thirty pompous noodles, you and me included, engaged in scribbling in the Rue de Grenelle? If those Departments decided that the Ministry of the Interior could be run by six competent men, at salaries of thirty thousand francs apiece, with ten thousand francs for office expenses, who would sign everything of secondary importance themselves, what would become of the three hundred and fifty (at least) clerks who are employed to wage such ruthless war on common sense? And, little by little, what would become of the King? All government is an evil, but an evil which preserves us from a greater. . . ."

"You talk just like Gauthier, the wisest man I have ever known, a republican of Nancy. If only he were here to argue with you! Besides, he is a man who understands Lagrange's *Theory of Functions* as well as you do, and a hundred times better than I. . . ."

The discussion between the two friends was endless. Not

being afraid to differ with Lucien, Coffe had won the latter's affection and felt obliged to respond to his remarks out of gratitude. Coffe could not get over his amazement at the fact that, although rich, Lucien was not more absurd. With this thought in mind, he asked:

"Were you born in Paris?"

"Yes, of course."

"And your father has always had a magnificent house, and you have always, since you were three years old, ridden in your own carriage?"

"But of course," Lucien repeated, laughing. "Why these questions?"

"Because I am surprised to find you neither absurd nor heartless. But let's hope that will come. You ought to see by the result of your mission that society resents your qualities. If you had been satisfied to get yourself covered with mud at Blois, the Minister would have presented you with the Cross on your return."

"Devil take me if I ever think of that cursed mission again!"

"You are wrong. It is the most valuable and the most curious experience of your life. Never, no matter what happens to you, will you ever forget General Fari, M. de Séranville, the Abbé Le Canu, M. de Riquebourg . . ."

"Never!"

"Well, the most trying part of the experience, morally, is over. Now begins the interpretation of the events. It will be interesting to follow in the different departments of the Ministry the fate of the men and the things still so fresh in your memory. But you must hurry, for it is very possible that the Minister has already some scheme up his sleeve for getting rid of you without offending your father."

"Speaking of my father, you knew, didn't you, that he is Deputy for Aveyron? He was elected after the third ballot by the flattering majority of two votes."

"You didn't tell me he was running."

"I thought it ridiculous. Besides, there wasn't much time to think about it. I learned it from my mother's letter brought by the special courier who had such a harrowing effect on M. de Séranville."

Two days later M. de Vaize said to Lucien:

"Here is a paper I should like you to glance at."

It was the first list of rewards in connection with the elections. Handing the paper to Lucien, the Minister smiled with an air of smug benevolence that seemed to say: "You have done nothing worth mentioning and yet see how I am treating you!" Lucien read over the list. There were three rewards of ten thousand francs with the word *successful* after the name of each recipient. On the fourth line appeared: "M. Leuwen, Master of Petitions, *unsuccessful,* M. Mairobert elected by a majority of one vote, but remarkable zeal displayed, a valuable subject: eight thousand francs."

"Well," said the Minister, "what do you say? Is that keeping the promise I made to you at the Opera?"

On the list, Lucien noticed, the few other agents who had been unsuccessful received only twenty-five hundred francs. After thanking the Minister, he added:

"I have a request to make, Your Excellency. It is that my name should not appear on the list."

"Ah," said the Minister, his face suddenly assuming an expression of the utmost sternness. "I understand. You expected the Cross. But really, after all your follies, I can hardly ask that for you. Your character is even younger than your age. Ask Desbacs of the amazement caused by your dispatches, coming one after the other, and then by your letters."

"It is because I know all that, that I beg Your Excellency not to consider me for the Cross, much less for a reward."

"Take care, sir," said the Minister, really angry now. "I

might take you at your word. Egad, sir, here is a pen—write down whatever you wish after your name."

Lucien wrote opposite his name: *"Neither Cross, nor reward, election a failure"*; then crossed out the whole line. At the bottom of the list he wrote: "M. Coffe, twenty-five hundred francs."

"Take care," the Minister repeated when he read what Lucien had written. "I am taking this paper to the Château. After that it will be useless for your father to bring up the subject again."

"No doubt Your Excellency's many important duties have made you forget our conversation at the Opera. I very explicitly expressed the desire that in the future my father should in no way be involved in my political career."

"Very well, sir. But kindly tell my friend, M. Leuwen, exactly what has taken place in the matter of the rewards. You were put down for eight thousand francs. You yourself effaced that figure. Good-day, sir."

His Excellency's carriage had hardly left the Ministry when Lucien was summoned by Madame la Comtesse de Vaize.

"The devil," said Lucien to himself as he saw her, "how pretty she is today. She seems less timid and there is a new sparkle in her eye. What is the meaning of this change?"

"You have treated us badly since your return, M. Leuwen. I have been waiting for an opportunity to speak to you on a certain matter in particular. No one at the Ministry, I assure you, defended your dispatches more warmly than I, and I never allowed anyone to say a word against them at my table—which, you must own, was courageous of me! After all, anyone can make a mistake, and I have good news for you. Your enemies must not be allowed to use your mission as an excuse to slander you, and although money, I know very well, is no object to you, they must be silenced. This morning I made my husband promise that he would present your name to the King for a reward of eight thousand francs. I wanted ten, but M. de Vaize explained that such a sum was reserved exclusively for outstanding successes. The letters which arrived from M. de Séranville yesterday are terrible for you! To counterbalance them I laid stress upon your father having been elected Deputy. M. de Vaize has had the list on which your name appeared at the very end for only four thousand francs, copied, so that now your name comes fourth, and is followed by the sum of eight thousand francs."

All this was said in many more words and, consequently, with greater reserve and feminine modesty, but also with many more marks of regard and interest than we can possibly note here. Lucien was touched, for in the last two weeks he had seen few friendly faces. He had begun to learn something of the ways of the world—at twenty-four it was about time!

"I should really make love to this timid little woman," Lucien thought to himself. "Dignities bore her, are really a burden to her. I would be her consolation. Her apartments are but a step from my office."

Lucien now told her how he had effaced his name from the list.

"My God!" she cried. "Are you crazy? I promise that you shall have the Cross at the very first opportunity."

"Which means," thought Lucien, " 'Are you going to leave us?' "

The tone in which it was said touched Lucien so deeply that he was on the point of kissing her hand. Madame de Vaize seemed much affected, Lucien filled with gratitude. Her sweet face, which expressed such friendliness, was all the more touching to Lucien since, during his mission, he had seen nothing but hate in the faces around him.

"But if I attached myself to her," he thought, "what boring dinners I should have to endure, with that face of her husband at the other end of the table and her cousin, that rascally little

Desbacs, always around." This reflection took less than half a second.

"Yes, I have effaced my name from the list. But, since you are good enough to take an interest in my future, I shall tell you my real reason. These lists of rewards may one day be published, and at that moment such celebrity may prove to be anything but pleasant. I am too young to expose myself to such a dangerous eventuality."

"Oh, God," cried Madame de Vaize with an accent of terror. "Do you really agree with M. Crapart? You think the Republic as imminent as that!"

Madame de Vaize's face expressed more than fear, it revealed, Lucien thought, an utterly mediocre soul.

"Fear," he said to himself, "makes her forget her fugitive sympathy and friendliness. In this age, privileges are dearly bought, and Gauthier was right to pity any man called *Prince*. He wouldn't, he said, admit this opinion to everybody for fear of being accused of abject envy. 'In this year of 1834,' I remember his saying, 'a young man, not yet as old as the century, who bears the title of prince or duke, is bound to have a touch of madness. Because of his name the poor fellow lives in constant fear, yet thinks he ought to be happier than other men.' This pathetic little woman would be much happier if she were plain Madame Le Roux. . . . To Madame de Chasteller, on the contrary, such thoughts of danger gave a charming glow of courage. I remember that evening when something led me to say: 'Then I should be fighting against you.' What a look in her eyes! . . . And what the devil am I doing in Paris? Why shouldn't I fly to Nancy? I shall beg her on my knees to forgive me for having been angry with her because she kept her secret from me. What a painful admission for a woman to make to a young man—especially to one whom, *perhaps,* she loved! Why should she have confessed? Had I ever spoken of uniting our lives before the world?"

"Are you angry?" Madame de Vaize asked timidly.

The sound of her voice roused Lucien.

"She is no longer frightened," he thought. "My God, I must have been silent for a whole minute at least."

"How long have I been dreaming?" he asked.

"Three whole minutes," Madame de Vaize replied with extreme gentleness; but in that very gentleness, intentionally stressed, could be detected the reproof of a powerful Minister's wife, unaccustomed to such absent-mindedness in company, and much less in a tête-à-tête.

"The reason is, Madam, that I am on the point of entertaining for you a sentiment for which I reproach myself."

After this bit of knavery, Lucien had nothing more to say to Madame de Vaize. He added a few courteous phrases, left her covered with blushes, and went to lock himself up in his office.

"I forget to live," he said to himself. "These absurdities of ambition prevent me from thinking of the only thing in the world that has any reality for me. I sacrifice my heart to my ambition and I have no ambition. How absurd! I am not altogether ridiculous, however, for I have been trying to give my father a proof of my gratitude. But there are limits! If I leave, people may think that I am piqued at not having obtained a promotion or the Cross! My enemies at the Ministry will perhaps say that I went to see the republicans in Nancy. And the telegraph I made talk so much will talk about me. But," he added, laughing, "why mention that diabolic machine?"

After his resolve to go to Nancy Lucien felt like a man again.

"I shall have to wait a few days for my father's return. It is my duty, and, besides, I shall be glad to have his opinion on my conduct at Caen, so ridiculed at the Ministry."

That evening his determination not to appear crestfallen made him extremely brilliant at Madame Grandet's. In the little oval drawing room, surrounded by thirty people, he was the center of the general conversation, and stopped all private chats for twenty minutes at least.

This success electrified Madame Grandet.

"With two or three moments like this every evening, mine will soon be the first salon of Paris."

When they went into the billiard room, she found herself standing beside Lucien, separated from the rest of the company. For a moment, while the men were busy choosing their cues, they were alone.

"And how did you spend your evenings in the provinces?"

"In thinking of a young woman in Paris I am desperately in love with."

It was the first word of the kind he had ever spoken to Madame Grandet, and came at a timely moment. For five minutes, at least, she let herself relish this remark before remembering the role she had decided to adopt in society. Ambition reacted violently, and, without having to make any effort, she was able to appear furious.

Fond words cost Lucien nothing at that moment. His mind had been filled with them ever since his decision to go to Nancy. For the entire evening he lavished all his tenderness on Madame Grandet.

CHAPTER TWENTY-ONE

M. LEUWEN returned from the Department of Aveyron thoroughly pleased with his election. "The weather was mild, the partridges excellent, full of savor, and the men incredible. One of my honorable constituents has commissioned me to send him four pairs of well-made boots. I am to begin by comparing the merits of the different bootmakers of Paris. The boots must be elegantly fashioned, but at the same time sturdy. After finding the perfect bootmaker, I am to give him the old boot which M. de Malpas has entrusted to my care. There is also the matter of a branch road of five quarters of a league from the royal highway to the country house of another valuable constituent, M. Castenet, which I have engaged to obtain for him from the Minister of the Interior. Fifty-three commissions in all, besides all those that I have been promised by letter."

M. Leuwen went on to describe to Madame Leuwen and his son the clever means he had employed to obtain the triumphant majority of two votes.

"It was all very amusing and had my wife been with me, I should have been perfectly happy. It's been years since I have talked so much and to such a quantity of bores. I am saturated through and through with official boredom and all the platitudes I've heard, and also uttered about our government. None of those ninnies of the *Juste-milieu,* who repeat the sayings of Guizot and Thiers without understanding them, could ever repay me in écus for the mortal boredom their presence inspires. After I leave such people I am stupid for an hour or more afterward—I even bore myself."

"If only," put in Madame Leuwen, "they were greater rascals but less chauvinistic, they might be less boring."

"And now," said M. Leuwen, turning to his son, "tell me all about your adventures in Champagnier and Caen."

"Do you want a long or a short story?"

"Long," cried Madame Leuwen. "It amused me vastly and I could hear it again with pleasure. I am curious to know what your father will think of it."

"Very well," said M. Leuwen with a mock air of resignation, "it is now ten-forty-five; we'll have some punch, and you can go ahead with your story."

Madame Leuwen motioned to the footman, and the door was closed. Lucien disposed of the outrage at Blois and the Champagnier election in five minutes. ("It was at Caen that I really needed your advice.") Then, at great length, he recounted to his father all that we, at great length, have recounted to our readers.

In the middle of his recital, M. Leuwen began to ask questions.

"More details, more details," he cried. "There's no originality or truth except in details. . . ."

Finally, at half-past-twelve, M. Leuwen remarked:

"So that is how your Minister treated you on your return!" He seemed violently incensed.

"But tell me," his son insisted, "how did I act, well or ill? The truth is, I don't know. On the field of battle, in the excitement of action, I thought I was a thousand times right, but now I am assailed by a multitude of doubts."

"And I," said Madame Leuwen, "I haven't any. You acted as the bravest man would have done. At forty you might have been a little more cautious in your behavior toward that little literary Prefect, for the animosity of writers is almost as dangerous as that of priests. On the other hand, at forty you would also have shown less energy and boldness in your handling of MM. Disjonval and Le Canu. . . ."

Madame Leuwen seemed to be soliciting the approval of her silent husband, to be pleading her son's cause.

"I must rebel against my champion," said Lucien. "What's done is done, and I don't care a straw for the Brid'oison of the Rue de Grenelle. But my pride is uneasy; what opinion should I have of myself? Am I worth anything? That," he turned to his father, "is what I want you to tell me. I don't ask if you are fond of me, or what you would say about me in society. But, as I may have twisted the facts in my favor in recounting them, thus justifying, according to them, the measures I adopted, I want you to hear M. Coffe's account as well as mine—and let me assure you, sir, he is never boring."

"He strikes me as a most disagreeable person," said Madame Leuwen.

"You are mistaken, mother. It is only that he is disgusted. If he had an income of four hundred francs, he would retire to the rocks of Sainte-Baume, a few leagues from Marseilles."

"Why doesn't he become a monk?"

"He believes that there is no God, or, if there is one, that He is wicked."

"Not so stupid!" put in M. Leuwen.

"Oh," cried Madame Leuwen, "he is even worse than I thought! That confirms me in my dislike."

"Then I have been very clumsy," rejoined Lucien, "for I wanted to get my father's consent to listen to the account of my campaign by a faithful aide-de-camp who did not always see eye to eye with me. And I shall never succeed in getting another session with my father if you don't second me."

"Not at all; this interests me. It reminds me of my recent laurels at Aveyron, where I had five legitimist adherents myself, and two of them, at least, thought themselves damned for taking the oath. But I swore that I would speak against the oath, and so I shall, for it is highway robbery."

"Oh, my dear, this is exactly what I feared," said Madame Leuwen. "Think of your weak chest."

"I shall sacrifice myself for my country and my two ultras! It was their confessor, at my instigation, who ordered them to take the oath and to vote for me. If your Coffe wants to dine with us tomorrow . . . Are we free tomorrow?" he asked, turning to his wife.

"We have a tentative engagement with Madame de Thémines. . . ."

"We'll dine here—the three of us and M. Coffe. If he is

the boring kind, as I fear, he will be less boring at table. We'll be out to everyone else, and Anselme will serve us."

Lucien persuaded Coffe to come, but not without some difficulty.

"You will find a dinner that would cost forty francs a plate at Baleine's Rocher de Cancale, and, even at that price, it's doubtful whether Baleine's dinner would be as good."

"Well, then, let's sample your forty franc dinner, by all means. It's just about the price of my board for a month."

Coffe made the conquest of M. Leuwen by his reserve and the simplicity of his recital.

"Ah, my dear sir, how grateful I am to you for not being a Gascon!" said the Deputy from Aveyron. "I've had an overdose of those bumptious fellows who are always sure of tomorrow's success until tomorrow arrives, then, when reproached with their failure, dish you up a platitude."

M. Leuwen asked Coffe a great many questions. Madame Leuwen was delighted to have this third edition of her son's exploits. And at nine o'clock, when Coffe was preparing to leave, M. Leuwen insisted on taking him with him to his box at the Opera.

"I am sorry that you are at the Ministry," M. Leuwen said to him before the evening was over. "I would have offered you a position at four thousand francs. Since poor Van Peters' death, I don't work enough, and, besides, since the Minister's stupid behavior toward this hero of ours, I have a sneaking desire to start a semi-opposition for six weeks. I don't feel at all sure of succeeding. My reputation for wit will frighten my colleagues, and I can't succeed without a squad of fifteen or twenty Deputies. . . . True, I shall be careful that my opinions do not disturb theirs. No matter what imbecilities they desire, I shall think as they do and say so. . . . But, by gad, Monsieur de Vaize, you are going to pay for your stupid blundering in regard to this young hero! As your banker, financial revenge would be beneath me. . . . Revenge is always costly to the avenger. . . ." M. Leuwen still spoke aloud, but as though to himself. "I cannot sacrifice one iota of my integrity as a banker. Thus, whenever the opportunity occurs, there will be the same profitable transactions on the Bourse as though we were still the best of friends. . . ." And he fell into a brown study. Lucien, who was beginning to find the political session a little long, just then caught sight of Mademoiselle Raimonde in a fifth tier box and disappeared.

"To arms!" cried M. Leuwen, suddenly coming out of his reverie and addressing Coffe. "We must get to work. . . . What time is it now?"

"I have no watch," Coffe replied stiffly. "Your son got me out of Sainte-Pélagie . . . and," Coffe's vanity could not resist adding, "in my schedule of bankruptcy I included my watch."

"Very honest, very honest, my dear Coffe," Leuwen replied absently. Then he added with great earnestness: "Can I count on your eternal silence? I must ask you never to pronounce my name or that of my son."

"That is my usual practice. I promise you."

"Will you do me the honor of dining with me tomorrow? If there are other people, I shall have our dinner served in my room; there will be just the three of us, my son, you and myself. Your sound, firm judgment pleases me, and I am most anxious to find favor with you, in spite of your misanthropy—that is, if you are a misanthrope."

"Yes, from having loved men too well."

Two weeks later the change that had come over M. Leuwen amazed his friends. He was constantly in the society of thirty or forty of the newly elected Deputies who were among the most idiotic in the Chamber. And what was even more incredible, he never exercised his wit at their expense. A certain diplomat among M. Leuwen's friends expressed his consternation: "He is no longer insolent toward imbeciles! He talks to them seriously. His character is changing. We are losing him."

"At last," M. de Vaize said to himself, "I've got the better of the audacious fellow." And he rubbed his hands with satisfaction. "I've brought him down a peg. All it needed was a little courage. I didn't make his son a Lieutenant, and now he eats humble pie."

The outcome of this happy reasoning was a little air of superiority which he adopted toward M. Leuwen, and which M. Leuwen noticed with great glee. As M. de Vaize, for a very good reason, did not surround himself with clever men, he was not aware of the astonishment caused by the change that had come over M. Leuwen, among those busy, brilliant men who make their fortunes out of the government in power.

The men of wit who had been in the habit of dining at M. Leuwen's were no longer invited. He gave them one or two dinners at a restaurant. He no longer invited any women, but every day five or six Deputies dined at his table. Madame Leuwen could not get over her amazement. He would say the strangest things to his Deputies, such as:

"This dinner—and let me say that I hope you will accept my hospitality any time you are not invited by one of the Ministers or the King—this dinner would cost more than twenty francs a person in the best restaurant in Paris. . . . For example, this turbot . . ."

Whereupon there followed the history of the turbot with the amount it had cost (invented on the spur of the moment, for he knew nothing of such things).

"But last Monday," he would add, "this same turbot, when I say this same turbot—naturally this one was still swimming around in the British Channel—I mean a turbot of the same weight and just as fresh, cost at least ten francs."

He was careful to avoid meeting his wife's eye when he expatiated on such interesting subjects.

Very skillfully, M. Leuwen contrived to hold the attention of his Deputies. He would generally take them into his confidence on such subjects as the extraordinary turbot, and when he told anecdotes they were about cab drivers who at midnight take imprudent Paris visitors, venturing to return home at such an hour and unfamiliar with the streets, out into the country.

Madame Leuwen's astonishment knew no bounds, but she dared not question her husband for she felt sure he would merely answer with a jest.

All the mental power of his Deputies M. Leuwen reserved for one abstruse idea, which he made them grasp by means of a thousand different examples, sometimes even bravely presenting it to them directly:

"In union there is strength. If this principle is universally true, it is, above all, true for deliberative bodies. There is no exception, unless there happens to be a Mirabeau in the Chamber. But which one of us is a Mirabeau? Not I *for one!* We can make ourselves count only if none of us insists upon holding stubbornly to his own point of view. We are twenty friends banded together. Very well. It is necessary for each one of us to think as the majority—that is as eleven of us think. Tomorrow an article of law comes up for discussion in the Chamber. After dinner let us take up this measure for discussion among ourselves. I have but one advantage over the rest of you in that, for the last forty years, I have been studying the perfidious practices of this city of Paris. But I shall always sacrifice my opinion to that of the majority of my friends. After all, four eyes are better than two. We are now about to deliberate on how we shall vote tomorrow. If there are twenty of us present, as I hope, and eleven vote *yes,* the nine others must absolutely vote *yes,* no matter how passionately they are wedded to *no.* That is the secret of our strength. If ever we should succeed in mustering thirty votes on every question, there is no favor the Ministers can refuse us. Let us now make a little memorandum of the thing each one of us would like to obtain for his family (I speak of things within reason). When each of us has obtained, through the Ministers' fear of us, a favor of approximately the same value, we will pass on to a second list. Now, gentlemen, what do you say to this plan of campaign?"

M. Leuwen had deliberately chosen, as subjects for the indoctrination of his theory and recipients of his hospitality, the twenty Deputies who were the most destitute of friends and connections, the most amazed by their sojourn in Paris, and by nature the dullest. They were almost all either from the Midi, Auvergne, or somewhere along the Perpignan-Bordeaux line. The only exception was M. N—— from Nancy, introduced by his son. M. Leuwen's greatest difficulty was to keep from offending their vanity, and even though he invariably gave in to them on every subject, he was not always successful. There was a mocking twist to the corner of his mouth which alarmed them. Several, thinking he was making fun of them, declined his dinners. These he replaced very happily by Deputies who had at least three sons and four daughters, and who were bent on finding good posts for all their sons and their sons-in-law.

About a month after the opening of the Chamber, and after twenty or more dinners, he decided that his little troop was sufficiently seasoned to take the field. One day, after an excellent dinner, he had them solemnly vote on a question of very minor importance which was to be debated the following day. In spite of all the trouble he had taken to make them understand, using the most indirect style possible and displaying the utmost caution, out of nineteen Deputies, twelve voted on the absurd side of the question. M. Leuwen had promised them in advance that he would speak in the Chamber next day in favor of the majority opinion. Nevertheless, confronted by such absurdity, he had the human weakness to try to enlighten this majority by a careful exposition which lasted a whole hour and a half. He was driven back with loss, when his Deputies appealed to his conscience. Valiantly, the following day for his maiden speech in the Chamber, he supported a glaring imbecility. He was properly vilified in practically all the newspapers without exception, but won the endless gratitude of his little troop.

We suppress the details, also endless, of his careful tutelage of the consciences of his flock of faithful Perigordians, Auvergnians, etc. He was determined that no one should seduce them, and he even, on occasion, went with them to look for lodgings or to one of those tailors who sell ready-made trousers in the arcades. If he had dared, he would have lodged them as well as practically boarding them.

Thanks to these daily efforts which, because of their extreme novelty, amused him, in a very short time he had mustered twenty-nine votes. He then decided never to invite to his dinners any Deputies outside his group of twenty-nine, and almost every day of the session he brought back a huge berlin full of them. One of his journalist friends, pretending to attack him, proclaimed the existence of a *Southern Legion,* twenty-nine votes strong. "But," inquired the journalist, "is it the Ministry that pays for this new Piet club?"

The day before the *Southern Legion* was, for the second time, to have occasion to show itself, to *reveal its existence,* as M. Leuwen said to them, he had them debate again after dinner. True to instinct, out of twenty-nine present, nineteen were once more for the absurd side of the question. Next day M. Leuwen ascended the rostrum and spoke in its favor. It won by a majority of eight votes. Fresh diatribes in the press against the *Southern Legion.*

M. Leuwen entreated his Deputies to address the Chamber

themselves, but in vain. None of them dared. In truth none of them could. Having friends in the Ministry of Finance, M. Leuwen was able to obtain for his followers one postmaster's place in a village of Languedoc and two tobacco shop concessions. Three days later, with the excuse that there wasn't time enough, he avoided a debate on a question in which one of the Ministers took a personal interest.

Next day this Minister arrived in the Chamber in full regalia, radiant and very sure of a successful outcome. He went around shaking hands with his principal friends, received others at his bench, and, turning toward the bench of his followers, gave them an ingratiating smile. The Chairman reported the bill and declared in favor of the Minister. A rabid *Juste-milieu* succeeded him, and seconded the Chairman. The Chamber was bored and about to approve the bill by a large majority. M. Leuwen's Deputies, not knowing what side to take, turned toward his place next to the Ministers. This time, his opinion untrammeled by his *Legion,* M. Leuwen ascended the rostrum and, in spite of his weak voice, obtained a religious attention. True, he managed to get in three or four witty and malicious strokes in the very beginning of his speech. The first made fifteen or twenty Deputies around the rostrum smile, the second brought a scattering of laughs and produced a general murmur of amusement. The Chamber was waking up. At the third, a great burst of laughter fairly shook the hall. The Minister, who wanted the bill to pass, asked for the floor and spoke, but without any success. Accustomed to obtaining the attention of the Chamber, M. de Vaize now came to his colleague's rescue. That was exactly what M. Leuwen had been praying for these past two months. He went over to one of the Deputies to ask him to yield his turn. As M. de Vaize in his speech had answered one of Leuwen's jibes rather well, Leuwen demanded the floor on a personal issue. The Speaker refused. M. Leuwen protested, and the Chamber accorded him the floor.

This second speech was a triumph. M. Leuwen gave free reign to his spite and got in several thrusts at M. de Vaize, which were all the more cruel for being couched in such a way as to preclude any reply. M. Leuwen's voice was exceedingly weak, and you could have heard a pin drop in the hall all the while he was speaking. It was a success similar to those the amiable Andrieux formerly enjoyed at the public meetings of the Academy. M. de Vaize fairly writhed on his bench and made frantic signs to the rich bankers, one after the other, who were Deputies and friends of M. Leuwen. He was in a rage, and spoke of challenging Leuwen.

"You want to fight against such a voice!" the Minister of War protested. "If you killed that old man, opprobrium would fall on the whole Ministry."

M. Leuwen's success surpassed his wildest hopes. His speech was the outburst of the bitter resentment he had kept pent up for the last two months. And during all that time, for the sake of vengeance, he had endured the dreariest boredom. His speech—if such a wicked, racy, charming diatribe, quite devoid of common sense, can be called a speech—marked the most agreeable session the Chamber had so far enjoyed. After it, no one could get himself listened to.

It was only four-thirty. The Deputies stood about talking for a few moments and then departed, leaving the Speaker alone with the ponderous *Juste-milieu* Deputy who had tried to confute M. Leuwen's brilliant improvisation by sensible arguments. M. Leuwen went home and to bed. He was horribly tired. But, toward nine o'clock in the evening, he felt somewhat revived and gave orders that he was at home to callers. Congratulations poured in. Deputies who had never spoken to him before came to shake his hand and compliment him.

"Tomorrow, if you will give me the floor," he said to them, "I shall effectively dispose of the subject, once and for all."

"But, my dear," protested Madame Leuwen, very much worried, "are you trying to kill yourself?"

Most of the journalists came during the evening to ask to see his speech. He showed them a playing card on which he had written five ideas to be developed. When the journalists saw that the speech had indeed been improvised, their admiration knew no bounds. The name of Mirabeau was pronounced without a smile.

Responding to this praise with charming wit, M. Leuwen feigned to regard it as an insult.

"You are still addressing the Chamber!" exclaimed a clever journalist. "And, by gad, it's not going to be lost. I have a good memory."

And sitting down at a table he began scribbling what M. Leuwen had just said. Seeing that he would be published right away, M. Leuwen added three or four sarcasms on M. de Vaize which had occurred to him after leaving the Chamber.

A little later the stenographer from the *Moniteur* came to bring him his speech for corrections.

"We always do this for General Foy."

The remark enchanted our author.

"This will relieve me of the necessity of speaking tomorrow," he thought, as he added to his speech five or six sentences in which he set forth with great clarity the opinion he wished to urge.

What was comical to watch was the rapture of the Deputies of his troop, who, all evening long, were witnesses of his triumph. Each of them was convinced that he himself had spoken. They kept coming to him with arguments which he should have advanced, and he, with perfect seriousness, agreed with them.

"In a month," he would whisper to one, "your son will be

an exciseman." To another: "Your son will be chief clerk in one of the departments of the Sub-Prefecture."

The next morning Lucien cut a strange figure in his office only a few feet away from the desk where the Minister, in a rage, no doubt, sat writing. His Excellency could not help hearing the commotion in the corridor made by the twenty or thirty clerks come to congratulate Lucien on his father's talents.

M. de Vaize was beside himself. Although he was in need of Lucien's services, he could not bring himself to see him. Toward two o'clock he departed for the Château. Hardly had he left when the young Comtesse de Vaize sent for Lucien.

"Ah, sir, do you really want to ruin us? The Minister is almost out of his mind, he never closed his eyes all night. You shall have your lieutenancy, you shall have your Cross, only give us time!"

The Comtesse herself looked very pale. Lucien was charming to her, almost tender. He consoled her as best he could, and convinced her that he had not had the faintest idea of his father's attack, which was true.

"I swear to you, Madam, for the past six weeks my father has not spoken a serious word to me. Since my lengthy account of my adventures at Caen, we have discussed nothing."

"Ah, Caen, that fatal name! M. de Vaize realizes how much he has been at fault. He should have rewarded you very differently. But today, he says, it is impossible after such an appalling declaration of war."

"Perhaps, Madam," said Lucien very gently, "it will be distressing to have the son of an opposition Deputy always around. If my resignation would be agreeable to your husband . . ."

"Oh, sir," Madame de Vaize interrupted him, "do not think of such a thing! My husband would never forgive me for having been so maladroit as to make you pronounce that word, so distressing for us both. On the contrary, it is a question of conciliation, and no matter what your father says, you must not desert us!"

And this pretty young woman began to weep without restraint.

There was never a victory, even a parliamentary victory, that did not start tears flowing.

Lucien did his best to console the young Comtesse, being careful, nevertheless, to make the distinction between what he owed a pretty woman and what he wished to have recounted to the man who had treated him so cavalierly on his return from Caen. For it was evident that the young woman was talking to him on her husband's order.

"My father is in love with politics," he explained to her once more. "He spends his whole time with boring Deputies. For six weeks he has not spoken a serious word to me."

Following his triumph, M. Leuwen stayed in bed for a week. A day would have sufficed to rest him completely, but he knew his country, where charlatanism added to real merit is like a zero placed after a number, increasing its value tenfold. In his bed, M. Leuwen received the congratulations of over fifty members of the Chamber. He refused the requests of eight or ten Deputies, not devoid of ability, who asked to be enrolled in the *Southern Legion.*

"We are really just a group of friends, rather than a political club. . . . Vote with us, second us during the session, and if your fancy, which is an honor to us, lasts until next year, these gentlemen, accustomed to seeing you share our point of view, will themselves invite you to join our friendly dinners."

"Even to manage my twenty-eight goslings," thought M. Leuwen, "requires the height of abnegation and all my skill. What would it be if there were forty or fifty, and clever ones at that, each wanting to be my lieutenant and bent on ousting his Captain at the first opportunity?"

One thing that made for the novelty of M. Leuwen's position, and his popularity, was that he dined his colleagues at his own expense. This was something which, in the memory of the Chamber, had never happened before. There had been the famous dinners of M. Piet during the Restoration, but for them the State had paid.

Two days after M. Leuwen's success, the telegraph brought news from Spain which would undoubtedly cause a fall in the Funds. The Minister hesitated, considering whether or not he should, as usual, send the information to his banker.

"It would be an added triumph for him," M. de Vaize said to himself, "if I showed that I was so piqued that I even neglected my own interests. . . . But, wait a moment! Would he be capable of betraying me? No, I hardly think so."

He sent for Lucien and, scarcely daring to meet his eyes, asked him to transmit the information to his father. The transaction was handled as usual. Two days later, when M. Leuwen sent M. de Vaize the latest profits, he took this occasion to include that of four previous operations, thus practically clearing the Minister's account with the banking house of Leuwen.

M. Leuwen's speeches hardly deserved that name. They were not elevated, they did not affect a tone of gravity, they were only clever society chatter, rapid and pungent. M. Leuwen had a horror of the periphrastic parliamentary style.

"Such grandiloquence would kill me," he remarked to Lucien one day. "First of all I could no longer improvise, and then I should have to work. I wouldn't join the literary clan for an empire! . . . I never dreamed that success was so easy."

Coffe now stood in high favor with the illustrious Deputy, entirely due to that one great virtue of his: he was not a Gascon. M. Leuwen employed Coffe on research, whereupon M. de Vaize dismissed him from his post of a hundred louis at the Ministry of the Interior.

"That is in the worst possible taste," said M. Leuwen, and promptly sent Coffe four thousand francs.

The second time M. Leuwen left the house it was to go to call on the Minister of Finance, whom he had known for a long time.

"Well," said the Minister, laughing, "are you about to make a speech against me?"

"I certainly shall, unless you repair the stupidity of your colleague, M. de Vaize."

And he told the Minister of Finance the story of the highly endowed M. Coffe.

The Minister, who was a sensible and practical man, refrained from asking questions about M. Coffe.

"I am told that M. de Vaize employed your son in the elections, and that it was young M. Leuwen who was attacked in the riot at Blois."

"He had that honor," replied M. Leuwen dryly.

"I did not see his name on the list of rewards submitted to the Council."

"My son effaced his name and put down M. Coffe for a hundred louis. But poor Coffe isn't happy at the Ministry of the Interior."

"Our worthy de Vaize is a capable man and speaks well in the Chamber, but he is altogether lacking in tact. What a splendid economy he has achieved at M. Coffe's expense!"

A week later M. Coffe was appointed Deputy Assistant Head Clerk at the Ministry of Finance with a salary of six thousand francs, but on the express condition that he should never appear at the Ministry.

"Are you satisfied?" the Minister of Finance asked M. Leuwen in the Chamber.

"Yes, with you."

Two weeks later, after a debate in which the Minister of the Interior had just enjoyed a signal success, the Chamber, before the voting began, buzzed with conversation, and all around M. Leuwen everyone was saying:

"A majority of eighty or a hundred votes for the government!"

M. Leuwen at that moment ascended the rostrum. He began by referring to his age and his weak voice. Instantly there was a profound silence. After making a terse and logical speech of ten minutes, he spent five holding M. de Vaize's arguments up to ridicule, while murmurs of amusement ran through the intensely silent Chamber.

"Vote! Vote!" shouted three or four *Juste-milieu* imbeciles, employed as hecklers.

"Very well, Mr. Hecklers," replied M. Leuwen, "I dare you to! And in order to give you time enough to vote, I shall go back to my place." As he passed by the Ministers' bench he cried in his feeble little voice: "Vote, gentlemen, vote!"

The whole Chamber and the galleries burst into a roar of laughter. In vain the Speaker insisted that it was too late to vote.

"It is not yet five o'clock," cried M. Leuwen from his bench. "Besides, if you do not want to let us vote, I shall have more to say tomorrow. Vote, vote!"

The Speaker was forced to allow the voting to proceed, and the Ministry won by a majority of only a *single vote*.

That evening the Ministers dined together and gave M. de Vaize a proper dressing down. The Minister of Finance took the initiative. He told his colleagues of the Coffe episode and the riot at Blois. . . . Throughout the dinner, M. Leuwen and his son occupied the attention of these grave personages. M. de Beausobre, the Foreign Minister, and M. de Vaize were strongly opposed to any reconciliation. The others laughed at them, and made them admit everything—the incident with M. de Beausobre over the Kortis affair, and the election of Caen, ill-paid by M. de Vaize. Finally, despite the indignation of the two

Ministers, to their *massimo dispetto,* that very evening, the Minister of War went to the King, and had two ordinances signed—the first naming Lucien Leuwen Staff-Lieutenant, the second awarding him the Cross for the injury sustained at Blois in carrying out a confidential mission!

At eleven the ordinances were signed, and before midnight M. Leuwen received copies, with an amiable note from the Minister of Finance. At one o'clock in the morning came an acknowledgment from M. Leuwen, in which he asked the Minister for eight little posts, and thanked him quite casually for the unprecedented favors accorded his son.

The next day in the Chamber, the Minister of Finance protested:

"My dear friend, one must not be insatiable!"

"In that case, my dear friend, one must be patient."

And M. Leuwen put himself down for a speech the following day. That evening he invited all his Deputies to dinner.

"Gentlemen," he said when they were seated at table, "here is a little list of the posts I have asked for you. The Minister of Finance thought he could silence me by giving my son the Cross. But if, before four o'clock tomorrow, we have not at least five of these posts which are so rightfully due you, we will use our twenty-nine black balls, as well as eleven others I have been promised, making forty in all. In addition, I intend to amuse myself at the expense of the worthy Ministers of the Interior and of Foreign Affairs, who were the only ones to oppose our demands. What do you think, gentlemen?"

Then, while ostensibly asking their opinions on the question to be debated the following day, he explained it to them.

At ten o'clock he went to the Opera. He had insisted upon his son's displaying the Cross on his uniform, which he never wore. While at the Opera M. Leuwen saw to it that the Minister was informed of his intention of speaking the next day and of the forty votes already assured, without the information seeming to come from him.

The following afternoon in the Chamber, fifteen minutes before the subject for discussion was announced, the Minister of Finance told him that five posts had been accorded him.

"As far as I am concerned, Your Excellency's word is as good as gold," M. Leuwen coolly replied. "But my five Deputies, whose cause I have espoused—all of them family men—know that MM. de Beausobre and de Vaize are our sworn enemies. Without an official notice, I am afraid they may be skeptical."

"Leuwen, you go too far!" exclaimed the Minister, and he flushed up to the roots of his hair. "De Vaize is right, you would exasperate . . ."

"War it is then!" said Leuwen. And a quarter of an hour later he made another speech.

The question was put to a vote and the Ministry won by a majority of only thirty-seven votes which was considered most alarming. In addition, M. Leuwen enjoyed the signal honor of having the Council of Ministers, presided over by the King, deliberate on his account, and for a considerable length of time. Beausobre thought they might try giving him a scare.

"He is a man of moods," said the Minister of Finance, "as his associate Van Peters often told me. At times he displays the sanest views, but at others, to satisfy a whim, he would sacrifice his fortune and himself with it. If we irritate him it will only serve to increase his epigrammatic fury, and among the hundreds of crazy things he says he will make one damning point, or at least one that will be taken up as such by the King's enemies."

"We can get at him through his son," M. de Beausobre insisted. "That solemn little fool they have just made a Lieutenant."

"It was not *they*, sir," cried the Minister of War, "it was I who made him a Lieutenant. And I think by profession I might be considered a judge of courage. It may be that when he was a Second-Lieutenant of Lancers he was not *very polite* at your house one evening, when he came looking for M. de Vaize to report on the Kortis affair, which, *I must say*, he handled remarkably well."

"Not very polite!" cried M. de Beausobre. "Why, he's a rap-scallion. . . ."

"*They* say: not very polite," repeated the Minister of War, emphasizing the *they*. "*They* even add certain details, such as an offer of resignation. *They* have described the entire scene, and to persons who have good memories!"

And the old warrior's voice rose angrily.

"It seems to me," interposed the King, "that there are times and places when it would be preferable to discuss things reasonably without raising one's voice."

"Sire," said the Comte de Beausobre, "the respect I owe Your Majesty silences me. But anywhere else . . ."

"Your Excellency will find my address in the royal almanac," retorted the Minister of War.

Such scenes were of monthly occurrence in the Council. The combination of the four letters K I N G had lost all its magic power in Paris.

A group of semi-fools, then called the *Dynastic Opposition,* which let itself be guided by a few men of vacillating spirit who *could* have been, but did not *wish* to be, Ministers of Louis-Philippe, sent overtures to M. Leuwen. He was profoundly astonished.

"So there are people who actually take my parliamentary chatter seriously! Have I really some influence then, some weight? It must be so, since a large party, or rather a large fraction of the Chamber, proposes a treaty of alliance with me."

For the first time in his life, M. Leuwen was filled with parliamentary ambition. But, as this seemed to him ridiculous, he was ashamed to speak of it to his wife who, until then, had shared his every thought.

CHAPTER TWENTY-TWO

WITHOUT THE KNOWLEDGE of his Ministers, the King summoned M. Leuwen. The old banker flushed with pleasure when M. de N——, the King's orderly officer, handed him the royal communication. (After all, he had been twenty years of age in 1793, when the monarchy fell.) However, for a man grown old in the drawing rooms of Paris, it took but an instant to recollect himself and control his sudden emotion. The coldness of his manner toward the King's officer might have passed either for profound respect or for total indifference.

In fact, returning to his cabriolet, the officer asked himself:

"Is it possible that this man, in spite of all his wit, is a Jacobin or just a fool impressed by a handshake?"

As he watched the cabriolet drive away, M. Leuwen regained his composure.

"I am about to play the well-known role of Samuel Bernard, whom Louis XIV once took walking with him in the gardens of Versailles."

This idea was enough to restore all M. Leuwen's youthful fire. He did not try to disguise from himself his moment of weakness, caused by His Majesty's message, nor was he afraid to admit all the ridicule with which he himself would have covered such a show of emotion had it been the subject of comment in the foyer of the Opera.

Until then, between M. Leuwen and the King there had been nothing more than a formal exchange of a few polite remarks at a ball or at dinner. He had dined several times at the Château in the early days following the July revolt. It was called by another name then, and M. Leuwen, who was not easily deceived, was one of the first to discern the anger which so pernicious an example inspired in the King. At the time, M. Leuwen seemed to read in that royal glance:

"I shall frighten the men of property; I shall make them believe that it is a war of the people who have nothing, against those who have something."

Aimed at this idea, which was never mentioned, M. Leuwen, to avoid appearing as stupid as the few country Deputies sometimes invited with him, allowed himself certain surreptitious pleasantries.

At one time, M. Leuwen had suspected an intention of compromising the little tradesmen of Paris by inciting them to shed blood. He had found the idea in very bad taste and, without hesitating an instant, had resigned as Battalion Chief of the National Guard. That position he had owed to the little shopkeepers themselves, to whom he had pretty generously loaned thousand franc notes, which had even been returned. In addition, he stopped going to the Ministers' dinners, on the pretext of finding them boring.

In spite of that, the Comte de Beausobre, in speaking to him, had used the phrase: *"A man like you . . ."* and had continued to ply him with invitations. But M. Leuwen had resisted all his wily flattery.

In 1792, he had taken part in one or two campaigns, and the name of the French Republic was for him like the name of a once loved mistress who had been guilty of misconduct. In short, his hour had not yet struck.

And now this summons from the King upset all his ideas. Not feeling entirely sure of his self-command he determined to keep a close watch upon himself.

At the Château, M. Leuwen's manner was admirably correct, and as free from embarrassment as it was from any undue eagerness. The cautious and subtle mind of the great personage soon caught this nuance, and was not at all pleased. He tried, by adopting a friendly tone, even marking a personal interest, to awaken this bourgeois banker's vanity, but to no avail.

Far be it from us to wish to detract from this celebrated man's reputation for wily finesse! What could one expect from a King without the prestige of military victories, and confronted by a malicious and witty press? Besides, as we have pointed out, this celebrated personage was conversing seriously with M. Leuwen for the first time.

Like his Minister, this sly pettifogger who occupied the throne, began by saying: "A man like you . . ." But finding his crafty plebeian guest impervious to fair words, and seeing that he was losing his time for nothing, besides being reluctant, by the length of the interview, to give M. Leuwen an exaggerated idea of the importance of the favor he was about to ask of him, the King, in less than half an hour, was reduced to plain-speaking.

Noticing this change of tone in so adroit a man, M. Leuwen was pleased with himself, and this initial success did much to restore his self-confidence.

"So," he thought, "His Majesty has decided to forego his Bourbon subtleties!"

With a truly paternal air, and as though to show that whatever urgency appeared, he was led and, as it were, constrained by circumstances, the King said:

"I wished to see you, my dear sir, without the knowledge of my Ministers. I am afraid, with the exception of the Marshal (Minister of War), they have given you and Lieutenant Leuwen little reason to be pleased with them. Tomorrow, in all likelihood, the final vote will be taken on the —— Bill. And I admit, sir, that I take a particular and peculiarly personal interest in this bill. I am very sure that it will pass by a standing vote. Is that not your opinion?"

"Yes, Sire."

"But by ballot, I shall be very properly defeated by eight or ten black balls. Do you agree with me?"

"Yes, Sire."

"Well then, do me a favor: speak against it if you like—your position I suppose makes that necessary—but give me your thirty-five votes. This is a personal favor I wished to ask of you myself."

"Sire, I have only twenty-seven votes at this moment, counting my own."

"Those poor noodles" (the King was speaking of his Ministers) "were terrified, or rather piqued, because of your list of eight little minor posts. I hardly need tell you that I approve your list in advance and, since the occasion has arisen, I invite you to add something for yourself, sir, and for Lieutenant Leuwen. . . ."

Happily for M. Leuwen, the King talked on in this vein for three or four minutes; during that time, M. Leuwen almost completely recovered his sang-froid.

"Sire," he replied, "I beg Your Majesty not to sign anything either for me or for my friends, but to allow me to present you with my twenty-seven votes tomorrow as a free gift."

"Gad, sir! You are a gallant gentleman!" cried the King, simulating, and not too badly, the frankness of a Henri IV; one had to remember the name he bore not to be deceived by it.

His Majesty talked for a good quarter of an hour along the same lines.

"Sire," said M. Leuwen, "it is impossible for M. de Beausobre ever to forgive my son. Your Minister betrayed rather a lack of self-control in the presence of that hotheaded young man, whom Your Majesty is pleased to call Lieutenant

Leuwen. I must ask Your Majesty never to believe a word of the reports on my son which M. de Beausobre will have brought to you by his police, or even by the police of my friend M. de Vaize."

"Whom you *serve with such probity.*" And the King's eyes shone with finesse.

. . . .

M. Leuwen was silent. The King repeated his question,* astonished at not receiving a reply.

"Sire, in replying, I should be afraid of yielding to my habit of candor."

"Answer, sir! Say exactly what you think, whatever it is."

M. Leuwen's interlocutor had spoken these words as a King.

"Sire, no one is unaware of the King's direct correspondence with the Northern courts, but no one mentions it to him."

Such prompt and unmitigated obedience seemed rather to surprise the great personage. He saw that M. Leuwen had no favor to ask. Not accustomed to giving or receiving anything for nothing, he had estimated that the twenty-seven votes would cost him twenty-seven thousand francs. "And it would be a bargain at that," this crowned calculating machine had decided.

He recognized in M. Leuwen all those ironic traits so often mentioned in the reports of General Rumigny.

"Sire," added M. Leuwen, "I have made a position for myself in the world by refusing nothing to my friends and by refusing myself nothing against my enemies. It is a very old habit. I beg Your Majesty not to ask me to change for the sake of your Ministers. They have assumed an air of arrogance toward me, even the worthy M. Bardoux, your Minister of Finance, who, when he spoke to me in the Chamber the other

*The question to which allusion is made is not in the manuscript— an oversight on Stendhal's part undoubtedly.

day of my eight posts, said in all seriousness: 'My dear friend, one must not be insatiable.' I promise Your Majesty my votes, which will be twenty-seven at the most, but I beg that you allow me to continue to make fun of your Ministers."

And that is what he did the next day with extraordinary verve and gaiety. After all, his so-called eloquence was really nothing more than an offshoot of his temperament. M. Leuwen was far more natural than it was permissible for any man to be in Paris. And now he was stimulated by the idea of having forced the King to be almost sincere with him.

The bill in which the King seemed to take such an interest passed by a majority of only thirteen votes, six of them being his Ministers'. When the result was announced, M. Leuwen, sitting on the second bench from the left, three steps from the Ministers' bench, exclaimed aloud:

"This Ministry is about to leave us. Bon voyage!"

The remark was instantly repeated by all the Deputies on neighboring benches. Alone in the room with a lackey, M. Leuwen would have been pleased with the approbation of that lackey; it may therefore be readily imagined how delighted he was with the success of this simple remark in the Chamber.

"My reputation stands me in good stead!" he thought, sustaining the scrutiny of all those bright eyes fixed upon him.

It was clear to anyone that M. Leuwen was not passionately attached to any one opinion. There were two things, however, to which he would never lend himself: bloodshed and bankruptcy.

Three days after this bill was passed, M. Bardoux, the Minister of Finance, approached M. Leuwen in the Chamber and said with some trepidation (he was afraid of an epigram and spoke very low):

"The eight posts have been granted."

"Splendid, my dear Bardoux," Leuwen replied, "but you owe it to yourself not to countersign these favors. Leave it to your successor in the Ministry of Finance. 'I shall wait, *Monseigneur.*'"

M. Leuwen spoke very distinctly so that all the Deputies around him heard his rejoinder, and were amazed. The idea of laughing at a Minister of Finance, a man who can make you a Receiver General!

He had some difficulty in winning the approval of the eight Deputies whose families would have benefited by the eight posts.

"In six months you will have two posts instead of one. We must learn to make sacrifices."

"Stuff and nonsense!" retorted one of the Deputies, somewhat bolder than the others.

M. Leuwen's eyes kindled; there were two or three rejoinders on the tip of his tongue. But he continued to smile pleasantly. "Only an idiot," he thought to himself, "would chop off the branch he's sitting on."

Every eye was turned on him. Another Deputy, emboldened by the first, cried:

"Our friend M. Leuwen sacrifices all of us for a bon mot."

"If you wish to sever our relations, gentlemen, you are your own masters," M. Leuwen returned gravely. "In that case, I shall be obliged to enlarge my dining room in order to receive all the new friends who, every day, keep asking to vote with me."

"Come, come! Let's not quarrel!" cried a Deputy who was blessed with a good deal of common sense. "What would we be without M. Leuwen? I, for one, have chosen him as general-in-chief for my entire legislative career. I shall never be unfaithful to him."

"Nor I!"

"Nor I!"

As the two rebellious Deputies hesitated, M. Leuwen went over to them and held out his hand. He took the trouble to make them understand that by accepting the eight posts the group would be reduced to the state of M. de Villèle's Three Hundred.

"Paris is a dangerous country. Within a week all the little newspapers would pounce upon your names."

At these words, the two opposition members shuddered.

"The least stupid of them," said the inexorable Leuwen to himself, "might very well have furnished articles."

And peace was restored.

The King had M. Leuwen invited frequently to the Château for dinner, and afterwards would retire with him to one of the window recesses, and engage him in conversation for a half or even three-quarters of an hour.

"My reputation for wit is dead and buried if I spare the Ministers." So, on the days following his dinners at the Château, he made a point of making fun of those gentlemen with almost complete unrestraint. The King complained to him.

"Sire," he replied, "I implored Your Majesty to give me carte blanche where your Ministers were concerned. I might grant a truce to their successors. This Ministry lacks wit, and, in peace time, that is what Paris will never pardon. What our worthy citizens demand is either prestige, like Bonaparte returning from Egypt, or else wit." (At the mention of that redoubtable name, the King was like a nervous young woman at the mention of the executioner.)

A few days after this conversation with the King, an affair was brought to the attention of the Chamber which caused all eyes to turn toward M. Leuwen. A Madame Destrois, ex-postmistress at Torville, complained that after being unjustly accused and convicted of a breach of trust, she had been removed. In making this petition, she explained, she wished simply to defend herself and vindicate her character. As for justice, *that* she did not expect as long as M. Bardoux enjoyed the King's confidence. The petition was trenchant, bordering on insolence, but not insolent; it might have been drawn up by the late M. de Martignac.

M. Leuwen spoke three times, and the second time was literally overwhelmed by applause. That day, the order of the day, asked for by M. de Vaize almost on bended knee, was obtained by a majority of only two, and by a standing vote at that. The ministerial majority was not more than fifteen or twenty votes. M. Leuwen said to the group of Deputies clustered around him as usual:

"M. de Vaize has changed the habit of timid voters. They usually stand up for justice, and vote for the Ministry. As for me, I hereby open a subscription for the benefit of the widow Destrois, the ex-postmistress who will certainly remain *ex,* and put myself down for three thousand francs."

Inexorable as he was with the Ministers, M. Leuwen took good care always to be the humble servitor of his *Southern Legion.* Only the twenty-eight Deputies were invited to dinner at his house. Had he so desired, his personal following (for his opinions were extremely accommodating) might have been increased to fifty or sixty.

"To split up my nice little party, the Ministers would gladly give those hundred thousand francs they sent to my son too late."

It was almost always on Monday that he invited his troop to dinner, in order to draw up a parliamentary plan of campaign for the week.

"Gentlemen, which one of you would like to dine at the Château?"

At these words the worthy Deputies saw M. Leuwen already Minister. They agreed that M. Chapeau, one of their number, should be given that honor, and that later, before the end of the session, the same honor should be solicited for M. Cambray.

"I shall add to these the names of MM. Lamorte and Debrée, the two gentlemen who thought of leaving us."

Whereupon the gentlemen in question began to hem and haw and make excuses.

M. Leuwen went to see His Majesty's aide-de-camp to arrange for these invitations, and less than three weeks later, four of the most obscure Deputies in the Chamber were invited to dine with the King. M. Cambray was so overcome by this undreamed-of honor that he fell ill and was unable to profit by it.

The day following this great event, M. Leuwen decided that he should take advantage of the weakness of these worthy gentlemen, whose lack of wit alone kept them from being mischievous.

"Gentlemen," he asked them, "if His Majesty should accord me a Cross, which one of you, do you think, should be the happy *Chevalier?*"

The gentlemen asked for a week to discuss the matter, but, at the end of that time, had been unable to reach a decision. After dinner it was decided to put it to a vote, a custom which M. Leuwen had found it expedient to allow to fall into abeyance. There were twenty-seven present. M. Cambray, ill and absent, received thirteen votes, M. Lamorte fourteen, M. Leuwen's own vote among the latter. . . . M. Lamorte was chosen.

There was apparently not the remotest chance of M. Leuwen's obtaining a Cross. "But the idea," he thought, "will keep them from revolting."

M. Leuwen went pretty regularly to see Marshal Soult, the Minister of War, since that Minister had made Lucien a Lieutenant. The Marshal showed him the greatest good will, and the two men were soon seeing each other three times a week. It was not long before the Marshal made his friend understand, but in such a way as not to call for a reply, that if the present Ministry should fall, and if the Marshal were charged with forming another, M. Leuwen would not be left out. M.

Leuwen was duly grateful, but he carefully avoided giving any similar assurance.

Sometime previously, M. Leuwen had screwed up his courage sufficiently to confess his dawning ambition to his wife.

"I am beginning to think very seriously about these things. Success has sought me out. The idea of myself as *eloquent* (according to friendly journalists) strikes me as comical. I talk in the Chamber exactly as I talk in a drawing room. But if the Ministry, which is on its last legs, should fall, I'd find myself with nothing more to say. For, to tell the truth, I hold no particular opinions on anything, and certainly, at my age, I am not going to begin to study in order to form some."

"But," put in Lucien, "you are so thoroughly versed in financial questions; you understand the Budget with all its dodges. There aren't fifty other Deputies who realize just how the Budget lies, and those fifty, you may be sure, are the first to be bought. Day before yesterday you had the Minister of Finance shaking in his boots on the question of the tobacco monopoly. You made the most prodigious use of the letter of Prefect Noireau, who had refused to allow a man to raise tobacco because he held the wrong opinions."

"All that is only sarcasm," M. Leuwen replied. "A little is effective, but too much, in the end, offends the stupid minority of the Chamber which, at bottom, doesn't understand anything about anything, and is almost the majority. My eloquence and my reputation are like a soufflé; a common working man would find them pretty unsubstantial fare."

"But you possess such a marvelous understanding of men in general," his son insisted. "Above all you know everything that has happened in Paris since Napoleon was Consul in 1800. That is enormous."

"The *Gazette*," remarked Madame Leuwen, "calls you the Maurepas of this age. I only wish I had as much influence with you as Madame Maurepas with her husband. Enjoy yourself, my dear, but, for mercy's sake, don't make yourself a Minister, it would kill you. You talk much too much as it is. Why, it gives me a pain in your chest!"

"There is still another objection to my being Minister," continued M. Leuwen. "I should ruin myself. The loss of Van Peters is beginning to be keenly felt at the bank. We have recently been caught in two bankruptcies in Amsterdam, for the simple reason that, since his death, no one has gone to Holland. It is the fault of this confounded Chamber. And this confounded son of yours is the primary cause of all my troubles. First of all, he stole half of your heart from me; secondly, he should have appreciated the value of money and taken his place at the head of my banking house. A man born rich, who does not dream of doubling his fortune! Has such a phenomenon ever been seen before? He deserves to be poor. His adventures over the election of M. Mairobert at Caen frankly nettled me. Had it not been for the stupid way M. de Vaize received him on his return, I should never have dreamed of making a name for myself in the Chamber. Now I've acquired a taste for this fashionable sport. And my role in the fall of the Ministry, that is, if it does fall, will be far different from what it was in its formation. But I am faced with a frightful obstacle: *what am I to ask for?* If I don't take something substantial, at the end of two months the very Ministry I helped to put in will laugh at me, and I shall be in a *ridiculous position*. To be Receiver General means nothing to me from the point of view of money, and it is a position too inferior to the one I already enjoy in the Chamber. To make Lucien a Prefect is simply to play into the hands of the friend who will be Minister of the Interior, giving him a chance to discredit me by removing Lucien from office. And that is exactly what would happen within three months."

"But what a splendid role—to do what is right without expecting a thing in return!" exclaimed Madame Leuwen.

"Something our public would never believe! That was M. de Lafayette's role for forty years, and he was always on the verge of being ridiculous. As a people we are too gangrened to understand such things. For three-quarters of the inhabitants of Paris, M. de Lafayette would have been a man really worthy of admiration had he stolen four million francs. Even if I refused the Ministry, but ran my house on a grand scale amounting to a hundred thousand écus a year, while at the same time buying land to show that I was not ruining myself, I should be more of a genius for them than ever, and I'd be able to keep the upper hand of these semi-rascals who are about to battle for the Ministry."

And turning toward his son M. Leuwen added laughingly:

"If you don't solve the problem: 'What shall I ask for?' I shall consider you totally devoid of imagination, and follow the only course left to me: I shall enjoy poor health and go to Italy for three months. The Ministry can then be formed without me. On my return I shall have been completely forgotten, but I shall not be ridiculous. Until I find some way of profiting by the combined favor of the King and the Chamber, which has made me one of the representatives of high finance, this favor must be taken into account and cultivated.

"And now," he said, addressing Madame Leuwen, "I must ask something rather boring of you, my dear. We shall have to give two balls. If the first is *well attended* we can dispense with the second, to which, I am sure, *all France,* as we used to say in my youth, would come."

The two balls took place and were an enormous success. Society accorded its unreserved approval. The Marshal had attended the first one to which the Chamber flocked, as it were, in a body, nor had the King failed to lend his presence. But what was even more significant, the Minister of War had

285

made a point of taking M. Leuwen aside for at least twenty minutes. And during this conference, which made the eyes of the eighty Deputies pop, curiously enough the Marshal had really talked business with M. Leuwen.

"I am very much embarrassed about one thing," the Minister had said. "What, within the realm of reason, can you ask for your son? Do you want him to be Prefect? Nothing simpler. Do you want him to be an Embassy Secretary? Unfortunately there is a tiresome hierarchy in the way. I could make him Second Secretary and, in three months, First."

"*In three months?* . . ." M. Leuwen had repeated with a dubious air, which was entirely candid, and without the slightest sarcastic intent.

In spite of this apparent sincerity, in anyone else the Marshal would have considered the remark offensive. To M. Leuwen he had replied in perfect good faith and with unfeigned perplexity:

"That's the difficulty. Show me a way of overcoming it."

M. Leuwen, finding nothing to reply to this, had fallen back on gratitude and friendship, the most genuine, most unaffected . . .

The two greatest dissemblers of Paris had been sincere. That is what Madame Leuwen had remarked when her husband told her of his confidential conversation with the Marshal.

The Ministers were forced to attend the second ball. Poor little Madame de Vaize was almost in tears as she said to Lucien:

"At the balls of the coming season it is you who will be Minister, and I who will have to come to you."

"I shall not be more devoted to you then than I am today, for that would be impossible. But I wish you would tell me which member of this house is going to be Minister. Not I, certainly, and my father even less—if that were possible."

"Then you are all the more wicked. You overthrow us without having anyone to put in our place. And all because M. de Vaize did not flatter you sufficiently when you returned from Caen!"

"Your grief makes me miserable. If only I could console you by the gift of my heart! But it was yours long ago as you very well know." And this was said with sufficient gravity not to appear impertinent.

But poor little Madame de Vaize was far from having enough wit to know what to reply, much farther from knowing *how*. She was satisfied to feel it vaguely, somewhat like this:

"If I were perfectly sure that you loved me, if I could have made up my mind to accept your homage, the joy of being yours would be the only possible consolation for the loss of the Ministry."

"Here," thought Lucien, "is another of the miseries of this Ministry which my father is flirting with at this moment. It was no pleasure to this poor little woman when M. de Vaize attained to the Ministry. Embarrassment and fear seem to have been her only sensations, and now she is in despair at losing it. She has a soul which only waits for an excuse to be sad. If de Vaize is turned out of the Ministry she will decide to be sad for the next ten years. At the end of those ten years she will be on the threshold of middle age, and unless she finds a priest who will occupy himself exclusively with her, ostensibly as her spiritual adviser, she will be bored and miserable for the rest of her life. No amount of beauty and charm could possibly make up for a character as tiresome as hers. *Requiescat in pace.* I'd be in a pretty pickle if she took me at my word and gave me her heart. Oh, what a dull and dreary age! In the time of Louis XIV I'd have been gallant and amusing, or at least tried to be, with such a woman. In this Nineteenth Century I am insipidly sentimental. It is the only consolation in my power to offer her."

If we were writing a *Memoirs of Walpole,* or any other book of that kind equally beyond our talents, we should continue to give the anecdotic history of seven semi-rascals, two or three of them clever, and one or two with fluent tongues, succeeded by the same number of arrant knaves. A poor honest man in the Ministry of the Interior who had devoted himself in perfect good faith to useful things would have passed for a fool; the whole Chamber would have scoffed at him. It was incumbent upon a man to make his fortune—not of course by flagrantly stealing—but, in order to be respected, it was of prime necessity to feather one's nest. As these little customs are on the eve of being replaced by the disinterested virtues of the Republic and of men who will die like Robespierre with thirteen écus and ten pennies in their pockets, we wanted to make a note of them.

But the story we promised our reader is not even the tale of this man of pleasure and of the pursuits by which he hoped to escape boredom. It is merely the story of his son, a simple soul who, in spite of himself, became involved in the fall of Ministers, that is as far as his melancholy, or, at least, his serious character allowed.

Lucien was filled with remorse in regard to his father. He felt no affection for him, and for this he often reproached himself, looking upon it almost as a crime or, at least, as a sign of an unfeeling heart. Whenever the pressing affairs of State gave him a little leisure, Lucien would say to himself:

"What gratitude I owe my father! I am the motive for almost all his actions. True, he wants to manage my life in his own way, but instead of commanding, he persuades. How carefully I should watch myself!"

Although the truth filled him with shame, he was forced to admit that he did not love his father. This was a constant torment to him, and almost a greater grief than to have been *betrayed by Madame de Chasteller* (that is the way he thought

of it on his dark days). Lucien's true character had not yet
asserted itself, which is surprising at the age of twenty-four.
Under an exterior, which had something singular and thoroughly noble about it, was hidden a naturally gay and heedless nature. Such he had been during the two years following
his expulsion from the École, but since his experience at Nancy,
this gaiety had suffered total eclipse. He appreciated the
vivacity and all the charms of Mademoiselle Raimonde, but
never thought of her except when he wanted to forget the
noblest side of himself.

During the ministerial crisis, to his ever-present cause of sadness was added the bitter remorse of feeling no affection for
his father. The *gulf* between them was too profound. Everything which, rightly or wrongly, seemed to Lucien sublime,
generous, lovable, everything for which it seemed to him noble
to die, with which it seemed beautiful to live, was a subject of
ridicule to his father and a delusion in his eyes. There was one
subject only on which they were in accord: that intimate
friendship of Lucien's parents which had stood the test of
thirty years. M. Leuwen was, it is true, of an exquisite
courtesy, which in the matter of his son's weakness fairly attained the sublime, and was an almost perfect replica of reality.
But Lucien had enough discernment to see that it was the sub-
limity of the mind, of subtlety, of the art of being polite, discreet, impeccable.

CHAPTER TWENTY-THREE

I T BECAME more and more obvious to everyone that M. Leuwen was going to represent the Bourse and the moneyed interests in the ministerial crisis which all eyes saw looming on the horizon and rapidly approaching. Disputes between the Minister of War and his colleagues were of daily, and even violent, occurrence. But as this detail may be found in all contemporary memoirs, and would take us too far afield, suffice it to say that more Deputies now crowded around M. Leuwen in the Chamber than around the Ministers.

Each day M. Leuwen's embarrassment grew. While everyone was envying him his existence and his position in the Chamber (with which he himself was not ill-pleased), he saw clearly that it could not last. While the better informed Deputies, the bigwigs of finance, and a small number of diplomats who understood the country in which they were envoys, admired the ease and casual air with which M. Leuwen had brought about so great a change, and steered the course of the Deputies at whose head he had placed himself, this clever man himself was in despair at not having any plan.

"I keep on delaying things," he said to his wife and son. "I send word to the Marshal that he must hound the Minister of Finance to the limit, that he might instigate an investigation into those emoluments of four or five million which that Minister awards himself. I prevent our friend de Vaize from doing foolish things. I have our fat Bardoux at the Ministry of Finance informed that we are not going to divulge more than a few of the lesser lies of the Budget, and so forth and so on . . . And in spite of all these delays, not a single idea has occurred

290

to me. Oh, where is that charitable soul who will spare me an idea!"

"You cannot eat your ice and yet you are afraid of its melting," laughed Madame Leuwen. "What a painful predicament for a gourmet!"

"And I am scared to death for fear I shall regret it as soon as it has melted."

Such conversations were resumed daily around the little table where Madame Leuwen took her evening lichen.

M. Leuwen now bent all his efforts to delay the fall of the Ministry. And the last three or four conversations he had with a great personage were conducted with this end in view. He could not be Minister himself, he could not decide on anyone else, and if the Ministry were formed without him he would lose his position in the Chamber.

For two months M. Leuwen had been extraordinarily bored with M. Grandet who, grown suddenly sentimental, had recalled that they used to work together at M. Perregaux's. M. Grandet courted him diligently, and could not seem to live without either the father or the son.

"Does this fatuous fool want to be Receiver General at Paris or at Rouen, or is he aiming at the peerage?"

"No," rejoined Madame Leuwen, "he wants to be Minister."

"Grandet Minister! Great God," cried her husband, bursting out laughing. "Why, his department heads would laugh in his face!"

"But he has all that ponderous and silly self-importance which is so popular with the Chamber of Deputies. Those gentlemen really abhor wit. What was it they disliked in MM. Guizot and Thiers but their wit? They accept wit only as a necessary evil. It is the result of their training under the Empire, and the insults which Napoleon on his return from Moscow heaped upon the ideology of M. de Tracy."

"I thought the Chamber could never sink lower than the

Comte de Vaize. That great man, like Villèle, has just the right degree of coarseness and cunning to be on a par and popular with the great majority of the Chamber. Will they really put up with this M. Grandet, so dull, so ordinary?"

"But in a Minister keenness and delicacy of wit would be deadly sins. It was hard enough for the Chamber, composed of the men of the old regime with which M. de Martignac had to deal, to forgive him his charming little light comedy humor, what would it have been had he also displayed that delicacy which is so shocking to wholesale grocers and people of wealth? If excess there must be, an excess of coarseness is less dangerous; it can always be remedied."

"Grandet understands only one virtue—that of facing a pistol or a revolutionary barricade. When a man, in any sort of an affair, refuses to capitulate for pecuniary profit or a post for a member of his family, Grandet immediately shouts: *hypocrisy!* He says he has seen only three dupes in France: MM. de Lafayette, Dupont de l'Eure, and Dupont de Nemours, who understood the language of birds. If he even had enough wit, or education, or vivacity to be able to cross swords in conversation, he might deceive people. But the least clairvoyant person recognizes in him at once the spice merchant who has made a fortune and wants to pass himself off for a Duke."

"M. de Vaize is a veritable Voltaire of wit and a Jean-Jacques of sentiment by comparison!"

"M. Grandet is like M. de Castries who in the days of Louis XVI was at a loss to understand how there could be so much talk about a d'Alembert and a Diderot, men who didn't keep carriages. Such ideas were fashionable in 1780; today they are even beneath a legitimist gazette of the provinces, and would compromise any man."

Since the success of his father's second speech in the Chamber Lucien began to notice that he himself had become quite a personage in Madame Grandet's drawing room. He tried to take advantage of this piece of good fortune to press his amorous suit in the midst of all the refinements of the most costly luxury. But he seemed to feel nothing but the genius of the cabinetmaker and upholsterer. The delicacy of these artisans made him all the more acutely aware of the less delicate traits of Madame Grandet's character. He tried in vain to banish the vision that kept fatally rising before his eyes of a mercer's wife who has just won first prize in one of those Vienna lotteries which the bankers of Frankfort are at such pains to advertise.

Madame Grandet was by no means what is called a goose, and was well aware of her lack of success.

"You pretend to have such an overpowering feeling for me, yet you show not the slightest pleasure in being in my little circle which normally should precede friendship."

"My God, how fatally true!" thought Lucien to himself. "Is she going to become witty at my expense?"

He hastened to reply:

"I am naturally shy, inclined to melancholy, and this misfortune is aggravated by that of being deeply in love with a woman who is perfect, and who feels nothing for me."

Never had he made a greater mistake than to voice such a complaint; from that moment it was Madame Grandet, so to speak, who courted Lucien. He seemed to take advantage of this position but—what was really very cruel—almost invariably when there were a great many people present. If he found Madame Grandet alone with only her intimate circle, he had to make the most heroic effort not to despise them.

"Are they wrong because their way of viewing life is diametrically opposed to mine? They have the majority with them."

But in spite of all his reasoning, which was eminently just, little by little he would grow cold, silent, interested in nothing.

"How can one talk of true virtue, of fame, of beauty, in

front of fools who misunderstand everything and try to spoil anything that is fine with their degrading jests?"

Distressed at being bored in the society of a woman he was supposed to adore, Lucien would have been even more distressed had he realized that his own state of mind was perfectly apparent. As he presumed that all these people were sticklers for polite behavior, he redoubled his attention and courtesy toward them.

During all this time Lucien's position, as private secretary to the man his father was engaged in tormenting, had become exceedingly delicate. By a kind of tacit agreement, M. de Vaize and Lucien rarely spoke to each other except to exchange polite formalities; an office boy carried papers from one to the other. As though to mark his confidence in Lucien, M. de Vaize fairly overwhelmed him with important ministerial business.

"Does he think he will make me cry mercy?" thought Lucien, and worked at least as hard as three department heads. He was often at his desk at seven in the morning, and sometimes during dinner he would have documents copied at his father's bank, and return to the Ministry in the evening to have them placed on His Excellency's table. And the Minister received these proofs of what in the departments was called talent, with the greatest possible ill-humor.

"It's more deadening than to calculate a logarithm to fourteen decimal places," Lucien remarked to Coffe, while M. de Vaize was complaining bitterly to his wife:

"M. Leuwen and his son evidently want to show me that I made a mistake in not offering the latter a Prefecture on his return from Caen. But what have they to complain of? He has his lieutenancy and his Cross which I promised him *only* if he succeeded, and he did not succeed."

Stealing Lucien's valuable time from those endless documents, Madame de Vaize would send for him three or four times a week. Madame Grandet also found frequent excuses for seeing him during the day, and, because of his feeling of gratitude to his father, Lucien tried to take advantage of these occasions and give a passable imitation of a man in love. He calculated that he saw Madame Grandet at least twelve times a week.

"If society is interesting itself in my affairs, it will think that I am terribly smitten, and I shall be forever whitewashed of the suspicion of Saint-Simonism."

To please Madame Grandet he took great care of his appearance and passed for one of the best dressed young men of Paris.

"It is a great mistake to make yourself look younger," objected his father. "If you were thirty-six, or at least had the disagreeable look of a *doctrinaire,* I could put you in the position which I should like to see you occupy."

This general state of affairs had now lasted six weeks, and Lucien was consoling himself with the thought that it could not possibly last six weeks longer, when one fine day Madame Grandet sent a little note to his father requesting an hour's conversation with him the following day at Madame de Thémines'.

"I am already treated like a Minister," thought M. Leuwen. "O enviable state!"

Next day Madame Grandet began with endless protestations of one sort or another. During these lengthy circumlocutions, M. Leuwen remained grave and impassive.

"Since I am asked for audiences, I must behave like a Minister," he said to himself.

After some time Madame Grandet went on to the eulogy of her own sincerity. . . . M. Leuwen counted the minutes by the clock on the mantelpiece.

"First and foremost, I must remain silent, I must not indulge in the slightest pleasantry at the expense of this young woman—so fresh and so young, yet already so ambitious! But what the deuce is she after? She is really lacking in tact. She ought to see how bored I am. . . . She may enjoy more aristocratic manners than our young ladies of the Opera, but less real wit."

But, when Madame Grandet at length asked him point-blank for a Ministry for her husband, M. Leuwen stopped being bored.

"The King, you know, is very fond of M. Grandet," she added, "and will be delighted to see him take his place in the affairs of State. We have proofs of the good will of the Château, which I shall be glad to particularize if you will give me the opportunity."

M. Leuwen assumed a cold and distant air. The scene was beginning to amuse him; it was worth a little play-acting. In spite of a natural tenacity of purpose which was not easily daunted, alarmed now and almost disconcerted, Madame Grandet began to speak of their longstanding friendship. . . .

At these remarks on friendship, which called for some response, M. Leuwen remained silent, and as though preoccupied. Madame Grandet saw her experiment miscarrying.

"I am ruining our chances," she said to herself. This thought decided her on extreme measures, and sharpened her wits.

Her position was rapidly deteriorating: M. Leuwen was not the same man he had been at the beginning of their interview. At first she was uneasy, then terrified. These emotions were most becoming, and lent some expression to her face. M. Leuwen encouraged her apprehensions.

Things arrived at such a pass that Madame Grandet decided to ask M. Leuwen plainly what it was he had against her. At this, M. Leuwen, who had for the last three-quarters of an hour maintained an almost solemn and ominous silence, had to struggle to keep from bursting out laughing.

"If I laugh," he thought, "what I am about to say will appear to her in all its ignominy. I shall have endured an hour of boredom for nothing, and shall miss an opportunity of *sounding* the depths of this famous virtue."

At last M. Leuwen, whose silence had grown more and more intolerable, seemed mercifully on the point of deigning to explain himself.

He asked a thousand pardons for what he was about to say, and for the painful expression he would be forced to employ. He amused himself by keeping Madame Grandet in a state of terror by implying the most terrible things.

"After all, she has no character, and that poor Lucien will be getting a boring mistress—if he gets her. These celebrated beauties are admirable for decoration and for show, but that's all. They must be seen in a magnificent drawing room surrounded by a lot of diplomats, covered with all their gewgaws, their medals and their ribbons. I'd be curious to know if indeed Madame de Chasteller is any better. Certainly not as far as physical beauty is concerned, or superb carriage, and it would be impossible to match the real beauty of these lovely arms. Aside from that, although it's rather amusing to poke fun at her, she bores me to death. At least, I keep counting the minutes by the clock. If she had the character her beauty seems to promise, she would have interrupted me a dozen times and driven me into a corner. She lets herself be treated like a victim who is forced to fight a duel."

At last, after several minutes of indirect propositions which kept Madame Grandet on tenterhooks, M. Leuwen pronounced the following words in a low and deeply emotional tone:

"Madam, I confess that I cannot bring myself to like you, for, because of you, my son will certainly die of a consumption." And he thought with amusement: "My voice stood me in good stead, it had just the right note of pathos."

But, after all, M. Leuwen was not made to be a great diplomat, a Talleyrand, an ambassador to serious personages. Boredom made him ill-humored, and he was never sure that he would be able to resist the temptation of launching some amusing or insolent sally by way of diversion. After speaking his solemn line, he felt such an irresistible desire to laugh that he quickly fled.

Left alone, Madame Grandet locked the door and for an hour remained motionless in her armchair. Her air was pensive, her eyes immeasurably wide open, like M. Guerin's *Phêdre* in the Luxembourg. No ambition-ridden man, tormented by ten years of waiting, ever coveted the Ministry as Madame Grandet coveted it at that moment.

"How wonderful to play the role of a Madame Roland, in the midst of this decaying society! I should write all my husband's ministerial circulars for him, for he has no style.

"Only through a great and unhappy passion with, as my victim, the most distinguished man of the Faubourg Saint-Germain, could I ever hope to attain a really important position. To what heights that would lift me! But I can grow old in my present situation before any such chance occurs. Whereas, if M. Grandet became Minister, men like that—perhaps not of the bluest nobility but of a very satisfactory hue—would flock around me. Madame de Vaize is just a little fool, but she has all of them she wants. Sensible people are sure always to come back to the master of the Budget."

Reasons swarmed through Madame Grandet's head, confirming her feeling that it would be a joy to be a Minister's wife. It was not exactly the way to contemplate such an eventuality. Such were hardly the thoughts that fired the great soul of Madame Roland on the eve of her husband's becoming Minister. But, alas, it is in the same way that our age imitates the great men of '93, the way M. de Polignac showed his character; the material fact alone is copied: to be a Minister, to bring about a coup d'état, create a "Day"—a 4th Prairial, a 10th of August, an 18th Fructidor. But how such triumphs are to be achieved, the motives behind the deeds—no one thinks of digging as deeply as that.

When it came to the question of the price to be paid for these blessings, Madame Grandet's imagination deserted her, she refused to think about it, her mind became blank. She was loath frankly to accept, and no less reluctant to refuse. She needed a long and superfluous debate to accustom herself to the idea. Fired by ambition, her soul could not be bothered by this disagreeable condition which was, after all, of secondary importance. She felt that she would certainly suffer remorse—not religious, but aristocratic remorse.

"Would a great lady, a Duchesse de Longueville, a Madame de Chevreuse, have given so little thought to this disagreeable condition?" she asked herself vaguely. But, her mind being completely absorbed by her dreams of the Ministry, she failed to answer.

"How many footmen will we have to keep? How many horses?"

This woman, so famous for her virtue, had so little time to spare in the service of that habit of the soul called chastity, that she forgot to reply to this question she kept asking herself, and, it must be admitted, purely as a matter of form. However, after enjoying her future ministerial status for more than three-quarters of an hour, she at last gave it her attention.

"Would Madame de Chevreuse or Madame de Longueville have consented? Yes, those great ladies undoubtedly would have consented. What makes them superior to me on the moral plane is that they yielded out of a sort of semi-passion, except when it was for a somewhat more physical reason. *They* could be seduced, *I* cannot." (And she admired herself enor-mously.) "With me judgment and foresight are the only considerations. Certainly the idea of pleasure does not enter into it."

Having regained her serenity, or at least feeling fairly reassured on this feminine point, Madame Grandet once more gave herself up to the sweet contemplation of the exalted position she would enjoy as soon as she became a Minister's wife. . . .

"A name that has once been associated with the Ministry is famous forever after. Among all the eminent men in the nation, thousands of Frenchmen know only the names of those who have been Ministers."

Madame Grandet's imagination soared away into the future, her youth stretching out before her, crowded with the most flattering events.

"I shall always be just, always kind—and to everybody, but with dignity. I shall be very active, and inside ten years all Paris will be talking about me. Already my house, my salon, my assemblies are well-known to the public. My old age will be like that of Madame Récamier—only with greater wealth."

Then, for a fleeting instant and only for form's sake, did she stop to wonder:

"But has M. Leuwen really enough influence to give my husband a portfolio? Or, once I have paid the price agreed upon, will he simply laugh at me? I must of course make sure! The first condition of any contract is the ability to deliver the merchandise sold."

The step Madame Grandet had just taken had first been agreed upon with her husband. She refrained, however, from giving him a verbatim account of her interview with M. Leuwen. She knew quite well that it would not be at all impossible to bring him to see things in a reasonable, philosophical and political light, but such a subject is always painful for a woman who respects herself. "It is better," she decided, "just to skip that part."

That evening it was not with unmitigated pleasure that she saw Lucien enter her drawing room. She lowered her eyes in embarrassment as her conscience told her:

"This is the person who will make it possible for you to be the wife of the Minister of the Interior."

Lucien, who knew nothing of his father's intervention, was immediately struck by something less formal and more natural about Madame Grandet, and later even noticed a hint of greater intimacy and warmth in her manner toward him. This manner which suggested, if only remotely, real simplicity and naturalness, pleased him far more than what Madame Grandet called sparkling wit. He remained by her side almost the whole evening.

But Lucien's presence, there was no doubt about it, embarrassed Madame Grandet. She was better acquainted with the theories than the practice of that high political intrigue which, in the time of Cardinal de Retz, constituted the daily life of those noble ladies de Longueville and de Chevreuse. She dismissed him early, but not without a little air of possession and friendly understanding which added to the pleasure Lucien felt at regaining his liberty at eleven o'clock.

Madame Grandet scarcely closed her eyes all night. It was only as day broke at five or six o'clock in the morning that the happiness of being the wife of a Minister finally let her get some rest. Had she been in the Ministry of the Rue de Grenelle, her sensations of happiness could hardly have been more violent. She was a woman for whom tangible blessings alone count.

During that night she had known one or two little vexations. For example, she began calculating the number and price of liveries at the Ministry. M. Grandet's were made partly of canary yellow cloth, which, in spite of all her recommendations, could not be kept clean for more than a month. How

much this expense would be increased, how much more super-
vision required by the enormous number of liveries needed at
the Ministry! She began to count: the porter, the coachman,
the footmen . . . Here she was stopped short in her calculations: she was not sure of the number of footmen at the Ministry of the Interior.

"Tomorrow I shall pay a little diplomatic call on Madame
de Vaize. Of course she must not suspect that I have come to
take stock of her household. How vulgar if she were to use
my visit as the subject for malicious gossip! But think of not
knowing the make-up of a Minister's household! M. Grandet
ought to know such things—but then he hasn't much of a
head."

It was not until she woke the next morning at eleven o'clock,
that Madame Grandet gave Lucien a thought. She soon smiled,
discovering that she was really fond of him, that he pleased
her more than he had the day before. For was it not through
him that all those grandeurs would come which were to in-
augurate a new life?

CHAPTER TWENTY-FOUR

WHILE LUCIEN was experiencing some astonishment at the singular reception accorded him that
evening at the Hôtel Grandet, Madame Leuwen
was engaged in serious conversation with her husband.

"Ah, my dear," she said, "ambition has turned your head,
such a good head too, God knows! Your lungs will suffer.
And what can ambition do for you? Is it money you want?
Is it decorations?"

Thus Madame Leuwen complained to her husband, who failed to defend himself.

Our reader will perhaps be surprised that a woman, still her husband's best friend at forty-five, should dare be so perfectly frank with him. It is because with a man of so singular a turn of mind, and a trifle mad, like M. Leuwen, it would have been exceedingly dangerous to be anything but entirely ingenuous. He might perhaps be deceived for a month or two through heedlessness, but one fine day the whole force of his really remarkable mind would, like the fire in a reverberatory furnace, become concentrated on the point about which a person was trying to deceive him; the deception would be discerned, made fun of, and all that person's credit with him lost forever.

Fortunately, for the happiness of husband and wife, they thought out loud in each other's presence. In the midst of such a lying world (and there is perhaps even more mendacity in intimate relationships than in society) this fragrance of perfect sincerity had a charm from which time could steal nothing of its freshness.

But never before had M. Leuwen come so near to lying to his wife as at that moment. Since his success in the Chamber had not cost him any trouble he could not believe in its duration, scarcely in its reality. Therein lay the illusion, the touch of madness, as well as the proof of the extreme pleasure he took in his success and the unbelievable position he had created for himself in three months. Had M. Leuwen brought to this affair the sang-froid which never deserted him in the most difficult financial matters he would have said to himself:

"This is a new way of using the power which I have always possessed. It is a steam engine which I had never thought of operating in this way before."

The flood of new sensations produced by such an astonishing triumph had quite got the better of M. Leuwen's habitual common sense, and it was this that he was ashamed to admit even to his wife. After endless discussion, M. Leuwen could no longer deny his weakness.

"Well then, yes!" he said at last, "I am suffering from an access of ambition, and the most amusing part of it is that I don't know what I want."

"Fortune is knocking at your door! You must make up your mind. If you don't open to her, she will knock at some other door."

"The miracles of the Almighty are wondrous to behold, especially when they operate on base and inert matter! I am about to make M. Grandet a Minister, or, at least, I am going to try."

"M. Grandet a Minister!" exclaimed Madame Leuwen, smiling. "But aren't you being unfair to Anselme? Why not consider him?"

(The reader has perhaps forgotten that Anselme was M. Leuwen's old and faithful valet.)

"Just as he is, with all his sixty years," M. Leuwen replied with that jocular seriousness he liked to affect, "Anselme would be far better for the affairs of State than M. Grandet, and, given a month to get over his astonishment, would settle questions, especially serious ones where great common sense is needed, much more wisely. But Anselme does not have a wife who is on the point of becoming the mistress of my son; and if I put Anselme in the Ministry of the Interior, the whole world would not see that it is really Lucien who is Minister in his person."

"Oh! but what is this you are telling me?" cried Madame Leuwen. And the smile, which had greeted the enumeration of Anselme's virtues, instantly vanished. "You are going to jeopardize my son's happiness. Lucien will be the victim of that restless spirit, of that woman who is always running about looking for happiness like a soul in pain, without ever finding it. She will make him as unhappy and uneasy as herself. How can Lucien fail to be shocked by the vulgarity of such a nature?"

"Ah, but she is the prettiest woman in Paris, or at least the most prominent. It would be impossible for a woman, so very virtuous till now, to have a lover without all Paris knowing it; and if the lover himself has a name at all well-known in society, this choice places him in the very first rank."

After a long discussion which was not without its charm for her, Madame Leuwen in the end conceded this point. She confined herself to insisting that Lucien was far too young to be presented to the public, especially to the Chamber, as a young business man and politician.

"Lucien makes a great mistake," M. Leuwen observed, "to affect such an elegant appearance and to dress so fashionably. And at the first opportunity I intend to speak to Madame Grandet on the subject. . . . In short, my dear, I count on driving Madame de Chasteller out of his heart. For, I can admit it to you now, I was really worried.

"I wonder," M. Leuwen continued, "if you know what admirable work Lucien is doing at the Ministry? I have excellent reports about him from Dubreuil, who has been assistant department head since the retirement of my friend Cretet twenty-five years ago. Lucien expedites more business than three section chiefs. He has not let himself be spoiled by any of the stupidities that fools call custom, the *daily round* of business. He decides questions promptly and boldly, in such a way as to dispose of them once and for all. He has declared himself the enemy of the Ministry's stationer, for he insists upon letters of only ten lines. In spite of his experience in Caen, he always acts in this bold, decided manner. And remember that, as we agreed, I have never told him my opinion of his conduct in the election of M. Mairobert. I have, of course, defended it indirectly in the Chamber, but he may have thought my remarks merely a matter of family solidarity.

"I shall have him appointed Secretary General if I can. Should they refuse me that on account of his age, the office will remain vacant. But even as private secretary Lucien will be Secretary General in fact, and take over those functions. He will either break his neck in a year, or he will make a reputation for himself, and I shall idiotically say:

> I have done my best
> All that friendship could do
> To make your fate blest
> And sweeter for you.

"For my part, I get myself out of a predicament. People will see that I have made Grandet Minister because my son is not yet ripe for office. If I fail, I'll have nothing to reproach myself with; fortune had not knocked at my door. If I succeed, my worries will be over for six months."

"Will M. Grandet be able to last that long?"

"There are reasons for and against it. He will have all the imbeciles with him, and he will run his house on a scale that will cost him a hundred thousand francs beyond his ministerial salary. That is enormous. He will lack absolutely nothing but wit in discussion, and common sense in business."

"A mere nothing!" commented Madame Leuwen.

"On the whole the best fellow in the world. In the Chamber you know how he will speak. He will read like a lackey the excellent speeches which I shall order from the best ghost writers at a hundred louis for every *successful* speech. And I shall speak myself. But will I have the same success in defense that I have had in attack? That is what I am curious to see, and the uncertainty intrigues me. My son and our little Coffe will furnish me with the body of my defensive speeches. . . . All this may be very dull, I really think . . ."

[*The chapter breaks off here. The fragment that follows was written in the manuscript on the back of the last page of the conversation between M. and Madame Leuwen.*]

But in reality Madame Leuwen was very much shocked by the feminine side of this arrangement.

"It is in very bad taste, and I am surprised that you would lend yourself to such things."

"But don't you know, my dear, that half the history of France is based on just such exemplary arrangements? Three quarters of the fortunes of our great families, now so high and mighty, were established by the hands of love."

"But what love, Great God!"

"Are you going to quarrel with the respectable name which French historians have adopted? Be careful or I shall use the exact word. From François I to Louis XV, the Ministry has always been the gift of great ladies, in the case of at least two-thirds of the vacancies. When our nation is not in the throes of an upheaval, she always reverts to these customs which are natural to her. And is it wrong to do what has always been done?" (This was M. Leuwen's true morality, but his wife, born under the Empire, had a sterner code more suitable to a budding despotism.)

She found some difficulty in reconciling herself to her husband's ethics.

CHAPTER TWENTY-FIVE

THERE WAS nothing romantic either in the character or in the habits of Madame Grandet, a fact which, for those with eyes to see and who were not dazzled by her queenly bearing and a complexion worthy of a young English girl, was strangely at variance with her conversational style as extravagantly sentimental and emotional as a novel by Nodier. She never said: *Paris,* but: *this vast city.* Romantic by affectation only, Madame Grandet brought to the management of her affairs a faultless judgment and the orderliness and meticulousness of a little shopkeeper who sells needles, and cloth by the yard.

When she had become somewhat accustomed to the joy of being a Minister's wife, she began to wonder whether perhaps M. Leuwen, because of his distress at seeing his son the victim of a hopeless passion, or at least in danger of making himself ridiculous, had not overestimated his strength. It never occurred to her to doubt Lucien's love. She knew love only through the bad replicas generally to be seen in society, and had not the eyes to perceive it where it sought seclusion. The great question to which Madame Grandet kept reverting was this:

"Is M. Leuwen really powerful enough to make a Minister? In spite of his almost inaudible voice, he is unquestionably a very popular orator, the only man the Chamber listens to— that no one can deny. They say the King receives him secretly. He is on the best terms with Marshal Soult, Minister of War. The combination of all these circumstances constitutes, without doubt, a brilliant position. But that does not necessarily mean that he can persuade a man as subtle and clever at dissembling as the King to entrust a Ministry to M. Grandet." And Madame Grandet heaved a deep sigh.

Tormented by this uncertainty, which in two days' time had almost completely undermined her happiness, Madame Grandet suddenly made up her mind. She boldly asked M. Leuwen for an interview, and had the temerity to fix the rendezvous at her own house. . . .

"This affair is so important *for us*," Madame Grandet began, "that I hardly think you will find it strange if I beg you to give me some further details in regard to the hopes you have led me to entertain."

"So," thought M. Leuwen, smiling to himself, "we don't discuss the price, we only want to be sure that the goods will be delivered."

In the sincerest and friendliest tone, M. Leuwen replied:

"It makes me happy indeed, Madam, to see the ties of our old and excellent friendship being more and more closely knit. From now on they must be intimate enough to admit of that degree of easy frankness and openhearted candor which will permit me to speak to you in a language free from all vain dissembling . . . as though you were already one of the family."

At these words, M. Leuwen could hardly refrain from giving her a sly wink.

"I have no need, I am sure, to ask you for absolute discretion. I shall not hide from you a fact which, indeed, with your penetrating as well as logical mind you must already have surmised: M. de Vaize is on the alert. One single indication, one single fact brought to him by one of his hundred spies—the Marquis de G——, for example, or M. R——, whom you know well, would be enough to upset all our little plans. M. de Vaize sees the Ministry about to escape him and he has not, one must admit, remained idle: he makes ten calls every day before eight o'clock in the morning. The Deputies are flattered because such an hour is unheard of in Paris. It reminds them of their own activity in the past when they were public prosecutors' clerks.

"Like myself, M. Grandet represents the Bank, and since July the Bank is the head of the State. The bourgeoisie has taken the place of the Faubourg Saint-Germain and now the Bank has become the nobility of the bourgeois class. M. Laffitte, believing that all men are angels, lost the Ministry for his class. Present circumstances call upon high finance to recapture control and once more to take possession of the Ministry. . . . Bankers have been accused of stupidity. Happily, the Chamber has given me a chance to prove that on occasion we are capable of overwhelming our adversaries with remarks which will not be so easily forgotten. I know better than anyone that such remarks are not arguments. But the Chamber dislikes arguments and the King likes only money. He needs a great many soldiers to check the working men and the republicans. It is to the interest of the government to keep on good terms with the Bourse. A Ministry cannot overthrow the Bourse, but the Bourse can overthrow the Ministry. The present Ministry cannot last much longer."

"That is what M. Grandet says."

"M. Grandet has sound enough views; but, since you allow me to speak to you as an intimate friend, I must confess to you, Madam, that if it had not been for you I should never have dreamed of M. Grandet for the Ministry. Let me ask you plainly: do you think you have enough authority with your husband to influence him when it comes to the capital decisions of his Ministry? It will take all your skill to handle the Minister of War. The King insists upon an army, and only the Marshal can administer and control it. But the King also loves money, wants piles of money, and he looks to the Minister of

Finance to furnish it. M. Grandet will have to keep a nice balance between the Minister of War and the Minister of *Money,* or else there will be an explosion. At present, for example, the differences between the Marshal and the Minister of Finance have caused more than a dozen ruptures, always followed, until now, by as many reconciliations. But the bitterness of the two sides has reached such a point that not even the most innocuous subjects can be discussed.

"Money is not only the sinews of war, but also of this kind of armed peace we have enjoyed since the July Days. In addition to money for the army, so indispensable against the workers, places must be found for the whole bourgeois general staff. They have at least six thousand gabblers who will turn their eloquence against you, if you don't silence them with posts worth six thousand francs. Constantly in need of money, the Marshal undoubtedly has his eye on a banker as next Minister of the Interior. Just between ourselves, what he wants is someone he can use, if necessary, against the Minister of Finance, someone who understands the fluctuating values of currency at different times of the day. The question now is, will the name of this Banker-Minister of the Interior, of this man who understands the Bourse and can, to a certain extent, control the maneuvers of M. de Rothschild or of the Minister of Finance, be Leuwen or Grandet? As for me, I am really too lazy for the job, and without mincing words, too old. I cannot yet make my son Minister. He is not a Deputy. I don't even know if he can speak in public or not—but I do know that for the last six months you have rendered him completely dumb. . . . But what I *can* do is to put into the Ministry of the Interior a suitable man who is the choice of the person who is going to save my son's life."

"I do not doubt the sincerity of your good intentions toward *us.*"

"Which, I take it, Madam, means that you rather doubt—

and in this I find another reason for admiring your prudence
—that you doubt my power to do so. In any discussion on the
high interests of the Crown or of politics doubt is a paramount
duty and cannot be considered an affront by either of the contracting parties. One may very well deceive oneself and jeopardize, not only the interests of a friend, but one's own as well.
I have told you that I might consider M. Grandet. You somewhat doubt my power. It is naturally not in my power to offer
you the portfolio of the Interior or of Finance as I would
offer you a bunch of violets. With things as they are today,
even the King cannot make you such a gift. A Minister, after
all, must be elected by five or six persons, each one with the
right merely to *veto* the choice of the others. He cannot absolutely guarantee the election of his candidate. Besides, Madam,
you must not forget that, in the end, it is necessary not only
to satisfy the King entirely and the Chamber of Deputies to a
certain extent, but also not to offend that poor Chamber of
Peers unduly. It is for you, lovely lady, to decide whether or
not you choose to believe that I intend to do everything in my
power to install you in the Ministry on the Rue de Grenelle.
Before estimating the degree of my devotion to your interests,
try to decide to your own satisfaction the exact weight of the
influence which for two or three times twenty-four hours
chance has put into my hands."

"I do believe in you, utterly," rejoined Madame Grandet.
"My very willingness to discuss such a subject with you is
proof enough. But it hardly follows that because I have confidence in your ability and your luck . . . that I am willing to
make the sacrifice you seem to expect."

"I should be miserable if I thought I was wounding in the
slightest degree that enchanting delicacy of your sex which
adds such charms to the bloom of youth, and even to the most
perfect beauty. But Madame de Chevreuse, the Duchesse de
Longueville and, in fact, all the women whose names have

left their mark on history and who—which is more to the point—have established the fortune of their house, sometimes had interviews with their doctors. Well, I am the doctor of the soul, the mentor of that noble ambition which your admirable position has inevitably kindled. In an age, in the midst of a society built on quicksands, where everything is unstable, where everything is crumbling, your superior intelligence, your great fortune, M. Grandet's well-known courage, and your own personal advantages have created for you a solid, impregnable position, independent of the caprices of power. There is only one enemy you have to fear: Fashion. For the moment, you are her favorite. But Fashion, without the least regard for personal merit, inevitably proves fickle. If in a year or eighteen months you present nothing new for the admiration of this society, which for the moment does you justice and places you in so exalted a position, you will be in danger. The least trifle —a carriage not in the best of taste, an illness, a mere nothing —and, in spite of your youth, you will be relegated to the ranks of past glories."

"I have known the truth of what you say for a long time," retorted Madame Grandet with a touch of annoyance, like a queen who has been inopportunely reminded of a defeat suffered by her armies. "Yes, I have known this great truth for a long time: Fashion is a fire which dies without fresh fuel."

"There is another truth," added M. Leuwen, "no less startling and no less pertinent: a patient who turns against his physician, or a litigant who turns against his lawyer instead of reserving his strength to fight his adversaries, is hardly on the eve of changing his position for the better."

M. Leuwen rose.

"My charming lady, moments are precious. Do you want to treat me as one of your adorers and try to make me lose my head? I must reply that I have no head to lose any longer, and will seek my fortune elsewhere."

"What a cruel man you are! Very well then, speak!"

Madame Grandet was wise to give up her high-flown style. M. Leuwen, much more a man of pleasure and of changing moods than a man of business or of ambition, found it sufficiently ridiculous to let his plans depend on a woman's whims, and was already turning over in his mind some other means of advancing Lucien's standing in the public eye.

"I am certainly not made for the Ministry," he had been saying to himself while Madame Grandet was talking. "I am too lazy, I am too accustomed to enjoying myself. I never take tomorrow into consideration. If, instead of a little Parisian society woman talking nonsense and beating about the bush, I were face to face with the King, I would be just as impatient, and would never be forgiven. I must concentrate all my efforts on my son."

"Madam," he said, as though bringing his thoughts back from far away, "do you want to talk to me as to an old man of sixty-five who is for the moment politically ambitious, or do you want to continue to do me the honor of treating me as a handsome young man, dazzled—as they all are—by your charms?"

"Speak! Speak, my dear friend," Madame Grandet returned eagerly, for she was quick to read in their eyes the decisions of her interlocutors, and she began to be frightened. It seemed to her—which was true—that M. Leuwen had reached the end of his patience.

"One of us must have confidence in the other's loyalty."

"In that case—to answer you with all the frankness you have insisted on as a duty—why should *I* be that one?"

"The force of circumstances, my dear lady, will have it so. What I ask of you—your stake, as it were, if you will permit me so common an expression, but at least perfectly clear" (and M. Leuwen's tone lost some of its urbanity and verged on that of a man selling a piece of land who has just named his final price), "what constitutes your stake in this grand intrigue of lofty ambitions, is entirely within your own control, while the quite enviable position I am offering you for sale depends on the King, and on the opinion of four or five persons who, for the moment, deign to place great confidence in me but who, after all, have ideas of their own. Besides, at any moment—after a failure on my part in the Chamber, for example—they might very well withdraw it. In this great combination of State and high ambition, the one who is already in a position to pay the price, or as you have permitted me to call it, the stake, must make the payment or, I am afraid, the other contracting party will have more admiration for her prudence than for her sincerity. And the other, whose stake is not at his disposal—myself, in other words—must do everything humanly possible which the other may demand to furnish her guarantees."

Madame Grandet remained thoughtful, and visibly embarrassed not so much over what her reply should be, as how best to formulate it. M. Leuwen, who was in doubt about the final result, for an instant had the malicious idea of putting off the decision until the following day. The night would bring counsel. But because of his natural indolence, his reluctance to return the next day, he was anxious to finish on the spot. So now, lowering his voice a little and speaking in the deep tones of M. de Talleyrand, he familiarly added:

"These occasions, my dear friend, which make or unmake the fortunes of a house, present themselves once in a lifetime, and present themselves in a more or less agreeable manner. The particular road to the temple of Fortune which I propose is one of the least thorny I know of. But will you have the strength of character? After all, the problem for you boils down to this: "Shall I or shall I not trust M. Leuwen whom *I have known for fifteen years?* In order to reply to that question coolly and wisely, ask yourself: 'What did I think of M.

Leuwen, and would I have deemed him worthy of my confidence two weeks ago, before there was any question of a political transaction between us?' "

"Perfect confidence!" cried Madame Grandet with relief, as though happy to do M. Leuwen a justice which relieved her of a painful doubt. "Perfect confidence!"

Then, with the resigned air of someone agreeing to the inevitable, M. Leuwen said:

"In two days, at the latest, I shall have to present M. Grandet to the Marshal."

"M. Grandet *dined* at the Marshal's less than a month ago," Madame Grandet, somewhat piqued, hastened to assure him.

"I underestimated this feminine vanity," he thought, "I judged her less stupid."

"Naturally, I cannot have the pretension of acquainting the Marshal with the person of M. Grandet. Everyone who knows anything of high finance in Paris knows M. Grandet, his financial genius, his wealth, his luxurious hôtel; he is known, above all, because of that most distinguished woman in Paris whom he has honored with his name. The King himself holds him in high consideration, his courage is famous. What I shall say to the Marshal is simply this: 'Here is M. Grandet, an excellent financier who understands all the intricacies of the money market, a man who, should His Excellency choose to make him Minister of the Interior, would be able to hold his own against the Minister of Finance. I should of course support M. Grandet with all the power of my feeble voice.' That is all I meant by presenting M. Grandet to the Marshal. In three days," added M. Leuwen, still speaking rather sharply, "if I do not say that, then, in justice to myself, I shall have to say instead: 'After due consideration I have decided that, with my son to assist me, if you will give him the title of Under-Secretary of State, I will accept the Ministry.' Do you think that after presenting M. Grandet, I am a man capable of saying to the Marshal in private: 'Don't believe a word of what I said to you in front of M. Grandet, I want to be Minister myself'?"

"But I do not doubt your good faith in the least," cried Madame Grandet. "You are putting a patch where there is no sign of a hole. You fail to realize how strange is the request you ask of me. You are a libertine, your well-known opinion of what constitutes the whole dignity of our sex prevents you from appreciating the full extent of the sacrifice. What will Madame Leuwen say? How can it be kept from her?"

"In a thousand ways; by an anachronism, for example."

"You must forgive me—I am in no state to continue this discussion. Do be good enough to postpone until tomorrow the conclusion of our conversation."

"As you wish! But tomorrow, will I still be Fortune's favorite? If you will have none of my suggestion, then I must make other arrangements, and endeavor to distract my son—who is my sole concern in this entire affair—by arranging a fine marriage. Remember that I have no time to lose. The absence of a definite reply tomorrow means a *no* which it will be impossible to reconsider."

Madame Grandet had just had the idea of first consulting her husband.

CHAPTER TWENTY-SIX

"M. LEUWEN is a passionately devoted father," Madame Grandet began by explaining. "His chief motive, his greatest worry in this whole affair, is the pronounced taste manifested by M. Lucien Leuwen for Mademoiselle Raimonde of the ballet."

"Like father, like son, egad!"

"That is what I was thinking," laughed Madame Grandet, adding more seriously, "You are going to have to make this matter your personal concern, or you'll lose M. Leuwen's voice."

"That's a fine voice you're promising me."

"You are intelligent, I know, but as long as that little voice is listened to, as long as his sarcasms are the fashion with the Chamber, he can, they say, make and unmake Ministers, and no one would take a chance of forming a Ministry without him."

"What a joke! A banker who is half Dutch, notorious for his charming friends at the Opera—and who refused to be Captain of the National Guard!" This last was added with a tragic air, for M. Grandet's ambition dated from the June Days. "In addition," he went on gloomily (he had been well received by the Queen), "in addition, a man known for his disgraceful jokes on everything which men in our station are bound to respect."

M. Grandet was fifty per cent a fool, ponderous and fairly well educated. Every evening he sweated blood for an hour *keeping up with French literature,* as he put it. But he would not have been able to tell the difference between a page of Voltaire and a page of M. Viennet. One can imagine his hatred for a man of wit who had had a triumph without making the slightest effort. That is what incensed him most.

Madame Grandet knew only too well that she could get nothing out of her husband until he had exhausted all the well-turned phrases the subject afforded. And the worst of it was that one phrase engendered another. M. Grandet had the habit of letting himself run on in this manner with the hope of developing some wit along the way. Had he lived in Lyons or Bourges instead of Paris, the method would have been justified.

After she had, by her silence, agreed with him on all M.

Leuwen's faults, this fertile subject occupying twenty minutes, Madame Grandet continued:

"You are now embarked on the road of lofty ambition. Do you remember the remark of Chancellor Oxenstierna to his son? . . ."

"Such remarks of great men are my breviary," cried M. Grandet. "I agree with them entirely: 'O my son, you will soon discover how little talent it takes to direct the great affairs of this world.'"

"There you are! For a man like you, M. Leuwen is only a stepping-stone. What difference does it make to you if he is worth anything or not? What is it to you if a Chamber made up of half-wits is amused by his bad jokes, and swallows his chatter from the rostrum as the significant eloquence of a true statesman? Remember that it was a weak woman, Madame de ——, who, by speaking to another weak woman, the Queen of Austria, introduced the famous Cardinal Richelieu into the royal councils. No matter what he is, it is the part of wisdom to indulge M. Leuwen's mania so long as the Chamber has that of admiring him. But what I should like you to tell me—for, mixing as you do in different political circles, you are able to gauge, with a practiced eye, all that is happening—is the credit M. Leuwen now enjoys solid? For it does not enter into the proud and pure system of ethics which I follow, to make promises and not to observe them scrupulously." And she added petulantly, "That wouldn't suit me at all."

"Well, yes," replied M. Grandet reluctantly, "M. Leuwen is indeed in high credit at this moment. His stupid witticisms in the Chamber have hypnotized everybody. I am of the same opinion as our friend Viennet of the Académie Française—even in the matter of literary taste we are in full decadence. Leuwen has the backing of the Marshal who, above everything else, wants money and M. Leuwen, I don't know how or why, is the representative of the Bourse. He amuses the Marshal with all his jests which are in execrable taste. It isn't difficult to be amusing if you allow yourself to say anything that comes into your head. The King, in spite of his exquisite taste, tolerates Leuwen's low wit. They even say that it was M. Leuwen who poisoned the King's mind against that poor de Vaize."

"Yes, but after all," cried Madame Grandet, "think of M. de Vaize as arbiter of the arts! What a farce! Did you know that when a picture of Rembrandt was proposed for purchase by the Museum, M. de Vaize wrote on the margin of the report: 'Find out what M. Rembrandt exhibited at the last Salon'?"

"At least," her husband retorted, "M. de Vaize is polite. Leuwen would sacrifice his best friend for a witticism."

"Tell me, do you think you would have the courage to appoint M. Lucien Leuwen, that silent son of a talkative father, as your Secretary-General?"

"What! A Second-Lieutenant of Lancers as Secretary-General? Such a thing has never been heard of! Is there no more seriousness left anywhere?"

"Alas, nowhere," sighed Madame Grandet. "There is certainly no seriousness left in our customs. It is deplorable. M. Leuwen was not even serious when he gave me his ultimatum, his condition *sine qua non*. . . . Only remember, my friend, if we make a promise we have to keep it."

"But to think of taking as Secretary-General a little sly-boots who even presumes to have ideas of his own! He would play the same role with me as that of M. de N—— with M. de Villèle. I am not anxious to harbor such an *intimate enemy*."

For another ill-humored twenty minutes, Madame Grandet had to endure the profound and witty remarks of this man, who, though more than half a fool, was trying to imitate Montesquieu, who failed to understand his position, and whose intelligence had been completely blocked by an income of a hundred thousand pounds. M. Grandet's heated reply, so fraught with interest, as he would have said, was as like as two peas to a newspaper article by M. Salvandy or M. Viennet. But we shall spare our readers who undoubtedly read something in a similar vein this morning in their journals.

Knowing quite well that his only chance of obtaining the Ministry was through M. Leuwen, M. Grandet agreed to leave the assignment of the post of Secretary-General to him.

"As to his son's title," pursued Madame Grandet, "M. Leuwen will decide. Because of the Chamber, it would perhaps be as well for his son to remain private secretary just as he is today under M. de Vaize, but with the functions of Secretary-General."

"I don't care for all this hocus-pocus. In a loyal administration everyone should bear the title which corresponds to his functions."

"If that's the case," thought Madame Grandet, "you ought to have the title of steward to a clever woman who makes you a Minister."

Once more several minutes had to be sacrificed. Madame Grandet knew that this brave Colonel of the National Guard, her husband, could only be silenced through pure physical fatigue. Talking to his wife, he was *practicing* his wit for the Chamber of Deputies. One can imagine what grace and congruity such pretensions lent to a perfectly prosaic merchant who totally lacked imagination of any kind.

At last Madame Grandet was able to proceed:

"It will be necessary to stupefy M. Lucien Leuwen with work, in order to make him forget Mademoiselle Raimonde."

"Noble function, indeed!"

"It's the mania of that man who, by a ridiculous stroke of luck, has obtained power, full power, at this moment. And what is more respectable than a man in power?"

Ten minutes later they again spoke of Mademoiselle Raimonde. When M. Grandet had quite finished laughing at M.

Leuwen's primitive tastes, and had exhausted the subject, he at last proposed:

"Well, then why don't you employ a little coquetry to make the young man forget this ridiculous passion? It's just the thing. You could offer him your friendship."

Until this moment, M. Grandet *had been displaying wit,* but now he spoke in that tone of unadorned common sense which was natural to him. (The conference had reached its seventh quarter hour.)

"Possibly," Madame Grandet rejoined with the most perfect artlessness, but secretly overjoyed. ("This is an enormous step in advance," she thought, "but I had to be sure.")

She rose.

"It is an idea," she said to her husband, "but hardly an agreeable one for me."

"But, my dear, your reputation is such—and at the age of twenty-six and with all your beauty, your conduct so virtuous, so far above suspicion to everyone, even above the envy aroused by my success, that you have every right, within the limits of modesty and, naturally, of honor, to permit yourself whatever may serve our advancement in the world."

("He talks about my reputation as he would talk about the good points of his horses.")

"It was not merely yesterday that the name of Grandet began to enjoy the esteem of respectable people. We were not born in a cabbage patch."

"Good Lord," thought Madame Grandet, "he's going to begin talking about his ancestor, the Captain of Toulouse!" And she hastened to interpose.

"Just stop to consider, M. le Ministre, the extent of the program you thus endorse. Any sudden change in my entourage might lead to gossip and damage my reputation. Once M. Lucien is admitted on a footing of intimacy, whatever he is to us during the first two months of your Ministry, such he must remain for two years at least, even if M. Leuwen should lose favor with the Chamber and with the King, or—which isn't likely—even if your Ministry should fall . . ."

"Ministries," replied M. Grandet, somewhat nettled, "last at least three years. The Chamber has still four Budgets to vote."

("And now I've called down upon my head another fifteen minutes of high politics in his best countinghouse manner.")

Madame Grandet was mistaken: exactly seventeen minutes passed before the conversation got back to the question of whether M. Grandet would consent to admit M. Lucien Leuwen as an intimate friend of the family for three years, if he admitted him for a month.

"But then people will say he is your lover."

"That is a misfortune from which I should suffer more than anyone. I expected you to try to console me. . . . But, to come to the point, do you or don't you want to be Minister of the Interior?"

"I want to be Minister, but only like Colbert, by honorable means."

"And where is the dying Cardinal Mazarin who is to present you to the King?"

This historic citation, so aptly brought forward, provoked M. Grandet's admiration. He mistook it for an argument and was convinced.

CHAPTER TWENTY-SEVEN

THAT EVENING Madame Grandet proposed a game of chess with Lucien. She was more animated and brilliant than usual, and her complexion was even more dazzling. Her beauty, which was of the first water, had nothing sublime or austere about it, in short, nothing to charm distinguished minds or terrify the vulgar. She enjoyed a conspicuous success with the fifteen or twenty persons who came up to the chess table during the game.

"And such a belle as this is practically running after me!" Lucien thought to himself as he gave her the pleasure of winning. "I must be a strange sort of animal not to be overjoyed."

All at once this thought occurred to him:

"I am in pretty much the same predicament as my father. I shall lose my standing in this drawing room if I don't profit by it. And who can tell if I won't regret it? I have always despised the position but I have not yet occupied it. I am a fool to despise it." Then, turning to Madame Grandet he said bitterly:

"For me, playing chess with you is a cruel privilege. Unless you respond to my fatal love there is nothing left for me but to blow out my brains."

"Very well then," she rejoined quickly, "live and love me! . . . But if you stay here any longer I feel that your presence will rob me of all my self-control. Leave me now. Talk to my husband for five minutes, and come back to me tomorrow at one o'clock."

"So now," Lucien said to himself as he climbed into his cabriolet, "I am a happy man."

He had hardly gone a hundred yards before he pulled up, and handed the reins over to his servant.

"I must really be happy," he decided, "since I am too upset to drive! And is the happiness society has to offer nothing more than that? My father is about to form a Ministry, he plays an enviable role in the Chamber, the most brilliant woman in Paris seems to be yielding to my so-called passion . . ."

But twist and turn his happiness as he would, the only comfort Lucien could squeeze out of it was summed up in his conclusion:

"Let us enjoy this good fortune lest, like a child, we regret it when it is gone."

A few days later, quitting his carriage at Madame Grandet's door, Lucien was suddenly beguiled by the loveliness of the moonlight flooding the Place de la Madeleine. Much to the astonishment of all the coachmen, instead of entering the house, he turned and walked away.

To escape their glances of curiosity, he went on a hundred paces and humbly lighted his cigar at a chestnut vendor's brazier. He then gave himself up to the contemplation of the beauty of the sky and to his own reflections.

Lucien had not been admitted to the secret of all his father's activities on his behalf, and we cannot deny that he was a bit flattered by his success with this Madame Grandet whose irreproachable conduct, rare beauty, and vast fortune added a certain glamour to Parisian society. Had she been able to add noble lineage to these other advantages, she would have been famous throughout Europe. But, do what she would, she could never entice any English *milords* to her drawing room.

Gradually, Lucien began to relish this good fortune of his, which had left him cold during the first few days. Madame

Grandet was the most impressive great lady he had ever known. For we must confess (although this may prejudice our hero in the eyes of those of our lovely feminine readers who, happily for them, enjoy too much nobility or too much wealth) that the infinite pretensions of the noble ladies de Commercy, de Marcilly, and other "cousins of the Emperor" destitute of fortune, whom he had met in Nancy, had always seemed to him ridiculous. . . .

"The cult of ancient ideas, of ultraism," thought Lucien, "is much more ridiculous in the provinces than in Paris. On second thought it is really less; for in the provinces, at least, that great body cannot be accused of energy. Filled with envy and fear, these two amiable passions make them forget to live."

These thoughts, summing up all Lucien's sensations in the provinces, spoiled for him Madame d'Hocquincourt's piquant charm, and the really superior wit of Madame de Puylaurens. That continual fear, that regret of a past one dares not defend, in Lucien's opinion, precluded all true superiority. But in Madame Grandet's drawing room, on the contrary, what luxury, what opulence, and what a complete absence of fear or envy!

"That is the only way to live," Lucien decided. And sometimes weeks passed by without his being shocked by any vulgar remark—the sort never heard in the drawing rooms of Madame d'Hocquincourt or Madame de Puylaurens. Such vulgar remarks, which betray a natural coarseness, were generally uttered by some Deputy of the Center who had sold himself to the Ministry for a decoration or a tobacco shop concession, and had not yet learned to wear a mask to conceal his ugliness. Much to his father's sorrow Lucien never addressed one word to these blockheads. As he passed by, he would hear them ponderously discussing the question of President Jackson's twenty-five million, or the sugar tax, or some other point of political economy, without even trying to understand the fundamental principles involved.

"They are the very dregs of France," thought Lucien. "They are both stupid and venal, but at least they do not live in constant fear, they do not cry over the past, nor do they stupefy their children by allowing them to read nothing but the *Journée du Chretien.*

"In this age when only money counts, and everything is for sale, is there anything comparable to a great fortune spent with a clever and cautious hand? This fellow Grandet never pays out ten louis without considering his position in the world. Neither he nor his wife allow themselves those extravagances which I, a young man still living under my father's roof, indulge in."

He often overheard them haggling about the price of a theater box, or soliciting one gratis from the Château or the Ministry of the Interior.

Lucien saw Madame Grandet constantly surrounded by universal homage. But despite all this philosophy, a certain monarchic instinct that still lingered in the carriage class insinuated that it would be more flattering to be admired by a woman who bore one of the great names of the old monarchy.

"Should I succeed (out of the question for me, of course) in being received in the legitimist drawing rooms of Paris, the only difference from those of Nancy would be that M. de Serpierre's and Madame de Marcilly's three or four Chevaliers de Saint-Louis would be replaced by four Dukes or Peers claiming, like M. de Saint-Lérant at Madame de Marcilly's, that the Emperor Nicholas had a treasure of six hundred million francs in a little chest bequeathed to him by the Emperor Alexander for the purpose of exterminating all the Jacobins in France whenever he got around to it. There is surely an Abbé Rey here too tyrannizing over the pretty women of the nobility, poor things, and terrifying them into spending two hours listening to the sermons of some Abbé Poulet. The mistress I should have then, even if her ancestors could be traced back to the Creation, would be obliged, in spite of herself, like Madame d'Hocquincourt, to join in discussions of twenty minutes, at least, on the merits of the Bishop of ——'s last charge to his clergy. The Holy Fathers who had burned John Huss at the stake would be lauded with the most finished elegance, but how that elegance would betray the underlying hardness of heart! The moment I meet with it I am on my guard. It pleases me in books, but in life it chills me, and, at the end of a quarter of an hour, arouses my antipathy.

"Absurdity of this sort in Madame Grandet, thanks to her bourgeois name, is entirely restricted to her morning calls on Madame de Thémines, Madame Toniel and other daughters of the Church. I should be let off with a few words of respect for all that is respectable, repeated once a week.

"The men I meet at Madame Grandet's have, at least, *done* something, if only to make a fortune. Whether they have acquired it through business, or newspaper articles, or by selling speeches to the government, they have at any rate been active.

"The society I mingle with at my mistress's," and Lucien laughed as he said the word, "is like a story badly written but interesting because of its subject matter. Madame de Marcilly's world is made up of absurd, or even hypocritical theories based on imaginary facts clothed in polite language. But the elegance of the style is constantly belied by the asperity of the glances. All that unctuous eloquence, in imitation of Fénelon, exudes, for anyone with somewhat keener senses, a delicate yet penetrating aroma of knavery and rascality.

"At a Parisian Madame de Marcilly's I might gradually acquire that habit of a total lack of interest in what I am saying, as well as the use of those expressions, so often recommended by my mother, which dilute the thought. Sometimes I really begin to regret that I never acquired those Nineteenth Cen tury virtues—but I should bore myself too terribly. I count on old age to take care of all that.

"I have noticed that the unfailing effect of this sort of elegance, which belongs to a handful of youthful inhabitants of the Faubourg Saint-Germain who have acquired it without, for all that, leaving their wits at school, is simply to spread around the *accomplished* person an atmosphere of profound distrust. His elegant conversation is like an orange tree planted in the middle of the Compiègne Forest—pretty, but out of place in our age.

"Fortune did not see fit to have me born into that world. And why change myself? What do I ask of their world? My eyes, as Madame de Chasteller told me a dozen times, would always betray me. . . ."

Abruptly Lucien's flow of words was interrupted by that name, as, by the crowing of the cock, were those of that weak man who, when taunted, denied his Friend, arrested for His political opinions. Like Bartolo in Rossini's *Barber,* Lucien stood motionless. Eight or ten times already, since Madame Grandet had made him a happy man, Madame de Chasteller's image had risen before his mind's eye, but never so vividly as at that moment. He had always banished it with some hasty excuse, such as: "My heart is not involved in this affair. This is purely and simply a matter of youth and ambition." Nevertheless, until this sudden evocation of Madame de Chasteller, he had done everything in his power to prolong his new liaison. Madame Grandet was not only causing him to break his relations with Mademoiselle Raimonde, but even with the cherished, the sacred memory of Madame de Chasteller. The iniquity was infinitely greater.

Two months before, in the collection of the heavenly porcelains of M. Constantin, he had come upon a head which, because of its resemblance to Madame de Chasteller, had brought a sudden blush to his cheek. He had had it copied by a young painter. While the work was being done, he haunted the artist's studio, who was touched by his tender eagerness and became his friend. Lucien would fly to the studio as though to do penance before this holy image. I wonder whether he will be eternally disgraced if we confess that, like the famous character with whom we have had the temerity to compare him, "when he thought thereon he wept"?

Toward the end of the evening, he decided to drop in at Madame Grandet's for a moment. He was a different man, and Madame Grandet at once noticed the change. A week ago this subtle spiritual change would have escaped her. Although she did not admit it to herself, she was no longer entirely governed by ambition. She had begun to have a taste for this serious young man, who was not dull like the others. She found in him an indefinable charm. Had she had more experience or more intelligence, she would have characterized Lucien's way of being different, which so attracted her, as *natural*. She had already passed her twenty-sixth birthday; she had been married seven years and, for the last five, had reigned over the most brilliant, if not the most aristocratic society of Paris. Even when alone with her, no man had ever dared to kiss her hand.

The next day a disturbing scene occurred between Madame Grandet and M. Leuwen. Acting with complete honesty in the whole affair, M. Leuwen had hastened to introduce M. Grandet to the old Marshal. A man of great good sense and energy, when he did not let himself sink into a state of torpor through laziness or ill humor, the Marshal had asked this future colleague four or five rather direct questions. Unaccustomed to such plain speaking, the great banker had replied in well-rounded, pompous periods. At this, the Marshal, who detested high-sounding phraseology, first of all because it is detestable, and also because he never knew what to do about it, had turned his back on M. Grandet.

"Why, your man's a fool!" he had said to M. Leuwen.

M. Grandet had arrived home pale and in despair, and for the remainder of the day did not have the heart to compare himself to Colbert. For he had just enough discernment to know that he had been supremely disliked by the Marshal. It must be said that the rudeness of the old General, bored and eaten up with bile, was in proportion to the alertness of M. Grandet's reactions.

The latter recounted his misfortune to his wife, who, while overwhelming her husband with flattery, at once jumped to the conclusion that M. Leuwen had deceived her. Madame Grandet despised her husband, as every honest woman should, but she did not despise him nearly enough.

"What is my husband's real function?" she had been asking herself for the last three years. "He is a banker and a Colonel of the National Guard. Very good, as a banker he makes money, as a Colonel he is brave. These two callings are of mutual aid to each other: as a Colonel he can get promotions in the Legion of Honor for certain regents of the Bank of France and of the syndicate of stockbrokers, who, in turn, from time to time arrange a thirty-six hour loan of a million or two with which he can manipulate the market. But M. de Vaize exploits the Bourse through the telegraph, as M. Grandet does through a rise in the market. Two or three other Ministers follow M. de Vaize's example, nor is the *Master of them all* less enterprising, by any means! He even ruins them on occasion, as in the case of poor Castelfulgens. On one score at least my husband is superior to all of them: he is a very brave Colonel."

Madame Grandet was under the delusion that no one ever noticed her ponderous husband's appalling mania for appearing witty. But no man was ever blessed by nature with less imagination for everything except hard cash lost or won on the money market. Everything people said seemed to him, unmitigated merchant that he was, simple persiflage for the sake of ensnaring the customer.

For the last four or five years, during which her husband, who considered M. Thourette's luxury a challenge to his honor, had been entertaining lavishly, Madame Grandet was accustomed to seeing him surrounded by flatterers. One day a M. Gamont, a little hunchback, clever, poor and not too well dressed, had dared express an opinion which slightly differed from that of M. Grandet on the greater or lesser beauty of the Auch Cathedral. On the instant, M. Grandet had driven him out of the house with such coarseness and such a barbarous display of the tyranny of money over poverty that it had shocked even Madame Grandet. Several days later she sent the poor man an anonymous letter enclosing five hundred francs, supposedly in payment of a loan. Three months later the poor fellow abjectly allowed himself to be invited once again to dinner by M. Grandet.

When M. Leuwen told Madame Grandet the truth—toned down considerably—on the subject of M. Grandet's replies to the old Marshal—their emptiness, their platitude, their affected elegance, she gave him to understand with that haughty disdain which suited her particular kind of beauty, that she believed he was deceiving her.

Whereupon, M. Leuwen behaved exactly like a young man: he was in despair over the accusation, and for the next three days his sole preoccupation was to prove to her the injustice of her suspicions.

What complicated the situation was that the King who, for the last five or six months, had become more and more averse to positive decisions, had sent his son to the Minister of Finance to arrange a reconciliation with the old Marshal (prepared, of course, when the reconciliation no longer suited him, to repudiate his son and banish him to the country). The reconciliation took place. The Marshal had been quite ready to agree to it since he was most anxious to have a certain supply of horses paid for before he left the Ministry of War. The agent responsible for the transaction, M. Salomon C——, had very wisely stipulated that the hundred thousand franc security from the Marshal's son, as well as the profits accruing to him, should be paid out of the funds provided by the order signed by the Minister of Finance. Although perfectly aware of the speculation on this purchase of horses, the King knew nothing of this last little detail. Hearing of it from one of his spies in the Ministry of Finance, who made his reports to the King's sister, the King was humiliated and furious not to have guessed it himself. In his anger he was on the point of sending the Chief of his Secret Police to Algiers in command of a brigade. The King's politics in regard to his Ministers would have been quite different had he been certain of the Marshal for two weeks longer.

M. Leuwen knew nothing of all this, and took the delay of two weeks as just another symptom of timid vacillation, or even of a deterioration of the King's capacities. But this explanation he failed to communicate to Madame Grandet. It was a principle of his that there were certain things one did not confide to women.

As a result, although he spoke with absolute frankness and perfect good faith on everything except this one point, Madame Grandet, her wits at this moment sharpened by the keenest anxiety, felt that he was holding something back.

Aware of her suspicion, and being an honest man, M. Leuwen was in despair; and, like all his reactions, his despair was intense and violent. That same evening after dinner, not caring to discuss certain subjects before his wife, he left early for the Opera, taking his son with him. As soon as they arrived in their box, he carefully bolted the door. This precaution completed, he had the audacity to relate in detail and in the most casual manner, the bargain he had made with Madame Grandet. He forgot that he was not talking to a politician, and thereby committed a stupid blunder.

Lucien's vanity was dismayed. Suddenly he felt cold all over. For, unlike the heroes of popular novels, our hero was not absolutely perfect. He was not even perfect. He had been born in Paris, and consequently with a propensity to vanity of an unbelievably powerful kind.

This inordinate Parisian vanity was not, however, united in Lucien with its vulgar companion, the stupid belief in perfections he did not possess. For example he had often said to himself:

"I shall never be successful with society women. I am too simple, too frank, I don't even know how to conceal my boredom, and am even less able to hide my love when it is sincere."

Then suddenly, and in the most unlooked-for fashion, Madame Grandet had burst upon the scene, with her queenly bearing, her incomparable beauty, her immense fortune, her irreproachable conduct, to give the lie to all these philosophic but pessimistic notions. Lucien had relished this good luck to the full.

"This success will certainly never be duplicated," he said to himself. "For, unless I am in love, I am incapable of winning a woman of strict virtue and one who enjoys a brilliant position in the world. Any success I may have, as Ernest has so often told me, will come through the dull and vulgar means of *love contagion*. I am too great a dunce to know how to seduce any woman at all, even a grisette. At the end of a week either she bores me and I drop her, or she pleases me too much, and knows it, and laughs at me. If poor Madame de Chasteller loved me, as I sometimes am tempted to believe, and still loved me after her misstep with that execrable Lieutenant-Colonel of Hussars—such a mediocre, dull, disgusting rival—it was not because I showed the least skill, but only because I loved her. . . . And how I do love her!"

Lucien paused a moment. His vanity was so acutely hurt at this moment, that this cry rose rather from the memory of love than from the actual sensation of its presence.

It was at the very moment when his affair with Madame Grandet was beginning to please him immensely, that his father's revelation came to destroy the whole scaffolding of his self-confidence. Only an hour earlier he had been saying to himself:

"For once Ernest was wrong when he predicted that never in my life would I win a respectable woman without being in love with her, in other words, that I could only succeed through pity and tears—what that miserable chemist calls the *watery way.*"

His father's perfidious disclosure, coming as it did after a day of triumph, plunged him into bitter gloom.

"My father has been making a fool of me!"

Vanity kept Lucien from permitting himself to be disconcerted by the keen, searching glance his father fixed upon him. From this pitiless scoffer he was able to hide his cruel disappointment. M. Leuwen would have been happy could he have read his son's mind; he knew by experience that the same fund of vanity which makes misfortunes of this kind so painful, prevents them from being felt for very long. What really worried him was the interest Madame de Chasteller had inspired. He suspected nothing of Lucien's present state of mind, and thought his son a politician, who understood perfectly the King's position with his Ministers, exaggerating neither the wary cunning, nor the baseness invariably awakened by the cruel whip of Parisian mockery.

After a moment or two, M. Leuwen thought of nothing but coaching Lucien in the role he was to play with Madame Grandet, in order to convince her that his father was not betraying her in any way; that it was M. Grandet, with his heavy

pompousness, who had caused the damage which M. Leuwen
was ready to do everything in his power to repair.

Happily for our hero, after an hour's session one of M.
Leuwen's friends came to the box to speak to him.

"You're going to the Place de la Madeleine, aren't you?"
M. Leuwen made a point of asking, as his son left.

"Yes, of course," replied Lucien with Jesuitical veracity.

He did indeed go, and with all haste, to the Place de la
Madeleine. It was the only place in the neighborhood where he
was sure of being alone and undisturbed, for he had now become quite an important personage, and much sought after.

"No," he said to himself as he paced up and down, "I can
never hope to win first prize in a lottery; yes, I am a simpleton
without wit enough to win a woman except through the
maudlin means of *love contagion*.

"My father is like all fathers, and I never saw it before. With
infinitely more intelligence—and even feeling—than the
others, like them he wants to make me happy in his own way,
not mine. And it is to satisfy someone else's whim that I have
been stupefying myself with a preposterous amount of bureaucratic work, and of the most imbecilic kind besides. The other
victims of the morocco armchairs are at least ambitious, like
young Desbacs, for example. All those high-flown, ready-made
phrases which I write with variations in the praiseworthy hope
of making some Prefect, guilty of permitting a liberal café
in his city, turn pale, or another swoon with delight who,
without compromising himself, has won over a jury and sent
a liberal journalist to prison, they find neat, suitable and *governmental*. They never stop to think that the man who signs
them is a scoundrel. But a fool like me, overburdened with
delicacy, has all the tedium of the job with none of its satisfac-
tions. I do with distaste things I find both disgraceful and
stupid. And sooner or later such flattering remarks as I now
address to myself in private, I shall have the pleasure of hear-

ing uttered aloud in public. It won't be pleasant. I am only twenty-four and, unless an excess of intelligence is mortal, as old women say, I have still some time ahead of me. How much longer, in all conscience, can this castle of cards, this flimsy structure of shameless knavery last? Five years? Ten years? Twenty years? Not ten, I should say. When I am not yet forty, and the reaction against these rascals sets in, mine will be the most ignominious of roles. And," he added with a smile of bitterness, "the whip of satire will lash me for sins which never even amused me.

> If you're going to be damned
> Be damned, at least, for amusing sins.

Desbacs, on the contrary, will have the best of it. But today he would be drunk with joy to find himself Master of Petitions, Prefect, Secretary-General, while I see in M. Lucien Leuwen only a perfect fool, an unconscionable blockhead. Even the mud of Blois couldn't wake you up. What can wake you then, poor wretch? Are you waiting for a personal insult?

"Coffe is right: I am a worse dupe than any of those vulgar souls who have sold themselves to the government. Yesterday, when he was talking about Desbacs & Co., didn't he remark with that inexorable coolness of his: 'The reason I don't despise them too much is that they haven't a penny to their names'?

"My rapid advancement—unheard of at my age—my talents, my father's position in the world, what has all that ever given me but this feeling of astonishment without pleasure: 'Is that all it amounts to?'

"It's high time I woke up. What do I need with a fortune? A five-franc dinner and a horse, isn't that all that I want at most? All the rest is often more of a bore than a pleasure, especially now that I can say: 'I am not despising what I know nothing about, like a silly philosopher à la Jean-Jacques.' Worldly success, smiles, shaking hands with country Deputies and Sub-Prefects on leave, glances of coarse good will from everyone in a salon, I have known you all! I'll meet you again in a few minutes in the foyer of the Opera.

"But what if I quit Paris without going back to the Opera, and went to the only place in the world where for me is the *perhaps* of happiness? . . . In eighteen hours I could be in Nancy in the Rue de la Pompe!"

This idea monopolized all his thoughts for a whole hour. In the last few months our hero had become much bolder. He had observed at first hand the motives which actuate men in high positions. That sort of timidity, which, to an intuitive eye, reveals a great, sincere soul, had not been able to resist the growing knowledge of great worldly affairs. Had he decided to spend his whole life in his father's countinghouse, he might have become and remained a man of merit, and been known as such to one or two persons. He had now reached the point where he dared follow his first impulse, and stick to it until someone proved to him that he was wrong. And thanks to his father's irony, he found it impossible to deceive himself with specious reasoning.

These thoughts occupied him for the hour or more he spent restlessly wandering around the square.

"After all," he said to himself, "my only concern in all this is to spare my mother's feelings and my father's vanity. In six weeks my father will have forgotten those castles in Spain he has been building for a son who is much too much a peasant from the Danube to play the part his father has in mind: a clever man who would make a mighty breach in the Budget."

With these ideas established in his mind as new and incontestable facts, Lucien returned to the Opera. The light music, and the charming dancing of Mademoiselle Elssler filled him with a delight which surprised him. He thought vaguely to himself that he would not be enjoying all these fine things much longer and for that reason they failed to exasperate him.

While the music gave wings to his imagination, his mind was engaged in reviewing life's many possibilities.

"If only farming didn't bring one into contact with rascally peasants, and priests who instigate them against you, and with a Prefect who has your newspaper stolen at the post office—as I insinuated to that numskull Prefect of ——, it would be the kind of work I'd like. To live in the country with Madame de Chasteller and to wrest from the land the twelve or fifteen thousand francs necessary for our modest comforts!

"Ah, America! No Prefects like M. de Séranville over there!" And all Lucien's old ideas on America and on M. de Lafayette came swarming back to him. When he used to meet M. de Lafayette at M. Destutt de Tracy's, he always imagined that all the people in America were imbued, not only with Lafayette's good sense, probity and lofty philosophy, but also with his elegant manners. He had been rudely undeceived. In America the majority rules and, for the most part, is made up of riffraff. "In New York the chariot of State has fallen into the opposite ditch from ours. Universal suffrage rules as a tyrant—a tyrant with dirty hands. If I don't happen to please my shoemaker he spreads slander about me which infuriates me, but I still have to flatter my shoemaker. Men are not weighed, they are only counted. The vote of the coarsest artisan is worth just as much as that of Jefferson, and often meets with greater understanding. Their clergy stupefies them, just as ours does— but they're even worse. They make travelers get out of the mail coach on Sunday, because traveling on Sunday is *mundane work* and a deadly sin. . . . Such universal, dismal barbarism would stifle me. . . . But I shall do just as Bathilde wishes. . . ."

For a long time he mused over this last thought, until suddenly it struck him with amazement. He was overjoyed to find it so firmly rooted in his mind.

"So there is absolutely no doubt about my having forgiven

her! It is not an illusion." Yes, he had entirely forgiven Madame de Chasteller her lapse from virtue. "Just as she is, for me she is the only woman in the world. . . . It would, I think, be more delicate never to let her suspect that I know of the consequence of her weakness for M. de Busant de Sicile. She will tell me of her own accord if she wants to tell me. All this stupid bureaucratic work has at least proved that I am capable, if necessary, of supporting myself and my wife."

"Proved it to whom?" sneered the opposition. "To people you will perhaps never see again and who, if you leave, will slander you the minute your back is turned."

Lucien was furious at this intrusion. "Ah, no, by heaven! It has proved it to *me,* and that is what counts. What do I care for the opinion of all those gentlemanly rascals who view with amazement my Cross and my rapid advancement. I am no longer that callow young Second-Lieutenant of Lancers leaving for Nancy to join his regiment, a slave to a hundred little weaknesses of vanity, and still smarting from that scorching remark of Ernest Dévelroy: 'Only too lucky to have a father who supplies your bread!' Bathilde told me some true things; and she made me compare myself with hundreds of other men, and the most highly thought of . . . Let's do as the world does and disregard the ethics of our official acts. Well then, I know that I can do twice as much work as the most plodding—consequently the most esteemed—department head, work, moreover, which I despise and which at Blois got me covered with mud —and well deserved, I'm afraid."

Absorbed by all this wealth of thought, Lucien knew almost perfect happiness. From time to time, the strains of a vigorous and virile orchestra and Mademoiselle Elssler's divinely graceful movements interrupted his reflections, lending them a seductive charm and potency. But more heavenly still was the image of Madame de Chasteller which almost constantly dominated his thoughts. This mixture of love and reasoning made this evening's end, in an obscure corner of the stalls, one of the happiest of his life. But the curtain fell.

To return to the house, to engage in an amiable conversation with his father, would be to plunge once more into the distressing world of reality and, we confess, of boredom.

"I must not go home before two o'clock, or beware the paternal dialogue!"

Lucien went to an apartment hotel and took a little suite. He paid in advance, but they insisted on seeing his passport. An agreement was finally reached with the proprietor. Lucien promised not to sleep there that night, and to come back with his passport the following day.

Overjoyed, he walked around his little apartment whose handsomest piece of furniture was the idea: "Here I am free!" He was as pleased as a child at the thought of the false name he was going to give himself.

The idea of renting this little apartment at the corner of the Rue Lepelletier marked a turning point in Lucien's life. The first thing he did the next day was to go to the Hôtel de Londres with a passport obtained from M. Crapart, which bore the name: M. Théodore Martin of Marseille.

"I have to have a false passport to insure my liberty," he said to himself as he wandered happily through his new rooms. "Here I shall be entirely free from paternal, maternal, sempiternal solicitude!"

Yes, this was the very unfilial remark pronounced by our hero. And it grieves me, not so much for his sake as for the sake of human nature. So true is it that the instinct of liberty is ingrained in every heart, and that one does not thwart it with impunity in a country where irony has discouraged stupidity. An instant later Lucien reproached himself for his rudeness to his mother. But, after all, this excellent mother, without realizing it herself, had also assailed his liberty. Madame Leuwen fully believed that she had acted with the greatest possible delicacy and address, for she had never once mentioned Madame de Chasteller. But a sentiment subtler than the wit of a Parisian woman, who has more wit, as everybody knows, than any other, made Lucien certain that his mother detested Madame de Chasteller. "But," Lucien thought, or rather felt without admitting it, "my mother should not be able either to like or dislike Madame de Chasteller; she should *not know of her existence*."

One can be sure that, occupied by thoughts like these, Lucien had no intention of letting himself be stifled by all the dry-as-dust ideas current in Madame Grandet's drawing room, and still less of enduring all the endless handshakings. Yet, with what anxiety was his arrival awaited in that drawing room! That dark mask, which sometimes obscured Lucien's amiable qualities and made him appear in Madame Grandet's eyes as a cold philosopher, had completely transformed this woman who had always been so sensible and so ambitious.

"He does not try to make himself agreeable," she thought, "but, at least, he is absolutely sincere."

This remark was the first step toward a headlong plunge into emotions until now completely foreign to her—and so impossible!

CHAPTER TWENTY-EIGHT

LUCIEN still had the bad habit and extreme imprudence of being natural in moments of intimacy, even when that intimacy had not flowered from true love. To dissimulate with someone whom one saw for four hours every day, seemed to him the most absurd thing in the world. This defect in Lucien, added to his air of candor, at first seemed to

Madame Grandet a mark of stupidity, later excited her amazement, and finally her keen interest—something Lucien could very well have done without. For, although Madame Grandet was the perfect example of the ambitious woman, supremely logical and solely preoccupied with the success of her schemes, she possessed, nevertheless, a woman's heart, but a heart which had not yet been touched by love. Lucien's naturalness should have been altogether ridiculous to a woman of twenty-six steeped in the cult of admiration and adoration for everything stamped with aristocratic approval. But, curiously enough, this very naturalness on the part of a man whose candid soul, foreign to all vulgar artifice, gave to everything he did a touch of oddness and a singular nobility, was the very thing best calculated to awaken a strange emotion in a heart which had remained insensible until then.

It must be admitted that when Lucien paid calls, after the first half hour he talked very little and not very well. In the first place he had never been known to stay anywhere more than half an hour, and, with the exception of Madame de Chasteller, he had never been on terms of intimacy with anyone. At present his relations with Madame Grandet disclosed this painful defect, one best calculated to wreck a man's fortune. Despite unbelievable efforts on his part, Lucien was absolutely incapable of dissimulating any change of mood, and never was there a nature more fundamentally changeable. This unfortunate trait, tempered somewhat by all the noblest habits of simple, exquisite courtesy instilled by a clever mother, had formerly seemed to Madame de Chasteller only an added charm. It had been for her a pleasing novelty, accustomed as she was to unfailing uniformity of temper, the masterpiece of that hypocrisy which is known today as a perfect education by people who are either too aristocratic or too rich, and which makes for an incurable dullness in the person who practices it, as well as in his *partner*. For Lucien, the recollection of an idea that was precious to him, a day of storm clouds and North wind, the sudden sight of some new piece of knavery (or some other equally common occurrence) was quite enough to transform him on the instant. He had found only one remedy for the ridiculous affliction, so rare in our age, of taking things seriously. It was to be shut up in a little room alone with Madame de Chasteller, sure that the door was well guarded and would not open to any intruder who might unexpectedly appear.

After making all these ridiculous allowances, it must be said, that for a Lieutenant of Lancers, Lucien was at this moment more attractive than ever. But a Madame Grandet could hardly be expected to appreciate such allowances on behalf of an odd and ailing mind, and would naturally find them tiresome and odious. However, Lucien was often silent and absent. This natural disposition of his was aggravated by the mentality, anything but encouraging to a noble soul, typical of the persons who formed the habitual court around this famous hostess.

Be that as it may, Lucien, at the moment, was being awaited in this drawing room with the greatest anxiety. For the first hour of that evening which had caused such a revolution in Lucien's heart, Madame Grandet had reigned as usual over her court. Gradually she began to be a prey, first to amazement, and finally to the most violent anger. She was able to think of nothing but Lucien. And for Madame Grandet to keep her attention constantly fixed on one person was something utterly unheard of. She herself was not a little astonished to find herself in such a state. She was, however, firmly convinced that it was entirely due to vanity and wounded pride. With swelling breast, and eyelids drawn and unblinking (as they always became under the effect of physical pain, and only then) she kept questioning Deputies, and Peers, and any of the others who fed off the Budget, as they arrived one after the other in her drawing room. To none of them did she dare mention openly the name which had been absorbing her attention all evening. In the hope that the name of M. Lucien Leuwen would sometime be inadvertently mentioned, she was obliged to hold them in interminable conversation.

Madame Grandet knew that Lucien had been invited to a hunting party which the Prince Royal was to give in the Forest of Compiègne, and that Lucien had made a bet of twenty-five louis against seventy that the first roebuck would be brought to bay in less than twenty-one minutes after it had been sighted. Lucien had been introduced into this exalted society through the favor of the old Marshal. This was by far the most flattering distinction that could be enjoyed by a young man attached to the government, or one bent on getting on in the world. And what a nice slice of the Budget could be expected within ten years by the man (the tenth) who hunted with the Prince Royal! The Prince had absolutely insisted on inviting ten persons only, for a writer of his suite had just discovered that *Monseigneur*, son of Louis XIV, and Dauphin of France, never permitted more than that number of courtiers on his wolf hunts.

"Is it possible," Madame Grandet wondered, "that perhaps the Prince Royal has sent word unexpectedly that he is receiving the future deer hunters of his party this evening?" But the poor Deputies and Peers who came to her drawing room were interested in more substantial things, and knew too little of that society where an attempt was being made to form a new Court, to be privy to such matters. This having occurred to her, she gave up trying to learn the truth from these gentlemen.

"But shouldn't he, in any case, have come here for a moment to let me know, or sent me a note at least? Such conduct is frightful!"

Eleven o'clock struck . . . eleven-thirty . . . midnight. Lucien did not appear.

"Oh! But it won't take me long to cure him of such charming ways!" thought Madame Grandet, quite beside herself with fury.

That night sleep never visited her eyes, as people who know how to write would say. Consumed by anger and grief, she sought for distraction in what her dutiful friends called her *historical studies*. She had her maid begin by reading to her from Madame de Motteville's *Mémoires,* the one book which only the day before had seemed the most perfect manual for a woman of the great world. Tonight these beloved memoirs appeared devoid of all interest. She finally even had recourse to the very novels she had for eight years been denouncing in long moral dissertations in her drawing room.

All night long poor Madame Trublet, her confidential maid, was kept trotting upstairs to the library on the floor above. She brought down novel after novel. None of them pleased her mistress, and at last sinking even lower, the sublime Madame Grandet, who had always had a horror of Rousseau, was obliged to fall back on *La Nouvelle Héloïse*. Everything read aloud to her at the beginning of the night had seemed cold and boring, nothing responded to her mood. But the rather pedantic rhetoric which makes readers with a somewhat fastidious taste close this book, proved just the thing for Madame Grandet's budding sensibility and bourgeois taste.

When she noticed the first light of dawn appear through the cracks of the shutters, she dismissed Madame Trublet. It had suddenly occurred to her that she was sure to receive a letter of excuse the first thing in the morning. "It will be brought to me at nine o'clock, and what an answer he will receive from me! I shan't mince matters!" Slightly calmed by the idea of vengeance, she fell asleep mulling over all the well-rounded sentences of her reply.

As early as eight o'clock Madame Grandet rang impatiently; she thought it was noon.

"My letters, my papers!" she cried petulantly.

The porter was sent for, and arrived with nothing in his hand but the journals in their dirty wrappers. What a contrast to the pretty little note, so elegant and so elegantly folded, which her avid eye looked for in vain among the papers! Lucien was famous for the art with which he folded his notes, and that was perhaps of all his elegant gifts the one which touched her the most.

She spent the whole morning making plans for forgetting Lucien, even for vengeance, but it seemed, nonetheless, interminable. At luncheon she was terrible to the servants and to her husband. Noticing that M. Grandet was in a gay mood, she took an acrimonious delight in telling him M. Leuwen's unvarnished account of his elephantine behavior during his interview with the Marshal, notwithstanding that it had been confided to her under the seal of eternal secrecy.

One o'clock struck . . . half-past-one . . . two o'clock. The reiteration of these sounds, recalling as they did her painful night, infuriated her. For a while she was virtually out of her mind.

All at once (who would have thought it of a character dominated by the most childish vanity?) she had the idea of writing to Lucien. For a whole hour she struggled against this horrible temptation: *to be the first to write!* She yielded at last, but without trying to hide from herself all the horror of her action.

"What an advantage it will give him! And how many days of severity will be necessary to make him forget his feeling of triumph at the sight of my note! But, after all," interposed love, hiding behind a paradox, "what is a lover? It is a friction instrument one scrapes to procure oneself pleasure. As M. Cuvier says: 'Your cat does not caress you when it rubs against you, it caresses itself.' Very well then, the only pleasure this young man can give me at this moment is that of writing to him. What do his sensations matter to me? Mine will give me pleasure. And," she added with ferocious glee, *"that* is what counts."

Her eyes at that moment were superb.

Madame Grandet wrote a letter. It did not satisfy her. She wrote a second and a third. Finally, she sent off the seventh or eighth which read:

My husband wishes to see you. We are expecting you, and in order not to go on expecting you forever, in spite of our appointment I have decided to write.

My compliments.

Augustine Grandet.

P.S. Come before three o'clock.

And when this letter, the one which seemed the least imprudent and, above all, the least humiliating to her vanity, was finally sent, it was already half-past-two.

Madame Grandet's footman found Lucien in his office in the Rue de Grenelle, looking perfectly serene. Instead of obeying the summons, Lucien wrote:

Madam,

I am doubly unhappy: I shall not have the honor of presenting my respects to you this morning, nor, in all probability, this evening either. I find myself chained to my desk by some pressing business which I was rash enough to undertake. You understand that being a dutiful clerk, I do not want to displease my Minister. But he will certainly never know the extent of the sacrifice I make to duty in not obeying the command of M. Grandet and yourself.

Please accept the renewed assurance of my most respectful devotion.

Lucien Leuwen.

Meanwhile Madame Grandet had been busy calculating the time it would take Lucien to fly to her side. She kept listen-

ing for the sound, now so familiar, of the wheels of his cabriolet, when, suddenly, there was a knock at the door and to her
great amazement her footman entered and handed her Lucien's
note.

The mere sight of it was enough to reawaken all Madame
Grandet's fury; her face became contorted and suffused with a
livid red.

"There might be some excuse if he hadn't been in his office.
But to have read my letter without immediately rushing to my
side . . ."

"Go!" she said to the servant, with a look that petrified him.

"The little fool will probably change his mind," she said to
herself. "He will arrive in a quarter of an hour, and it would
be better if he saw his letter still unopened. Better still," she
decided after a moment, "if he didn't even find me at home."

She rang and ordered her carriage. She began restlessly pacing up and down the room; Lucien's note lay on a little round
table by her armchair, and, in spite of herself, she kept glancing at it every time she turned.

Her carriage was announced. As the servant left the room,
she snatched up Lucien's note and opened it in a movement
of rage without, as it were, consenting to her own action. The
woman in her had triumphed over the diplomat.

Lucien's icy letter drove her practically out of her mind. To
excuse such weakness, we should like to observe that she had
reached the age of twenty-six without ever having been in love
before. She had even sternly refrained from indulging in any
of those casual flirtations which might lead to love. Now, love
was having its revenge. For the last eighteen hours it had been
struggling against the most inveterate pride for the heart of
this woman whose conduct was so exemplary, whose name
was so exalted in the annals of contemporary virtue!

Never was struggle more cruel. At each recurrence of her
pain, pride, poor thing, lost ground and was defeated. Ma-

dame Grandet had obeyed it for too long and had grown weary of the kind of pleasure it procured.

At length this long-standing habit and her cruel passion in their struggle for supremacy succeeded, by their united efforts, in driving her to despair. What! A man had eluded, disobeyed, despised her commands!

"But he hasn't the slightest notion of how to behave!"

After two hours of the most atrocious suffering, all the more painful for being experienced for the first time, she finally tried to console herself with the thought of all the flattery, homage and respect she enjoyed, and from the most important men of Paris. For a moment it seemed as though pride would triumph. But suddenly in a fresh outburst of grief, so painful that she could no longer endure passively waiting, she hurried downstairs and got into her carriage. She was scarcely seated when she changed her mind, thinking:

"If he were to come now, I should miss him!" And she gave her footman Lucien's address:

"Rue de Grenelle, the Ministry of the Interior."

She was actually going to seek Lucien in his office.

She refused to reflect on what she was doing. Had she stopped to think, she would have fainted. Prostrated by despair, she lay back on the cushions; being roughly shaken by the jolting of the carriage seemed to act as a diversion, and bring her some relief.

CHAPTER TWENTY-NINE

W HEN LUCIEN SAW Madame Grandet coming into his office, he felt a sudden gust of anger.

"What! Will this woman never leave me in peace! She takes me for one of her numerous flunkeys. From the tone of my letter, she should have known that I had no desire to see her."

Madame Grandet threw herself into an armchair with all the arrogance of a person who, for six years, has been spending a hundred and twenty thousand francs a year. This hint of money in her manner struck Lucien unpleasantly, and destroyed any sympathy he might have felt.

"I am dealing with a grocer's wife *demanding her due*. To be understood I shall have to speak plainly."

Madame Grandet remained silent in her armchair. In a position more bureaucratic than gallant, Lucien sat motionless in his, his hands resting on the arms, his legs stretched out at full length. His expression was exactly that of a merchant who has got the *worst of a bargain*. There was not a sign of any generous sentiment; on the contrary, he showed every evidence of being dominated by inflexible severity, strict justice and self-interest alone.

After a moment, Lucien felt rather ashamed of himself.

"Ah! if Madame de Chasteller should see me now! But, my answer would be: courtesy would only mask what I wish to make this grocer's wife realize."

"Sir," said Madame Grandet at length, "must I beg you to tell your usher to retire?"

Madame Grandet's language tended to glorify all functions.

The person in question was a humble office boy who, seeing a beautiful lady with a fine equipage arrive at the Ministry looking so distraught, was hanging about through curiosity, with the apparent excuse of poking up a fire which had no need of his services. At a glance from Lucien he left the room. The silence continued.

"Well, sir," Madame Grandet finally burst out, "are you not astonished, stupefied, aghast at seeing me here?"

"I confess, Madam, that I am surprised by a certainly very flattering occurrence, but one which I do not deserve."

Lucien had not been able to bring himself to be impolite in words, but the tone in which his remark was spoken was enough to discourage any idea that it was an amorous approach, and made it appear coldly insulting. The affront came just in time to strengthen Madame Grandet's faltering courage. For the first time in her life Madame Grandet was timid, because, during the last few days, her cold and arid heart had known, for the first time, a feeling of tenderness.

"I always thought, sir," she went on in a voice that trembled with anger, "if I have rightly understood your protestations—quite lengthy at times—on the subject of your lofty principles, that you had the pretension of being an honorable man."

"Since you do me so much honor as to speak of me, let me say that I am endeavoring to be just, and to view my position as well as that of others, without flattering myself."

"Will your solicitous *justice* stoop to consider how very dangerous my coming here is? Madame de Vaize might recognize my livery."

"It is precisely because of the danger that I find it difficult to reconcile this action with the idea I have always entertained of Madame Grandet's superior prudence, and the wisdom that permits her to calculate in advance all the circumstances which might render any act more or less useful to her lofty projects."

"Apparently, sir, you have borrowed that rare prudence of

mine, and find it *useful* to alter all those sentiments, so endlessly reiterated, with which I have been daily importuned."

"The devil," thought Lucien, "if I'll be so good-natured as to let you disarm me with your empty phrases."

"Madam," he resumed with the greatest composure, "those sentiments which you do me the honor to remember, have been humiliated by a success not altogether due to them. They have fled blushing in confusion at their mistake, but not before learning the painful truth that they owed their apparent triumph merely to the prosaic promise of an introduction to a Minister. A heart which they had fondly and, of course, erroneously believed they had touched, had really only yielded to calculating ambition, and all the apparent tenderness was merely words. In short, I found out that I had been . . . duped. That is the explanation which my absence was intended to spare you. That, Madam, was my way of being an honorable man."

Madame Grandet did not reply.

"So be it," Lucien said to himself, "I'll make it impossible for you to pretend not to understand." And he added in the same tone:

"No matter with how much unswerving courage a mind that aspires to high positions may endure the qualms which assail vulgar natures, there is a kind of misfortune such a mind cannot endure without chagrin, and that is to have been wrong in one of its calculations. And so, Madam, and I say it with regret and only because you have forced me to do so, perhaps you have been . . . wrong in the role your superior wisdom thought to assign to my inexperience. These, Madam, are the not very agreeable words I had hoped to spare you, believing that I was thus acting as an honorable man. But you have surprised me in my last redoubt—my office. . . ."

Lucien might have gone on indefinitely with this all too simple explanation. Madame Grandet was thunderstruck. The pains of wounded pride would have been atrocious if, happily for her, a less callous sentiment had not come to soften her suffering. At the fatal, and all too true, words: *introduction to a Minister,* Madame Grandet had covered her eyes with her handkerchief. A moment later, Lucien thought he noticed, in the gilded depths of the ministerial armchair, certain telltale movements of her body. Without even realizing it, Lucien became wary.

"This," he said to himself, "must be the way Parisian actresses reply to reproaches that admit of no answer."

But, in spite of himself, he could not help being somewhat touched by this well-acted imitation of extreme suffering. Besides, the grief-shaken body before his eyes was so beautiful!

In vain, Madame Grandet felt that this fatal discourse of Lucien's should be stopped at any price. He was getting more and more angry at the sound of his own words, and would, perhaps, bind himself to resolutions which had never occurred to him at first. She knew that she should make some sort of reply, but felt incapable of uttering a word.

At last Lucien's discourse, which Madame Grandet had found so interminable, came to an end, whereupon she found that it had ended too soon. She would have to reply, and what could she say? This frightful situation entirely changed her way of feeling. At first she had said to herself out of habit: "What humiliation!" Soon she became insensible to the misery of wounded pride and became aware of a different and much more poignant pain: she was about to lose what had, for the last few days, been her only interest in life! What would her salon mean to her now, and all the pleasures of her brilliant soirées, so highly appreciated by everyone, and frequented by only the best society of the Court of Louis-Philippe?

Madame Grandet knew that Lucien was right. She saw how ill-founded her own anger had been. She had forgotten it. She went even further: she took Lucien's side against herself.

The silence continued for several minutes. Finally, Madame Grandet removed her handkerchief, and Lucien was struck by the most startling change of physiognomy he had ever seen. For perhaps the first time in her life, her face wore an expression that was wholly feminine. Those extraordinarily beautiful features now possessed the added fascination of expressiveness they usually lacked. She had just tossed her hat carelessly aside, and the slight disorder of her hair only added to her charms. And yet, that lovely youthful countenance, which Paul Veronese would have been delighted to have as model, was quite literally painful to Lucien's eyes. To him it bespoke only the prostitute who gloried in being beautiful enough to be able to sell herself for a Ministry. But the greater the wealth, consideration and social advantages she enjoyed, the worse this seemed to him. "How much lower she is than a poor little streetwalker who sells herself to buy bread or a new dress!" And so, Lucien noticed this change in Madame Grandet without being touched by it. At that moment, everything—his father, Madame Grandet, Paris—was anathema to him. Nothing could touch him now except the thought of what might happen to him in Nancy!

"I admit," Madame Grandet said at last, "I am very much to blame. But what has happened is extremely flattering to you. In all my life, except for you, I have never deviated from the path of virtue. Your courtship amused me, flattered me, but seemed to me without the least danger. I was seduced by ambition, I confess, and did not give myself to you out of love. But my heart has changed" (here Madame Grandet blushed deeply and could not look at Lucien), "I have had the misfortune of becoming attached to you. It took only a few days, and without my being conscious of it, for my heart to change. I forgot what I considered my duty—that of elevating the name of Grandet. Another sentiment began to dominate my life. Now the idea of losing you, most of all the idea of losing your respect, is unbearable. . . . I am ready to sacrifice everything to merit your esteem once more."

With this Madame Grandet buried her face again, and, from behind her handkerchief, found the courage to say:

"I will break with your father, give up all hope of the Ministry . . . but you must not leave me!"

And with a grace he found irresistible, as she said these last words, Madame Grandet held out her hand to Lucien.

"This grace," said Vanity, "this change, amazing in so proud a woman, are entirely due to your attractions. Isn't that better than to have made her yield through the arts of seduction?"

But Lucien remained cool to the flattering voice of Vanity. His expression did not change from one of cold circumspection. And it was now the voice of Skepticism that added:

"Here is a remarkably beautiful woman, and one who counts on the effect of her beauty. Now let's try not to be a dupe. Let's stop to consider. Madame Grandet proves her love for me by a quite painful sacrifice—that of her lifelong pride. So, I should believe in her love . . . but just a moment. This love would have to be proved by somewhat more conclusive and more enduring tests. But if it is real, at least I don't owe it simply to pity. It is not a love inspired by *contagion,* as Ernest says."

It must be admitted that while indulging in these reflections, Lucien's expression was not that of a romantic hero. He had rather the air of a banker weighing the advisability of an important speculation.

"Madame Grandet's vanity," he mused on, "may consider that being jilted is the worst of all calamities, and that she must *sacrifice everything to avoid this humiliation,* even the interests of her ambition. More than likely, it isn't love that is making these sacrifices, but simply vanity, and mine would be blind indeed if it gloried in any such doubtful triumph. The thing to do then is to show the greatest deference and respect.

Her presence here is really most embarrassing. Since I feel incapable of submitting to her demands any longer, and her salon bores me, I must try politely to make her realize the truth.

"Madam," he said, "there will be no change in the respectful devotion I have always shown you. Although the sympathy which for a moment brought us into a relation of intimacy may have been due to a misunderstanding, an error, I am nevertheless everlastingly your debtor. I owe it to myself, Madam, I owe it even more to the tie that united us for a brief moment, to confess the truth. Gratitude and respect still fill my heart, but love, I no longer find in it."

Madame Grandet looked at him with eyes reddened by tears checked now by the intensity with which she hung upon his words.

After a little silence, she began to weep again without restraint. Through her tears she looked up at Lucien, and dared pronounce these extraordinary words:

"Everything you say is true. I was dying of ambition and pride. Finding myself so immensely rich, my one aim in life —I dare confess this bitter absurdity to you—was to have a title. I gave myself to you through ambition alone. But now I am dying of love. I am unworthy, I know. Humiliate me . . . I deserve your scorn. I am dying of love and shame. I am at your feet; I beg your forgiveness; I have no more ambition, no more pride. In the future tell me what you want me to do. I am at your feet, humiliate me all you like! The more you humiliate me, the more human you will be to me."

"Is all this still affectation?" Lucien asked himself. He had never before witnessed a scene of such violence.

She had thrown herself at his feet. Stooping, Lucien was trying to lift her when, suddenly, he felt the arms in his hands go limp, and soon he was holding the whole weight of her inanimate body. Madame Grandet had fainted.

357

Lucien was embarrassed but not moved. His embarrassment came entirely from the fear of failing in this precept of his moral code: *never to hurt anyone unnecessarily*. But a recollection, utterly ridiculous at such a moment, suddenly drove away all idea of compassion. Two days before, Madame Grandet, who owned an estate near Lyons, had been approached for a contribution to the collection being raised in behalf of the unhappy Lyons prisoners who had taken part in the April insurrection, and who were to be tried in Paris. They were to be brought from Lyons to the Perrache prison in Paris in open carts, thinly clad, in the middle of winter.

"I must say that I find your request extraordinary, sir," she had replied to the men making the collection. "You are apparently not aware of the fact that my husband is connected with the government, and Monsieur le Préfet of Lyons has forbidden this collection!"

She herself had recounted the incident in her drawing room to her assembled guests. Lucien had looked at her in amazement before remarking:

"In such weather, many of those poor wretches will die of cold in their carts; they have nothing but summer clothing, and are not given blankets."

"What of it?" cried a fat Deputy and a July hero. "All the less trouble for the Paris Court."

Lucien had kept his eyes fixed on Madame Grandet: she remained unmoved.

Seeing her now in a state of unconsciousness, her features devoid of all expression except that of her habitual haughtiness, he remembered the same impassive look on her face when he had spoken of the prisoners dying of cold on the road. And even in the midst of a love scene, he remained a republican.

"What am I going to do with this woman?" he asked himself. "One must be human. I must give her some good advice and, at all costs, get her home."

He propped her gently against the armchair, and went to lock the door. Then, dipping his handkerchief into a plain china pitcher full of water (the only household utensil the office afforded), he moistened her forehead, cheeks and neck, without all this beauty having the slightest effect upon him.

"If I wanted to take a mean advantage, I would call Desbacs to the rescue! He keeps all sorts of smelling salts in his desk."

At length, Madame Grandet gave a little sigh.

"She mustn't find herself on the floor," thought Lucien. "It would remind her of the painful scene."

He lifted her up bodily in his arms, and placed her in the great gilded armchair. This time, the contact of this charming body did, at least, remind him that he was holding in his arms and had at his disposal, one of the most beautiful women of Paris. And her beauty, not being dependent on expression or charm, but a *sterling* and plastic beauty, lost almost nothing in this state of unconsciousness.

Madame Grandet roused slightly, and looked at Lucien through half-open eyes, the upper eyelid being still too weak to open fully.

Lucien decided that the thing to do now was to kiss her hand, and nothing could have more effectually hastened the resurrection of this lovesick woman.

"You will come to see me, won't you?" she murmured in a hardly audible voice.

"Yes, of course. You may count on it. But now it is too dangerous for you to remain here. The door is closed, someone might knock; young Desbacs, perhaps, might come . . ."

The thought of that malicious young man seemed to restore Madame Grandet's strength at once.

"Will you be good enough to help me to my carriage?"

"Don't you think it might be a good idea to say something about a sprained ankle to your servants?"

"Oh, generous friend! You are not the kind of man to wish to compromise me, and to flaunt your triumph. How good you are!"

Lucien felt touched, and was annoyed with himself for his weakness. Taking the hand that was resting on his arm, he placed it on the back of the armchair, and hurried down to the courtyard.

"Madame Grandet," he said to the servants in a tone of concern, "has just twisted her ankle. A bone may be broken. Come quickly!"

One of the Ministry attendants held the horses while Madame Grandet's coachman and footman hastily followed Lucien, and helped Madame Grandet to her carriage.

With all the little strength she had regained, she pressed Lucien's hand. Her eyes grown eloquent again, eloquent with supplication, she said to him from inside the carriage:

"Until tonight!"

"Of course, dear Madam, I shall call to find out how you are."

Amazed at the strange agitation of their mistress, her servants were suspicious of the whole thing. These people become very wise in Paris. They knew well enough that hers was a distress due to something else than mere physical pain.

Lucien locked himself in his office once more. With long strides, he paced from one corner of the room to the other.

"What an unpleasant scene!" he said to himself. "Was it put on? Did she exaggerate her feelings? The fainting fit was real enough . . . as far as I can judge. That would seem to be a triumph for my vanity; I don't even feel pleased."

He tried to go on with a report he had begun, but soon perceived that he was writing nonsense. He went home, mounted his horse, rode over the Grenelle bridge, and soon found himself in the Meudon woods. There, reining in his horse to a walk, he began to think. What remained, above all else, was remorse at having been touched when Madame Grandet had lowered the handkerchief from before her face, and worse still, at having been affected for a moment when he had lifted her unconscious form in his arms, and placed it in the armchair.

"Ah! if I am unfaithful to Madame de Chasteller, she will have reason to be unfaithful to me."

"It seems to me," the opposition retorted, "she hasn't made a bad start. Having a baby . . . a mere trifle!"

"Since nobody knows," replied Lucien resentfully, "there's no ridicule attached to it. Ridicule has to be apparent, or it doesn't exist."

Returning to town, Lucien went straight to the Ministry. He had himself announced to M. de Vaize, and asked for a month's leave of absence. The Minister, who for the last three weeks had been only half a Minister and had kept praising the pleasures of repose (*otium cum dignitate,* as he often said) was surprised and altogether delighted at the flight of the enemy's aide-de-camp.

"I wonder what it means?" he asked himself.

Armed with his leave of absence in proper form, written by himself and signed by the Minister, Lucien went to say goodby to his mother. To her he spoke only of a little jaunt to the country.

"Where in the country," she anxiously asked.

"Normandy," replied Lucien, for he understood very well that look on his mother's face.

The slight remorse he had felt at deceiving so excellent a mother was dispelled by her question: "Where in the country?"

"My mother hates Madame de Chasteller," he said to himself, and that settled everything.

Leaving a line for his father, he rode over to Madame Grandet's whom he found still quite weak. He behaved with the utmost courtesy, and promised to return in the evening.

In the evening, regretting nothing in Paris and hoping with all his heart to be forgotten by Madame Grandet, Lucien departed for Nancy.

[*Stendhal once more leaves numerous blank pages to be filled in later with an account of this second flight of Lucien's to Nancy. It was never written.*]

CHAPTER THIRTY

FOLLOWING THE SUDDEN DEATH of M. Leuwen, Lucien returned to Paris. He spent an hour with his mother before going to the bank. M. Reffre, the judicious gray-haired manager and an experienced man of affairs, even before speaking of his employer's death, said to Lucien:

"I must talk to you about your affairs, sir. But perhaps we'd best go into your private office, if you don't mind."

They had barely entered the room, when he began:

"You are a man—and a brave man. You must be prepared for the worst. Will you permit me to speak frankly?"

"Of course, my dear M. Reffre. Tell me plainly the very worst."

"You will have to go into bankruptcy."

"Great God! How much do we owe?"

"Just exactly what we have. If you don't go into bankruptcy, you will have nothing left."

"Isn't there some way to avoid bankruptcy?"

"To be sure, but then you wouldn't even have a hundred thousand pounds, and besides, it might take from five to six years to realize the whole amount."

"Wait here for me a moment. I want to consult my mother."

"But your mother knows nothing about business, sir. Perhaps it would be better not to mention the word bankruptcy. You could, you know, pay sixty per cent, and still be comfortably well-off. Your father was loved by everyone in the business world. There isn't a little shopkeeper who hasn't, at one time or another, received a couple of banknotes of a thousand francs from him. You will have your certificate of bankruptcy for sixty per cent signed within three days, even before the books are audited. And," added M. Reffre, lowering his voice, "all the business transactions of the last nineteen days are entered in a separate book that I lock up every evening. We have sugar to the amount of one million one hundred thousand francs, but without this book no one can find them."

"And this," said Lucien to himself, "is a perfectly honest man."

Seeing him so thoughtful, M. Reffre added:

"M. Lucien has somewhat lost the habit of the banking business since he has enjoyed such great honors. He no doubt attaches to the word bankruptcy the false idea held in society. M. Van Peters, whom you were so fond of, went into bankruptcy in New York, and was so little dishonored that our largest business has been with New York and all North America."

During this speech, Lucien was thinking: "I shall have to find a job." But M. Reffre, believing he had convinced Lucien, went on:

"You could even offer forty per cent, and I have arranged everything with that in mind. Should any disgruntled creditors try to force our hand, you will reduce them to thirty-five. But, as I see it, forty per cent would not be strictly honorable. Offer sixty per cent, and still Madame Leuwen will not be obliged to give up her carriage. Madame Leuwen without her carriage! There isn't one of us who wouldn't be pierced to the heart at such a spectacle! There's not one of us who has not received presents from your father amounting to more than his salary."

Still trying to think how the true state of affairs could be kept from his mother, Lucien remained silent.

"There's not one of us," M. Reffre went on in the same vein, "who is not determined that you and your mother shall be able to count on six hundred thousand francs. And besides," he added, raising his black eyebrows over his little eyes by way of emphasis, "even if none of the others should acquiesce, even if they should prove traitors, I, who am their chief, say that you will have six hundred thousand francs as surely as though you held them in your hands at this very moment, as well as all the household furnishings, silver, and so forth."

"Please wait for me here, M. Reffre!" was all Lucien replied.

He was shocked by this reference to the furniture and silver. He seemed to be seeing himself dividing the loot in a robbery.

After a somewhat prolonged quarter of an hour, quite ten minutes of which was spent preparing his mother for the news, he returned to M. Reffre. Like Lucien, his mother had a horror of bankruptcy and had offered to sacrifice her dowry, amounting to one hundred and fifty thousand francs, requesting only a life annuity of twelve hundred francs for herself, and twelve hundred francs for her son.

M. Reffre was dumfounded by their decision to pay their creditors in full. He begged Lucien to take twenty-four hours to reconsider.

"That is the one thing, my dear M. Reffre, I cannot grant you."

"Well then, M. Lucien, don't breathe a word of our conversation. This is a secret between Madame Leuwen, you and myself. The other employees have only the faintest idea of the situation."

"Good-by then, my dear Reffre, until tomorrow. My mother and I look upon you, nonetheless, as our best friend."

The next day, M. Reffre renewed his offers. He begged

Lucien to consent to go into bankruptcy, giving even ninety per cent to the creditors. A day later, after another refusal, he said to Lucien:

"The name of the banking-house can be turned to good account, provided all debts are paid . . . here is a complete list," and he handed Lucien a huge sheet of grand-eagle paper covered with figures. "Meanwhile, I, Jean-Pierre Reffre, and M. Gavardin (the cashier) are prepared to offer you one hundred thousand francs cash, and guarantee to pay all outstanding debts left by M. Leuwen, our honored chief, no matter of what sort, even his tailor's or his saddler's bills."

"Your proposition pleases me enormously," replied Lucien. "I should rather deal with you, my good and honest friend, for one hundred thousand francs than receive one hundred and fifty thousand from anyone else, who might not have the same regard for my father's good name. I make only one request: give M. Coffe an interest in the firm."

"I must be frank with you, M. Lucien. To work with M. Coffe mornings takes away my appetite for dinner. He is a thoroughly worthy man, but just the sight of him brings bad luck. However, it will never be said that the House of Reffre and Gavardin refused a request made by a Leuwen. To sum up our purchase price: one hundred thousand francs in cash, a twelve hundred franc annuity for Madame Leuwen, and the same for her son, all the furniture, silver, linen, horses, carriages and anything else you care to keep. All this is fully set forth here in this agreement. I want you to show it to a man whom all Paris respects, and who is spoken of with veneration in all business circles: M. Laffitte. And now," he continued, going over to the desk, "I shall add a life annuity for M. Coffe."

The whole transaction was completed in the same frank and loyal manner. Lucien consulted his father's friends. Several, when he pressed them for their opinion, blamed him for not going into bankruptcy with sixty per cent to the creditors.

"You can't be paupers, after all," they said; "no one will want to receive you."

Lucien and his mother had not hesitated for a second. The agreement was signed with MM. Reffre and Gavardin. Madame Leuwen received an annuity of four thousand francs instead of twelve hundred, one of the other employees having offered the additional amount. With this one exception, the agreement contained all the clauses mentioned above. M. Leuwen's two old employees paid one hundred thousand francs cash, and the same day Madame Leuwen put up for sale horses, carriages and silver services. Her son made no objection. He told her that he would not hear of taking anything but his annuity and twenty thousand francs of the capital.

During these transactions Lucien saw scarcely anyone. Unshaken though he was by the loss of his fortune, the commiseration of most of his acquaintances would have exasperated him.

The effect of the calumnies spread by the Comte de Beausobre was soon apparent. The public believed that the change in his fortunes in no way troubled Lucien's tranquillity because he was, at heart, a Saint-Simonian. If he didn't have this religion, they said, he would have invented another.

Lucien was altogether amazed when a letter arrived from Madame Grandet, who was staying at a country house in Saint-Germain, fixing an appointment with him in Versailles, at 62 Rue de Savoie.

Lucien was on the point of excusing himself when he thought:

"After all, I've behaved rather shabbily toward her. I'd better sacrifice one more half hour."

He found a woman quite desperately in love, and almost without strength enough to speak intelligibly. She did manage however, with remarkable adroitness and delicacy, to make him the following scandalous proposition: she begged him to accept an income of twelve thousand francs and, in return, asked only that he should come to see her (intentions purely honorable) four times a week.

"All the rest of my time I shall spend waiting for you."

Lucien saw that if he made the reply her offer invited, he would only provoke a violent scene. To avoid this, he told her vaguely that for certain reasons such an arrangement could, in any case, not begin for six weeks, but that he promised within twenty-four hours to give her his answer in writing. In spite of all his precautions, this unhappy meeting did not end without tears, and lasted for two hours and a quarter.

Previous to this trip to Versailles, Lucien had been engaged in a very different sort of negotiation with the old Marshal who, on the point of losing his portfolio for the last four months, was still Minister of War. Several days before, one of the Marshal's officers called upon Lucien to ask him, in the Minister's name, to be at the Ministry of War at six-thirty the next morning.

Still half-asleep, Lucien kept the appointment. He found the old Marshal looking like a sick country priest.

"Well, young man," the old gentleman began in a gruff voice, *"sic transit gloria mundi!* Another one ruined! Good God, one doesn't know what to do with one's money these days. There's nothing really safe but land, and the farmers never pay you. Is it true that you refused to go into bankruptcy? And that you sold your banking-house for a hundred thousand francs?"

"Perfectly true, Marshal."

"I knew your father, and while I'm still in this penitentiary, I am going to ask His Majesty for a six or eight thousand franc post for you. Where do you want to be?"

"Far away from Paris."

"Ah, I see, you want a Prefecture. But I refuse to owe anything to that scoundrel de Vaize. . . . And so, *nothing like that, my Larrirette,*" and he began singing the last words.

"I was not thinking of a Prefecture. Out of France, I meant to say."

"Better speak frankly between friends. The devil! We're not here to be diplomatic. All right—Secretary of an Embassy?"

"I am not entitled to be First Secretary. I know nothing of the duties of the office, and, as I have only twelve hundred francs a year, Attaché wouldn't be enough."

"I will make you, not first nor last, but second. M. le Chevalier Leuwen, Master of Petitions, cavalry Lieutenant! and he says he's not *entitled!* Write me tomorrow and let me know if you want to be Second Secretary or not."

And the Marshal dismissed him with a wave of his hand, saying:

"Honor!"

The following day Lucien, who for form's sake had consulted his mother, wrote to tell the Marshal that he accepted his offer.

Returning from Versailles, he found a note from the Marshal's aide-de-camp asking Lucien to be at the Ministry the same evening at nine o'clock. Lucien did not delay.

"I have asked His Majesty for the post of Second Secretary to the Embassy at Capel for you," the Marshal began. "If the King signs, you will have a salary of four thousand francs, and in addition, a pension in recognition of the services rendered by your late father without whom my law on —— would never have passed. I don't say that this pension is as solid as marble —but still, it ought to last at least five years, and in four or five years, if you serve your Ambassador as well as you have served de Vaize, and if you hide your Jacobin opinions (it was the King told me you were a Jacobin)—in short if you are clever, before the pension of four thousand francs is suppressed you will be getting six or eight thousand in salary. That's more than a Colonel gets. And so, good luck and good-by. I have paid my debt. Never ask me for anything else, and don't write me."

As Lucien turned to go, the old Marshal added:

"If you haven't received anything from the Rue Neuve-des-Capucines in a week, come back here at nine o'clock in the evening. As you go out tell the porter that you are coming back in a week. Good evening. Good-by."

There was nothing to hold Lucien in Paris. He did not wish to return until his misfortune had been forgotten.

"What!" all the imbeciles in the foyer of the Opera exclaimed. "You, who had a right to expect millions!"

And several persons bowed to him in a way that plainly said: "Don't speak to us."

His mother had displayed great force of character and an attitude in the very best taste. Never a complaint. She could have kept her magnificent home eighteen months longer. But before Lucien's departure she had settled down in an apartment of four rooms on the third floor of a house on the Boulevard. She sent announcements to a small circle of friends that she would be at home Fridays for tea, and that, during the time of her mourning, she would see no one on any other day.

The eighth day after his last interview with the Marshal, Lucien was wondering whether he should call on him again or not, when a large packet was brought to him addressed: *M. le Chevalier Leuwen, Second Secretary to the Embassy at Capel.* Lucien went immediately to the embroiderer to see about his uniform. He called on his Minister, received a quarter of his salary in advance, and, at the Ministry, studied the correspondence of the Embassy of Capel, except for the confidential letters. Everyone talked to him about buying a carriage but, three days after receiving his nomination, he bravely left by the mail coach, and heroically resisted the temptation of going to his new post via Nancy, Bâle and Milan.

He stayed for two delightful days on the Lake of Geneva, visiting all the places made famous by *La Nouvelle Héloïse*. At Clarens, in a peasant's cottage he came across an embroidered bed-set which had belonged to Madame de Warens.

The complete apathy which had so distressed him in Paris (hardly the place for receiving condolences) now gave way to a gentle melancholy: he was going far away from Nancy, perhaps forever!

This sadness opened his heart to the emotions of art. With more pleasure than befits an ignoramus, he visited Milan, Saronno and the Charterhouse of Pavia. Bologna and Florence threw him into a state of emotion and enthusiasm which would, three years before, have caused him the greatest remorse.

And when, finally, he arrived at his post at Capel, he had to lecture himself severely in order to adopt toward the people he was about to see a proper degree of coldness.

STENDHAL'S NOTE FOR THE END OF LUCIEN LEUWEN

Madame de Chasteller and Lucien are married while Lucien still believes that she has had a child. After their marriage in Paris: "You are mine," she cries as she covers him with kisses. "Now you must go to Nancy. And you must go at once, sir, at once! You know, alas, how my father detests me. Question him, question everybody! Then write to me. When your letters show that you are convinced (and you know that I am a good judge) then come back to me—but not till then. I shall certainly be able to distinguish the philosophy of a sensible man willing to pardon a fault which antedates his lease, and the natural impatience of a lover, from the sincere conviction of that heart which I adore!" At the end of a week Lucien returns.—End of novel.

APPENDIX

The following notes were left by Stendhal, either at the beginning of the second part of Lucien Leuwen, *or on the margins and backs of his manuscript pages.*

FEBRUARY, 22, '35.—Chronology.—Outline for me; I write it out solely for the purpose of avoiding contradictions in the little words describing the seasons or anything else. Probably the exact dates will remain vague. Nothing ages a novel so much as the last digit of a date. Thus in the text, instead of 1835, say 183-.

The essential periods in chronological order: eleven months in Nancy (three of boredom, eight of love), nine in the Ministry of the Interior in order to become, and prove to the world that he has become, a worker. Opening of the Chamber after the revolt of November.

Lucien leaves Paris for Nancy, April 25, 1833.

After a stay of eleven months in the provinces, he returns to Paris, March 25, 1834.

Seven months later, he leaves for the elections, Blois, Caen, etc., October 25, 1834. (In Nancy they were beginning to prepare for the elections seven months ago—that's stretching the point a bit.)

His father's stupid confession of his bargain with Madame Grandet, December 1834, nine months after Lucien's first return from Nancy.

Lucien's third trip to Nancy: January 24, 1835. Ministerial crisis in January or February. There had been a short trip to Nancy incognito, like Dominique's [Stendhal's name for himself] to Renne. Sentimental journey undertaken out of curiosity. He had not yet forgiven her for the baby; he forgives her November, 1834.

I write out the plan after having written the story . . . to make the plan first freezes me, because after that, memory is the active agent instead of the heart.

*　　　*　　　*

"I entrust to your mother, my dear Lucien, the painful duty of scolding you when necessary. I think, having put you in a position to receive some honorable saber scars, I have done all that can be demanded of a good father. You are familiar with life in a regiment; you are familiar with life in the provinces; do you prefer life in Paris? Command us, my Prince. There is only one thing we will not agree to, and that is marriage."

"I assure you, father, there is no question of that."

M. Leuwen to his son on another occasion: "Your words betray your feelings too plainly. You are not without wit, but you talk too freely of what you feel too strongly. That encourages all the knaves. You should always try to entertain people by talking of things that don't interest you in the least."

*   *   *

When office work is proposed: "Very well," he (Lucien) said to himself, "I shall at least learn a trade which will supply me with my daily bread, and I shall not win a horse merely, as Ernest says, because I have a rich father."

*   *   *

"I didn't think you were so young. You are a pebble not yet rubbed smooth. At the first audience you gave yesterday you were a poet." [Coffe to Lucien after leaving the Prefecture of the Department of Cher.]

*   *   *

To be incorporated: After eight months at the office, Lucien wrote letters that were too short, too clear, too exempt from ambiguous phrases, in other words, much too dangerous to sign. But he had a rare talent for getting things done, and could expedite more work than three of the best department heads together.

*   *   *

It seemed to Lucien he had managed to speak in such a way that if his remarks were repeated, they would prove that he had not been privy to the suggestion of administering opium.

Leaving the Rue de Braque, Lucien, who had expected to be horribly unhappy until this affair was over, felt very well pleased with himself.

"I may be on the verge of public disgrace and death, but at least I have played my cards well."

      *   *   *

It remains to be decided: when should Mmes. de Chasteller and de Constantin appear (in Paris)?

THREE ADDITIONAL CHAPTERS

Interesting as these chapters are in themselves, they seemed either too fragmentary, or too unrelated, to be left in the text, where, in the French editions, they appear between chapters twenty-one and twenty-two.

DU POIRIER IN PARIS

ARRIVING in Paris, Du Poirier was completely dazzled by all the luxury. Soon a wild, unreasoning longing to enjoy some of this astonishing luxury took possession of him. He observed the admiration bestowed upon M. Berryer by the nobility and the great landowners. M. Passy was at home with all the complicated figures of the Budget. But the enormous majority of France, the people who want a badly paid *King Log,* were not represented.

"They won't be for a long time, either, for they can't elect a Deputy. And here am I for five years. I intend to be the O'Connell and the Cobbett of France. I'll stop at nothing, and I'll make an important, a unique place for myself. There's no danger of any rival appearing until the day when all the officers of the National Guard can vote . . . in ten years perhaps. I am fifty-two—later, come what may! I'll object that they have gone too far, and I'll sell myself for a lifetime sinecure, and rest on my laurels."

In two days' time the conversion of this new Saint Paul was decided, but the how of the matter was more difficult. He dreamed about it for a week. The main thing was not to sacrifice religion.

At last he hit upon a banner the public could understand. *Words of a Believer* had enjoyed a great success the year before. Dr. Du Poirier adopted it as his gospel, had himself introduced to M. de Lamennais and displayed the keenest enthusiasm. I even wonder if this ill-bred disciple did not make the illustrious Breton regret his celebrity. Yet had not M. de Lamennais himself, after beginning as the Pope's adorer, become a lover of liberty? Great-hearted Liberty is sometimes a little absent-minded and forgets to ask: "Where did you come from?"

The day before in the Chamber, when attacked by the laughter of the right and the heavy sarcasms of the bourgeois aristocracy, with the aid of gestures and facial expression, Du Poirier had displayed sufficient skill to make them swallow this astonishing piece of egotism:

"I fully expect to be attacked for my way of expressing myself, of gesticulating, of ascending this rostrum. Underhanded warfare, all that! Yes, gentlemen, it is true, at the age of fifty-two I am seeing Paris for the first time. But where have I been spending those fifty-two years? Have I been buried in some provincial château, flattered by my lackeys and my notary, entertaining the priest at dinner? No, gentlemen, I have spent all those years learning to know men of all ranks, and in helping the poor. Inheriting a few thousand francs, I boldly sacrificed them to get an education.

"When I left the university at the age of twenty-two, I was a doctor, but I didn't have five hundred francs to my name. Today I am rich, but I have struggled for that fortune against talented, energetic competitors. I have made that fortune, gentlemen, not—like my fine adversaries—by just taking the trouble to get born, but by dint of visits at three sous, then three francs, then ten francs; and, to my shame, I confess that I never had time to learn how to dance! Now these fine gentlemen, these orators and accomplished dancers, make fun of the poor country doctor who has failed to acquire all the graces. Truly a memorable victory! While they were taking lessons in style, and in the art of talking without saying anything, after the manner of the *Athenaeum* or the *Académie Française,* I was visiting huts high up in snow-covered mountains, and I became acquainted with the wants and the desires of the poor. I am here to represent one hundred thousand Frenchmen deprived of the right to vote with whom I have conversed all my life—but they make the terrible mistake of not being impressed by airs and graces."

*   *   *

Lucien, who had noticed Du Poirier's name among the new Deputies, was surprised one day to see him walk into his office. He embraced the doctor with emotion, and tears came to his eyes.

Du Poirier was disconcerted. For three days he had hesitated before coming to Lucien's office; on being announced he was terrified, his heart started beating violently. He trembled for fear the young officer had learned of the strange trick the doctor had played on him to get him out of Nancy.

"If he knows, he will kill me!"

Du Poirier possessed wit and method and a talent for intrigue, but he had the misfortune to be pitifully lacking in courage. His profound medical knowledge was made to serve his cowardice (a shortcoming most uncommon in France) and his imagination evoked all the tragic consequences of a punch in the jaw or a well-aimed kick in the posterior. For that was exactly the treatment he anticipated from Lucien. And for this reason, although he had been in Paris for ten days, he had not come to see Lucien before. For this reason also he had finally come to Lucien's office, which was more or less public, where he would be surrounded by clerks and other attendants, rather than to Lucien's home. The day before he had caught sight of Lucien on the boulevard, and had hurriedly turned tail, and ducked down the nearest side street.

"At least," his caution prompted, "if a misfortune should befall me [he meant a punch or a kick] it's better to be in a room without witnesses than in the middle of the street. I can't very well remain in Paris without meeting him sooner or later."

Suffice it to add that, despite his avarice and fear of firearms, the wily doctor had bought himself a pair of pistols which even at that very moment reposed in his pockets.

"During the elections, when so much bitterness is always aroused, M. Leuwen may well have received an anonymous letter. In that case . . ."

But Lucien embraced the doctor with tears in his eyes.

"Ah, he hasn't changed!" said Du Poirier to himself, and was thereupon filled with inexpressible contempt for our hero.

Seeing the doctor, Lucien immediately imagined himself back in Nancy, a stone's throw from the Rue de la Pompe. Only a very little while ago perhaps Du Poirier had talked with Madame de Chasteller! Lucien looked at him with the tenderest interest.

"But what can this mean?" Lucien asked himself. "He isn't dirty! He has a new suit, new trousers, a new hat, and new shoes! It's unheard of! What a change! How could he possibly bring himself to spend so much money?"

*   *   *

Like all provincials, Du Poirier exaggerated the sagacity as well as the crimes of the police.

"This is a very lonely street," he said to Lucien. "What if the Minister I made fun of this morning in the Chamber should have me seized by four of his men and thrown into the river? I can't swim, and besides it doesn't take long to catch pneumonia."

"But his four men have wives, mistresses, cronies; they would gossip," replied Lucien. "Besides, do you really think that Ministers are such knaves?"

"They are capable of anything!" Du Poirier retorted warmly.

"Ah," thought Lucien, "there's no cure for fear." And he decided to escort the doctor to his door.

As they walked along the endless wall of a vast garden, the doctor's fear increased. Lucien felt his arm tremble.

"Are you armed?" he asked Lucien.

"If I tell him I have only my cane he is capable of fainting with terror, and I shall be here for an hour." So Lucien replied in a brisk military tone:

"Only my pistols and a dagger."

This completed the doctor's panic; Lucien could hear his teeth chattering.

"If this young officer knows the trick I played on him in Madame de Chasteller's anteroom, what a chance for revenge he has now!"

As they were going along a ditch which had overflowed during the recent rain, Lucien suddenly stepped to one side.

"Ah, sir," cried the doctor in heart-rending tones, "you wouldn't think of vengeance against an old man!"

"He is certainly crazy," thought Lucien.

"My dear Doctor, I realize that you like money, but if I were in your place I'd hire a carriage and resign myself to being less eloquent in the Chamber."

"That's what I keep telling myself," moaned the doctor, "but I can't help it; when I get an idea I feel myself drawn to that *rostrum* as though I were in love with it; I make eyes at it, and am furiously jealous when anyone else is there. When I'm up there and there's silence all around, when everybody in the visitors' balconies is so attentive, especially all those pretty women, I feel as strong as a lion, I'd speak my mind to God the Father Himself. It's only in the evening, after dinner, that I'm seized with fright. I've thought of renting a room in the Palais Royal. As for a carriage, I've thought of that too, but they would bribe the coachman to overturn it. I could very well have a coachman come up from Nancy, only before he left, M. Rey or M. de Vassigny would promise him twenty-five louis to get rid of me. . . ."

A drunken man was coming toward them. The doctor clung desperately to Lucien's arm.

"Ah, my friend," he said after a moment, "how lucky you are to be brave!"

GENERAL FARI

ONE DAY, in great distress, Lucien burst into the Minister's office. He had just seen a monthly police report, a copy of which had been sent by the Minister of the Interior to the Minister of War, stating that General Fari had been guilty of propaganda at Sarcey where he had been sent nine or ten days before the elections of —— to nip in the bud an incipient liberal movement.

"Nothing could be farther from the truth!" cried Lucien indignantly. "The General is devoted heart and soul to his duty. He would be horrified at the mere idea that anyone sent on a mission for a certain purpose should do the contrary."

"Were you present, sir, on the occasion mentioned in this report, the accuracy of which you challenge?" the Minister haughtily rejoined.

"No, Your Excellency, but I am sure that the report was made in bad faith."

The Minister was about to set out for the Château. He left the room in a passion, and began abusing the footman who was helping him on with his coat.

"If he got a penny out of this slander, I could understand," Lucien said to himself. "But what's the good of such mischievous lying? Poor Fari is almost sixty-five. If there happens to be a department head at the War Ministry who has a grudge against the General, he can take advantage of this report to have one of the best officers in the army retired—and one of the finest men in the world. . . ."

There happened to be in Paris at the moment the former secretary-general of the Comte de Vaize in the last Prefecture the Comte had occupied before Louis XVIII called him to the Chamber of Peers. Running across him the next day at the Ministry of War, Lucien spoke to him about the report on General Fari.

"What has our Minister against him?"

"His Excellency once had the notion that General Fari was paying undue attentions to his wife."

"What! At the General's age!"

"The young Comtesse was dying of boredom at —— and General Fari amused her. But I'd be willing to wager not a word of gallantry ever passed between them."

"And you think for such a trifling reason . . ."

"Ah, you don't know our Minister. His pride takes offense at the slightest provocation, and he never forgets. That man's heart—if he has a heart—is a storeroom of hatreds. If he had the power of a Carrier or a Le Bon, he would have at least five hundred persons guillotined for purely personal offenses, and at least three-quarters of them would have even forgotten his name—if he didn't happen to be a Minister. If ever he has supreme power, I advise you, who see him every day and probably oppose him on occasion, to betake yourself to the other side of the Rhine as fast as ever you can go."

Lucien hurried back to the Ministry to find Crapart, chief of the Ministry's secret police.

"What reason can I give that will affect this rogue?" Lucien pondered as he made his way across the courtyard and down the corridors that led to the police headquarters. "The truth—the General's innocence, his probity, my friendship for him—would all be equally ridiculous in his eyes. He would think me childish. . . ."

The attendant, who had great respect for the Hon. Private Secretary, whispered to him that Crapart was engaged at the moment with two or three spies of the highest society.

Still trying to think what he should say, Lucien gazed out of the window. Nothing came to him. He saw the men get into their carriage.

"Charming spies, indeed," Lucien said to himself. "No one could be more distinguished-looking."

The attendant returned and Lucien, still thoughtful, followed him. When he entered M. Crapart's office he seemed pleased.

"There is a certain Field Marshal Fari somewhere in the world," Lucien began.

Crapart's manner became grave and somewhat hostile.

"He's a poor devil," Lucien went on, "but not without a certain honesty. He pays my father regularly two thousand francs yearly on a debt. In an imprudent moment, my father loaned him a thousand louis, and the General still owes him about nine or ten thousand francs. So it is to our interest that General Fari should continue to be employed for four or five years longer."

Crapart remained thoughtful.

"I'll not beat about the bush, my dear colleague. . . . But you can see for yourself—I'll show you the Minister's own handwriting."

For five or six minutes, Crapart searched through his files.

"F . . . ! Someone's always mislaying my papers!"

An ugly-looking clerk entered and was roundly abused.

While being berated, he in turn examined the files, and finally handed Crapart the document he had been looking for:

"Here is report No. 5 of—" he began.

"Get out!" shouted Crapart with shocking rudeness, and, turning to Lucien, remarked calmly, "Here's what we're after."

He began turning over the pages:

"Hm . . . hm . . . hm . . . Ah! here it is," and he accented the words as he read:

"'*General Fari acted with firmness and moderation; he talked to the young men in the most persuasive manner. His reputation as an honest man carried weight.*' And now," Crapart exclaimed, "what do you think of this? All that is crossed out, and this is what has been added in His Excellency's own hand: '*Everything would have gone smoothly but for this deplorable fact: all the time General Fari was in —— he engaged in propaganda, and never stopped talking about the Three Days.*' Under the circumstances, my dear colleague, I'm afraid I can do nothing to help you get back your ten thousand francs. That last sentence went over to the Ministry of War this morning. Look out for the explosion!" And Crapart gave one of his coarse laughs.

Lucien thanked him cordially and hurried over to the Ministry of War. He went directly to the department of the military police.

"I am sent by the Minister of the Interior on a most urgent matter," he explained. "By some mistake a deleted page of a rough draft was inserted in the Minister's last letter."

"Here's your letter. I haven't opened it yet," replied the department manager, handing Lucien the letter. "Take it along with you if you like, but let me have it back before I begin work tomorrow morning at ten o'clock."

"If the page is in the middle, I'd prefer correcting the letter at once."

"Here are erasers and pumice . . . make yourself at home "

As Lucien installed himself at a table, the official asked:

"And how is your great study on the Prefectures after the elections coming along? For the past two years they've been promising my wife's cousin, now Sub-Prefect at ——, either Le Havre or Toulon . . ."

Lucien showed the greatest interest in the manager's family affairs, and gave him the most gratifying replies. While chatting, Lucien recopied the middle sheet of the letter signed Comte de Vaize. The sentence in question was next to the last one on the back of the page to the right. By cleverly spacing the words and the lines, Lucien succeeded in suppressing the seven lines concerning General Fari without the change being noticeable.

"I'll just take our page along with me," he said, after working for three-quarters of an hour.

"As you wish, sir . . . and may I take this opportunity to recommend our little Sub-Prefect to your attention?"

"I'll look up his dossier and add my recommendation," Lucien promised him. ("Here I am doing for General Fari what Brutus would not have done for his country.")

One of the clerks of the firm of Van Peters, Leuwen, and Co. was leaving for England the following week. Lucien entrusted him with a letter for General Fari to be mailed when he got within twenty leagues of the General's place of residence. The letter informed the General of the hate the Minister still harbored against him. Without signing the letter, Lucien cited two or three remarks of their private conversations that would reveal to the worthy General the author of this salutary warning.

M. DES RAMIERS

EVER SINCE the beginning of the session, Lucien had found his duties more amusing. The most ethical, the most Fénelonian editor of the government newspaper par excellence, M. des Ramiers, recently elected Deputy from Escorbiac in the Midi by a majority of two votes, was engaged in paying assiduous court both to the Minister and to Madame la Comtesse de Vaize.

"He is an unpolitically-minded man," Lucien decided, "who believes that he can reconcile things which are utterly incompatible. If men were as good as he pretends, there'd be no more need of a police force or courts of law. But, after all, he errs only out of the goodness of his heart."

In consequence, M. des Ramiers was very well received when he came to see Lucien one morning on a matter of business.

After a preamble in the very best style, which, if reproduced here, would cover at least eight pages, M. des Ramiers explained that there were some exceedingly painful duties connected with public office. For example, he found himself under the strictest moral obligation to demand the removal of an exciseman of spirituous liquors, one M. Tourte, whose brother had twice, in the most scandalous fashion, opposed his, M. des Ramier's, nomination. But even this was said with ingenious precautions; otherwise Lucien might not have been able to control the irresistible desire to laugh which had seized him at the first hint of the Deputy's motives.

"Fénelon demanding a removal!"

Lucien amused himself by replying in des Ramier's own style. He pretended not to understand the question, not to realize what the Deputy was aiming at, and wickedly forced this modern Fénelon to ask point-blank for the removal of a poor devil of a semi-skilled worker who, on a salary of eleven hundred francs, supported himself, his wife, his mother-in-law, and five children.

When he had sufficiently enjoyed M. des Ramier's embarrassment, caused by Lucien's seeming obtuseness, which had forced the poor Deputy to speak in the plainest and therefore the most odious terms, Lucien advised him to take the matter up with the Minister, and tried to make him understand that the interview was at an end. As M. des Ramiers persisted, Lucien, sick of the rascal's mawkish expression, felt tempted to try harsher methods.

"But wouldn't you, my dear sir," insisted the Deputy, "do me the inestimable service of explaining to His Excellency the painful necessity I am faced with? My mandators seriously reproach me with being unfaithful to the promises I made them. But, on the other hand, to ask His Excellency for the removal of the head of a family . . . ! After all, I have my duty to my own family to consider. If the government should show its confidence in me by appointing me to the Auditor's court, for example, there would have to be a new election. And how could I present myself to my astonished mandators unless the behavior of M. Tourte is censured by a conspicuous mark of disapprobation? As I see it, having had a majority of only two votes, the slightest preponderance on the other side might be fatal to the future deputation. But I interfere as little in the elections as possible, sir. I must admit that in the interests of our social mechanism I fully realize the necessity of certain actions —quite indispensable I agree—but which I wouldn't for the world be mixed up in. The decrees of the courts must be executed, it is true, but God forbid that such duties should fall to my lot!"

M. des Ramiers flushed very red, and at last realized that he was expected to retire.

"M. Tourte will be removed," thought Lucien, "but I shall henceforth call this new Fénelon by his right name: executioner."

Barely four days later, Lucien came upon a long letter from the Minister of the Interior to the Minister of Finance enjoining the Collector of Indirect Taxes to recommend the removal of M. Tourte. Lucien called in a clerk famous for his skill in erasing words neatly, and had him write in Tarte for Tourte, wherever the name appeared.

It took des Ramiers two weeks to discover why the removal of M. Tourte was being delayed. Meantime, Lucien had found occasion to give Madame de Vaize a full account of the scene enacted in his office by this new Tartuffe. The Comtesse was much too kind ever to recognize evil unless it was very plainly explained and proved. Now, seven or eight times she reverted to the subject of poor M. Tourte, whose name had struck her, and several times she forgot to invite M. des Ramiers to the ministerial dinners given to Deputies of minor importance.

M. des Ramiers realized whence came this sudden turn of fortune. He began to insinuate himself into a very exclusive social set where he was considered a philosopher and a somewhat too liberal innovator, and was able to spread some malicious gossip.

Lucien had completely forgotten the scoundrel when one day young Desbacs, who envied des Ramier's wealth and was paying court to him, came to inform Lucien of the Deputy's remarks. This was going a bit far, even for a Desbacs, Lucien thought.

"One rogue denouncing another!"

He went to see M. Crapart to ask him to verify the truth of Desbacs' slander. Rather a novice in Parisian salons, Crapart never doubted for a moment that Lucien was on the most intimate terms with Madame de Vaize, or at least on the point of attaining to that post which was the envy of all the young clerks: lover of the Minister's wife. M. Crapart displayed the greatest zeal in doing Lucien's bidding, and a week later was able to bring Lucien the confirmation of M. des Ramier's remarks about Madame de Vaize.

"I'll be right back," said Lucien, and, taking the misspelled reports of the society spies, he went off to see Madame de Vaize.

The open-hearted confidence the Comtesse felt toward Lucien was closely akin to a much tenderer sentiment. Although vaguely aware of this, Lucien was so sick of his affair with Madame Grandet that he felt a horror of all intrigues of this kind. Since he had left Nancy, the one thing which came the nearest to a state of happiness for him was to ride for an hour at a slow walk through the Meudon woods.

During the days that followed, Lucien found Madame de Vaize really incensed against M. des Ramiers, and as she possessed more sensibility than social tact, she made the Deputy feel her anger in the most humiliating fashion. I don't know how, but this usually gentle nature thought up the cruelest expressions to apply to this modern Fénelon. And as she employed them without the least circumspection in the midst of the numerous court that always surrounds a Minister's wife, they proved extremely damaging to this Deputy-journalist's aureole of philanthropy and virtue. His friends were worried, and there was an unmistakable allusion in the *Charivari,* a periodical which very neatly poked fun at the Tartuffery of the gentlemen of the *Juste-milieu.*

Finally came a letter from the Minister of Finance enclosing the reply of the Collector of Indirect Taxes: there was no M. Tarte among the excisemen in his Department. But M. des Ramiers, much to his credit, had managed to get a postscript added in the

Minister's own hand: "Could this perhaps be M. Tourte, excise-man at Escorbiac?"

A week later M. de Vaize replied:

"Yes, it is precisely M. Tourte who behaved so badly, and whose removal I recommend."

Lucien stole the letter and hurried to show it to Madame de Vaize.

"What can we do now?" she asked, with an air of concern which Lucien found charming. He took her hand and kissed it rapturously.

"You mustn't," breathed the Comtesse in a scarcely audible voice.

"I shall be careless and put this letter in an envelope addressed to the Ministry of War."

Eleven days later it was returned by the Minister of War with a note explaining the mistake. That day the correspondence clerk had placed three letters just received from the Minister of War in a large folder (called a chemise in the Ministries) and had written across it: "Three letters from His Excellency, the Minister of War." For a week Lucien had been holding in reserve another letter from the Minister of War, in which the Minister claimed authority over the mounted municipal guard. Lucien substituted it for the one in which the communication concerning M. Tourte had been returned. M. des Ramiers, who had no direct connection with the Minister of War, was obliged to have recourse to the famous General Barbaut, but in the end it took fully six months before his demand for the removal of M. Tourte was finally granted. As soon as the news reached Madame de Vaize, she gave Lucien five hundred francs to be sent to the poor official out of a job.

Lucien encountered twenty or more affairs of this kind. But, as you see, it takes eight printed pages to make all the details of such low intrigues understandable, and that is too costly!

Actuated by a sentiment new to her, the gentle Comtesse declared to her husband with a firmness which greatly astonished him, that if ever M. des Ramiers dined at the Ministry, she would be indisposed and dine in her own room. After two or three experiments, M. de Vaize ended by crossing M. de Ramiers' name off his list of Deputies. When this became known, over half the Deputies of the Center stopped shaking hands with the mealy-mouthed editor of the ministerial paper. As a last straw, M. Leuwen, who had only learned of the anecdote later through the indiscretion of Desbacs, went to his son for a full account. The name of M. Tourte seemed to furnish a unique opportunity, and soon the story made the rounds of the salons of high diplomacy. M. des Ramiers, who succeeded in worming himself in everywhere, had somehow obtained an introduction to the Russian ambassador. When des Ramiers was presented to him, the famous Prince loudly exclaimed: "Ah! the *des Ramiers de Tourte!*" Whereupon the modern Fénelon turned purple, and the next day M. Leuwen set the anecdote circulating through Paris.

NOTES

PAGE 4. *Non ragioniam di loro, ma guarda e passa:* Let us not speak to them, but look and pass. (Dante, *Inferno;* Longfellow translation.)

PAGE 5. *the great banker M. François Leuwen:* As one of his models for Lucien's father, Stendhal mentions the banker Pillet-Will (1781-1860) who was one of the founders of the Caisse d'Epargne (Savings Bank) and Regent of the Banque de France. There is still a Rue Pillet-Will in Paris.

PAGE 6. *sommations respectueuses:* Formerly in France children who were of age and who intended to marry without their parents' consent were required to serve notice on them to that effect, and to call upon them to give their consent. This extrajudicial notice was called a "sommation respectueuse" or respectful notification.

PAGE 7. *a clever and brave freebooter like Soult:* Nicolas Jean de Dieu Soult (1769-1851) who entered the army as a private, became Marshal of France and Duke of Dalmatia. He was one of Napoleon's most famous and popular generals. In Louis-Philippe's government Soult, at different times, held the portfolios of War and of Foreign Affairs, and was Premier from 1839 to 1840. He was always at swords' points with the doctrinaires, Guizot and de Broglie who, according to Louis Blanc, considered him, "a rude soldier, proud of his renown which his ability did not justify." Soult could not stomach the haughtiness and intellectual arrogance of the doctrinaires. In his manuscript, Stendhal substitutes N—— for Soult, except in one instance when the name has been written and crossed out. At the end of his novel, becoming even more careful, he avoids "Marshal" and calls him "General N——." At the time Stendhal was writing his novel, which so mercilessly lampoons the government, Soult was actually Minister of War, and he himself was "feeding on the Budget" as Consul at Civita-Vecchia. Following the example of Henry Debraye, editor of the Champion Edition, 1927, and to avoid more of those confusing "N——s" I have in every instance substituted the name Soult.

PAGE 9. *I mean a politician, a Martignac—I won't go so far as to say a Talleyrand:* The Vicomte de Martignac, liberal Minister of Charles X, who believed in a representative monarchy and lent his charming eloquence and his gentle and bewitching voice to that cause. He was not a favorite with Charles, who said of him: "He is just a beautiful organ of speech." He was a politician, but not an unscrupulous rascal like the great Talleyrand. Jean-Baptiste de Talleyrand de Périgord began in holy orders and was appointed Bishop by Louis XVI; was representative of the clergy of his diocese in the States General; Minister under the Directory, the Consulate, and the Empire; was made a Prince of the Empire (Prince de Bénévent); continued in favor after the July Revolution and was Louis-Philippe's Ambassador to London.

PAGE 9. *Colbert:* See note for page 331.

PAGE 9. *Sully:* Maximilien de Béthune, Duc de Sully (1559-1641), friend and Minister of Henri IV.

PAGE 9. *Cardinal Richelieu:* (1585-1642), famous statesman, Minister of State to Louis XIII, and arbiter of policy.

PAGE 9. *had Frotté shot by the gendarmes, who were taking him to prison:* The Comte de Frotté, leader of the rebel royalists (les Chouans) in Normandy, was shot after his surrender in spite of the promise of Bonaparte (then First Consul) that if he surrendered "he could count on the generosity of the government which wished to forget the past and to unite all Frenchmen."

PAGE 10. *the great actor Monvel:* Jacques-Marie Boutet, called Monvel (1745-1812), actor, playwright, and father of the famous actress Mademoiselle Mars.

PAGE 10. *the Abbaye:* Prison of the Abbaye, built in Paris between 1631 and 1635 as the seignorial prison of the Abbaye de Saint-Germain-des-Prés; became a military prison in 1789; scene of the massacres of September 1792; torn down in 1854.

PAGE 11. *as the Débats would say: Journal des Débats,* founded as a moderate republican newspaper in 1789. It made a practice of publishing articles of literary value.

PAGE 14. *after the manner of Vauvenargues:* Luc de Clapiers, Marquis de Vauvenargues (1715-1747), moralist of lofty character who enjoyed the friendship of Marmontel and Voltaire. His *Introduction à la connaissance de l'esprit humain* is famous for its moral aphorisms.

PAGE 14. *the Bouffes:* The Théâtre-Italien, Stendhal's favorite theater in Paris where Italian opera was given, where "all Paris" went to hear the greatest Italian singers of the day, such as Giuditta Pasta (Stendhal's friend), Malibran, Rubini, and where every lady of fashion *had* to have her box.

PAGE 17. *the Emperor's Comte Daru:* Pierre-Antoine Daru, Henri Beyle's cousin, through whose powerful patronage Stendhal became a prosperous government official under the Empire. Daru was Commissary General of the Grand Army, and later Napoleon's Secretary of State. He was also a man of letters and member of the Académie Française.

PAGE 18. *50 louis to twelve or fifteen thousand francs:* francs livres, écus, napoleons, and louis d'or at this period had the following relative values: Francs and livres were almost equivalent. A livre was equal to 20 sous; an écu to 6 livres; a louis d'or to 4 écus or 24 livres; a napoleon to 20 francs.

PAGE 18. *There you have the doctrinaires:* During the Restoration this name was given to certain politicians who sought to elevate politics to the level of a philosophy. They were intellectuals and, for the most part, academic professors. They supported the Bourbons and the Charter, advocating a constitutional government on the British model. Their leaders were Royer-Collard and Guizot. After the July Revolution, the designation became very elastic. As Louis Blanc says, it was "a word which everyone employed though no one was able to define it, not even those to whom it was applied." There was really little difference between their objectives of peace and prosperity for the prosperous, and those of the left-center party made up of former liberals such as Lafayette, Laffitte, Thiers. The doctrinaires were extremely unpopular because of their dogmatic arrogance and haughtiness, and Louis Blanc sums them up by saying: "Pride was what, in fact, constituted them a school." M. Leuwen here adds another characteristic: duplicity.

P A G E 2 0 . *the Moniteur:* Government newspaper, devoted to official announcements.

P A G E 2 0 . *M. le Comte de Vaize, Minister of the Interior . . . MM. N——, N——:* There is a really disturbing confusion of N——s throughout the book, referring to a variety of persons. Whenever Stendhal indicates in his notes the name of the real person he had in mind, or the name is obvious from the text, I have, therefore, substituted it for the ubiquitous N——, as in this case "M. de Vaize" for "M. N——, Minister of the Interior."

P A G E 2 0 . *Master of Petitions* (Maître des Requêtes): A sinecure in the Council of State comparable to that of English Privy Councilor.

P A G E 2 2 . *like Dupont de l'Eure the one honest man of the party:* See note for page 292: *three dupes in France.* . . .

P A G E 2 3 . *Madame Cunier:* Stendhal has forgotten that in the first part of his novel he gave the name of Mlle. Prichard to the right-thinking postmistress of Nancy.

P A G E 3 0 . *E sotto l'usbergo del sentirsi pura:* Sheltered by the consciousness of her own purity. (Dante, *Inferno.*)

PAGE 30. *I am dying to hear Rubini:* The Italian tenor, Giovanni Battista Rubini (1795-1854), who was all the rage at that time. From 1831 to 1838 he sang almost exclusively in Paris and London.

PAGE 31. *Madame d'Hocquincourt had forgotten the very existence of M. d'Antin:* Opposite this sentence, Stendhal has the following note: "For me. Thus, to be woven into the fabric of my Paris scene, I shall introduce six or seven Nancy characters: MM. Du Poirier, d'Hocquincourt, d'Antin, de Vassigny, Mmes. d'Hocquincourt, de Constantin, de Chasteller."

PAGE 32. *The law of sacrilege:* This refers to the bill against sacrilege introduced in 1825, when mutilation was discussed in the Chamber as punishment for profanation of the Host. "This mention of the amputation of the hand," Martineau notes, "appears over and over again in Stendhal's works as one of his chief grievances against the politics of the ultras." As a matter of fact, the law that was enacted making sacrilege punishable by death and putting profanation of the Host on a par with parricide, was never enforced.

PAGE 36. *M. Dumoral:* Stendhal never corrected his inconsistencies in regard to the Prefect of Nancy. He had first thought of placing the action of the first part, *The Green Huntsman,* in Montvallier, a sub-Prefecture, with Fléron as sub-Prefect and Dumoral as Prefect of the Department. Later he changed to Nancy, which is a Prefecture. In the second part of the novel, wherever the name Dumoral appears, Henry Debraye substitutes Fléron, since, he says, Stendhal would have done so if he had revised his novel. But Stendhal would certainly also have made the necessary alterations in the text. For this reason I have retained the name Dumoral (as Henri Martineau does), and also because the description of Dumoral here does not agree with that of Fléron in the first part of the story, and Stendhal is known to have had two different living models in view.

PAGE 36. *his eight months in Sainte-Pélagie:* Famous prison in Paris dating from 1792, torn down in 1899. Here political prisoners were held, especially those arrested for violation of the laws governing the press. According to Stendhal, debtors were also sent to Sainte-Pélagie, as witness Lucien's former fellow-student at the École Polytechnique, Coffe, whom Lucien rescues from that prison by paying his indebtedness.

PAGE 44. *a painter . . . Lacroix:* Martineau suggests that this is the great romantic painter Eugène Delacroix whose talent Stendhal was one of the first to recognize. Delacroix formed one of the circle of artists and writers frequented by Stendhal after his return to Paris from Italy in 1821, when Delacroix was in his early twenties.

PAGE 44. *M. de Polignac:* The unpopular Minister of Charles X, who headed his reactionary ultra-royalist Ministry which signed the famous Ordinances, thereby setting off the July Revolution. He was sentenced to life imprisonment in the Castle of Ham, but was set at liberty by the amnesty of 1836.

PAGE 46. *the fever over the elections and the Spanish question:* The Spanish King Ferdinand VII died September 29, 1833. This raised the question in France of whether to recognize the young Queen Isabella or not. The government was unanimous in favor of recognition. But Thiers went even further, and became the advocate of armed intervention against the Carlists, a project opposed by the majority of the Ministers. The elections here referred to were those of June, 1834, when new elections were to be held to replace the Chamber, dissolved at the end of the last session.

PAGE 48. *but at the word telegraph he understood:* This is the first of Stendhal's many references to the semaphore telegraph, invented by Claude Chappe in 1792, used for the first time in 1794. These semaphores were set up at intervals on hilltops and high towers. Stendhal was fascinated by these devices and for a moment thought of calling his whole novel *The Telegraph.* This obviously was too particular for a general title, but admirably suits the second part where it plays such an important role. On the margin of his manuscript of *The Life of Napoleon,* Stendhal left the following note (published by Henri Martineau in *Mélanges Intimes et Marginalia*): "Telegraph. 'It is easy to govern since the invention of the telegraph. News is received in Paris from Calais in three minutes—there are 27 telegraphs; from Lille, two minutes—there are 22 telegraphs; from Strasbourg 6½ minutes, 45 telegraphs. From Lyons 8 minutes, 50 telegraphs. From Brest, 8 minutes, 80 telegraphs.' (*Monthly Review*, No. 313, p. 546.)" The telegraph at this time was controlled by the government.

PAGE 54. *Villèle used to consult him:* Comte de Villèle (1773-1854), the leader of the ultra-royalists during the Restoration, Premier, 1821-1828.

PAGE 56. *Saint-Simonism:* A socialistic system based on the doctrines of Saint-Simon (1760-1825), called the father of French socialism. He was a descendant of the author of the *Mémoires*. When industrialism was still in its infancy, Saint-Simon predicted that the future lay with the industrial state. After his death his disciples Olinde Rodrigues, Enfantin, and Bazard formed a school, and developed Saint-Simon's principles into the utopian philosophy called Saint-Simonism or Saint-Simonianism. Their ambitious program had as its objective the abolition of competition and of war by the creation of a league of all nations and the international organization of industry, as well as the distribution of wealth by following the maxim, "to each man according to his capacity, to each capacity according to its works." To these tenets were added a mystical religion, and although perfectly sincere, the Saint-Simonists made themselves ridiculous by their antics. They were persecuted by the government, and one of the "Fathers," Père Enfantin, when arrested on an absurd charge (of which he was acquitted), appeared at his trial with the words "Le Père" inscribed on his chest, his hair long, and a beard like a Hebrew prophet. The upper classes, secure in their wealth and power, did not take seriously the theories of the Saint-Simonists so far in advance of the times, but they laughed at their eccentricities. They were a natural butt for the sarcasms of M. Leuwen, who throughout the book taunts his son for his Saint-Simonist gravity.

PAGE 56. *first and second floors:* Second and third floors in America—that is the first and second floors above the rez-de-chaussée, or ground floor, where persons of wealth had their apartments. Only the less affluent who lived in the attics appreciated Saint-Simon's hopeful socialistic doctrines.

PAGE 60. *a falling out with Barrême:* Bertrand François Barrême (1640-1703), a French arithmetician who invented a ready-reckoner, since called in French a barême or barrême.

PAGE 62. *Troppo aiuto a Sant' Antonio:* Too great an aid for St. Antony.

PAGE 62. *Victor Cousin:* (1792-1867) The founder of systematic eclecticism, and spokesman for the German transcendentalist philosophers whom Stendhal detested. Of Cousin, Stendhal once remarked: "Except for Bossuet, Cousin is the cleverest dealer in serious humbug." When his friend Guizot became Premier, Cousin was made a member of the Council of Public Instruction.

PAGE 62. *the same character as Blifil:* The mealy-mouthed villain in Fielding's *Tom Jones*. Stendhal was a great admirer of Fielding, and several times in his notes contrasts his own style and method with that of the English novelist.

PAGE 63. *Béranger was once a clerk at eighteen hundred francs:* Pierre Jean de Béranger (1780-1857), famous political song writer who, in his early years, had a clerkship in the office of the Imperial University. During the Restoration he became the champion of the opposition to the Bourbons, and was twice imprisoned for his libelous songs. Lucas-Dubreton says that Béranger "accomplished more for the liberal cause than all the speeches and newspaper articles . . . under the Restoration, Béranger was really the *vox populi*." After the fall of Charles X he became "the soul of the Orleanist party." Although remaining in the background, he exerted an influence on affairs of State by acting through the leading statesmen, Laffitte in particular.

PAGE 64. *He is a Guizot minus the intelligence:* François Guizot (1787-1874), professor of modern history at the Sorbonne, entered politics after the Restoration as a member of the opposition and follower of Royer-Collard, the founder of the doctrinaires (see note for page 18). In the July Monarchy he held different portfolios and, with Casimir-Périer, was spokesman for the more conservative of the two parties representing the wealthy bourgeoisie in the Chamber.

PAGE 66. *and is anxious for another Rue Transnonain:* This is a reference to a shocking incident which occurred in Paris during the April riots of 1834. The insurgents had already dispersed when there was a rumor that the troops were being fired on from No. 12 Rue Transnonain. Thereupon the soldiers burst into the house and shot or bayoneted men, women, and children with bloodthirsty cruelty. Stendhal shared the general horror over this butchery, referring to it several times as a sample of the government's bloody methods. A famous Daumier lithograph gruesomely recalls the event.

PAGE 69. *That devil of a General Rumigny:* Cautious as usual, Stendhal in his text substitutes N—— for Rumigny, but writes "Mignyru"—that is Rumigny—between the lines. General Rumigny was responsible for the ruthless suppression of the insurrection in Paris in 1834 during which occurred the massacre of the Rue Transnonain

PAGE 69. *Chief of Police of the Château:* The Château de Neuilly, near Paris, Louis-Philippe's principal residence, destroyed in the revolution of 1848.

PAGE 69. *see to it that the soldiers and civilians don't get too friendly:* See following note on the "Kortis Affair."

PAGE 70. *the Kortis affair:* Stendhal borrowed this incident from an "affaire Corteys" which actually occurred in Lyons in 1834. To understand the situation it is necessary to recall the political unrest existing in France at this time. Although the July Revolution of 1830 had been accomplished by the uprising of the working class of Paris led by republicans, it was the politicians, the bankers, and industrialists, that is the wealthy bourgeois class, who profited by the people's victory. The government looked upon the embittered working class, underpaid and overworked and constantly prodded by the liberal journalists (such as the famous Carrel whose articles did much to launch the April riots in Lyons), as a constant menace. Even with its standing army increased to the unheard-of number of 360,000 men for the purpose of putting down strikes and riots (waging "cabbage-wars") the government still did not feel secure. A supplementary army of agents provocateurs was therefore employed to stir up quarrels between the citizenry and the military.

Kortis, an agent of the King's secret police, in trying to pick a quarrel with an armed soldier had been mortally wounded, and the government was afraid he might reveal its unsavory methods. At this time the administration of opium was regarded with suspicion as a means used by the government to silence those who might embarrass them by their revelations. The republican press had already hinted at this possibility. Lucien's mission is therefore to silence this rumor and at the same time to keep Kortis from betraying the government.

PAGE 73. *I know how M. de Caulaincourt died:* General de Caulaincourt (1772-1827), Napoleon's Ambassador to Russia and representative at the Congress of Châtillon, was supposed to have died of remorse for the part he had played in the arrest and execution of the Duc d'Enghien. D'Enghien had been condemned by a commission, acting under the order of Napoleon without the observation of any of the forms of law, and shot at Vincennes. This execution left a stigma on Napoleon's name, and on all those who carried out his orders. De Caulaincourt's last years must have been anything but agreeable with his resentful enemies, the royalists, in power. He died in 1827, but, according to Martineau, of cancer of the stomach.

PAGE 74. *Corneille's tragedy* Horace: The subject of this tragedy by the French poet Pierre Corneille (1606-1684) is the combat between the three Horatii and the three Curiatii brothers, in the reign of the Roman King Tullus Hostilius, who fought to decide a quarrel between their respective cities of Rome and Alba Longa.

PAGE 74.

[*"By Albe, now appointed, I no longer know you."
"But I know you still, and that is what kills me. . . ."*]

["Albe vous a nommé, je ne vous connais plus."
"Je vous connais encore, et c'est ce qui me tue. . . ."]

Stendhal left a blank with the note: "Two lines of verse here." The above lines from Corneille's tragedy were chosen by Debraye as the ones in the drama which fitted "least badly" with the text.

PAGE 75. *representatives from the* Nationale *or the* Tribune: The two most important republican newspapers. The editor of the *Tribune* was the brilliant young Armand Marrast, who after the Revolution of 1848 became a member of the provisional government. Armand Carrel was editor of the *Nationale*. (See next note.)

PAGE 76. *Ah, why did M. Guizot fail to make Carrel a Councillor of State?*: Armand Carrel (1800-36), the famous journalist and republican leader who with Thiers and Mignet founded the *Nationale,* which vigorously opposed Charles X. When his colleagues deserted to the *Juste-milieu* government, Carrel continued to edit the paper alone. He was the most courageous and spirited of all the republican journalists, and the one most feared by the government. A great admirer of Carrel, Stendhal several times in *The Green Huntsman* speaks of the republicans' desire for a war to avenge the treaty of 1815 which was Carrel's ruling passion. Carrel was killed in a duel with another journalist, Emile de Girardin.

NOTES

PAGE 78. *belonged to the Congrégation:* A Catholic religious and political organization founded in the days of the Republic, and directed largely by the Jesuits. Supporting the ultra-royalist faction, it became powerful under the Restoration. Its avowed purpose was "the development of the sphere of good works, and the defense of the Faith against bad examples"—in other words, against all signs of liberalism.

PAGE 98. *M. Pozzo di Borgo:* Count de Pozzo di Borgo (1764-1842), the Corsican patriot and lifelong enemy of the Bonapartes. He entered the service of Russia in 1803, and was sent as Russian Ambassador to Paris under the Restoration.

PAGE 102. *because Italian singers are not excommunicated:* In a marginal note Stendhal adds: "When she dares go to the Théâtre-Français once or twice a year, it is only on the order of her confessor in order that she may accompany her husband."

PAGE 103. *taken the place of the Rohans and the Montmorencys:* Two of the most illustrious families of France, whose members for centuries had been foremost in the councils of the Kings of France.

PAGE 104. *Madame Adelaide:* Adélaïde d'Orléans, Louis-Philippe's sister. *Madame de Polignac:* (about 1749-1793) Intimate friend of Marie-Antoinette.

PAGE 113. *unless there is some chance of a grand cordon:* That is, of being made a Commander of the Legion of Honor, whose distinguishing mark is a broad ribbon worn across the chest.

PAGE 116.

Make your arrest yourself, and choose your own punishment.

Fais ton arrêt toi-même, et choisie tes supplices.

(Corneille's tragedy *Cinna*)

NOTES

P A G E 1 1 7 . *Just as Dangeau was not a great nobleman but patterned after a great nobleman:* Philippe, Marquis de Dangeau (1638-1720), a witty courtier at the court of Louis XIV. Stendhal in *Souvenirs d'Egotisme* calls his cousin Martial (younger brother of "Napoleon's Comte Daru") "a Dangeau of the Emperor's court."

P A G E 1 1 9 . *a long ordinance relative to the National Guards:* The National Guard, disbanded by Charles X, had been reorganized in 1831 by the *Juste-milieu* government with the idea of making it a thoroughly middle-class body whose interests would be neither royalist nor proletarian. Anyone who could buy a uniform was eligible, and it chose its own officers, except for those of the highest rank who were still appointed by the King. Stendhal may mean that since the government had become so unpopular, the loyalty of the National Guards throughout France could no longer be counted on. In 1830 the disbanded members of the Guard, who still retained their arms, had gone over to the insurrectionists. This recollection undoubtedly worried the July Monarchy.

P A G E 1 2 1 . *the political committee of Henri V:* The legitimists were no longer considered politically dangerous. Their own ranks were divided. They all refused to recognize Louis-Philippe, but did not agree as to which of the legitimate Bourbons was their sovereign. To some he was still Charles X. Others, while accepting the abdication of Charles, looked upon the Dauphin as his successor, and called him Louis XIX. But the majority gave their allegiance to Charles' grandson, Duc de Bordeaux and Comte de Chambord, in whose favor Charles had abdicated, and called him Henri V.

P A G E 1 2 6 . *But I must forget her to be happy here:* "Mais il faut l'oublier pour être heureux ici." The source of this quotation is unknown.

P A G E 1 2 8 . *five or six savants . . . two or three celebrated writers:* Stendhal's note on the margin: "The real ones: Cuvier, Laplace,

401

Dumas, Audouin, Villemain, Cousin. Seen by me at M. de Pastoret's."

PAGE 130. *Abbé Jean-Jacques Barthélemy:* (1716-1795) An erudite scholar who wrote *Voyage du Jeune Anacharsis en Grèce,* a study of the political and private life of the Greeks in the Fourth Century. *Marmontel:* Jean-François Marmontel: (1723-1799) Mediocre author of books of various types, including *Mémoires. Abbé Delille:* (1738-1813) French poet and translator of Milton and Virgil. *Antoine-Léonard Thomas:* (1732-1785) An elegant but pompous poet. Apparently feeling that this conversation overheard by Lucien is rather flat, Stendhal makes a memorandum on the margin: "Introduce a real anecdote about Thomas and Barthélemy."

PAGE 133. *trying to understand a denunciation of the Algerian policy:* Algiers had been captured July 5, 1830, but the conquest of Algeria was proving a long drawn-out affair. After the wily Emir had shamefully outwitted General Desmichels in negotiating a treaty in February 1834, the question arose as to the advisability of abandoning the country altogether, and saving France further expense and humiliation. A commission of inquiry was appointed, and, in spite of the precariousness of the French occupation, it advised the government to maintain its position in North Africa. A Governor General was then appointed. The conquest of Algeria was not completed until 1844, and the Algerian question remained the subject of perennial dispute, and the government's policy subject to constant criticism.

PAGE 134. *the General tried to silence him with 15,000 louis:* Stendhal's marginal note: "The real Flandin insists that General Mouton gave him 40,000 francs, and no one contradicts him. Newspapers of 1st and 2nd December 1834."

PAGE 134. *They discussed Algiers . . . forty million francs:* When Algiers was captured, forty million francs had been found in the Bey's treasury, which was just about what the expedition had cost.

PAGE 141. *Mademoiselle Elssler:* The Viennese dancer Fanny Elssler (1810-1884), the most famous ballerina of her day. She made a grand tour of the United States in 1841 with her sister Thérèse, who later became the morganatic wife of Prince Adalbert of Prussia.

PAGE 143. *the Caron affair:* Reference to an episode of the insurrectional movement of the French Carbonari in 1821, known as the Saumur Conspiracy. The government had been warned in time to circumvent the conspiracy and arrest most of the conspirators. Some of them, however, escaped, and in order to recapture them and to round up all suspects, the police in conjunction with the military authorities organized a fresh conspiracy. Lieutenant-Colonel Caron was persuaded by agents provocateurs that it was possible to rescue the prisoners in Belfort, and was then arrested by his own troops, tried, and executed.

PAGE 145. *tobacco concessions:* Tobacco has always been a government monopoly in France. A tobacco shop was a favorite bribe or recompense for political services.

PAGE 180. *that the* Tribune *was now at its four hundred and fourth lawsuit:* For some time the government had been waging unremitting war on the stubborn republican press, but neither fines nor imprisonment stopped their bold attacks on both King and government. "The *Tribune,*" writes Louis Blanc in his *History of Ten Years,* "staggered under the weight of the prosecutions which were, one after the other, directed against it. Having lost all hope of quelling it, the Minister (Casimir-Périer) had sworn to destroy it completely. The witty editor of *Caricature,* M. Philipon, and the author of the poetical *Némésis,* M. Barthélemy, were in like manner vigorously proceeded against without succeeding in crushing the pencil of the one or the pen of the other."

PAGE 180. *the increate light of Mount Tabor:* Mount Tabor was a hill in Galilee known as the Mount of the Transfiguration. Montesquieu says that in the Eastern Empire, "the question was disputed as to whether the light which appeared around Jesus Christ on Mount Tabor was create or increate."

PAGE 183. *Carnot and Turenne:* Both men who had rendered signal service to the State. Lazar Carnot (1753-1823) was a member of the Committee of Public Safety, organized the fourteen armies of the Republic, and drew up the plans of campaign. He was called the "Organizer of Victory." Henri de la Tour d'Auvergne, Vicomte de Turenne (1611-1675), a great French general in the days of Mazarin and the Fronde. He was made Marshal for his services in the Thirty Years' War, and was later created Marshal-General of France.

PAGE 184. *the bludgeoners of the Bourse:* After the abortive insurrection of June 5th and 6th, 1832, on the occasion of the funeral of the popular liberal Deputy General Lamarque (in which Lucien with some of his fellow-students of the École Polytechnique took part, and for which they were expelled), the republican party had had to limit its activities to propaganda. The republican press kept hounding the government by harping on its corruption, its financial scandals, the dishonest influence of bankers on the affairs of State as well as on the voting in the Chamber, and on its persecution of the press in violation of the Charter. Many new democratic associations, like "Les Droits des Hommes," were formed, which distributed violent pamphlets against the government. These seditious circulars were hawked through the city by public criers. In 1834 two laws were passed, one against public criers on February 6th, the other against associations on March 29th. The first caused tumultuous rioting which the police repressed by the most discreditable means. The event here described by Coffe, in which he took part, occurred when the government police sent hired thugs armed with heavy clubs, but dressed as respectable citizens, to the Place de la Bourse. They assaulted not only the rioters but curious and peaceable passersby as well. The republican papers dubbed them "the bludgeoners of the Bourse." The law against associations was the last straw which roused the people of Lyons to rise in the first of the April riots of 1834.

PAGE 189. *before a nice court-martial like that of Colonel Caron:*
See note for page 143 on *the Caron affair.*

PAGE 189. *our politicians will be Tom Joneses like Fox, or Blifils
like M. Peel:* Tom Jones the honest amorous hero, and Blifil the
slick villain, of Fielding's novel. Charles James Fox (1749-1806),
the great Whig statesman, was a strong opponent of war with
America, and the only English politician who favored the French
Revolution and was opposed to the wars with France. Several times
Foreign Secretary, he invariably supported liberal measures. Sir
Robert Peel (1788-1850), conservative English statesman, was a
confirmed Protectionist until 1841; he was Prime Minister in 1834
and again in 1841. When Home Secretary in 1822 he reorganized
the London police force, giving his name to the English "cops"
who have ever since been familiarly called "bobbies," just as the
Irish had bitterly nicknamed his police "peelers," when he was
Secretary for Ireland from 1812 to 1818. The clearest thing about
this comparison is that Stendhal detests Peel.

PAGE 196. *would require a Carrier or a Joseph Le Bon:* Two of
the most notorious instigators of atrocities during the French
Revolution.

PAGE 198. *because they want a King Log:* A king without authority, alluding to La Fontaine's fable in which Jupiter sent down
a log to be king of the frogs.

PAGE 198. *Telegraphic dispatch:* The word "telegram" was not
used until much later, and when first introduced into the language
was considered a shocking barbarism. In 1852 the following paragraph appeared in *The Albany Evening Journal* of April 6th: "A
New Word: A friend desires us to give notice that he will ask
leave at some convenient time, to introduce a new word into the
vocabulary. . . . It is telegram instead of telegraphic dispatch or
communication. . . . Telegraph means to write from a distance,
telegram the writing itself executed from a distance."

405

PAGE 206. *the eloquence of M. Berryer:* See note for page 217.

PAGE 212. *whose moral disgust almost amounted to physical nausea:* In *Henri Brulard* Stendhal wrote: "I loathed Grenoble—no, loathe is too refined a word—Grenoble made me sick at my stomach."

PAGE 217. *Concordat of 1802:* This provided that Archbishops and Bishops should be appointed and supported by the government and confirmed by the Pope.

PAGE 217. *Ah, so you are afraid of M. Berryer:* Antoine Berryer (1790-1868), famous orator of the legitimist party, feared by his opponents because of his power to sway people by his eloquence. Lucien's condition eliminates Berryer, who is not an elector nor an inhabitant of the Department.

PAGE 217. *Thanks to the works of M. de Chateaubriand:* François René, Vicomte de Chateaubriand (1768-1848), the great French romantic writer whose celebrated style was so abhorrent to Stendhal. An ardent royalist, Chateaubriand was made a Peer during the Restoration, served as Ambassador to Great Britain and Minister of Foreign Affairs. Louis XVIII declared that a pamphlet Chateaubriand wrote in 1814 against Bonaparte and in favor of the Bourbons was worth an army to the legitimist cause. His most famous works are: *Le Génie du Christianisme, Mémoires d'Outre Tombe,* and his American Indian novel *Atala.* Stendhal called him the "Grand Lama."

PAGE 221. *David allied with the Amalekite:* Stendhal's note: "To be verified. Quotation from sermon." The ancient nomadic tribe of the Amalekites and the Israelites were constantly at war. The Amalekites were finally crushed by David with merciless cruelty.

PAGE 235. *Hampden stands for Mairobert:* Because the government feared Mairobert for his liberal views, Lucien and the Minister, to conceal his identity in their telegrams, gave him the name of the great English patriot and opponent of Charles I, John Hampden, a cousin of Oliver Cromwell.

PAGE 241.

A shade less good fortune, but sooner encountered . . .

Un peu moins de fortune, et plus tot survenue . . .

The quotation is from Corneille's *Polyeucte*. Stendhal made a slight error, writing *survenue* in place of *arrivée*.

PAGE 246. *Never will you forget General Fari, M. de Seranville, Abbé Le Canu, M. de Riquebourg* . . . : In Stendhal's text this list ends with "M. le Maire Rollet." According to a marginal note Stendhal intended to introduce this character, the Mayor of Caen and a friend of M. de Séranville. But as he is not mentioned before, I have omitted his name here.

PAGE 254. *I don't give a straw for Brid'oison of the Rue de Grenelle:* Lucien ridicules de Vaize by giving him the name of an absurd comic character in Beaumarchais' *Mariage de Figaro*.

PAGE 256. *Rocher de Cancale:* A famous restaurant in Paris famous for its sea food, especially oysters. There is still a restaurant of that name in Paris.

PAGE 261. *this new Piet club:* Under the Restoration a Deputy from Mans, Jean-Pierre Piet, made himself chief of a club of royalist Deputies, and acquired real influence in the Chamber, giving his colleagues frequent dinners. Chateaubriand, one of its members, has thus described their meetings: "We used to sit around in a circle in a room lighted by a lamp that smoked. In this legislative fog we discussed the law that had been proposed, the motion to be carried, and which of our members were to be raised to office."

PAGE 263. *Andrieux formerly enjoyed:* François Andrieux (1759-1833), author of fables, comedies, and stories.

P A G E 2 6 4 . *a playing card on which he had written five ideas to be developed:* Suggested by Stendhal's own method. His book *De l'Amour* was composed from ideas jotted down on playing cards in Milanese drawing rooms.

P A G E 2 7 3 . *well-known role of Samuel Bernard:* The powerful banker who, in the reign of Louis XIV, so often came to the rescue of the King's treasury. The anecdote here referred to took place not at Versailles but at Marly. Samuel Bernard, having refused another large loan, is summoned by the King's Controller of Finance. "By chance" he encounters Louis XIV himself, who graciously shows him over the gardens. The ruse is successful and Samuel Bernard almost ruins himself to oblige a prince who has done him so great an honor. Ennobled by Louis XV, he became the Comte de Coubert.

P A G E 2 7 7 . *The King repeated his question:* An oversight on Stendhal's part: the question alluded to here does not exist in his manuscript.

P A G E 2 7 9 . *'I shall wait, Monseigneur':* This refers to an anecdote about Cardinal Fleury, Minister to Louis XV, and the witty prelate and poet Abbé Bernis, who later became a Cardinal. The severe Cardinal Fleury, reproaching the Abbé for his dissipation, said: "You have nothing to hope for as long as I live." Whereupon the Abbé rejoined: "I shall wait, Monseigneur."

P A G E 2 8 0 . *M. de Villèle's Three Hundred:* An allusion to the subservient royalist majority returned to the Chamber in 1824. Louis XVIII's ultra-royalist Premier had so successfully manipulated the elections that only nineteen liberals were returned.

P A G E 2 8 3 . *calls you the Maurepas of this age:* Jean Frédéric de Maurepas (1701-1781), Louis XVI's favorite Minister.

P A G E 2 9 1 . *where Madame Leuwen took her evening lichen:* Iceland lichen or moss was at one time made into a tonic, and was also considered a nutritious article of diet. Stendhal does not say whether Madame Leuwen took her lichen in liquid form or as a gelée.

PAGE 291. *the ideology of M. de Tracy:* Antoine Louis Claude Destutt de Tracy (1754-1836), the utilitarian philosopher whose works profoundly influenced Stendhal's thinking, had won Napoleon's displeasure in the early days of the Empire by his liberal doctrines. The ideologue was a friend of Jefferson and of Lafayette, whose son married de Tracy's daughter. After his return from Italy in 1821, Stendhal became an habitué of the de Tracy salon in Paris, which he describes at length in *Souvenirs d'Egotisme.*

PAGE 292. *three dupes in France: M. de Lafayette, Dupin de l'Eure, and Dupont de Nemours who understood the language of birds:* After the July Days, Lafayette, the legendary hero of freedom in the eyes of the populace, had vouched for Louis-Philippe as "the best of republicans." Like Stendhal himself, Lafayette had been mistaken. Dupont de l'Eure (1767-1855), a modest, sincere, and courageous liberal, accepted with some reluctance the post of Minister of Justice in Louis-Philippe's first Cabinet. Louis Blanc describes a most enlightening interview between the real and the make-believe democrat: "he (Dupont de l'Eure) said he was not a courtier and that his habits and affections were republican. The Prince replied that there would be no court, and that he himself regretted that he could not live in America." Pierre Samuel Dupont de Nemours (1739-1817), "who understood the language of birds," a statesman and a writer on finance. He believed with the physiocrats that the standard of precious metals is false and that the only true wealth is that of the land and its manufactured products. The Stendhalian touch about the birds, Martineau believes, was suggested by Nemours' interest in rural economy. During the Revolution, Dupont de Nemours favored a constitutional monarchy, was imprisoned under the Terror, and only saved by Robespierre's fall. He emigrated to the United States but returned to France in 1802, and served on the commission which arranged the transfer of Louisiana to the United States. Made Councilor of State in

1814, on Napoleon's re-appearance he returned to America where he spent the remainder of his life with his two sons, who were powder manufacturers in Wilmington, Delaware. In 1802, his son Eleuthere Irenée had founded the E. I. Dupont de Nemours Company, ancestor of the present colossus of that name. Stendhal quotes Talleyrand as saying of him: "except for a few hopeless intransigents like Dupont de Nemours, who cares about liberty in France today?"

PAGE 292. *M. Grandet was like M. de Castries in the days of Louis XVI:* Marquis de Castries, Minister of the Marine in 1780.

PAGE 292. *d'Alembert and Diderot:* The two famous editors of the great French *Encyclopédie* (published between 1751 and 1765), who, with Voltaire, revolutionized French thought in the eighteenth century. The *Encyclopédie* was the arsenal of the new philosophy which armed leaders for the coming Revolution.

PAGE 293. *the bankers of Frankfort:* The famous family of bankers, the Rothschilds, originated in Frankfort. Meyer Amschel Rothschild (1743-1812), the founder of the family as financial magnates, left five sons, all of whom were made Barons by the Austrian Empire; Meyer, the eldest, succeeded his father as head of the firm of Frankfort, Salomon established a branch in Vienna, Nathan in London, Karl in Naples, and James in Paris.

PAGE 299. *a 4th Prairial, a 10th of August, an 18th Fructidor:* Stendhal probably had in mind the 1st Prairial, Year III (May 20, 1795) when an insurrection was started by the Jacobin party against the Convention, or as Carlyle more picturesquely puts it: "Sansculottism has risen once again. . . . Saint-Antoine is afoot: 'Bread and the Constitution of Ninety-three!'" The mob from the Faubourg Saint-Antoine burst into the Convention hall where Boissy-d'Anglas was presiding, murdered Deputy Feraud and paraded his head on the end of a pike. For ten hours most of the members, following the example of their courageous president, remained in session until rescued by the troops. After three days of rioting the insurrection was quelled and Sansculottism was dead.

On the 10th of August 1792 occurred the insurrection which assured the triumph of the Jacobin party. On that day the mob stormed the Tuileries and murdered the Swiss Guards. Louis XVI, who had taken refuge in the Assembly, was arrested and imprisoned in the Tower of the Temple. This date marks the end of royalty.

The 18th Fructidor (September 4, 1797) is famous for the coup d'état of the republican party over the party of reaction in the Council of Ancients and the Council of Five Hundred. The three republicans, Barras, Rewbell and La Revellière defeated their colleagues, Barthélemy and Carnot. The latter escaped, but Barthélemy and many of his adherents—deputies and journalists—were deported to Cayenne.

PAGE 306.   *I have done my best*
             All that friendship could do
             To make your life blest
             And sweeter for you.

             J'ai fait pour lui rendre
             La destin plus doux
             Tout ce qu'on peut attendre
             D'un amitié tendre.

Both Martineau and Debraye are silent on the subject of these verses.

PAGE 307. *born under the Empire:* This is obviously impossible. According to Stendhal's calculations, Madame Leuwen in 1834 was eighteen years older than Lucien, who was then twenty-three. Napoleon was made Emperor in 1804. Debraye suggests that Stendhal meant to say "married" instead of "born."

PAGE 310. *M. Laffitte, believing that all men were angels:* Jacques Laffitte (1767-1844), banker and statesman; with Lafayette a leader of the liberals. His influence was a determining factor in placing Louis-Philippe on the throne of France; he was Premier and Minister of Finance in 1830-1831. As Stendhal here suggests, Laffitte enjoyed an exaggerated optimism and replied to everything, "It will turn out all right." Lucas-Dubreton adds: "It was said that his whole political, intellectual, and moral code could have been packed into one of Béranger's songs."

PAGE 318. *and a page of M. Viennet:* Guillaume Viennet (1777-1868). His biographical note in the *Petit Larousse* is sufficient commentary: "An Academician, last of the classicists, author of epistles, fables, and tragedies." Henri Martineau says that he bore Stendhal a grudge because of the latter's unflattering criticisms.

PAGE 319. *Chancellor Oxenstierna:* (1583-1654), a Swedish statesman made Chancellor by Gustavus Adolphus in 1611.

PAGE 321. *M. Salvandy:* Achille, Comte de Salvandy (1795-1856), writer and statesman. He imitated the style of Chateaubriand, Stendhal's pet aversion, and is mentioned contemptuously in one of the marginal notes: "The present regime is ideal for intrigants without talent like M. de Salvandy." He served as model for M. de Torpet, author of the pamphlet which started the mud-throwing at Blois.

PAGE 326. *President Jackson's twenty-five million:* An allusion to the indemnity claimed by the United States for the ships seized by Napoleon. A settlement was finally made in 1835.

PAGE 328. *unctuous eloquence in imitation of M. Fénélon:* François de Salignac de La Mothe Fénélon (1651-1715), the famous French theologian and writer, Archbishop of Cambrai. He was the tutor of the young Duc de Bourgogne for whom he wrote his well-known *Télémaque.* His other writings include a treatise on the education of young girls, used by Madame de Maintenon in her fashionable school at Saint-Cyr. Fénélon's defense of Quietism led to a quarrel with Bossuet which was settled by the Pope in Bossuet's favor. Fénélon was banished to Cambrai. The Archbishop's noble and flowery ecclesiastical style was not to Stendhal's taste.

NOTES

PAGE 329. *the divine paintings on porcelain by M. Constantin:*
Abraham Constantin, a Swiss painter who copied famous pictures
on porcelain. A friend of Stendhal's.

PAGE 331. *to compare himself to Colbert:* Jean Baptiste Colbert
(1619-1683). Recommended to Louis XIV by Mazarin on his deathbed, Colbert became the King's chief Minister. On the fall of
Fouquet, he was made Controller-General of Finance. Endowed
with keen intelligence and indefatigable energy, he effected important changes, not only in the department of finance where he
introduced order and economy, enormously increasing the State's
revenues, but in all branches of government.

PAGE 331. *that poor Castelfulgens:* Or Chateaubriand. Stendhal's
marginal note: "Episode about his mistress, Mme. ——, a dose of
clap at Trautmannsdorf."

PAGE 337.

> *If you're going to be damned*
> *At least be damned for pleasant sins.*

> Si vous vous damnez
> Damnez vous au moins pour des péchés aimable.

Henri Martineau notes: "These often-quoted lines have never been
definitely attributed to anyone."

PAGE 337. *à la Jean-Jacques:* Jean-Jacques Rousseau (1712-1778),
the famous romantic writer and philosopher whose works caused
such a furore in France that he was obliged to flee Paris. Like
most boys of his generation, Stendhal came under his influence, and
at an early age was devouring *La Nouvelle Héloïse* and the *Confes-
sions.* Although still often behaving like a Rousseau hero when
hopelessly in love, after he had finally dedicated himself to a cult
of happiness and energy, and adopted the Civil Code as his ideal of

a perfect style, he repudiated the melancholy Jean-Jacques and his romantic rhetoric.

PAGE 349. *The woman in her had triumphed over the diplomat:* Or, as Stendhal puts it more bluntly in a note: "To be exact, her uterus triumphed over her head." Unlike today, in Stendhal's time the language of literature was obliged to stay in the drawing room.

PAGE 368. *the Embassy of Capel:* Although Stendhal's note at this point indicates that Capel stands for Madrid, he was in reality thinking of Rome. According to his original plan Rome was to have been the setting of a third part of the novel, with a new cast of characters. When he abandoned this idea, he failed to indicate how he intended to wind up his hero's adventures. The one thing which seems certain from his various notes is his intention of giving the novel a "happy ending" with the reconciliation and marriage of Lucien and the beautiful and innocent Bathilde.

PAGE 370. *Madame de Warens:* The Baronne de Warens (1700-1762), with whom Rousseau lived in her house in the picturesque hamlet of Les Charmettes in Savoy.

PAGE 375. *the O'Connell and the Cobbett of France:* The "Great Daniel O'Connell" (1775-1847), Irish national leader and agitator, idolized by the Irish people. William Cobbett (1762-1835), English political writer and reformer.

PAGE 376. *had himself introduced to M. de Lamennais:* Abbé Félicité de Lamennais (1782-1854), priest, philosopher, theologian and reformer. He started a paper called *L'Avenir* (The Future) professing the doctrines of freedom of the press, of instruction, and of discussion, which displeased the Jesuits and the Bishops, and was suppressed. His first book *Essai sur l'indifférence en matière de religion,* de Maistre called "a clap of thunder in a leaden sky." Lamennais, a sincere Christian, wished the Church to be entirely independent of the "atheistic State" and of political parties. *Paroles*

NOTES

d'un croyant, which Du Poirier adopted as his gospel, was one of Lamennais' later works. In his *Revolution and the July Monarchy,* Lucas-Dubreton says of Lamennais: "This philosopher, who was at once a Christian and a revolutionary, was acceptable neither to the ecclesiastical nor to the lay authorities . . . he was the Savonarola of the Nineteenth Century."

PAGE 386. *the Charivari:* A satirical review founded in 1832 by Charles Philipon, author of the caricature of Louis-Philippe as a pear, *La Poire,* mentioned in *The Green Huntsman.* His outstanding collaborators were Honoré Daumier, the greatest caricaturist of the Nineteenth Century, and Paul Gavarni, the witty delineator of Parisian life and society. In 1832 Daumier was imprisoned for six months for his lampoon of Louis-Philippe as Gargantua.